GOD'S ADAMANTINE FATE

GOD'S ADAMANTINE FATE

COLIN ALEXANDER

DONALD I. FINE, INC.

New York

HOUSTON PUBLIC LIBRARY

This novel is a work of fiction. Names, characters, places and incidents are either the product of the author's imagination or are used fictitiously. Any resemblance to actual events, locales, organizations or persons, living or dead, is entirely coincidental and beyond the intent of either the author or publisher.

This one is for Cello, who always believed and who anchors my rather skewed orbit. I would also like to thank my agent Don Gastwirth for his sage and spirited representation.

Because God put His adamantine fate
  Between my sullen heart and its desire,
I swore that I would burst the Iron Gate,
  Rise up and curse Him on His throne of fire.
Earth shuddered at my crown of blasphemy,
  But Love was as a flame about my feet;
  Proud up the Golden Stair I strode; and beat
Thrice on the Gate, and entered with a cry—

All the great courts were quiet in the sun,
  And full of vacant echoes: moss had grown
Over the glassy pavement, and begun
  To creep within the dusty council-halls.
An idle wind blew round an empty throne
  And stirred the heavy curtains on the walls.

—Failure
BY RUPERT BROOKE

PART
I

Doctors pour drugs, of which they know little,
for diseases, of which they know less,
into patients—of whom they know nothing.

VOLTAIRE

Chapter 1

"Good evening New Jersey! This is Acey Henson, your Ace in Space, coming at you from her slightly skewed orbit here at WCZY, 990 AM on your radio dial, in Flemington, New Jersey. I do hope that you've all had a good evening so far, or at least that you've made it through the day alive, and now you're set to fly with me from nine to two. We're going to have a couple of good guests tonight and, in between, I'll make my usual smart-ass remarks, or maybe my unusual smart-ass remarks would be closer to the truth! We'll also have open lines later for 'Sound Off To The Ace' and you can call in and, if you're coherent, make your own smart-ass remarks. First things first though, we have a message from our sponsor, Ed Newin's Chevrolet on Route 202 where every buy is a good buy, so why don't you sit back, close your eyes, pop the top on some fruit juice, yeah right, and we'll fry what's left of your little minds. And while your doing that, let's not think of what might be in that fruit juice, and I don't mean the ingredients on the label. One of these days, something may get fried for real. I'll be back in a couple."

THE WOMAN'S voice that came out over the radio was a little like the radio itself, scuffed from use with a crack in the plastic cover, but still serviceable. The rapid fire delivery drilled the words into the listener, where they stayed. Twelve-year-old Jerry Inman knew Acey Henson's opening spiel by heart. He fiddled with the tuning control on the clock radio by his bed to eliminate the static, then he sat back on the bed with his pillow propped between him and the bedroom wall. He was still dressed in his Little League uniform, minus the sneakers of course, because he could not wear them when he lay on the bed, but the uniform showed none of the telltale dirt and grass stains that should have been there after a game. He had not, in fact, gone to the game. He had put his sneakers on and pulled his glove out of the closet, but that was as far as he had gone. The sneakers had come off, now lying on the floor with the glove, and he had climbed back onto the bed. When his mother had called upstairs to tell him that he would be late, he had simply said that he did not want to go. She had not asked why, which was good, he had thought. He could not have told her. He just did not feel like playing baseball. He did not feel like doing anything, really. He had just sat on the bed watching the western sky as it had begun to darken. Then, at nine, he had put on WCZY because he could listen to Acey Henson without having to do anything. He just sat in the dark with the chatter.

Charley Inman came home about an hour later. He was a weathered stick of a man, a carpenter to whom sun and wind and the vagaries of thinning hair had conspired to give an appearance beyond his forty-five years. It was not work that had kept him out late, although it was a busy time for carpenters in the state of New Jersey just then. No, he was out late because it was Thursday night and Thursday night, as he had told Ellen the day they were married twenty-seven years before, was boys' night out. The locale for this weekly event had changed over the years, but for the last five years it had been Milardo's Bar and Grill. Thursday night, however, was a constant. It was sacred.

He drove slowly down Birch Street and turned his pickup into the gravel driveway. Behind him, across the road, the land sloped downward through high grass and bramble to Scheuermann's Run, a modest stream that eventually flowed into the Delaware. He parked the truck but did not get out immediately. Of late, whenever he came home he would sit a minute and look at his house. It was a three-bedroom split-level without a garage, and its red paint could have used a freshening. All day he spent working on houses twice the size of his own, he thought. It only seemed reasonable that a carpenter should fix up his own place, too, even if it was small. Ellen voiced that opinion at intervals. Somehow it never happened.

He let the screen door bang behind him (it needed a patch) and walked through the short passageway to the kitchen at the rear of the house. Ellen was sitting at the table with a cup of tea in one hand, the television on, and one of those silly television crossword puzzles on the table in front of her.

"Hi."

She looked up with a start. "Charley! You scared me. You're early tonight."

Inman shrugged. "I guess. Is there any beer in the fridge?"

Ellen moved to get a bottle from the refrigerator while Charley settled down at the table. When she brought him the beer, he twisted the top off and took a long draught.

"Did you eat?" she asked.

"Not really. A few fries." He took another swig of beer. "Danny's back is still hurting him and Sam somehow managed to put a nail through his hand today. Damned if I know how he did that. One thing and another, nobody felt much like eating tonight."

Or drinking, Ellen added silently. Normally, midnight would be an early return home on a Thursday.

"Did Jerry win his game?" Charley asked.

She shook his head. "He didn't go."

"What?" That statement stopped Charley's mind from half-thinking about the house and Danny's back and Sam's hand. "What do you mean, 'he didn't go'?"

"Just what I said, Charley." Ellen Inman had a square face with a generous mouth that set firmly when she thought she was being questioned. "He said he didn't want to go and he didn't. He's been upstairs all evening."

"That's crazy," Charley Inman said. "All Jerry ever wants to do is play baseball. Did he say why?"

"No."

"Christ, that boy's been acting weird ever since it got warm. I thought you took him to the doctor."

"I told you I did, two weeks ago. He said there's nothing wrong. It's just a phase he'll work his way out of.

"Christ," Charley said again. I better go upstairs and see what's the matter."

Inman shook his head as he moved to the stairs leading to the bedrooms. He and Ellen had raised two children before Jerry. The boy was in the Army now; the girl was married. It always seemed to him that those two had gone smoothly. Jerry was a different matter. He had come along late and unplanned. Bringing Jerry up was a chore. Sometimes Charley thought that he had lost his knack for children somewhere in the years between Amy and Jerry. Sometimes he thought Jerry was perverse, although Ellen always insisted that he had simply forgotten how much trouble children could be. Of course, Ellen was also much closer to the children. Baseball, though, had been Charley's favorite sport when he had been Jerry's age, and he saw his passion for the game mirrored in Jerry. Baseball, it seemed, was the one area where father and son saw eye to eye. The idea that Jerry might lose his interest in baseball held frightening implications for Charley Inman.

Jerry's door was closed, which was typical, but no light showed underneath, which was not. Charley could hear the noise of the radio through the door. He pushed the door open and walked into the room. Moonlight coming in through the window showed him his son's stockinged feet near the edge of the bed. The rest of the boy was hidden in shadow.

"Jerry?"

"Yeah, Dad?"

"Your mom says you didn't go to the game."

"She's right."

"How come? Is something wrong?"

"No. I just didn't feel like it."

That was essentially the same information that Ellen had given him. Since he was already upstairs with Jerry, it brought Inman to a mental stop.

Thanks to that lacunae in his train of thought, and a sudden rise in the voice of Acey Henson, he noticed for the first time what was on the radio.

"After she told you *that*," Acey Henson was saying, "all you could come up with was 'it's no big deal'? And then, after that, you are coming to me looking for sympathy? Now I have heard everything. You want sympathy, I'll tell you where to find it. Check the dictionary between shit and syphilis. Good grief! This is one we ought to vote on. All of you out there who think I'm right, call us at 1-900-999-2020 to vote yes. If you happen to think that an abortion is no big deal and Acey's a jerk, call 1-900-999-4040 to vote no. Either call is fifty cents and I'll give you the tally an hour from now. Meanwhile, we're going to a commercial 'cause I'm going to be sick."

Charley looked at the radio as the voice was replaced by an announcer plugging Channel home centers. There was displeasure on his face. "Dammit, Jerry," he said, "didn't I tell you that I don't want you listening to that goddamn show?"

"But everybody listens to it."

"Everybody does not listen to it," Charley said, now with an edge in his voice. "Anyway, it was you I told not to listen to it, not everybody. Right?"

"Yeah," came the grudging answer.

"Is that why you didn't go to your game? So you could sit up here and listen to that damn punk talk about abortions and sex? Is it?"

"No! Acey doesn't come on until nine o'clock anyway."

"Then why didn't you go? And turn that damned thing off!"

There were a great many things that Jerry did that made Charley unhappy, but in most cases, such as not listening to his parents or playing loud rock music, Jerry seemed no different from any other child in the nation. Charley's knowledge on this subject was grounded in a poll he had read in the *Daily News*. Acey Henson, however, seemed to be a local problem. Charley had no idea if anyone else listened to her, although a couple of the guys at work seemed to know about the show.

While Charley was beginning to regret that Jerry had not been blasting his stereo, Jerry reluctantly snapped the volume control to "off." "I didn't feel like going," he said again.

"What?" Thinking about the radio, Charley forgot his original question.

"I said I didn't feel like going to the game."

"That is not an answer."

"All right! I didn't go because Mr. Sobel said I couldn't start because I'm not playing hard enough, that's why! But I am! I really am! I'm just tired and it's not fair," and he burst into tears.

The explosion brought Charley to a mental stop again. Jerry was a natural athlete, no telling where he had it from but it was there, and baseball was his best sport. He had been able to throw a ball and swing a bat, at least a whiffle bat, well before his fourth birthday. He had been the star of every team he had played on. It was the kind of talent Charley often wished he had had. Jerry being benched was inconceivable.

Without thinking, Charley flicked the light on, as though the light bulb would also shed some light on the question in his head. Jerry blinked, taken by surprise. The light showed Charley nothing but Jerry, however. Jerry was a good-looking boy. Charley had always said that. There was a little brown mole on his right cheek, close to the small mouth and firm chin. He had Ellen's brown eyes and soft brown hair, which fell halfway across his forehead. Tall for his age, he was lean with the thinness children have between the time of losing their baby fat and gaining adult muscle. Jerry was maybe thinner than he had been, which was not surprising since Ellen had said that he had not been eating well. It showed mostly in his face. Then Jerry looked up at him and Charley Inman felt a chill. There was a faint but definite yellow tinge to Jerry's eyes.

Within the following ten minutes, Charley had hustled downstairs, hustled Ellen back upstairs where they both peered into Jerry's eyes and then retreated with Ellen to the kitchen leaving a baffled and frightened boy alone in his room. Once in the kitchen, Charley found that he could not sit down.

"You saw his eyes?" he asked his wife, looking for some contradiction of his own memory.

"I saw them," Ellen said, "same as you."

"Well, have they looked like that before?"

"Not that I've noticed."

Charley kneaded his hands together before he spoke again. "The doctor didn't say anything when he saw Jerry, did he?"

"Nothing about his eyes, that's for sure."

"Well, there's something there now. That's for sure."

"I'll take him back, first thing tomorrow."

"Yeah. No! Not there. I mean, maybe that doc's no good. After all, we're seeing something now, shouldn't he have seen it two weeks ago? That's the whole idea isn't it, that they're supposed to see things before you do? Take him to someone else."

"Now, Charley Inman, you calm down!" Ellen stood up, hands on hips. "How am I going to get him in to see a new doctor? Even if I find one who'll see someone new, do you have any idea how long it takes to get an appointment? I doubt it. You haven't done anything like that in ten years."

Charley quieted a bit, but did not change his stance. "I still say he should go to someone else. You call up, tell them your kid has the yellow jaundice and they'll see you. Believe me."

"Yellow jaundice?"

"Yeah, that's what they call it when your eyes look like that. Yellow jaundice. They'll see him." Precisely who called it that Charley could not have said. He did remember hearing it though, probably in regard to someone else. Probably at Milardo's.

Ellen did not know what yellow jaundice might be, but she did have an idea about what might be wrong, one that formed sharp and clear in her mind while Charley talked. Her eyes narrowed.

"Could it be the insulation?"

"Insulation?"

"Yes. Weren't you telling me the builders were using some new kind of insulation this year that they blow into the walls?"

"Pro-Insul. Sure, what of it?"

"Don't you remember? A few years ago, they had all that trouble with that other insulation and now it's almost impossible to sell a house if you've got it in the walls because people can get cancer. Did you bring any of this new stuff home? You've had it on your clothes. Did you bring any home on your clothes or anything?"

"I don't think so," Charley said dubiously. Then, more sharply, "Dammit, Ellen, that was the whole point of using this stuff. There aren't any of those problems."

"So they say," Ellen snapped. "Everything's safe until it isn't."

Charley tried to counter. "If it's so damn unsafe and I brought it home 'cause it was all over me then how come I ain't sick? My eyes ain't yellow." He leaned forward at Ellen, pulling his lower lids down as he did so. The eyeball was white.

"How should I know why? Jerry's a kid and you're not; maybe that's all there is to it. You should think about those things, that's all."

"Fine." Charley was irritated because, somehow, it seemed that it was his fault Jerry's eyes were yellow. "You take him to the doctor tomorrow and he'll tell you. Meantime, don't tell me it's the insulation."

Upstairs, Jerry had heard enough of his parents' discussion to be thoroughly frightened, even though he understood little of it. He did not want to go downstairs and ask, because he could figure from the way they were acting, that his parents thought they were hiding something from him. From experience, he knew it was better to let them think that. Instead, he turned Acey back on. Somehow, she had the Mayor of Somerville on the air. Jerry did not understand much of what the discussion was about, but he enjoyed listening to Acey make the Mayor squirm. He wished that he could do that to important people too. He fell asleep as Acey started to take callers.

The next morning, after feeding her husband breakfast and sending him off to work, Ellen Inman settled down with the phone book. Actually, she had two phone books, the current one and the one from the previous year. Charley would insist on Jerry seeing a new doctor, with no concept of how difficult that could be to accomplish. It did seem reasonable, however, that a doctor who was in the new phone book but not in the old one would be new to the area and, therefore, more likely to take a new child.

There was one name in the book that fit Ellen's criterion, a Dr. Michael Flowers, and her logic paid off with one call to his office. The office nurse said that Dr. Flowers would be glad to see Jerry. If Mrs. Inman could bring him over right away, the doctor would fit him in before his regular appointments started. She took a little information from Ellen, who made certain to emphasize that Jerry had yellow jaundice, and then passed a note to Dr. Flowers to tell him that he had a new patient coming by shortly.

Dr. Flowers, as Ellen had surmised, was happy to see the note. He had completed his residency training in Trenton the year before and then done what he had always wanted to do, move to the country and hang out a shingle. The practice had grown slowly, however, so new patients were still welcome. He spent perhaps thirty seconds thinking about Jerry when he saw the note. It would almost certainly prove to be a case of viral hepatitis, probably from bad clams. Unless this child was sick enough to need the local hospital, there would be nothing to do except explain about contagion and wait. As a nice by-product, he might be able to add the family to his practice on a regular basis.

The doctor's assurance lasted through his brief conversation with Ellen Inman and ended almost as soon as he started to examine Jerry. He spent another ten minutes on his exam, but that was more for the sake of appearances than because he expected to learn anything else. He already knew that he was in over his head. Once he finished, he excused himself and went to the front desk. There was a tension in his gut and it was only partially due to the sight of his morning appointments beginning to fill up the waiting room, unaware that they would have to wait much longer than expected.

"Nancy," he said to his nurse, "would you call the Childrens' Hospital in Trenton for me. Have them page Dr. Zeke Schwartz. I'll take it in my office."

I just hope the bastard didn't decide to take the day off, he added silently.

Chapter 2

_____

"Hi there, Bob," the radio in the nurses' conference room said, *"what's on your mind?"*

"Hi, Acey," a man's voice answered. *"I just wanted to say something about what you told that last guy."*

"Oh, Lord, here it comes! Wait! I know what you're going to say. You hate my advice. Go ahead, say it. Beat me, whip me, lash me verbally—I'd say give me a tongue lashing but with my reputation God knows what the censor would think—but go ahead, do it, let's get it over with, I won't even kick you afterward. You want me to put it to a vote?"

"No, no, no." There was a laughter-filled gap before Bob's voice picked up again. *"I want to agree with you."*

"You do?"

"Yeah. I work a farm down in Hunterdon and, I tell you, I'd die before I take some handout to sit on my ass. If he can work he should work, and if it's not enough money for him, well shit, he probably isn't worth it anyway."

"No argument from me, Bob. That's about what I said. I've got no problem, and I don't think you would either, with supporting somebody who can't work or can't find work, but I'll be damned if I'm going to pay for somebody to say 'If you won't pay me what I want, then I'm just going to sit around and suck on a brew.' That match what you think?"

"Yeah, pretty much. Listen, what I really wanted to ask was sort of along that line. I heard somewhere that you used to drive a truck. Is that true?" Skepticism was evident in the question.

"Definitely true," was the answer. *"More than once."*

"How did you go from driving a truck to being on the radio?"

Acey gave a short laugh. *"One summer, I found a job driving truckloads of fertilizer down in Iowa. Fertilizer, hell. You're a farmer, you know what I mean. Shit. I guess the station figured that if I could haul it, I could shoot it."*

"CHRIST," SAID Dr. Dan Broda. "Let's shut that damn broad off."

His female colleague winced at the coarse phrase. The conference room where the radio was playing was a square, nine feet on a side, set into the inside corner of a corridor. It was not a very private place. Windows ran the full length of both corridor walls and doors opened onto mirror image nursing stations, one along the interior side of each hallway. Set on its tile floor was a round table with a fake wood surface and a number of metal-and-cloth chairs. It spite of the sign on the doors that designated it a nursing conference room, there were no nurses in it. Aside from the charts in bright blue plastic binders piled on the table, the only occupants were two physicians.

Both doctors were young, but the woman was clearly younger. She sat in one of the chairs at the table, dressed in a clean pair of green scrub pants and a white coat that looked pressed. The copy of the Harriet Lane handbook in her jacket pocket had neither crease nor stain on it. From ten feet away, she screamed "new" at anyone who might care to wonder, and not just from her dress but the still way she sat and the intensity on her face. Intense and worried. Broda was only three years older, but his posture, casually perched on the cabinet next to a microwave unit, bespoke a vast gulf between the two, similar to the gap between a veteran and a soldier fresh from boot camp.

The analogy ran through Broda's head as he sat there swinging his legs and looking at his new intern. The hospital had a policy of starting its new interns one week before the previous year's seniors, veterans of three campaigns in the trenches of medicine, packed up and left. It probably made sense from the point of view of taking care of the patients, Broda thought, but it meant that he was going to spend his last week in the Childrens' Hospital of Central New Jersey nursemaiding a bunch of kids who might or might not someday be competent.

Broda frowned, trying to size up the intern in front of him. This would be her first night on call, the first time she had been alone in a ward and responsible for the children there with her. He looked at the tension in her posture, the uneasy way she sat on the chair, and he tried to guess how she would react if trouble developed. Would she go to pieces or freeze, forcing Broda to make a mad dash in the middle of the night to try to remedy the situation? It was hard to tell beforehand. Broda watched her without speaking. She was transferring information from a number of sheets to her notepad. Each time, before she started to write, she pushed her plastic rimmed glasses up the bridge of her nose. It was obviously a nervous habit. Broda wondered if she would do it while she was gloved for a procedure. If she did, she might give some unlucky child a nasty infection.

While a part of Broda's mind was cataloguing the various kinds of trouble she might cause, another part of his mind was performing a different kind of assessment. That part of him looked at her face and saw that it was full and oval, coming to a sharp point at her chin. Her nose was drawn straight, which was why those glasses always seemed to slip part way down it. The glasses were thick and magnified the size of her dark brown eyes when she looked up. Her hair, which was the same color, was thick. It fell to her shoulders and covered her forehead. It was not a bad-looking face, in Broda's opinion, although it could have benefited from a little makeup. Few of the female house officers wore any, probably because they were afraid it would cause people to take them for nurses. That was okay with Broda. It gave fair warning of what she would look like in the morning.

Her figure was harder to judge, hidden as it was by the baggy scrub top and white coat. The way she sat, however, pulled the scrub pants tight across her hips. From that, he was able to infer that she was on the stocky side. Somewhere, she had learned the trick of using a safety pin to pull the sides of the V-necked scrub top closed. That deprived Broda of the view he had expected, down the front of her shirt, which was the principal reason he had seated himself on the cabinet above her. That was irritating. He wondered if it was worth trying to sleep with her. One of the other interns, the one with the Italian name, Tony something, had made a joke about this one not being worth the effort. Probably tried and was shot down, Broda thought. Might this one be worth it?

This one. What the hell was her name? Her last name, which was on the call roster, was too hard to even try to pronounce. Somewhere, he had a sheet with pictures and full names of the new interns, but since he did not have it with him, it was useless. He squinted as he tried to read her first name off her nametag.

"Jolanta?" he tried, giving it a hard American "J."

The young woman flushed. "That's Jolanta," she said. "It's like a 'Y' at the front." The way she said it, the name sounded much more fluid and was finished more quickly.

"Everybody calls me Jo," she said before Broda had an opportunity to speak again. She pronounced the diminutive in the American style.

She wondered if she was still blushing for her cheeks continued to feel hot. The matter of her name was a touchy one. All her life she had loved her name. It was her grandmother's name and it reminded her of her grandmother and the way her grandmother would slip into something other than English when she was saying something little Jolanta was not supposed to hear. Back then, everyone called her Jola. The problem had first surfaced in medical school. There, she discovered that some of her American-born classmates, and her teachers and her patients looked down on the foreign physicians as being half-trained, and not as bright or as competent as the American ones. Jola was actually as American as any of them, born in the

United States of parents born in the United States. It was the name that made people think otherwise. Not her last name, of course, Polish surnames being as common in America as Smith, but the foreign-sounding first name that seemed to be equated with foreign-born. At first, it had irritated her. Eventually, though, she just wanted the issue to go away. In an odd way, it was her family that settled the problem with their harping on her lack of husband and children. She wanted to be a doctor, not a housewife as the family would have dictated. Jola became Jo, and that was the end of it. Unfortunately, when the hospital processed her paperwork at the beginning of her internship, they used her legal name. Consequently, her ID badge read "Jolanta Marienkiewicz" and she had been too busy to have it changed.

She let out a little sigh of relief when Broda simply shrugged and made no other comment on the name. In fact, he had given it no thought at all. He had decided that his prime interest was finding out what chances he had of sleeping that night and the possibility of sleeping with Jo or Jolanta or whoever could wait until next week when he would be a Fellow.

"Okay, Jo," Broda said. I heard about the floor at sign-out. I just want you to go over your trouble spots with me. Shall we take it from the top?"

"Sure. There's only one, I think." Jola pushed a lock of hair off her forehead, settled the glasses more comfortably on her nose and hoped that was the right answer. Every child on the floor was sick, of course, some more so than others, but she thought most of them would make it through the night without doing anything unexpected.

"Fine," Broda said, "why don't you present your problem child?"

Jola coughed. Then she shuffled through a small deck of index cards, each stamped across one end with a name and having several lines of writing below. She selected one and pulled it out.

"Jodie Schmidt. She's a twelve-year-old white female with acute myelogenous leukemia. No match so no transplant. She's on some Boston protocol. Anyway, she got her drugs twelve days ago. Went to the beach yesterday and started feeling not so good in the afternoon. Was nauseous last night but her parents didn't check her temperature until this morning, when it was up. She's got no white cells and I do mean none, she keeps spiking temps, now she's saying her belly hurts, and she won't let me look at it."

Broda looked briefly at some notes he had made on his clipboard. "Considering the poisons they gave her, I'm not surprised she's got no white cells. She's on antibiotics, which is all you can do about that for now. What's the story with her belly?"

"I don't know. She won't eat but when I try to examine her, she goes berserk. I paged the Fellow just before you came up."

Broda gave her a puzzled look. "There is no Fellow on Oncology. Who did you talk to?"

"Uh, wait a sec." Jola looked back at her card. "Schwartz. He said he'd be right up."

"Oh, great!" Broda pushed both hands through his hair. "Schwartz is an attending. He's in the house?"

"I guess."

"Crap."

"What's wrong," Jola asked. "Is there a problem with him?"

"Oh, no. It's just that Zeke Schwartz is the Great Black Cloud of Central New Jersey. When he's on, things happen. You'll find out. What you did wrong was you called him instead of me. You always call the senior before the attending, unless you want to have a short and unhappy life. *Capiche?*"

Jola blushed and tried to cover it by nodding vigorously. Then she tried to apologize. Broda cut it off with a quick, "Never mind." He, in turn, was interrupted by his beeper. He stared at the red numerals flashing on top of its plastic case.

"The Emergency Room calleth," he said with a grin, "so I'm off." He left with the ritual comment that seniors have given uncounted classes of interns. "Don't hesitate to call me if you need help. Just remember, it's a sign of weakness."

The expression on his face as he said it was somewhere between a grin and a smirk. It was hard for Jola to know if he was being serious.

At about the same time that Broda left for the Emergency Room, the Great Black Cloud was headed up to 4 North to see Jodie. The two did not meet because Schwartz, as was customary, took the stairs. He hated waiting for elevators. Climbing the stairs also allowed him to work off some of the evening's aggravation, and there was plenty of that. He had actually been finished, ready to leave, at five that afternoon, with the ticket for an excellent seat at the Phillies game tucked in his coat pocket. He had almost been out the door, would have been out the door had he not stopped to banter with the secretary. That was when the phone rang. It had been Mrs. Fisher about her son. He had spoken to Mrs. Fisher the day before, when she had wanted to wait until next week before bringing the boy in so that she could see if he would get better without treatment. That had been fine with Schwartz and he had said the same thing when she called back in the morning to make sure it was really okay. Naturally, she had waited until five o'clock to panic, calling in hysteria, saying she could not possibly make it through the night without knowing what was going on. Barlow was on call, not Schwartz, but Barlow did not answer his page. It had seemed reasonable to see the boy quickly in the Emergency Room—the family lived only fifteen minutes from the hospital. They had not arrived until eight-thirty, however, and Barlow still did not answer his page, which left Schwartz cooling his heels at the hospital. The Fishers, having finally arrived, were still in the waiting room, the Emergency Room with its new staff of interns having backed up like a plugged drain, when the floor called about Jodie. Schwartz figured that Mrs. Fisher's son, who could have waited until tomorrow or even next week, could sit a while longer in the Emergency Room while he checked on Jodie. He allowed himself a little grin as he thought about what piss-and-vinegar little Jodie might do to a poor new intern.

The corridor lights on 4 North had already been dimmed for the night when he walked out onto the floor. Only the nursing station remained brightly lit. It was quiet. Only the sounds of a television or a heart monitor were audible as he passed open doorways. He liked working on the floors in the evening. There was less noise, less hustle and bustle, more time to think.

He did not cut an imposing figure coming down the hall, not in his hightop walking shoes and the knot of his tie hanging below the second button of his shirt. He was of average height, with enough bulk properly distributed on his frame to appear athletic. His open boyish face would have had trouble buying a beer in a strange bar, and it had a little grin that never quite left it. Only the sprinkle of gray at the temples amidst his brown hair gave credence to his claim of thirty-four years. He walked behind the desk at the nursing station and poked his head into the conference room.

"Hi! You called about Jodie?"

"Yes. You're Dr. Schwartz?"

"Please, Zeke." He stuck his hand out while giving silent thanks that the intern spoke recognizable English.

Jola took the proffered hand, a bit uncertainly at first. Schwartz's grip was brisk and firm. "I'm Jo Marienkiewicz. I'm sorry I bothered you. I thought you were the Fellow."

"Well, until we have enough of a program to attract a couple, I might as well be. What's up?"

Marienkiewicz repeated her story about Jodie. Schwartz frowned as he listened to it.

"A lot of kids are quirky about being examined," he said. "When they're sick, though, you have to work around it. I'm not *always* in the house." He saw her flush under the criticism and he softened his tone. "Come on, let's go see what the problem is."

Jodie's room was a semi-private one directly across from the nursing station, good placement for a child who would need careful watching. The other bed was unoccupied, so the only people in the room were Jodie and her parents. The Schmidts looked much the same as every other pair of nervous parents Schwartz had seen, so much so that their individual characteristics were masked by their tense stances and drawn faces. The first comment to Schwartz was the stereotyped, "What's wrong?" followed closely by Mr. Schmidt's concern that they should have come in the previous night. He did not say it in so many words, but Schwartz had heard enough variations on the theme to know the intent. Schwartz did not know the answer to the first question, not yet, and had no trouble saying so. It was the second question that always gave him trouble. Internally, he knew that the Schmidts had, in fact, endangered Jodie's life by waiting. Part of him wanted to drill that into them. He was also aware, though, that both parents knew the truth as well as he. There was probably nothing he could say that would punish them any more than they were already punishing themselves, and it certainly would not help Jodie. He swallowed his first thoughts and told them that it probably would have made no difference. There would be time later to emphasize the need for haste. He saw them relax a little, which gave him a chance to turn to Jodie.

Jodie Schmidt was a skinny collection of arms and legs, mostly hidden under the blanket. She sported big brown eyes that seemed to take up half her face, and a set of freckles. In the past, she had also had shiny brown hair falling almost to her waist. That was gone now, but its loss had never seemed to upset her. Schwartz did not notice. He was used to bald kids.

"Hi, sport," he said. "How are you doing?"

Jodie just shook her head and said nothing.

"I hear your tummy is bothering you."

This time her head nodded up and down.

"I need to look at it." Schwartz sat down on the bed next to her.

"No."

"Hey, sport, you know I have to. Tell you what, I'll do it so you won't see it. How's that?"

This time she gave a grudging assent. Schwartz piled up the bedsheets in such a way as to create a ridge between Jodie's face and her stomach. It gave him a fair view of her abdomen while hiding it from her. He listened with his stethoscope for a moment, then felt briefly with his hand.

"That wasn't so bad, was it?"

"Yes."

"Oh come on, Jodie, give me a break, will you?"

There was a quick smile on her face that pulled dimples under freckled cheeks. "I don't want to give you a break, Dr. Zeke."

"Yeah. I think if you did, I'd really be worried." He turned to Jo. "Doctor, ah, what?" he said, puzzling over the name.

"Marienkiewicz," said Marienkiewicz.

"Marienkiewicz," he said, trying to repeat it.

"No. It's Marien-KAY-vitch. The accent is in the middle."

"Oh, so you're really Dr. Kay Vitch," Jodie piped up from the bed.

Schwartz grinned. "That's my Jodie. As long as she talks back to you, things are okay. Anyway, Dr. Kay Vitch will be here tonight so she needs to feel it also. Okay? She'll go just as easy as I did."

After Jodie nodded again, he surrendered his spot on the bed to Jola. "You don't need much pressure," he advised as she sat down. She copied his exam, noting where the muscles tensed and the face winced. When she was finished, Schwartz gave a noncommittal statement to the parents and led the way back to the conference room.

"What did you think?" he asked her.

"I don't know. She's guarding a little, but there's no point-tenderness. Nothing specific."

"I agree, except for one thing. She looks sick. That's not specific either, but she's a tough little kid, pretty good gymnast actually, and something's wrong. Make sure you get a film of that tonight. I'd get another set of cultures, too. You should also reexamine her in like four to six hours. You call me if anything changes."

"That will be about three in the morning," Jola protested.

"So?" He raised one eyebrow. "I assume you are planning to be here."

She flushed again, but this time snapped back at him. "I have no problem seeing her at three. I was not sure you wanted to be called then."

"My apologies, but yes, I do want to be called if there is a problem. Look, Doctor, ah, what should I call you outside of Kay Vitch?"

"Jo is fine."

"Okay. What you have to realize, Jo, is that kids like Jodie can go sour just like that." He snapped his fingers. "I don't expect you, at this stage, to handle everything yourself. I just want to be sure you get a hold of me quick if something happens. Okay?"

"Sure." Her face was still red. She was sure of that.

It was not really okay, Schwartz thought to himself. I think I still have a lot to learn about teaching. He sighed and tried to think of something else to say. In the silence, he became aware of the radio behind him.

"Are you telling me, then," a woman's voice said, "that you're afraid of eating almost anything in a supermarket?"

"I wouldn't touch any of that stuff, Acey. You don't really know what they put in it."

"Oh Lord. Why on my show? What would you like me to tell you?"

"What do you think I should do about it, Acey?"

"What do I think? I think that the shrink comes on in a few hours and you should call back then."

"What was that?" Schwartz asked.

"It's a local talk show. Someone called Acey Henson. I guess one of the nurses likes it."

"I've heard that name mentioned, not in any good way. Although," he laughed, "I'd probably tell the lady to call a shrink, too. Listen, I've got a kid in the ER so I've got to go. If you need me, you call. Don't worry about the time."

After Schwartz went downstairs, Jola went back to Jodie's room to get the cultures. She had not needed to ask, "Cultures of what?" They needed to be certain that nothing was growing in Jodie's blood. Jola set out her equipment on the nightstand by the bed: two bottles half-filled with culture medium, three syringes, a small bottle of saline, and an assortment of antiseptic pads. Jodie eyed the preparations apprehensively.

"You know I got a line," she told Marienkiewicz. "I don't get any more needles."

"I know that," Jola said. "Let's have a look at it."

"Don't touch my belly!"

"I won't."

Carefully, Jola pulled the hospital johnny out of the way. The "line" was a short plastic tube that dove through a little hole right over Jodie's breast-bone. From there it ran just under the skin—it could easily be felt—until it reached her neck where there was a small scar. That marked the spot where the tube had been threaded into the jugular vein, through which it contin-ued until the tip hung just outside the heart. The tube was actually two tubes, side by side, in a single sheath. On the outside of Jodie, each one ended in a small sealed port. One of them connected Jodie to her intrave-nous fluids. The other was free. Jola started to wipe its surface off with an antiseptic pad.

"Are you sure you know what you're doing?" Jodie asked.

"Yes, I know what I'm doing," answered Jola.

"How long have you been a doctor?"

Three days, thought Jola, although I have done this lots of times. Wrong answer to give a scared child, she decided. "Long enough," she said.

"Maybe we should ask Dr. Zeke to do it."

"I don't think so. He's got too many other things to do."

"I just don't want you to screw up my line," Jodie said.

"I'm not going to screw it up." Jola smiled. "Dr. Ivory from Surgery told me these lines are so sturdy, if you get a good grip, you can twirl a kid around on it like a lasso."

Jodie looked up at her. "You are so full of shit, Dr. Kay Vitch. I bet that's why your eyes are brown."

"Yours are brown, too, kiddo."

"Yeah, but I was born with them." Jodie broke off as a spasm of pain crossed her face. She put her head back on the pillow and drew a few quick breaths. "Oh boy. It hurts. Come on, Kay Vitch. Do something to make my stomach feel better. Quick!"

"I'm trying, Jodie. That's why I've got to get this blood."

"Okay, okay. Just do it quick."

A couple of minutes later, Jola retreated to the nursing station, the contents of each culture bottle red with Jodie's blood. That kid was scary, the way she looked when the pain hit her. Jola decided to sit at the nursing station and wait for the portable X-ray machine to roll up. While she sat, she wondered if Schwartz had really been serious about being called at three in the morning. She wondered what Broda would think about being called at that hour. Or, about not being called.

Chapter 3

TRENTON, NEW JERSEY _____

"GODDAMMIT, Barlow, I cannot deal with this!" Zeke Schwartz's hand came down with a crack like a rifle shot on A. Barlow Worthington's desk. "I've been real polite for a year, but enough is enough."

Barlow Worthington looked up into Zeke's face with a look of pure astonishment. He was a portly sixty-year-old with iron gray hair combed straight back from a broad face on which deep furrows set off the mouth from plump cheeks and lines almost as deep crossed the forehead. Norman Rockwell might have painted that face on a country doctor. His mouth and hazel eyes were opened wide as Zeke's hand landed next to a crystal paperweight. The cigarette he had been reaching for stopped halfway out of the pack.

"Zeke, if you object to my smoking that much, you could have said something." Worthington had a soft, gentle voice. It sounded wounded.

"Huh?" There was a confused look on Schwartz's face. "Barlow, if you want to smoke here, go ahead. I'm allergic to it, but, right now, I could not care less. I'll just huff and puff and if I can't take it, I'll probably rain snot all over your paperwork. That's not why I'm pissed."

"Then what is it?" An edge began to form under Barlow's voice. "You're in here almost before I have a chance to sit down, you slam my door, and then you pound on my desk. This is not how I want to start a Friday morning. I will not have you pounding on my desk. And will you please sit down? It's nine in the morning and you look like you need to go to sleep."

"Yeah, funny thing about that." Zeke took a deep breath and flexed his hands before settling into one of the leather chairs in front of Worthington's desk. "Barlow, may I ask where you were last night?"

"I had dinner in the city," Worthington answered. His face settled back into a benign, slack-jawed response. "Why? Did you have trouble last night?"

"In a manner of speaking. I think Jodie Schmidt is brewing something in her belly that we're not going to like. Then there is the kid down on 3 South with heart failure. I didn't even know that kid was in the house until the house staff paged me at midnight. I'm on service this month, Barlow, you've got to let me know who you bring in. But what really frosts me is that you were supposed to be on call last night. It's just a damn good thing I was around, but I'm on this weekend and I really would have appreciated taking it easy last night."

Worthington's eyebrows came together as Schwartz finished speaking. "Zeke, I don't think I was on last night. Here, wait a minute." He opened the appointment book that lay on his desk. "No. See, I had that dinner scheduled from a while ago. Nothing else."

Schwartz sighed and pulled a piece of paper from his pocket. "Here's the call schedule we have posted. I've circled yesterday in red."

"Zeke, I'm sorry. Doris didn't put it in my book."

"Christ, Barlow." Zeke jammed his hands into the pockets of his long white coat and slumped down into the chair. What was he going to say? Nothing he had not said before. He looked up at Worthington and said nothing.

How did I land myself in this armpit? he asked himself instead. Actually, it had been very easy, as he knew. He had been a hotshot junior faculty member in Boston a year and a half ago when he had been offered the position. It had seemed like a dream. The Childrens' Hospital had just moved into a new building all its own. The medical center was expanding its faculty and wanted to create a Childrens' Cancer Center at the hospital. Would Dr. Zeke Schwartz like to join the faculty and build up the program? Of course he would! There would be money to hire Fellows so that he could establish a training program, another faculty position he could fill with a person of his choosing, and the promise of a second faculty position to fill once the program was running. It would be difficult at first, of course, but Barlow Worthington, who was scheduled to become Dean of the Medical School, was going to put off his retirement to help out in the clinic and at night. Zeke had certainly heard of Worthington, who had been an often-quoted authority while Zeke was in medical school. True, Worthington was not, anymore, an up-to-date oncologist, but that would not really be a problem.

Unfortunately, the program Zeke had been promised was not the program he found. The money to run the new cancer center proved to have been depleted before Zeke had ever arrived. There was enough to run the center, but not enough to pay for research or to hire Fellows. Frank Wehmer, the physician Zeke had brought with him, had stayed only six months. "This isn't what I was promised, buddy," Wehmer had said. "I need research funds to run my lab and time to spend in it." He had no trouble finding a position that would give him both. Wehmer's defection meant that Worthington had to do more than merely "help out," because without the funds it proved impossible to hire any other faculty. Unfortunately, Worthington had not carried a clinical load for years. A lot had happened in the treatment of childhood cancer in the eighties, but Worthington had not been part of it. Sadly, Zeke had concluded that while Barlow could write one hell of a textbook, he could not take care of patients to save his life. Or theirs.

"Zeke, I did mean to talk to you this morning anyway," Worthington was saying. For him, the storm was over with Schwartz's silence and he dismissed it from his mind. "About the program funds."

"Oh?" Zeke looked up from studying his feet. Blowing up at Barlow never seemed to do any good. It just slid right off without effect. The mention of the program funds, however, had Zeke's attention. "What about the funds?"

"The people I had dinner with last night are from one of the pharmaceutical companies. I think they'll be willing to fund a fellowship position here." Worthington beamed as he said it.

"Which company?"

"Meldrum Products. You know anything about them?"

"Not a whole lot. They make that new antifungal, Aspergicin, which I've used, but they don't make a chemotherapeutic. How come they're going to bankroll us? Or do I have to wear their logo on a sweatband when I make rounds?"

Worthington chuckled. "Really, Zeke, they are not the Devil Incarnate. As it happens, their Vice President of Medical Affairs is an old classmate of mine. I told him about all the work you've done here and that we all think you'll be able to build a really top-notch program. They will be happy to set up the Meldrum Products Oncology Fellowship to start next year. I know it's not right away, but we can still have one of the docs from Camden cover now and again when you need it. If this runs well, and especially if you can get that faculty slot filled, they might go for two positions the year after. This is where those connections help, you know, although it's also a big vote of confidence in you. Well deserved if you ask me. After all, it could just as easily have been the Meldrum Products Infectious Disease Fellow-ship."

Zeke studied Worthington through narrowed eyes without changing his position in the chair. He could feel his anger slipping away and he rather resented that. It was as though he should feel grateful to Worthington for handing him the means to put his program back on track, even though it should not have been necessary in the first place. Zeke knew that he should have stayed angry, knew that he should have pushed the argument with Barlow to a conclusion, knew that he should have forced Barlow to deal with his problems instead of smiling and saying "I'm sorry" and going on to something else the way Barlow always did. It made Zeke seethe inside and, when it did, the anger was directed against himself. Why was he like this? If one of his patients was being mistreated, he would have raised hell and not stopped until the matter was resolved to his satisfaction. He had done just that often enough. Why was it that when it was he who was being pushed around he did not stand up for himself? He always ended up accom-modating, stretching himself a little thinner, to keep the peace. He ought to say something.

"So, what do you think, Zeke?"

Worthington's question made Zeke realize he had been silent for a while. I wonder what would happen if I really told him what I thought, he won-dered. Neither of them, however, found out what Zeke might have said because they were interrupted by a knock on the door. Doris, Zeke's secre-tary, stuck her head into the office.

"Excuse me, may I interrupt for a minute?"

"You already have," said Zeke.

"My, aren't we premenstrual today?" she shot back.

Schwartz grimaced and sat up straight. "Sorry. Do you need one of us or both?"

"Just you. There's a Dr. Michael Flowers on the phone about a new patient. Says he needs to speak to you right away. It looks like your Friday is off to a flying start."

Zeke grumbled to himself as he walked over to the division's outer office. He had noticed, ever since he had become a specialist, that local physicians would piddle around all week with a patient and then refer them on Friday, so as to keep the weekend free. Typically, the Friday dumps started around three in the afternoon. When they started in the morning, it generally meant a very long day. He stood at Doris's desk and picked up the phone there. It took only a few minutes to realize that this was not going to be an ordinary dump.

"Look, Dr. Flowers," he said, "I think I really need to see this kid before

I'm going to guess what the problem is. Since it's Friday, the sooner the better because I would like to get the workup started before the weekend. I have clinic this morning. If they can get over here, I'll fit them in when they show up."

"That would be fine," Flowers replied. "I appreciate it."

"Incidentally," Zeke added, "what do they know about what's going on? What have you told them?"

Flowers had told the family nothing. "I wanted to talk to you first," he said.

Sure, Schwartz thought. Given half a chance, he figured Flowers would ship them over without saying anything. Not out of any lack of sympathy for the family, of course, but to spare himself a difficult conversation.

"I would suggest telling them," Zeke said, in a manner that made it more than a suggestion, "that there is a mass there. You don't need to be specific, but they have to know they're coming to see an oncologist. Otherwise, if they come in cold, they will go crazy and I will spend the first hour peeling them off the walls." He was speaking from sad experience.

"I have no problem doing that," Flowers replied. "I would expect that they should be at the hospital in about an hour. Maybe a little less."

Mentally, Schwartz crossed his fingers. He had seen enough people stop for lunch, do their shopping and then roll in around five P.M.

"One last thing," Zeke said. "What's the kid's name?"

"Jerry Inman," Flowers answered.

It was about noon when the clinic nurse informed Zeke that the Inmans had arrived, not as much delayed as Zeke had feared if not quite as promptly as Flowers had promised. He looked at the stack of clinic charts on the table in front of him, then at the list of names behind him on the blackboard, and tried to calculate his chances of making a dash to the cafeteria while the Inmans filled out forms. They did not seem good. Hopefully, he told himself, there would be peanut butter and crackers by the coffee machine in the ICU later on. He could raid their supplies while he made rounds. In the meantime, he forced himself to plough through the chart work so that, if the Inman boy needed work, he would not be too far behind at the end of the afternoon.

Once the Inmans had been placed in an exam room, he walked down the short corridor of the clinic to find them. The chart was in the wall clip by room three. He left it there; it would have nothing in it he had not already heard. Inside, Ellen Inman stood up to greet him. Jerry was already sitting on the examining table and said nothing. Zeke shook Ellen's hand, then leaned back against the wall because the room, like all the exam rooms, was too small. It was as though the architect, realizing that he was designing a clinic for children, had designed the rooms on a child scale. It was all very well for the young patients, but those rooms had to hold a doctor and parents as well, all of whom were adult sized. Seated at the low desk, Zeke felt as though everyone was huddled around him.

They talked for a while, more for the sake of talking than for information about Jerry, the story not having enlarged since the earlier visit to Dr. Flowers. The conversation did give Zeke a chance to watch Jerry. Even aside from the yellow eyes, he did not like what he saw. Jerry was too subdued, not at all like the boy Ellen Inman was describing. The thinness of his face and hands also bothered Schwartz. Most children were thin when they grew rapidly, but sick children were thin in a special way—the way Jerry was thin. Zeke had Jerry lie down on the table and pull his shirt up so that Zeke could see his stomach. The problem was pretty obvious. Normally, the liver tucks up under the rib cage, where it cannot be felt by a hand pressing on the abdomen. If it is felt at all, it is just as a thin shelf with a sharp edge. Zeke could feel the edge of Jerry's liver a good three inches below where the ribs left off, and it was hard and knobby. Schwartz decided Flowers had not been exaggerating.

"Okay," Schwartz said finally, "what did Dr. Flowers tell you earlier?"

"He said there was something wrong with Jerry's liver. That there might be a tumor in it."

"I'm afraid that looks like a good possibility."

"So, what do we do now?" Ellen Inman's face had a stoic set to it, as though she had discounted the bad news long before.

"First, we need to know exactly what is happening. When your eyes are yellow, I worry about how well the liver is working. We'll need to admit Jerry for some tests."

Ellen did not have a chance to ask "What kind of tests?" because Jerry broke in with, "You mean I have to stay?"

" 'Fraid so, sport. Lousy food and my ugly face twice a day. Can you stand it?"

"Maybe. Does this mean I hafta have an operation?"

"It might. I don't know just yet."

"You'll tell me first?"

"Absolutely. Whatever we do, we'll tell you and your folks first."

"Then it's okay, I guess."

Zeke gave him a quick smile. He had a feeling that he was going to like this kid. "Do you have any other questions at the moment, Mrs. Inman?" he asked. "If not, I should see about getting Jerry a bed and then we ought to talk about what needs to be done today."

"Just one question now," she said. "When you find out what it is, will you know why it happened?"

That brought a slight frown to Schwartz's face. There were two stock questions that every parent asked, "What can you do for it?" and "Why did it happen?"

"Before I can tell you why," he said, "or even what we can do, we have to find out what it is. To be honest, most of the time we don't know why kids get tumors. It's not that there isn't a reason, it's just that we don't know the answers yet." Something about the way she was looking at him told him not to stop. "Is there a problem of some kind around where you live?"

"No, I don't think so," Ellen Inman shook her head. All of a sudden, what she had said to Charley the other night sounded silly. She pursed her lips tightly. So what if it sounded silly? "It's just that I'm wondering. Charley, that's my husband, he works construction. They've been using a new kind of insulation, the kind you blow into walls. It gets on his clothes."

"Is he sick?"

"No."

"Hmmm. What is this stuff called?"

"Pro-Insul. I don't know who makes it. I think it's pretty new."

Schwartz made a note on his clipboard. "I'll check on it once I have a better idea what the problem is," he said.

He headed back to the phone in the clinic conference room with Mrs. Inman's question turning over in his head. It was always a long shot to turn up any association between something in the environment and any particular tumor, but that did not mean that such associations had never been found. Most of the time, though, it ended like the frustrated mother who finally answers her six-year-old's eternal "Why?" with "Because." Take your own advice, Zeke, he told himself. Worry about it when you know what the kid has.

The more immediate problem was finding a place to put Jerry and then finding room on various schedules to have his tests done. By age, Jerry belonged on 4 North. Schwartz hoped that a bed had opened on that floor. It was bad enough for an adolescent to be hospitalized for the first time, but to be stuck on an infant division just made it worse. The senior resident indeed had one bed available on 4 North. Schwartz spent five minutes describing the case and claimed the bed. Then he paged the admitting intern to make certain that Jerry was handled the way he wanted. When the phone rang with the return call, it was Jo Marienkiewicz.

"Well," he said, "if it isn't the infamous Dr. Kay Vitch. I thought I called the admitting intern. I could swear you were on last night." There was a silence and he could imagine her blushing on the other end of the line.

When she finally answered, she said, "I am admitting. The way they arranged the schedule, the other two interns are in clinic this afternoon, so I have the admission even though it's not my day."

"Well, that certainly sucks," he commiserated. Then he went on to describe Jerry. "I'll have all the blood work drawn down here," he finished, "can you get him on for a body CT scan this afternoon?"

"I can try."

"Please. If they won't do it today, call me back. I can always go over and kick the radiologist."

The scan was crucial, he thought. A fancy X-ray device that rotated inside a large doughnut, it converted a human body into a series of salami slices on film. It made diagnosis faster, easier, far more precise. It came at a price, though, he thought. Reliance on technology made his physical examination skills less exact than those of the generation that had taught him. The young doctors he was teaching would probably be less skilled that he. Of course, it was not a problem as long as there was a machine to spit out the answer. He walked back to the exam room to explain this marvel of medicine to Ellen and Jerry Inman.

Late that afternoon, Worthington strolled onto the infant ward looking for Zeke Schwartz. A fresh cigar stuck in the breast pocket of his white coat, projecting upward to partially cover his name, which was stitched in red thread. It was near feeding time and cries echoed incessantly from both sides of the corridor, but Worthington ignored them. They were just the normal background noise for that floor. He went over to the nursing station to ask after Schwartz when he saw him come out of one of the patient rooms. Schwartz had a chart tucked under one arm and quickly crossed the corridor to the desk, where he pulled one of the wheeled chairs under him and sat down to look at the chart he was holding. He did not notice Worthington at all.

"Zeke, can I interrupt for a minute?"

Schwartz looked up, a little surprised, as though Worthington was not the person he had expected to see. "What's up, Barlow?"

"I need to talk to you for a few minutes, if I can."

"Sure." Zeke swept his arm around the desk. "Grab a loose stool and have a seat."

Worthington grimaced, then walked around to the end of the desk to sit next to Schwartz. "You know, Zeke," he said, "your sense of humor leaves something to be desired."

"No doubt. However, that's old news and I'm sure that was not what was on your mind."

"True." Worthington hesitated. "Zeke, I just wanted to apologize for yesterday, I mean about being on call. Doris did leave me a note, I just didn't see it, or it didn't register. I found it under some stuff this morning."

"Geez, Barlow." Zeke flipped the chart closed and looked up. He could not think of anything else to say immediately. "It's over and done with. I'm sorry I blew a fuse. Why don't we just forget it?"

"Consider it forgotten," said Worthington, as though he, not Schwartz, had been wronged. "I just want you to know that I am here to try and help out. I know it's a difficult situation and I know an old retread like me probably isn't what you need, but I'm just trying to take some of the load off. I'm sure that's why that mixup happened. The grant money from Meldrum is so important that it's all I was focusing on."

Worthington should have left well enough alone. At the mention of the grant money, Schwartz's face turned grim again.

"I appreciate that you're trying to help, Barlow, I really do. However, this whole business about the money should never have come up. I came here to build up this program and there was supposed to be money earmarked for that. Well, the money isn't all there anymore because some of it was used up. You helping out and panhandling Meldrum doesn't change that."

"Zeke, we've been through this before. At the time, you weren't here yet and we had other needs for equipment and personnel that couldn't be met any other way."

"Yeah, so the hospital ripped off my program money. Please," he said as Worthington started to interrupt, "that's what it amounts to. If this hospital has such trouble balancing its books, maybe we need new management."

"It's not that simple, Zeke."

"No, I'm sure it's not, but it's me and my program that got screwed so I'm not very happy about it."

"Maybe you should be at the budget meetings," Worthington suggested. "Then you would see just how big a problem it is."

"Maybe I should be there. Is this an invitation?"

Worthington looked at Schwartz's face and decided to reconsider. "Whoa, whoa, slow down!" he said. "Let me check it out with the administration. If you start showing up at the budget meetings then the whole faculty will want to be there and it will turn into a circus."

"Fine, I'll wait. Because even if I'm there, I still don't have the money, and if I don't have the money we can't get any researchers or any Fellows or even get *accredited* to train Fellows, and I have to spend all my time on the wards because there's no one else to do it. I can't build a program from scratch if I'm on the wards or in the clinic all the time."

"No question it makes things more difficult but, you know, I do think you spend more time than is really necessary. You don't have to be doctor and social worker rolled into one."

"Barlow, I only know one way to practice. Either I do it right or I don't do it."

Worthington sighed. "Nobody disputes that you take good care of your patients, but you need to be a bit more pragmatic about your time. Anyway, I don't want to get into an argument over this again. Will you call this guy Woodward at Meldrum? It's not everything, but it's a start. Okay?"

"One fellowship position is not going to solve the whole problem, Barlow."

"I know that; I just said that. However, it's one more Fellow than you have now. So, you will call him?"

Reluctantly, Zeke agreed. There really was no alternative.

Five-thirty that afternoon found Schwartz in the Radiology suite. The lights in the reading room were dimmed, almost like a movie theater. Along each wall stood banks of backlit, white, plastic panels that held hundreds of X-rays. Each bank of panels was labeled, either by specialty or by in-patient division, to make it easier to find a set of desired films amidst all the others that had been taken that day. Schwartz was standing in front of the bank tagged as "Body CT." His hands were jammed deep into the pockets of his coat while the expression on his face seemed to jam his eyebrows together at the bridge of his nose. His attention was fixed on a sheet of X-ray film displayed on the panel in front of him. The film was divided into twelve equal rectangles and each rectangle held the picture of a cross-sectional slice of Jerry's belly.

"Goddamn," Schwartz said.

"I agree with you there," said the radiologist standing next to him. "It looks like it has completely replaced the left lobe of the liver and is probably into the right, too." He tapped his finger against the appropriate spot on the film to emphasize his point.

"And it's all in the liver?" Schwartz asked. "Nothing anywhere else?"

"Nothing distant, no. Nothing that you could call a metastasis or a primary elsewhere. It may be invading tissue posteriorly—I can't tell you for sure—but that's the primary tumor. How jaundiced is he?"

"Starting to resemble a pumpkin, I'm afraid."

The radiologist gave a barking laugh. "I'm not surprised. See here? The bile duct is obstructed and it's backing up like a New Jersey storm drain."

"Yeah." Schwartz stared at it a minute longer, then came to a decision. "I think we're going to have to do something about that, and sooner rather than later."

He picked up the telephone at the side of the viewer and punched in four numbers.

"Hello, page operator," came the answer.

"Yes, please page Dr. Neil Ivory for 5798."

When Ivory answered, Zeke asked him to come to the reading room as soon as he could. It took no more than fifteen minutes for him to arrive. Ivory was a big, barrel-chested man dressed in a green scrub suit. Despite his garb, Schwartz had not called him out of the operating room. Ivory was never seen in the hospital wearing anything other than green scrubs. Whether this was his way of announcing to all and sundry that he was a surgeon or whether, as most of the women suspected, it was because the V-neck of the scrub top allowed him to show off a shag of brown chest hair, was a matter of lunchroom debate. His skill in the operating room was beyond question. Schwartz was not alone in considering him the best pediatric surgeon on the staff.

"Hi, Zeke," he said. "What's the disaster?"

"That's a fine how-do-you-do if I ever heard one," Schwartz replied.

Ivory laughed. "I've worked with you long enough, Zeke, to know that a phone call from you on Friday afternoon is not about tee-off times for the weekend. Who do you want me to see?"

Schwartz told him about Jerry, then stepped away from the viewer so Ivory could have a good look. He spent little time with the film.

"I can do him tomorrow, if you like," he said, turning away from the viewer. "We can decompress him and see how much of that thing we can get out, although I doubt we can get it all. Any idea what it is?"

"No."

"Well, we'll find out for you. Funny place for a primary tumor in a kid his age, isn't it?" Schwartz nodded. "Any particular reason he should have one?"

"That's the same question his mother asked," Zeke replied. "I'll tell you the same thing I told her: I don't know. You tell me what it is, maybe I'll have an answer for you. Maybe. By the way, did you see Jodie this afternoon?"

"Yeah."

"What do you think?"

"Nothing good. We might get by, but I think we're going to have to take that chunk of bowel out. The way luck usually runs when you're on, I'd say the middle of the night is a good bet."

"Thanks." Zeke let his mind drift back to the CT scan in front of him. Mrs. Inman's other question of the morning surfaced again, the one about the insulation. What had she called it? Pro-Insul, that was the name. I wonder if it is possible, Schwartz asked himself. I wonder.

Chapter 4

_____

"Hiya, Acey."

"Hi yourself, kid. What's your name?"

"Andrea."

"Well, Andrea, you got the last call of the show. What's on your mind?"

"I wanted to ask you about a boyfriend."

"Don't have one. That was easy."

Giggles came from the other end of the line. *"No, no. I meant mine."*

"Oh, your boyfriend. Right. How old are you, Andrea?"

"Fifteen."

"Fifteen? Isn't it a little late for you to be calling in?"

"There's nobody home but me, so I can."

"Ah hah! Well, Andrea, when I was fifteen, if there was nobody home but me at almost two in the morning, I wouldn't be home either. Okay, what's with the boyfriend?"

"Well, Acey, it's like we have a real relationship, you know, and he's nice too, but he wants to, you know, and I don't know what I should do."

"Ah, yes, the eternal question. Listen, it may be real, and he may be nice but that doesn't mean that sleeping with him is going to be real nice, if you get my drift. No matter how it starts, it always ends up with the girl on her back with her arms and legs up in the air like a dead cockroach. You want to look like a dead cockroach?"

There were more giggles, with a *"No,"* spliced in the middle.

"Good. Good night, Andrea, and thanks for calling. Damn, but that brings me to the end of 'Sound Off To The Ace,' and for sure your Ace in Space has been swinging in a wide orbit tonight! We're going to break for a commercial message from Larsen's Motorcycles of Lambertville, the people who put power where you sit, but before we do, I have a quick message for you sports fans out there. It's real simple. No glove, no love. You gotta make it clear and you gotta make it firm, so to speak of course. Got it? I'm sure you did. And now, as they say, a word from our sponsor and then I'll be back to wrap up."

THE TALK came streaming out of a low brick building, set back by thirty feet of lawn from US Route 202. Most of the building was dark, but a spotlight played on WCZY, 990 AM, set in big block letters across the front, so that anyone driving past could not help noticing. The parking lot at the back still held a few cars, since the station stayed on the air twenty-four hours a day. Light showed from some of the windows facing the lot, where the night shift kept the signal flowing out to the transmitter located five miles away to the southwest. Normally, the engineers and the night-time talent had the station to themselves. This particular night, though, one of the offices was also occupied.

"So, Johnny, what do you think of the place?"

The speaker was Howard Firman, who was the general manager of the station, and it was his office in which he sat with an old acquaintance, John Lawrence Thigpen.

Thigpen took a moment to formulate his reply. Had someone asked him, earlier that day, what the odds were of his sitting in a low-budget AM station at two in the morning, he would have laughed. Twentieth high-school reunions are funny things though, and Howard had been so insistent about showing him the station that Thigpen had wound up accepting the invitation. Why had Howard dragged him out to the middle of nowhere in northern New Jersey? Probably because I was stupid enough to mention that I have evaluated broadcast properties, he said to himself. Actually, it might have happened anyway. Howard wanted to show off, Thigpen was certain. To prove that he, Howard, had made something of himself. What did Thigpen think? A tough question to answer. Howard, himself, looked like a grosser edition of the boy Thigpen remembered from high-school graduation. He was fat now, where he had been pudgy then, with a great moon face whose jowls were already starting to sag. The black hair had thinned on the crown so that the front had to be combed back to cover it. Howard's blue shirt had been opened at the collar, as if to give the double chin room to breath, and stretch lines radiated from the buttons over his paunch where the shirt held his expanse at bay. Howard looked more fifty than thirty-eight, Thigpen thought. Unconsciously, Thigpen gave a tug at his shirt to reassure himself of his own trimness. Say something polite, he told himself, but don't talk about Howard. What about the station?

Thigpen figured he could probably shock Howard into a heart attack if he started reeling off, based on just what he had gleaned from Howard's rambling commentary, where this station stacked up against similar stations in cash flow and return on assets. Quad Industries had bought the station, Howard had said, because they were smart enough to recognize undervalued property caused by poor management. Howard was probably correct, there. Unfortunately, it was Thigpen's opinion that Quad Industries did not know how to manage radio stations either.

"It's really interesting, Howard. I mean, I never thought you'd wind up in radio."

"Yeah, it's funny how these things turn out. But what do you think of it, really?" There were a few beads of sweat forming on Howard's upper lip, even though it was not hot in the office. He cursed himself for that and wished he had grown a moustache to hide that tendency of his. He cursed himself a second time for caring what John Lawrence Thigpen thought.

Really? Thigpen was thinking. He looked around at Firman's office, so cramped that Howard's body barely fit behind his desk, which was cluttered with loose-leaf binders and computer printouts. He looked at the chair he sat on, an ancient metal thing with green vinyl on the backrest and seat cover, except where a chunk had been torn out and yellowed foam was visible. The balance sheet sounded better, at least to the extent he could estimate. He could not sit on the balance sheet, however.

"It's nice, Howard. Nice compact outfit. Must be fun to run."

"Hey, that it is. I guess that's something you miss out on in what you do." Firman grinned. A little wheeze came out with his exhalation. "You really like it?"

"I said yes, Howard." Change the topic quick, Johnny, he thought. "Tell me, who's that chick you've got on the air?"

"Acey Henson, you mean? Why do you want to know?"

"She looks sharp," Thigpen said. He had had a look into the broadcast studio when Howard had given him the grand tour. The studio had been plain vanilla. Seen one, seen them all, and the equipment was old. He had thought that the girl in there looked sharp though. Sharper than anything else in the building. That was definite.

"Henson?" Firman looked confused. "What's to know about Henson? Did you see that tee shirt she was wearing?"

"You mean the one that says, 'If you can read this, you're too fucking close' in big block letters? Yeah, I saw it when she stood up."

"She means it."

Thigpen allowed himself a little grin. Perhaps the evening would not prove to be a total waste. "I like that kind of style," he said. "Now, you're the boss here, right?"

"Right," Firman answered, a little warily. He did not like the way Thigpen said it.

"So, bossman, can you get me a date with her?"

"What!" Firman could feel the sweat breaking out on his scalp also. "Johnny, you don't understand something. She calls herself the Ace in

Space on the air and, let me tell you, it's for a reason. She's *weird*. Believe me, Johnny, you don't want a date with Acey Henson."

Thigpen could feel himself relax even as Firman so obviously began to tense. He had hit the right button. Whether he was more interested in the possibility of the date or in watching Howard sweat was unclear even to him, but he was enjoying it in any case.

"I don't see the problem, Howard," he said. "She looks sharp, she sounds feisty. I like the combination. You can swing it, can't you?"

"I can try. Her show finishes at two, if you want to stick around."

"Why not?" said John Lawrence Thigpen.

Why not, indeed, thought Howard sourly. After twenty years, Thigpen had gotten to him again, just as he had done for four years of high school, and he had done it on Howard's own turf. Goddammit!

Down at the end of the corridor that ran past Howard Firman's office were the broadcast studios. They were small rooms, soundproofed against the outside. In one of them, Acey Henson was winding up her show, unaware that she had become the topic of conversation in the station manager's office. She sat at the main console, earphones on her head, dual turntables to her right. The turntables showed no sign of having been used. That was not the case with the large ashtray by her left hand. It was filled with a small forest of cigarette butts, each one crushed out and left vertical. The air in the room, had she bothered to look up at the fluorescent lighting, held a smoky haze. She did not look up. Her attention was on the clock and the microphone. More smoke drifted from a half-finished cigarette in her left hand.

"All right boys and girls," she said into the microphone, "it's two o'clock. Do you know where *you* are? Do you have any idea? Even if you don't it does mean that this is all for me tonight, so thank God I know where I am. I'll be back again at six this evening with the evening news, if you can believe that. Well, you can believe that I will be doing the news, 'cause I will, whether you can believe the news is something else again. Anyway, I'll be here at six for a half-hour, but I'll be back in a proper orbit at nine. Until then, this is Acey Henson, your Ace in Space at WCZY 990 AM, saying good night and I'll talk to you tomorrow."

At the last word, she caught the cue from the man sitting across from her on the other side of a glass partition. The clock over the console showed two A.M. exactly. With an air of finality, she crushed out the cigarette she held. She waited until she heard the network programming that followed her come on, then she leaned back in her chair and stretched.

"God, it seems like they slipped an extra hour in between nine and two. You sure nobody set the clocks back, Gordy?"

The man on the other side of the glass just grinned at her and shook his head.

"Bet you wouldn't tell me if they did." She returned the grin, pulled off the headset, and stood up. Once up, she stretched again. As she came up on her toes, she reached five and a half feet, settling back to an inch less than that when she stood straight. The figure revealed by the shirt that Thigpen had noticed and by her skintight blue jeans was a sturdy one, broad through the shoulders with small breasts. There could be no question of the muscles in her thighs and calfs; the jeans could as well have been painted on from the wide leather belt to where their zippered bottoms disappeared into heavy black boots. She tucked the shirt back in at her waist where it had pulled up. The waist was not as thin as she would like, but there was no flab in evidence. The sleeves of the shirt were cut off at the shoulder. Their absence revealed a tattoo on her upper right arm. It showed a dagger, with a red rose twined around it.

It was not her body that usually caught one's attention, though. Her face did that, pale skin over elfin features, dominated by a pair of wide, blue eyes that said, "Keep out," when they looked at someone. Her hair was ash blonde, a color that might prompt a quick look for dark roots, but hers was the same color right down to the scalp. It was cropped short on the right, hung to her jawline on the left and the short top part was gelled into standing up straight. There were two streaks, one orange, the other blue, colored in from her right temple to behind her ear.

She picked up a nearly-empty pack of Winstons from the console, then walked over to the coat tree by the door. From that, she took a black leather jacket and put it on. It was an old jacket and had seen hard use: the finish had worn away in places. She zipped it up, feeling that the bulk of the jacket had magically added an inch or two to her height. She picked up a helmet from the base of the coat tree and, with a wave to Gordy, walked out of the studio.

Howard Firman did not need a camera to know when Acey left the studio. There was nothing subtle about the sound of her boots on the tiled corridor. He waited until she was even with his office door, then called out, "Hey, Spaceshot! Hold up a moment."

She stopped at the shout and came back to the doorway. Her face held a frown. It was unusual to see anyone in the station manager's office at two in the morning, much less two anyones. Howard she knew, of course, although—thanks to her schedule—she did not have to deal with him all the time. The other was a stranger, a small slim man with curly brown hair wearing a two-piece suit. Bizarre pair, she thought, looking at Howard's bulk and wildly askew tie.

"Isn't this past your bedtime, Howard?" she asked.

He refused to rise to the bait. "Come on in, Acey," he said waving her into the office, "I want you to meet a friend of mine from high school."

Acey came to a stop a couple of feet from where Thigpen was sitting and stood there, right thumb hooked casually into the front pocket of her jeans. From where he sat, Thigpen could see scars over the first two knuckles of that hand. Feisty with a capital F, he thought.

"Acey," Firman continued, "I want you to meet John Lawrence Thigpen. Like I said, we knew each other in high school. Now he's a big shot with some venture capital people on the West Coast. John, this is Acey Henson."

Thigpen made a polite noise while Acey responded with the merest tip of her head. Firman frowned and sweated some more. He had expected Acey's silence, but he had hoped that Johnny would be a little more forthcoming about what he wanted. As it stood, Firman was going to have to do it all by himself. Either that, or he would have to explain to Johnny later why he had not.

"Uh, Acey, hang on a minute. I need to ask you a favor."

"A favor?" Howard asking for a favor instantly made her suspicious. "You can go ahead and ask."

"Well, it's like this, Acey. John's just out here for a few days, our high-school reunion you know, and he caught your show, which he really liked, so I was wondering if you could, tonight or tomorrow night."

"Tonight or tomorrow what, Howard?" She pulled a cigarette out of her pack and lit it.

"Maybe you could go into New York and have dinner or something," Howard finished lamely.

Acey looked at him coldly. "You asking me to go out with him?"

"Uh, yeah. Basically."

She inhaled, then blew smoke at them. "Howard, I have a contract with this station that says what I do for you. Look it up. I do not work on my back."

"Now Acey, I didn't," he started.

"Bullshit, you didn't. If your curly haired friend is so damned horny, why don't you take him home and let him grease his pole on your butt?"

Firman squeezed his fingers against his temples. Trust Henson to make him look foolish in front of Thigpen.

"Christ," he said, "I think I'm losing my mind."

"What can I tell you?" asked Acey. "Small things are easy to misplace."

Howard turned crimson. He started to say, "Now Acey," again but this time he was cut off by a burst of laughter from Thigpen.

"Christ, Howard," he said, "is this how your employees usually talk to management?"

Howard's face went even redder but he said nothing. It was Acey who answered the question.

"Actually, Mr. Thigpen," she said in a voice as icy as her eyes, "I talk as I please, here or anywhere else. Sure, Howard doesn't like it but, you know what? I don't give a shit. I fill a lot of holes around here and my show consistently pulls good ratings, the best this station gets, so Howard isn't going to fire me no matter how I talk. And you know something else? If I didn't get those ratings, I could be nice as pie and sleep with every one of his damned friends and I'd still get canned because Quad Industries owns the station and all QI cares about are the ratings. So, how should I talk?"

"Any way you please, obviously, Miss Henson," Thigpen said. He was still grinning.

"Damn straight," said Acey. She turned her attention back to Firman, who had recovered his normal coloration. "By the way, Howard, as long as you are here, I'll be by in the mid-afternoon. I have the programming schedule set up. I just want to go over it with Rog before I give it to you."

The abrupt change in tone took Howard by surprise. It showed in the jerk of his head, as though he was searching for a part of the scene that he had missed. "Sure, fine," he got out while he collected his wits. Then, "Dammit, Acey, when is he coming back? I'm paying him to be the programmer, not you."

"Yeah, well, you're not paying me to do the news or specials either, but until he can come back I'm doing them. Anyway, I check everything with him, so it's not like I'm doing it off the top of my head. As to when he'll be back, I'll ask him. Next week, I hope."

"That's what I heard last week."

"What can I tell you, Howard? He was feeling better, then he had a fight with his girlfriend. She pushed him down the stairs. You want me to tell him to have his doc send another letter?"

"No, No! Forget it, Acey. Just go home, get out of here, I can't deal with this at two in the morning."

"Sure, Howard, no sweat." She turned to Thigpen with a grin. "See, sometimes I do what he tells me to."

A few minutes later the roar of an engine reached them in the office. Thigpen cocked an eyebrow at the sound.

"That's her Harley I saw out back?"

Firman nodded. "Trust me, you're just as well off she said no. Although, if you're so damned keen on it, come back in the afternoon and try it yourself."

"I think I'll pass," Thigpen said. The idea had served its purpose. "Unless there is anything else you want to show me, I'd like to get back to my hotel and go to bed."

Chapter 5

_____

THE ALARM clock pulled Acey Henson out of a deep sleep at six-thirty in the morning. She looked at it with one eye while trying to decide if she should throw it across the room for its temerity. I'll let you live another day, she decided. Then she sat up with a groan. Six-thirty was just too early to get up after a late show, but she had to see Rog, and that meant going to Philly, and she would rather do that early. She thought about that necessity in order to keep herself moving around the apartment as she took care of her morning chores. It was a small one-bedroom apartment sparsely furnished with a couch, chair, and low table in the living room, all covered with papers and bound volumes. There was a table with one chair in the kitchen. A potted avocado plant struggled for life by the living room window. She ignored the scattered debris and concentrated on her business.

A quick shower, suitably cold, helped her wake up. Afterward, she stood in front of the bathroom mirror and looked at the image of her body with her usual disappointment. It was an adequate body, but not a great one. Too small on top, she told herself for what had to be the ten-thousandth time. Of course, Momma had always told her whenever she had moaned about it, that anything more than a handful was a waste, but Momma had hardly had to worry about it. Otherwise, she was at least trim and firm, although she was certain that a couple of extra pounds had attached themselves to her waist. Where had they come from? Too much sitting on her butt, no doubt. Such was the price of success. The color scheme in her hair was growing old, but this morning was not the time to change it. She settled for growling at it instead. She pulled on tee shirt, jeans, and boots and headed for the kitchen.

Reposing on the bottom shelf of the refrigerator was half of last evening's pizza, still in its cardboard box. Pizza always tasted better cold the next morning. What else? One cup, fill with water, into the microwave and buzz for a minute and a half. One spoonful of coffee and a packet of Sweet 'N Low. Ah, breakfast! Moments later, she was on her bike, headed for Philadelphia.

She parked her bike in front of one of the Society Hill townhouses, then paused a moment on the sidewalk to look at them. She had always liked them, from the day she had first seen them. Maybe someday she would be able to buy one. Maybe.

The door opened quickly after the first knock. On the other side was a handsome man of about forty years dressed in a blue business suit.

"Hi there, Acey," he said. "I'm a little surprised to see you so early."

"I'm surprised to see myself this early, Jimmy," she replied. "I wanted to see how Rog is doing, so I figured I should get here before you went to the office."

Jimmy gave her a brief nod. "Sure. Come on in. I'm actually just about to run. He led her inside, back to the kitchen. "Can I get you something?"

"Glass of milk would be fine."

"No problem. Something to go with it? Bagel? Cream cheese?"

"Bagel yes, cream cheese no," she said. "I don't want to find out how strong Levi's seams really are." Jimmy chuckled at that as he poured the milk.

"So, how is Rog," she asked after a gulp of milk. "He was at the doc's yesterday, right?"

"Right." Jimmy let out a long sigh. "You probably should talk to Rog about it. Physically, he's feeling better, no fevers at least, but mentally not so hot. He'd like to talk to you."

"Absolutely will. He's up to it?"

"Yeah. He's sitting out back in the sun room. Just go on back."

"Sure." She took a bite out of the bagel and another look at Jimmy. His face seemed to have added more lines and more gray at the temples even in the short time since she had last seen him. "How are you doing?" she asked.

Jimmy let out another sigh. "As well as can be expected, I guess." It looked as though he was going to say something after that but thought better of it. Instead he looked at his watch. "Christ! I'm going to be late and my desk is still buried from last week. Go on out back now, but wipe your mouth first. You've got milk on your lip."

"Sure." She grinned and gave his arm a squeeze. "You're a dear, Jim."

"So I have been told," he replied. "Do me a favor and put the glass in the sink when you go. Rog never bothers."

The route to the sun room led through the living room, a spacious area made cozy by wicker furniture and a forest of plants. It was a place she envied, in part for the contents, which she could now reproduce in her own living room if she wanted, but also for the memories that went with them. The sun room had been a patio off the living room when she had first come there, three and a half years ago. About two years ago, it had been enclosed with glass walls. She could remember Rog and Jim wrangling for hours over the plans. Roger Bannerman was sitting out there now, wrapped in a blue bathrobe in a chair in the sun. An uneaten plate of eggs and bacon lay on the table next to him. He looked up as she opened the sliding door from the living room.

"Well, if it isn't the fastest mouth in the east," he said. "How are you doing, Acey?"

"I'm fine. How are *you* doing?" In some ways, the question was rhetorical. Roger Bannerman was a tall man at six foot three and his height had always made him look thin. He had lost nearly thirty pounds over the past few months, and Acey thought he looked skeletal. His cheeks were sunken as were his eyes. Acey knew the answer to her question in absolute terms; what she was interested in was a change from the week before. At least, his eyes lit up a bit when he saw her. That was an improvement.

"How am I doing?" he said back to her. "Could be worse I suppose. Sit down. Would you like some breakfast?" He pushed the plate to her side of the table.

"Thanks, but Jim fed me. What I want is for you to eat the breakfast." She pushed the plate back to him.

Bannerman shook his head. "Not right now, Acey. I just feel that if I eat now, I'll be in the bathroom in ten minutes. That's really the worst of it, is this damn diarrhea. If it weren't for that, I think I could get back to work."

"Yeah." She had heard him say that before. "What did the doc say yesterday?"

Bannerman made a face at her before he answered. "Same thing he told me before. That I should take AZT."

"You say it like you're still not going to do it."

"I'm not sure. Maybe not."

"Why not? Dammit Rog, we've had this conversation before. It's supposed to work."

"Work! Oh Christ, Acey, what the hell do you know about it?" He thumped the glass tabletop, rattling the plate. "All it really buys you is about a year. That's all, mostly. I don't want to do that until I have to. It's like, once I do, my clock starts running."

"The clock is running anyway, Rog," she said evenly. "You might as well feel better. Anyway, if it buys you a year, maybe then something else will come along."

He stared at her for a moment, the way he used to do when he was about to get angry over some foolish thing she had done at work. Then it passed.

"Blunt as always, aren't we? You may be right about the first part, but don't delude yourself about the second. We'll all be dead and buried before there is something that really works. Sometimes I think that's what they want. Maybe you're right and maybe I'll take it, but I don't know. Lord knows, it's not cheap."

"You've got insurance."

"Oh sure." Bannerman gave a bitter laugh. "I do that and that means that the station will know and then it's good-bye Roger. I can't do that. I have to keep that job."

"They can't throw you out over this."

"Come on, Acey. There's always a way to do it. I tell the station and I won't keep the job. That's a guarantee."

"You won't keep it like this, that's for sure," she said sharply. "You've been out more than in for months and not at all the past few weeks. It's getting harder to come up with reasons. I actually told Howard that you got hurt when your girlfriend pushed you down the stairs."

"Jesus, Acey, that's not even funny."

"It wasn't meant to be funny. I was rushed and I was pissed. It was as serviceable a lie as I could manage on short notice. Don't worry, though," she added, "he didn't want a letter and he still thinks you are still doing most of the work here while I run the stuff back and forth. He swallowed it."

"Yeah. Howard always was lazy and he's not terribly bright. Of course, I'm not lazy and I am terribly bright but he'll still be there when I'm long dead and that's damned unfair."

There was a silence after that. Acey looked at Roger and thought that he might start to cry and wished that would not happen. I just do not think I can deal with that, she thought. In the meantime, though, no words were coming into her head, and that was a rare event.

Finally, she forced herself to say something just to end the silence. "The important thing is, Rog, that, Howard being Howard, this works. He doesn't care where the work comes from as long as he doesn't have to do it."

Bannerman shook his head and then rested it on the back of the wicker, looking up at the ceiling. "Of course, the fact is that you're doing all of it. I've really taken advantage of you haven't I?"

"Not in the least," she said. Then she waited for his eyes to return to level and fixed on them, blue eyes looking straight into his brown ones. "I've wanted to learn this stuff, so doing it is good for me. I don't mind. But, I can't do it forever."

"Meaning you want to stop carrying Roger Bannerman. Hard to blame you."

"Goddammit, Roger, that is not what I said!" She leaned over the table and stabbed her index finger at the top to emphasize the sentence. "You listen to me for a moment, okay? You're the one who took on a twenty-four-year-old girl with a loud mouth, three years of knocking around the country for experience, and five million rough edges, and believed her claim that she had the talent for radio, and then you had the patience to develop it. I haven't forgotten and I never will. I said can't, not won't. You were the one who told me, 'pay your dues here for a couple of years and bigger offers will come.' It's three years now. I'm established and I'm ready. The offers will come. I can't carry you if I leave WCZY."

Another embarrassed silence followed her outburst and dragged on for several minutes. In Bannerman's mind was the thought that taking out his bitterness on the one person, other than Jim, who had stood by him was a foolish thing to do. He managed to avoid saying the thoughts that rose in his mind out of fear that she would walk out. Acey, for her part, went nowhere. It was hard to see her friend and mentor reduced to clinging to her for survival. Hitting him over the head with reality made her feel worse.

It was Bannerman who finally spoke up. "Could I ask you to get me a Coke?" he said. "Then, when you come back, maybe we should change the topic."

It was a relief, Acey found, to walk out of the sun room back to the kitchen. The tension had become too thick too fast. Roger had picked just the right way to defuse it—get her out of the way for a moment so she could cool down. How many times had he bailed her out that way her first year at the station, always just before she would have shot her mouth off and said something unforgivable? She took the bottle of Coke out of the refrigerator and poured him a glass. Then she took a deep breath, telling herself to calm down and watch her mouth. Thus fortified, she went back to the sun room.

"Sorry, Rog," she said putting the glass down next to the now cold eggs.

"Don't worry about it. Tell me what's going on at the station."

"Nothing much new," she said settling back into the wicker chair. "Howard is still Howard. He grew up listening to WABC blow everybody away playing nothing but Top Forty, so that's all he wants to do. It's the same goddamn argument every time. You tell him that no AM station today, most especially not a small one, can survive with a short playlist of rock music. He goes, 'Uh, huh.' You tell him that we need unique programming to give people a reason to tune us in. He goes, 'Uh, huh.' And then he starts fighting over the schedule as though nothing had ever been said." She threw her arms up in the air.

Roger chuckled. "Sounds like old times. He'd do the same with me. I suppose we shouldn't complain. At least, he doesn't have the guts to overrule me, or you. It also sounds like you've learned something. He lets you do your show the way you like."

"I pull the numbers."

"I'm not surprised. It's good. We get your signal down here at night."

Both of Acey Henson's cheeks flashed red.

"How's the big special coming?" Bannerman asked, ignoring Acey's reaction.

"You had to ask. It sucks. You know, I figured toxic stories are hot in New Jersey these days and that we could really pull together one hell of a program on it. But I have got reports on just about every goddamn creek, lake, and cesspool in the state. Makes me sick just looking at the file drawer, but I can't seem to make a story out of it. It needs a hook and I don't have it."

"Welcome to the world, Acey." He took a long swallow of Coke. "I'd keep at it. Eventually something will click. But, seriously, why the big push? I mean, the news and the programming is saving my ass, and honestly I'm grateful, but why this special? You don't need it."

"Yes I do."

Acey pushed her hands down into her pants pockets and slumped in the chair. All of a sudden, it was three and a half years ago and she was a brash, nervous punk trying to tell Roger Bannerman that she ought to be on the air.

"Rog, I want to do serious stuff, or at least I want to be able to do *some* serious stuff."

"As I recall, you have. That business with the medical center in Trenton for one."

"True. But it didn't start with me, I just picked up on it. When I get my next shot, I want to have this to show them what I can do from scratch. I don't want to stay just a radio personality with a show."

"Why not? You're good at it." He was rewarded by a renewed flush on her cheeks. "Why? What's the problem, Acey? You're doing well. Hell, you draw an incredibly broad audience, I mean, you have kids listening to you. Kids don't normally tune in talk shows, but they listen to you. That's a success. It may be unique. For my own selfish reasons, I'm hoping you stay at WCZY, but what you said before is right. Offers will come in and if you can take this act to a big station you could be set."

"Kids go with the fads, Roger. Right now, I'm a fad. It may not always be that way."

"I seem to recall you telling me you drew them before."

"That was a college radio."

"All right, forget the kids. It's still a good show."

"I can do more," she said simply.

"You may be right. I hope you are." Roger gave her a smile, which would have looked better had he not lost so much weight. "Look, I appreciate your coming down, but you need to get back and I need to take a nap."

"Sure thing. Just tell me, how is Jim doing?"

Bannerman shrugged. "Okay, I guess. Watching me is kind of hard, you know."

"I think so." She stood up and reached over to squeeze his hand. "You take care. Give me a call if you think you can start coming in. If not, I'll stop by next week."

When she left, Bannerman had never looked at the station's programming materials.

Chapter 6

FLEMINGTON, NEW JERSEY _____

THE URGE that drove Howard Firman to the washroom was real enough but it had been brought on less by the volume of coffee he had consumed than by the sound of Acey Henson's motorcycle in the parking lot. He *had* to talk to Henson when she came in—he had been telling himself that ever since he had left Thigpen at the latter's hotel earlier that morning—and he had to talk to her about matters beyond the programming schedule. That necessity was what had motivated his bladder.

Firman knew exactly how he ought to go about it. When discussing problems with a subordinate, he had been taught, make a list. Go through the list carefully, item by item, and document the conversation. Howard had the list on his desk. It was a lengthy one, mostly because he had been putting off and putting off the things that bothered him. He had justified the delay to himself on the grounds that this was really Bannerman's job and that as soon as Bannerman came back, Howard would give him the list and have Bannerman take care of it. The scene the previous night, however, had made him resolve to have The Discussion today. He could hardly avoid it. Still, it ought to be a simple task. So why was he in the bathroom with a sense of urgency but no output?

Mostly, he decided, talking with Henson was never easy. In fact, it was a pain and had always been so. He never would have hired her, but that had been Bannerman's decision, of course. Even when the conversation was strictly about programming, it was difficult. He never liked what she brought, it was never what he wanted, and yet somehow he was never able to change it. Firman did not really understand how that happened. He was, after all, the boss. The problem, as he saw it from in front of the urinal, was that she was crazy. It was not hard to find the proof. Only a crazy would have staged a fund-raiser at the Speedway, where part of the program had Acey trying to jump her bike over two schoolbuses. She had made the jump but had not quite been able to control the landing. The fall had cost her a row of stitches in one leg and left Howard wondering how to fill her air time. Henson, of course, had shown up, limp and all, and spent half the night talking about it. Not normal at all, and that probably explained why he had so much trouble dealing with her. It was not as though, he told himself, she outwitted him. Henson was not that smart. Her college degree was real enough, which had actually surprised him when he had corporate security investigate it, but it was from some cow college in the Midwest. Firman had been educated at Williams and he doubted that Henson would have lasted a semester there.

He was also troubled by her popularity. Some of the not-too-bright radio personalities made a living out of talking dirty on the air. Henson did not do that, at least not to any great extent. She also did not follow any standard format for her show, a tendency he noted creeping into the rest of the programming since Bannerman had been out so much. It was surprising anyone listened to her. He heard the back door swing open, then closed, and prayed for relief, sweat beginning to start on his lip.

It was Roger Bannerman that weighed on Acey's mind the whole drive back from Philadelphia. In some ways, she thought, he looked worse now than he had two weeks before when he had been running a high fever and had a horrible case of shingles. He looked worse, she decided, because when he had been obviously sick it had been easier to discount his depressed spirits. With his body appearing normal, well fairly normal, Roger's mood seemed perilously close to giving up. Acey had a hard time contrasting that with her memory of the man who had yelled and screamed and actually torn his own jacket in response to "I quit this shitty job" from a frustrated Acey Henson, who had tripped over her own tongue and messed up a show. How could a person be so beaten down?

Part of her also worried that the limit to her ability to cover for Roger was fast approaching an end. Not because she was tired of doing it, or even as she had told him because she might leave the station, but because the longer she tried to do it, the more likely it was that she would fail. She would tell one quick lie too many and trip herself up, or Howard would finally bestir himself and discover that Roger had done no work for the past two months and precious little for the three before them. That would be an ugly scene.

When she reached the station, she dropped the folder with the programming materials on Howard's desk, thankful that he seemed to be down the hall exercising his kidneys. Then she ducked into her office to have a quick cigarette before Howard looked through the folder. As an office, it was not much, barely a cubicle really, holding an overstuffed file cabinet, a metal desk of uncertain vintage, a telephone and piles of manilla folders organized in a way only her mind could fathom. It was *her* office, though, the nameplate next to the door said so. For Acey Henson, that was not bad.

The cigarette had not quite reached the filter when her phone rang. True to form, it was Howard, telling her to come to his office.

"Close the door, Acey," he said when she walked in. That was usual too. Given a choice, Howard would have left the door open, so that anyone in the corridor could hear him discipline the other occupant. Since the other occupant was Acey, however, Howard had to close the door. An open door would have let everyone hear her replies.

"We need to talk, Acey," he said. That was not part of the program and it made her frown. Usually, Howard would start off by pronouncing her schedule to be "shit" and then proceed to tell her what he wanted. The first time he had done it, she had nearly brained him with the ashtray she had been holding. Fortunately, Roger had taught her how to handle Howard. Acey had reached the stage where she could leave Howard flushed and sweating, her schedule intact, without even raising her voice.

"Talk about what?" she said warily.

"Last night for starters. Is there some reason you had to be so rude?"

Inwardly, Acey relaxed a little bit. "Sure. He was a jerk to put you up to proposition me and you were an asshole to do it."

Howard winced, jiggling the roll of fat below his chin. "A simple no would have sufficed."

"Possibly, but I think I made my point anyway." She smiled at him. "Is there something else?"

"Yes, damn it!" You are supposed to be her boss, Howard kept thinking. He could not push Thigpen's mocking smile of the previous night out of his mind. "What is the story with that freak you hired for the night shift?"

"What freak? Do you mean Pam?"

"Whatever her name is. She looks like a goddamn junkie."

"Pammy is not a junkie," Acey said. "She does her job, which is more than I can say for some people, and if you were where you belong at midnight it wouldn't have bothered you. Do you want to talk about programming or what? I'm tired and I have a headache."

"Ah, yes, the programming." Howard's eyes refocused on Acey, as though business had been the farthest thing from his mind. Perhaps, it had been. He was still berating himself for letting Thigpen push him into a situation where he knew Acey would humiliate him, and also for letting Acey do it. "Right, programming." He shuffled around on his desk until he found a small pad of paper with a checklist scribbled on it. The folder Acey had left for him lay closed, off to one side.

"First, I want to talk to you about this voting business on your show. One of these days we're going to get a complaint that the tallies are rigged and then we'll have the FCC on our backs. I don't need that, so I want you to stop it."

"Did you talk to Legal?"

"No, why?"

"Because I did," she countered. "I talked to them when we started. They said as long as there was a record of calls that could be checked, there was no problem. The phone company has the record of how many calls those numbers get. So, what's the big deal?"

"And we have to pay for them to keep count, too? Those calls probably end up costing us money."

"Dammit, Howard, no they don't!" Acey could feel her carefully constructed cool facade dissolving. It took her longer now to reach the flash point than it had in the recent past, but it still happened regularly. "You listen to me for a minute," she said. "Those calls cost the caller fifty cents apiece. When they connect, before the caller is told his vote is registered, there is a quick promo spot we sell to our regular customers. We make money on that. Also, a listener has to dial our number and hear our slogan, which is free advertising for us. Plus, people like it. When I'm out of sync with them, they let me know it. It helps match the program to what our audience wants. No way should we be giving this up."

She wanted to yell that Howard should have known all of that without her having to tell him. Handling the advertisers and the budget was part of the station manager's job. Howard, of course, had sloughed it off on Roger years ago. As Roger did less and less, the tasks had gravitated down to Acey. I bet I know the details of every account we have, she thought bitterly. I know whose checks are on time and who waits until the last minute. I am the one who knows what advertiser to tap when there is unsold time. I am the one who knows about every damn cent that comes into this station, not you. That was what she wanted to say, but she didn't say it. Had she said it, then it would have been obvious that Roger was no longer doing the work. Careful with the mouth, Acey, she thought.

Firman had no immediate rebuttal since he did not know, off the top of his head, what the account balance was. The financial printout for the last month should have been on his desk—he had seen it but not read it three days before—but a quick glance to either side failed to disclose it. To sidestep the argument, he made a check mark on his pad and changed the topic.

"Speaking of making money," he said, "I'd like to know what all those checks for Freedom of Information stuff are about. Whatever it's for, it's too damn much."

"I need the FOI reports for this toxic special that I'm working on with Roger. That's the only way I can get the stuff, and we can afford it."

"Well, even if we can afford it, what the hell do we need it for?"

"Oh come on, Howard. Toxic is real hot right now. Nobody has made a big story out of anything in this part of the state yet, but it doesn't take a rocket scientist to know there has to be stuff around here."

"Yeah? And just who do you think you are? If I saw you on the street, I'd figure you for a rock groupie like that little twerp you hired, not Woodward and Bernstein."

"Oh really? Well, it's better than a . . ." She chopped the sentence off right there, before she said, "fat-assed pig." Getting into a name calling match was just another way of losing. Roger had taught her that also.

"Roger thinks the idea will sell," she managed to say evenly.

"Roger thinks it will sell." Howard sighed. "What is he doing, speaking *ex cathedra* from Philadelphia?" He was thinking that, dammit, he was Roger's boss, too. "Acey, this is just a small station out in the country. We can't be fooling around with this sort of stuff. People listen to music on the radio; that's what they want. If we go to a music format, stick to just the hot music, the very top stuff, that's how we can really do well. I've talked about it with Roger before and I really think it's time we made the move. If we do well enough, we'll get noticed at corporate. Once that happens, it's onward and upward. Don't you find that an exciting concept?"

"Howard," she said, "that concept is so exciting, the piss is just drizzling right down my leg. Sure, we're a small country station, but we're also smack in between New York and Philadelphia. Anyone who wants that formula can tune in one of the big stations and get it in FM stereo too. The only way we are going to survive is to be different. It works, too. We make money, so why fiddle with it?"

As he usually did at this stage of an argument, Firman gave up and fiddled with his pen. He wanted to tell the little punk in front of him that radio was supposed to be thousands of people listening to the Top Forty countdown, the way he remembered MusicRadio WABC dominating the ratings. It was, as he had read, Alan Freed spinning record after record, to start the pop music format. It was not supposed to be some little girl renegade spinning outrageous conversations and having people vote by phone on her equally outrageous opinions. That was not radio no matter how many people listened to her. In his gut, Howard was certain of this, but he knew that if he said it, she would laugh at him and quote numbers. He felt aggrieved at Roger Bannerman for all this trouble because Bannerman, as Howard knew, was where all these ideas had come from in the first place. If Bannerman was present, he thought, he could reason with the man. Bannerman had been in radio for over fifteen years. Thinking that, he conveniently forgot that Bannerman had never given in to him either. It was easier to forget that and conclude that there was no point arguing with an errand boy, or girl as the case might be.

All he said to Acey was, "I guess you're just a little bit different, right?"

"No. Howard," she said, "I'm a lot different. Now are you going to sign off on that or not?"

Firman reached over and pulled up the top cover of the folder, then scrawled his name on the first sheet underneath it. He closed the folder again, without looking at any of its contents, and chucked it across the table.

"You'll go over it with the day crew also?" he asked.

"Naturally," answered Acey Henson.

R Y E ,   N E W   Y O R K _____

John Lawrence Thigpen woke up and for one wildly disorienting moment could not figure out where he was. That happened to him periodically. One hotel room was very much like any other hotel room. Given the amount of traveling he did, it was not surprising that every now and then he was unable to place the room or the city. Not surprising, perhaps, but that did not mean he liked the sensation much. He sat up with a groan, holding his head in his hands.

With the motion, his head oriented itself. He was in the Rye Town Hilton. It was his customary New York base, close enough to the city to be convenient for business while allowing him to stay away from Manhattan, which he hated. Convenient that is, except for being dragged into the New Jersey hinterland until two in the morning. Dear God, he asked again, why did I go out there? His amusement over being able to tweak Howard in his own station had vanished during the long ride back. It had not reappeared in the morning.

Thigpen looked at his watch and gave a start when he saw that it was eleven o'clock. The late night had combined with his California-time internal clock to wake him up later than he ever allowed himself. It was a minute before his mind took control of his racing heart rate. Calm down, he told himself, no schedule today. You are off.

He clung to that thought as he cleaned himself up in the bathroom. It was a damn good thing he had held himself to two drinks the night before. A genuine hangover on top of this would be too much to take. In God's name, what idiot had scheduled a twentieth high-school reunion for a Thursday night? If it was Saturday or Sunday morning his internal monitor would not care that it was eleven, but it was Friday and his insides were screaming that he should be at work. How long had it been since he had last taken vacation days? Long enough that he had forgotten what it was like to wake up late on a weekday.

"So, what idiot told you to go to this thing?" he asked his reflection in the mirror.

He grinned at the reflection which, predictably, grinned back. For the effort and planning he had put into taking three days off, he could have spent the weekend in Paris or Montreux instead of coming to the reunion. He was not curious about Paris or Montreux, however, and he was curious about his former classmates. What had happened to the demigods of the football team? Which of the prissy "just a good night kiss" girls would have been divorced several times with children by each man and which of the easy ones had turned out prim and proper? Who was successful and who was not? Most especially, who had fallen flat on his or her face because, given the underlying affluence of the community where Thigpen had grown up, that took a special skill. Who was now in a position to be useful to John Lawrence Thigpen? No one really, it had turned out, which had been very disappointing. Those were the questions that had drawn him to the reunion. He had not gone there to boast. Certainly not. He had not even been entirely truthful about what he did.

"Hey, Johnny! Remember me? What are you up to?" was how the conversations would start.

"Doing venture capital," would be his reply. "You know what that is?"

"Yeah, sure. I'm doing [fill in the blank] myself," and then Thigpen would let the conversation roll along whatever line the other was interested in. Usually, it was themselves.

Venture capitalist! He chuckled over that while he pulled on his clothes. Venture capitalist my ass, he thought. I am an adventure capitalist! It was not something he cared to discuss publicly. Not with that crowd. They would have been on him like jackals on a kill, all wanting an inside line, even a hint of what might be happening that no one knew about yet. Sammy Noto had been just like that anyway, as though Thigpen having slept twenty years ago with the girl who was now Sammy's wife had written Sammy a call on Thigpen's knowledge. Wrong. Except for that, it had been amusing, or it had until Howard had hijacked him. If there was a more unlikely person to have leeched onto him, Thigpen could not think of one.

It had almost spoiled the evening. He shook his head at the memory as he pulled a blazer over his polo shirt. He wondered if Howard had ever figured out who had put the Ben-Gay in his jock one long ago spring day. Probably not. Howard just wanted to show off his job, never mind that he held it only because his father knew the right people. Thigpen put it out of his head and wondered if the restaurant was open.

On his way to eat, he picked up a copy of the *New York Times*. It was his habit to read the paper with his breakfast and, even though it was closing in on noon, it was still his first meal of the day. It was equally his habit to turn directly to the business section. He skipped the articles. Anything that appeared in an article was old news, even if it was true. As for the rumors, Thigpen had no interest in reading about them. He had started too many of them to pay much attention to someone else's rumors. Instead, he went straight to the stock prices. Vacation day it might be, but Thigpen had a list of fifteen or twenty companies in his head whose prices he automatically checked. It would not have been breakfast had he not. In the middle of his journey through the New York Stock Exchange listings, his eye stopped at the line for Quad Industries. Twenty-nine and a half dollars per share, down one from the day before.

He lingered over that line, scratching his chin. Quad Industries was not on his list, never had been, but something was tickling his brain, an invisible finger scratching at its base the way his forefinger was on his chin. Ah, yes. Quad Industries owned Howard's station. The company was a large conglomerate, he knew, put together over the past fifteen to twenty years. It was a rather diffuse conglomerate, without any recognizable theme. There was a subsidiary in defense electronics and another in children's toys (although maybe there was a synergy there the humorless analysts had missed), one that made lawn furniture and one that made fertilizer. There were about thirty different subsidiaries in all, and many of them had subsidiaries of their own. Thigpen could recall only a few of them. He could not remember whether there was a single subsidiary that owned the radio stations, the logical way to do it, or whether they were split up. Thigpen always looked at such organizations as being inefficient. It was the radio station that kept his mind on the company. The station would have a broadcast license, of course, which was valuable. Then, looking beyond the old equipment, there was the building and the adjoining acreage that Howard had boasted about the station owning. If there was any truth to Howard's babbling, the station itself was comfortably in the black. How much was a station like that really worth and how much could one be bought for? The price of television stations was high enough to give buyers nosebleeds, but not radio stations. How many radio stations did Quad Industries own? Thigpen wondered if anyone had bothered to look at the value of the company as the sum of its parts rather than the amorphous blob it appeared to be on the surface.

Twenty-nine and a half dollars a share. Damn! The paper told him nothing that was worth knowing. The market price of a single share, in isolation, was worthless knowledge.

His interest having been piqued, it was all Thigpen could do to sit at the table and eat the meal he had ordered. Once he finished eating, with a reasonable amount of decorum, he bolted for the elevators. Back in his room, he called his California office and was put through to his secretary.

"Maria," he said, "I need you to get something for me."

"No problem, Mr. Thigpen. None of us thought you'd hold out until the weekend."

He ignored the jest and plowed ahead. "Listen, can you get me the latest 10-K for Quad Industries?"

"I can get it, but I know we don't have that one in the office. I'll have to order it."

"Damn! Well, if that's what you have to do. Meanwhile, can you find whatever we do have? Clippings, brokerage reports, that sort of thing."

"Of course I can."

"Good, good. Put it together and Fedex it to me here will you? You have the address."

"No problem. You enjoying your time off, Boss?"

"Absolutely," he said, and hung up.

Thigpen lay back on the bed, hands behind his head, and permitted himself a daydream about what the financial picture of the company might truly look like. What it would look like, that is, after he was through sorting out the chaff. The reality might not live up to his expectations, but until the documents arrived, he could enjoy his fantasy. Who knew? Maybe it would be even better. It did look as though there had been one useful person at that reunion, unlikely a prospect though he would have seemed in advance.

John Lawrence Thigpen smiled a broad smile. He liked to style himself an adventure capitalist. Most people would have called him something else. If they were being polite, they might have called him a raider. Most people were polite, at least, to his face.

Chapter 7

_____

SUNDAY MORNING Jodie Schmidt was lying flat on her back on a bed without a top sheet. She was staring up at the ceiling, or would have been, except for the fact that her eyes were held shut by pieces of tape. She looked rather like a butterfly in a lepidopterist's collection, limbs carefully staked out away from the body for better viewing. She breathed, but only in synchrony with the machine at the bedside, which let out a sigh every three to four seconds. A plastic hose from the machine disappeared up her right nostril. Other plastic tubes ran from pumps that either sat on the shelf behind the bed or hung from poles alongside it. One tube led into a dressing on the center of her chest, the others to sites along her arms. The pumps whined and clicked, liquid crystal displays showing how much liquid had run from each one into Jodie, in much the same way as the ventilator beat out her breaths with the precision of a metronome. Yet another tube snaked down one leg, leading to a bag tied to the bed rail. A tiny amount of yellow liquid had collected at its bottom. In the midst of this, Jodie made not the slightest move. That was not surprising because one of the drugs given to her had paralyzed every muscle in her body. It was easier to run a human body by dials and switches if the body was not moving.

Zeke Schwartz stood, almost as motionless, at the foot of the bed. His eyes were fixed on the numbers displayed by the monitors on the wall, bright green numerals on the black screens. The expression that had congealed on his face was not pleasant.

Jolanta Marienkiewicz pulled back the sliding glass door that was the entrance to Jodie's room and stepped inside. Her face was flushed and her breathing rapid, as though she had run up four flights of stairs, which she had. Schwartz turned around at her entrance.

"Have you seen her yet?"

"Not today, yet. I was just getting sign-out from Tony and there was a problem on the floor. I came in to say hello yesterday and she looked fine."

"There is a problem here. Did he tell you that her blood pressure was down this morning?"

"Yes. He said she was probably dry." *Dry, of course, in the sense of being* a little dehydrated. Marienkiewicz checked her notes briefly. "She got two boluses of fluid over the last three hours."

"Dry my left big toe!" Schwartz snapped. "You practically don't even need a stethoscope to hear her gurgle. If she gets any wetter, she's going to need scuba gear. Come outside with me."

He gathered up the clipboard from the bedside table and went out through the glass door. There he spread the papers out on a small rolling table. Jodie might be paralyzed, but that did not guarantee that she was not awake. If she was awake, she could hear. They were joined by two nurses wearing scrubs. Both looked as tense as Schwartz.

Zeke stood over the flowcharts and ran his finger along one column of figures, much the way Patton might have traced Rommel's line. "Look at the ins and the outs. What do they tell you?"

"She's not dry." Jola felt a knot in her stomach. Had Tony come down to look? She did not know. She had simply assumed it.

Her unspoken question was answered almost immediately by one of the nurses.

"I tried to tell Tony about this twice last night," she said. "I couldn't get him to come down."

"Did you try the Senior?" Zeke asked.

"Yeah. He had an emergency and told me to page Tony."

"Shit. If that happens, you can call me. Always." He shook his head. "There are assassins everywhere, Jo. You have to watch out for them. Okay." He shifted his attention back to the charts. "She's not dry. I sent off a blood gas and I've given her some Lasix already. Now what?" It might be an intensive care unit, and the patient might be ill, but there was still time for a quiz.

"Pressors?" Those were a class of drugs that by squeezing the heart and the blood vessels could increase the blood pressure of a failing patient.

"Right," Schwartz replied. "They are being mixed up right now."

"But what is wrong?"

"Septic. Almost certainly."

"How?" Jola looked puzzled. "I thought when we took out that bowel that we fixed the infection."

"Old saying, Kay Vitch, 'a patient can have as many diseases as she pleases.' Maybe the bug went from bowel to bloodstream, maybe it came from somewhere else. All I know is that she's got no white cells, she's losing her blood pressure, and that spells infection. Now, you tell me. We haven't had a positive culture yet, she's getting her Rambocillin and she's still sick. What's going on?"

"Rambocillin?"

"Yeah. A drug that kills any bug that it meets. She's getting the latest and greatest. So, what's wrong with her?"

"Fungus?"

"Bingo! My bet exactly. Now you're halfway there. What are you going to treat her with?"

"I'm not sure."

"Reasonable answer. These days, you get a choice. My preference, right now, would be Aspergicin. It's fairly new, been around about three years, but I also had some experience with it in Boston while it was being tested. I like it. Less side effects than the others and it's great at sterilizing those indwelling catheters. I don't want to lose her central line." To himself, he thought that if it worked, he would be a lot happier about the Meldrum Products Oncology Fellowship. He might even say so to this Woodward character, assuming of course that the man ever called him back.

"Zeke, are we going to lose her?"

"We might." He looked at her face and guessed that there was more there than just routine concern. "You like her, don't you?"

Jola's face went bright red. "Yes, I do. I think she's a neat kid, even if she does call me Dr. Kay Vitch."

Schwartz grinned. "That's your fault for making a big deal out of the pronunciation in the first place. She is a neat kid, though. Let's see if we can keep her alive, shall we?"

Keeping Jodie Schmidt alive, it turned out, was easier said than done. Her blood pressure stubbornly refused to come back up, even to the low pressures that were normal for a child. They boosted the dose of the pressors as high as they dared, then in desperation switched to a more powerful drug. No matter what they did with the ventilator settings, the oxygen content of Jodie's blood barely budged from where it teetered at the lowest limit of adequate. It was as though, Schwartz remarked with exasperation, Jodie's numbers were every bit as obstinate in their refusal to do what they were supposed to do as Jodie herself, when she was up and playing hide-and-seek in the clinic.

"This is getting ridiculous," Zeke muttered as he looked at the latest set of numbers on Jodie's blood. "If this is going to go on all day, I need better access. How come she doesn't have an arterial line?"

"It clotted off last night," one of the nurses told him. "Tony said just to pull it."

"Well, she still needs it."

It was one thing for Schwartz to say that Jodie needed an arterial line, but that did not make it happen. Jola had never put one in before and, in fact, had never seen one put in. The concept was simple enough. An arterial line was nothing more than a small, plastic catheter, usually placed in the radial artery at the wrist. Hooked to a pressure transducer, it allowed the pulse and blood pressure to be continuously displayed on a monitor. It also made it easy to take blood samples. One merely stuck the needle of a syringe into the hub of the line and the blood pumped right into the syringe. The problem was putting the catheter in place. One of the nurses already had all the tubing in place before Jola muttered for the second time to Schwartz that she did not know how to do it.

Zeke simply lifted one eyebrow and said, "No problem. Just watch this one."

He went to work quickly with a padded board and a roll of tape. Soon Jodie's arm was swathed in tape, her hand held as though reaching out for a ball, the wrist exposed and facing upward. The catheter Zeke held was the same as they used for intravenous lines. It was a thin tube of plastic mounted on a plastic hub. The plastic fit flush over a needle so that the point of the needle projected just past the end of the plastic tube. Zeke swabbed off the wrist with antiseptic and felt for the pulse. He grumbled under his breath, as he always did, about the gloves he wore. He had learned his techniques in the days before AIDS, back when no one worried about a little blood on the hands. It always seemed that the glove interfered with his touch.

When he was satisfied with the location of the pulse, he kept one finger lightly over it, the catheter poised in his hand. He looked a lot like a spear fisherman, patiently waiting to strike at a fish below the surface. Smoothly, he stuck the needle into the wrist and felt it hit the artery below. The artery, however, was muscular and rubbery. It rolled to the side and the needle sank down striking bone.

"Sorry, Jodie," he murmured, pulling the catheter back and feeling again for the artery.

The apology was as automatic as it was unnecessary. Being paralyzed, Jodie did not flinch. Beyond that, Schwartz had loaded her with enough morphine and Valium that she would feel nothing. Thank God for those drugs, he thought. The paralytic drug did nothing more than that; it did not impair consciousness. Zeke could imagine nothing worse than being paralyzed, breathing by a machine and getting stuck with needles, all while being awake.

On his second try he felt a pop as the needle speared the artery. Bright red blood spurted back through the hub and onto the towels under Jodie's hand. With his forefinger, Zeke pushed the plastic off the needle and up into the artery. A moment later, he had the tubing connected and a green line traced Jodie's pulse on the monitor above the bed.

"Got it?" He looked up at Jola.

"I think so."

"Good. You know the saying, 'see one, do one, teach one'? You do the next one."

Jola looked troubled. "I'm not sure it's that easy."

"It never is, not for any of us. You just have to do it anyway." Zeke pulled the knot of his tie away from the collar so he could open the top button. "Okay," he said, "back to business. Where is that damn Aspergicin?"

"I don't know. I ordered it right after we discussed it, but it hadn't come up when we started on that line."

A quick check disclosed that it had not arrived since then either. A quick call by Marienkiewicz to the Pharmacy uncovered the problem. Aspergicin was classed as a new antibiotic and, as such, could be used only with the approval of the Infectious Disease service.

"You mean you're not going to send it up?" Jola was incredulous.

"I can't," the pharmacist told her. "ID has to approve it before I can give it out."

"I don't think you understand," Jola said. "This is the ICU. I've got a septic kid up here who's going down the tubes. I need the drug."

"Page whoever is on for ID," she was told. "All they have to do is call me and I can release it."

Doing as she was told, Jola hung up and asked the operator to page the Infectious Disease Fellow. It took a while for the Fellow to respond, as she happened to be having brunch at the Hilton. When she did call back, she listened to Jola's story and said that she would come by in the afternoon to see Jodie. Marienkiewicz protested that they could not wait for the consultant to finish brunch but found it to no avail. Yelling "Wait!" into the phone to keep the Fellow from hanging up, she waved frantically for Schwartz to pick up the receiver.

"I am sorry, Dr. Schwartz," the ID Fellow said after listening to Schwartz recount the same story, "but we have to restrict the use of these agents. It's not always clear that they are more effective than the older drugs. Also they are much more expensive and the more indiscriminately we use them, the quicker we get resistance."

"All of which is correct," Zeke said, "as far as it goes. However, I have enough experience to know that her chances are going to be real poor if she doesn't get treated quickly and I can't see starting with second best in this situation."

"I said I would come by in the afternoon and evaluate her."

"I see. Well, obviously you understand this case far better than I do, so I will explain to her parents that you have made this decision and that you will be here this afternoon to explain to them why we have to be so careful with these new drugs. In fact, I think I'll sit in on your explanation. I may learn something."

"That is totally inappropriate, Dr. Schwartz."

"So are you, Doctor. Do I get the drug?"

It reached the ICU from the Pharmacy about fifteen minutes later.

Aggravating as that problem was, it paled in comparison to the beepers. In theory, the beepers were a convenience since a person wearing one was accessible without the constraint of having to stay in a prescribed location. In practice, they were a constant annoyance. Jola was responsible for a floor full of children aside from Jodie. They did not vanish simply because she was completely tied up with a sick child. Many of the calls could probably have waited, but there was no way of knowing that without answering them. Finally, Schwartz called the Senior Resident and handed him Jola's beeper. She was both relieved and chagrined by that move. Relieved because she could not, as Schwartz pointed out to the Senior, take care of Jodie if she had to run back and forth to the phone and, in any case, she was in no position to take care of a real problem on the floor if one arose. She was chagrined at the same time because she thought it might look as though she could not handle her job.

There could be no such succor for Schwartz and it seemed that his beeper went off every fifteen minutes. Jola caught bits and pieces of his conversations as she shuttled between Jodie's room and the small office where they had spread out the charts. There were two children with ear aches, followed eventually by two pediatricians seeing the children with the ear aches, a child who had thrown up his medicine and one who had lost a battle with the family cat. Since all of these children were being treated for cancer, each call required consideration. It all had to be done with one eye kept on the room where the nurses worked over Jodie. Finally, there was a call from the Emergency Room. Jola had just walked into the office with a handful of lab results as Schwartz hung up the phone. He had that tight little grin that she had come to associate with trouble on the way.

There was a mischievous tone, it was almost playful, in Schwartz's voice when he said, "Kay Vitch, you are about to find out why people hate being on with me. I have a package from the ER for you."

"Can Don see the kid in the ER?" Jola asked. The standard procedure would have been for her to go down to the ER and see the new patient there. She wondered if Schwartz was thinking Jodie stable enough for her to resume her regular responsibilities. If so, Jola was not ready to agree.

"Not going to the floor," Zeke said. "Coming straight here." He sounded just like a younger cousin about to spring an intricate practical joke.

"Why is that?"

"I'll tell you. By the way, do you speak Spanish?"

"No."

"Then you better call an interpreter. Neither do I. We'll work out the details as we go, but the basic outline is this. There is a nine-year-old boy down there named Diego Aguilar. They are from Venezuela, family up here on the south shore or some such. Anyway, the kid had been feeling ill for a few weeks so finally, on Saturday, they went to a clinic down there. The lab called the doc this morning to tell him that the kid has leukemia. He went ahead and did the bone marrow himself. The slides are coming with the family. The kid has a sky high white count and the doc thinks it's the promyelocytic type. You know anything about that?"

"Just from hematology lectures. I've never taken care of one. What happens?"

"They bleed all over the place."

"How do I treat that?"

"Plasma. That and heparin, sometimes."

Jola stared at him, not believing that he could be joking. "Heparin is an anticoagulant," she said slowly. "Why would you give that to someone who is bleeding?"

"Because you have to think about what the basic problem is. These leukemia cells contain granules that trigger the clotting mechanism. When the cells break down, and they go fast when we start treating, they dump the granules and you get microscopic clotting everywhere. It uses up the clotting factors and you can't stop real bleeding."

"I know about disseminated intravascular coagulation," Jola said. "I never heard of using heparin to treat it. Does it work?"

"Sometimes yes, and sometimes no. Depends who you talk to. It's worth trying if we get stuck, which we may. I'll give you the doses before I go downstairs."

"You're not planning on leaving are you?"

He grinned at her. "Only briefly. I have a kid coming in tomorrow morning for a second opinion and I need to look at the slides. I know Carlos is in Pathology today because he promised me a reading on Jerry's tumor by this afternoon. My guess is that now will be the best chance I get." Marienkiewicz had gone quite pale while he was talking, so he added, "Just get everything set up the way I set it out. It won't really hit the fan until we start treating him. If there's a hitch, just page me. Lord knows, everyone else does."

Once he left the unit, Schwartz hustled. For all his glibness to Marienkiewicz, he was not happy at the prospect of leaving for any length of time with an unstable Jodie Schmidt and a new disaster in the making. Still, he had to see those slides, not because he could read them any better than

Carlos, he could not, but because he needed to see them himself and ask his questions of the pathologist before he gave an opinion. He slept better that way. He made a quick detour to the Emergency Room to see the slides the clinic doctor had made of Diego Aguilar's bone marrow. It took little more than a glance to satisfy himself that the diagnosis was correct. Sometimes, things were obvious. The child had already been sent upstairs, so Schwartz headed for his next stop.

The Pathology Department looked deserted when he arrived. Since he knew Carlos had to be around, he headed for his office and pushed the door open. Carlos Ibanez was at his desk, swivel chair tilted dangerously far back, blowing smoke at the ceiling. He seemed lost in thought, for he did not look up when Schwartz entered.

"Hey, Earth to Carlos!" Zeke called out.

The other man was startled and almost went over backward. "Christ, Zeke, next time knock. You could kill a man that way."

"I did knock. You were out in the ozone."

"Oh. Well, I wasn't expecting you yet. Jerry's slides won't be ready until three. I'll call you the moment they're done. Promise."

Schwartz laughed. "I wasn't here about Jerry. You said three, and I'll be here at one minute after three. You know that. I've got something else." He held up a box of slides, a clear plastic case about the size of a cigarette pack. The glass slides inside jiggled when he shook it.

"Ah. What have you got there?"

"A tumor I need to give an opinion on tomorrow morning. The ER just handed me a brand new leukemic, so I thought I should do this now."

"Ah hah. The usual luck of Ezekiel Schwartz. Are you sure they don't announce your call days on the evening news?"

Ibanez got up and took the box of slides from Schwartz. He settled in again at a big multi-headed microscope. He spread the slides out on the table in front of him, then picked up one after another and scanned through them slowly. Then, he waved Schwartz to a seat in front of the eyepieces opposite his own.

"So, how's your group coming," Ibanez said as he focused up and down on a slide, moved it left to right and then changed the magnification. "You enjoying your job?"

Zeke's first response was a chuckle. "More than likely, I'll be ready for a padded cell soon."

"What's the matter?" Ibanez demanded. He tossed the slide off the stage and replaced it with another. "I thought Barlow was supposed to help out."

"That's why I'm going to need the padded cell. If I had no help, at least I would know I had no help. With Barlow, I'm never sure."

"Ah. Here, look at this field. Here and here." He varied the magnification and pushed the slide around with his fingers as he spoke.

Watching the slide move around under magnification made Schwartz seasick. It had from the time he had been in school and he often wondered how a pathologist could stare at slides all day.

"What did they say it was?" Ibanez asked. Zeke swallowed and handed him the papers that had come with the slides.

"No argument from me," Ibanez said, after thumbing through them. "It is what they say it is. That what you need?"

"Yup. Thanks, Carlos." Zeke stood up, immediately relieved once his eyes were away from the microscope. "I have a feeling I had better get my ass back upstairs. Call me when you have a look at Jerry's sections will you?"

Upstairs, the unit, which had been busy before, now resembled a stirred anthill. Some of that still revolved around Jodie, but the center of the activity was the newly admitted child. Schwartz examined him briefly, checked over the preparations Marienkiewicz had made, looked at the laboratory results that had been obtained, and retired to the little office they had used earlier to calculate the doses he wanted. Once that was done, he gathered up Marienkiewicz and went to speak to the parents. It was a difficult conversation, made more so by the necessity of funneling everything through the interpreter, who was fluent enough in English and Spanish but less so in the language of medicine. Schwartz came away with a feeling of frustration, that too little information had been conveyed. At least, he thought, the gravity of the situation was understood by everyone. If the boy was still alive in a day or two, there would be time for another discussion.

There was no crisis just then, however. Schwartz and Marienkiewicz made their preparations, drew up drugs they might need and taped them by the bed, and tried to bring the child as close to normal as they could. Schwartz's drugs arrived and were given and there was still no crisis. It came suddenly, about two hours later. The Aguilar boy coughed and what came up was bloody. Then his right hand began to twitch and a moment later his body was in the throes of a grand mal convulsion.

Zeke popped into the room and ordered anticonvulsants. Then he went to check the boy's eyes while Jola came up by his side.

"What's happening?" she asked.

"Bleeding more. Probably into his head as well. Better get him another bag of plasma and order some more platelets from the blood bank."

No sooner had he said that, than the pattern on the heart monitor went awry. Almost simultaneously, the blood pressure dropped.

"Get the crash cart," Schwartz snapped. Then he leaned over to the shelf behind the bed to grab the laryngoscope and an endotracheal tube, six inches of clear plastic that could be used to connect a patient to a ventilator. He rattled off a string of medication orders to deal with the cardiac arrest all the while using the blade of the laryngoscope to pull up on the jaw and tongue so that he could fit the tube down the windpipe.

The anesthesia resident came running from the other side of the unit and fitted a bag hooked to an oxygen line to the end of the tube Schwartz had inserted. That allowed him to breathe the boy by squeezing the bag until a technician showed up with the ventilator.

Jola stopped asking questions; she was standing at the boy's side when the trouble started, so she started pumping on his chest the way she had been taught. To her surprise, nobody pushed her out of the way. She barely noticed when two of the nurses slid a board under the child to give her a firm surface to pump against. For Jola, the events seemed to be on videotape, albeit on fast forward. People crowded around the bed with medications, tubes and needles. There was blood everywhere. It spattered up against the inside of the plastic tube every time the anesthesiologist forced in a breath. It dribbled from every needle puncture in the skin and puddled on the bedsheets. Jola tried not to think of the bleeding her pumping must be causing where she could not see it. Eventually, the flurry died down. The child was still alive, his heart beating normally on its own, and the seizures had been stopped. She realized that a pool of sweat had soaked her shirt under each arm. She looked over at Schwartz. His tie was gone, but otherwise he looked unchanged from before.

"Zeke," one of the nurses was saying, "you had a page about half an hour ago. Dr. Ibanez in Pathology. I told him you were tied up."

"Fair assessment," Zeke said. "I hope he's still there."

"He said he would wait."

Carlos proved as good as his word. "Hi there," he said when he picked up the phone. "I heard you were having fun."

"Loads," said Zeke. "You have news for me on Jerry?"

"Yup. Have a question for you first."

"Shoot."

"This kid ever have hepatitis?"

Schwartz paused for a moment. "Not that I know of. Why?"

"Well, my friend, because you've got, or more accurately he's got, a hepatocellular carcinoma. That's why."

"I will be damned. A primary liver tumor. That explains why his CT scan looked like it did. Thanks, Carlos."

"No problem. I'll leave the slides out for you if you want to come down later."

Zeke looked up to find that Jola had walked over during the conversation. He repeated Carlos's findings to her.

"That's odd isn't it," she asked. "At least, it's odd for a child."

"Damn odd, in this country anyway," Zeke replied. "Common enough
in Asia, but not here. Most of the time, people who get it have a chronic
infection with hepatitis. That's why Carlos asked. We didn't get a history of
that, did we?"

"No. I can screen for that, though."

"Do that," he said. "You can do me a favor also. When you call the floor,
can you ask them to send the Inmans down here? I told them to meet me on
the floor to talk about the results and, frankly, I'd rather stay close to here."

"No problem," she said. "I'd rather you stay close to here too."

Zeke smiled at that. "Don't shortchange yourself. You did real well back
there, Dr. Kay Vitch. It was nice work."

Marienkiewicz blushed. "Not really. Everything sort of blurred. I was
just following what you said."

"Yeah, well, you didn't screw up and you didn't freeze and you didn't
wet your pants and I've seen all three. But, don't worry. I'm sure you'll get
another chance tonight."

Part of Schwartz hoped that the Inmans were not there, that they had
found some reason not to come to the hospital, that they would come on
Monday. Surely, that would be a sane thing to do. It had been Schwartz
who had the crazy idea, "I'll have the results Sunday, so if you want to
come in late afternoon I can talk to you about them." It had seemed sensible then. He had to work Sunday anyhow, and with new housestaff it had
been reasonable to suppose that he would be there the whole day. Why not
talk to them Sunday rather than Monday, when he would be tired from the
long weekend and up to his neck in problems. Unfortunately, it no longer
seemed like a good idea, not with Jodie teetering on the brink and the new
boy bidding fair to slide over it. Worst of all, there was no cavalry to call.
He was the cavalry. Serve you right, he thought, for having the temerity to
think you could build a brand new program in this subspecialty. Briefly, he
closed his eyes and felt overwhelming fatigue. He opened them as he heard
the ward clerk announce that, yes, the Inmans had been waiting and they
would be right down.

Zeke Schwartz had come to the conclusion years before that trying to
talk around a difficult subject in the hopes of making it more palatable was
a losing proposition. There was no way of turning bad news into good
news, so it was best given quickly. That way, one could move on to the
topic of what to do about it. Once they had seated themselves in the ante-
room outside in the unit, he did just that. He told them the diagnosis Carlos

had given and the outlook, which in his opinion was no more than a month or two of life if nothing was done. It bothered him to give a diagnosis without a personal look at the slides, the way he had done with Monday morning's case, because he could remember one episode where he had been given a diagnosis over the phone only to have the senior pathologist change it at the Tumor Board meeting and then deny that the phone call had taken place. That had been a nightmare.

After he finished speaking, Schwartz watched Charley and Ellen Inman to see what they did with the news. Every family was different when it could no longer hope that the diagnosis would be something benign. Sometimes parents blew up; sometimes they broke down. Outwardly, the Inmans did neither. Tears glistened at the corners of Ellen Inman's eyes and she fished in her purse for a tissue to wipe them away before they ran out. Charley just stared off into nowhere.

When her eyes had been dried, it was Ellen Inman who took the lead in asking about what was to be done. Schwartz had little in the way of good news in that regard either. The tumor was inoperable. Ivory had relieved the blockage, which had been the immediate cause of Jerry turning yellow, but the tumor had grown too widely within the liver and through the liver's capsule, for it to be completely removed. There was no effective treatment known, although modest success had been reported with a variety of drugs. Schwartz offered to check the latest information and then use whatever seemed most promising. It was not much to offer. Ellen Inman had a number of questions after that, specific ones about the different drugs, about why there was no good treatment, about how to pay for all of it. She wanted to know why it had happened. Schwartz, in turn, asked about hepatitis, but neither the Inmans nor any of their children had had it, as far as they knew. Then she came back to the Pro-Insul. Had that caused Jerry's tumor? Charley looked uncomfortable, but Ellen insisted on asking the question. Schwartz found it more disturbing than the first time. Some chemicals did odd things to the liver, and this was a liver tumor.

"There is nothing in particular that I know of," he said, "but I agree that it is worth looking into. I can check it out better during the week and I'll let you know what I find. It won't affect anything that we do, though."

Charley asked nothing, not even at the end.

Schwartz walked back to the unit feeling drained. Two meetings like that in one day was about as much as he cared to handle. It looked quiet in the unit, enough so that he began to think of dinner as a possibility, especially since he had missed lunch. That was when his beeper went off again.

"Hello, Ezie?" said a female voice when he picked up the phone.

"What?"

"I said 'hello.' Don't you recognize your Aunt Gussie?"

"Oh. Of course, I do, Aunt Gussie. Why are you paging me?"

"Is it a bad time, dear?"

Was it a bad time? It probably could be worse. "It's okay. What's up?"

"I just wanted to remind you about Danny's bar mitzvah next Saturday. Everyone is looking forward to seeing you. I didn't want you to forget."

"I didn't forget." Actually, he had. "Thank you for reminding me, though."

"That's all right. Listen, Ezie dear, can I ask you a question about my arthritis?"

"Aunt Gussie, I'm really sorry, but I have to go now. Can I call you during the week?"

He hung up the phone and turned around to find the charge nurse looking at him with a bemused expression on her face.

"Aunt Gussie?" she asked.

"If you're lucky, I'll be polite and not say what I'm thinking," said Schwartz.

Whether he would have said anything remained unknown, because just then Jodie's blood pressure began to fall again.

They spent most of the evening stabilizing Jodie, only to have the Aguilar boy begin to deteriorate. Around midnight, it looked as though he might die, but somehow, they turned him around. It was only a temporary respite, however. In the early morning hours he began to have seizures again and then he died again. This time nothing worked, no medicines, no electric shock, no pounding on his chest brought him back.

After an hour of trying every trick he knew to coerce a body into functioning, Schwartz brushed sweaty hair off his forehead and declared, "Enough."

Ten heads looked up at him in a stillness broken only by the EKG machine as the pen drew a straight line, marred only by an occasional irregular hump.

"Thank you, everybody, for your help," Schwartz said, "but I'm afraid that's it." He reached over and turned off the ventilator, a symbolic end for the struggle.

Zeke looked around the room and saw Jola at the window, staring out into a gray morning. He was not sure if she was crying.

"You okay?" he asked, putting a hand on her shoulder.

"I don't know. To have—oh, I don't know."

"You mean, to have somebody die when you are responsible?"

"Yes." She looked around. Her eyes were dry. "It feels horrible."

"It doesn't get easier. We just learn to hide it better."

"But what did we miss?"

Schwartz knew that was a safe way of asking what they had done wrong. "Nothing," he said, "at least nothing that I can think of. There are some fights you can't win and I'm afraid this was one of them. Look, I need to talk with the family for a little while. Why don't you get cleaned up and I'll meet you for a cup of coffee?"

"Sure." Then she managed a faint smile. "Don't you think you need to get cleaned up more than I do?"

Schwartz took a quick look in the room's mirror and conceded that she had a point. During the night, he had exchanged his shirt for a green scrub top. It was stained with sweat, brown blotches of Betadine and blood. His face needed a shave.

"I think you're right," he said.

Safely ensconced in the tiny bathroom of the ICU, Schwartz exchanged his grimy scrub top for a fresh one pulled off the supply cart. Then he stepped over to the sink and splashed his face with cold water. After several splashes, he looked up at the mirror. The face he saw was haggard, eyes bloodshot, water dripping off his stubble.

"God. I do this for a living?"

He shook his head, flinging droplets against the mirror. The only place to sit in the bathroom was the toilet, so he put the lid down and sat on it. His body felt like an inert lump.

He always felt that way after a wild night. As long as there was action, as long as things were happening fast, Schwartz would barely notice his fatigue. He could go all night into the next day and still feel, if not fine, okay as long as there was a continuous stream of action. The moment the action stopped, the moment he could relax, it all caught up with him. He felt as though he could go to sleep right there on the toilet seat. That was a dangerous sensation because he had a full day's work ahead of him.

The night had been bad, even for him. It would, doubtless, embellish his image with the housestaff as a black cloud, someone whose call nights were to be avoided at all cost. He chuckled at the thought. Cloud colors were a funny thing, a bit like karma. Some people had white clouds. It was always quiet when they were on call. It could be so quiet that one would think a "closed" sign had been posted outside the hospital. Then, there were those like Schwartz with black clouds. Trouble seemed to find them. It had been that way for Schwartz ever since the day he had first walked onto a ward as a medical student. From all appearances, it would be that way until the day he retired. At least, people with black clouds were frequently excellent physicians. Certainly, they had plenty of practice.

With a groan, Schwartz dragged himself off the toilet seat. He knew from experience that if he could keep moving, he would be all right. It was giving in to the desire to vegetate that was dangerous.

The storage room of the ICU held a Mister Coffee and a box of crackers. Above the machine, a hand-lettered sign had been taped.

"Keep 'em alive 'til eight o'five," it read.

Schwartz shook his head at the sight. While that might be the sole objective of a tired intern, it would be unfortunate if one of the families saw it. He took the sign down, then poured himself a cup of coffee from the ICU's pot. That would get him through the meeting with the Aguilars. Then he could finish his notes and probably put away a full pot of coffee while he was doing it. That would see him through clinic.

Chapter 8

SCHEUERMANN'S RUN, NEW JERSEY _____

CHARLEY INMAN was quiet the whole of the long drive back from the hospital. In the passenger seat next to him, Ellen was quiet as well, looking out the window most of the time. That was fortunate because Charley was no more interested in responding to conversation than he was in initiating it. He had expected the doctor to tell him that something was wrong with Jerry—no kid went around with yellow eyes without something being wrong—but he was totally unprepared for the way he felt following their talk with Schwartz. When Schwartz had said, "This is what it is," it was like having a prison door slam shut behind him.

His mind still had trouble believing it. Cancer was something that happened to old people, not to kids. It had happened to Charley's father. Bert Inman had been sixty-eight years old and sick for months before the doctors told him that he had a growth on his intestines. They had taken it out, but it had already spread to his liver and he died soon after. Schwartz had said that Jerry's had started in his liver. Was that right? Did Schwartz really know? Charley wished he knew the answer to that.

He was no more talkative when they reached the house. It was late for starting dinner, and Ellen really did not feel like cooking, which was just as well because Charley did not feel like eating anyway. Instead, he dropped some ice cubes into a tall soda glass and poured it full of scotch.

"What are you looking at me like that for?" Ellen had been watching him pour from her usual seat at the kitchen table. Her expression was disapproving.

"Jerry's got cancer and you're going to have a drink."

"Why shouldn't I?"

"Because we need to figure out what to do and getting drunk won't help."

"There's nothing to figure. That's Schwartz's job."

"There's stuff to figure."

Charley's eyes narrowed. "You're thinking the Pro-Insul did it, aren't you?"

"Well, don't you? It makes sense. Jerry didn't have no infection. You heard Schwartz ask. You know the answer, same as I."

"Oh, so now it's my fault Jerry is sick." Charley took a swig of his drink, then topped it off again.

"Charley Inman, I did *not* say it was your fault. But, maybe it is someone's fault and you need to be thinking and not drinking."

Charley mumbled a response into his glass. He could see that it would get around to being his fault, no matter how the conversation started. He wanted no part of that. Rather than face that, he took his glass upstairs and left Ellen and her disapproval in the kitchen.

Upstairs was no better. It was too quiet. It was strange, because usually he was yelling at Jerry to be quiet or turn off the radio or turn down his stereo, but now there was no Jerry and it was too quiet. Just a few days before, he remembered, he had been ready to wring Jerry's neck over some stupid song the kid had played five times in a row. Now, he missed him. Drink in hand, he walked into Jerry's room and sat down on the bed. About halfway through the scotch, he decided that he wanted to do something to cheer up Jerry. He was nearly to the bottom of the glass before the idea crystallized, or, at least, precipitated, in his mind. In the hospital, without Charley to tell him what he could and could not listen to, it was a sure bet that Jerry would have the radio on at that hour. There was a telephone in Jerry's room, a gift from last Christmas. Charley picked up the receiver and dialed WCZY.

The first two tries resulted in a busy signal. The third attempt went through. Charley told the operator who answered the phone that he wanted to call in to Acey Henson's show. The man wanted Charley's name and the reason for his call. Charley gave his name, but danced around the reason. He did not want to sound silly to whoever was on the other end. It was enough to satisfy the man, apparently, because Charley was told to hold, his call would be queued and he would be notified when he was going on the air. Charley sat back and finished his scotch. He had no idea how long he would have to wait. In fact, he almost hung up twice before the man cut in again to tell him that he was being connected.

In the broadcast studio, Acey Henson looked at her monitor. The only call waiting was from someone named Charley; the board showed no reason for the call.

"He sounds a little slurred, Acey," Gordy's voice said into her headset. "If you want, I can cut him out. What do you think?"

Acey wasted no time thinking about it. "Go ahead and put him through," she said. It had been a dull evening. A drunk caller might be entertaining. If not, she could always cut him off in the middle. She caught the signal that her microphone was again live to the outside.

"Good evening, Charley!" There was a silence after the greeting. "Hello Charley. Earth to Charley, are you there?"

In spite of the cue from Gordy, Charley Inman's mind had wandered far from the phone. Belatedly, he realized that Henson was talking to him. "Uh, I'm here," he said, just in time to avoid a hang up.

"Okay, Charley, I thought for a moment that we'd lost you. What do you think of the show tonight?"

"I don't know. I haven't been listening to it. I mean, I'm sure it's fine, but it's not the sort of stuff I like, so I don't listen to it."

"Well, I'm sure there are a few people around who are like that. But tell me, Charley, you don't like my show and you don't listen to it so why, if I may be so bold, are you calling in?" In the studio, Acey crossed her fingers. Every now and then, there was a call like this. Sometimes, they could be a great deal of fun.

"I wasn't calling for me," Charley said hastily. "It's really for my kid."

That changed Acey's thinking. This was going to be an oddball call. No way of guessing where it would go. "Tell me about it," she said.

"My kid, Jerry, he's twelve. He listens to you all the time, at least he does if I don't catch him." Charley suddenly realized what he was saying and started to laugh. "Sorry about that," he said.

"No sweat. I've got broad shoulders. I can take it. Actually, if I keep sitting in this chair all the time, it won't just be broad shoulders. Anyway, your kid knows a good show when he hears one, even if you don't. What's with Jerry?"

"He's in the Childrens' Hospital, you know down in Trenton. The doctor there, Dr. Schwartz, told us he's got cancer. He told me what type, but I can't remember the name right now."

At the word "cancer," Acey sat bolt upright in her chair. Gordy was frantically signaling that it was time to cut the call and go to a commercial. She waved him off. Don Biederman's Chrysler-Plymouth was unlikely to know or care if its spot was a few minutes late. This was a call she wanted to play out.

"God, I'm awfully sorry to hear that, Charley. Is there something I can do for him?"

"Uh, I don't know." Suddenly, Charley was at a loss. He had never thought it through to what he would do in this situation. "Maybe you could do something for him on the radio?"

"Absolutely. Can you give me an idea what he would like?"

Inman hesitated again. All he knew of the music coming out of Jerry's room was that he hated it. He was about to admit to his ignorance when he happened to look up at the posters that adorned the walls of Jerry's room.

"Uh, would you have anything by Guns 'N Roses you could play?"

"Charley," Acey said dryly, "you may have noticed that this is a talk show. I mean, yes, there is a turntable in the studio but I use it to slice pizza. Why don't we give Jerry a big hello on the air and then, while we go to a commercial, I'll think of something. If you stay on the line, Pam will pick up in the office to get your name and address and we'll send him one of our WCZY sweatshirts. We sure do wish him well."

When Charley hung up, she could see Gordy become agitated again. Not only was the commercial late, but he could tell that she was going to change the focus of the show. Gordy probably thought that she was caught up in the conversation and had forgotten her schedule. If so, he was wrong. She knew the schedule to the half-minute without needing to refer to the printed one on the clipboard by the console. She was going to ad-lib it for a while. That was one advantage of being the host. The planned program had not been too hot anyway.

While the commercial ran, she leaned back and lit another in her usual series of cigarettes. By the time it was over, she had her idea.

"Okay, Jerry, I hope your dad's right and you're listening, because this one's for you." It was a story about a young Acey in a hospital, a mean nurse and a joke played with bedpans. It was a good story to gauge by the hue of Gordy's face. Then she turned back to open lines. Jerry had a lot of well-wishers throughout the evening.

FLEMINGTON, NEW JERSEY _____

Henson was up early Monday morning, less because she intended to be than because her weekend shows started and ended two hours earlier than the shows during the week. She sat in the bed trying to organize her thoughts, a process that included a mental review of the previous show. Inevitably, that review brought up the episode with Jerry. One raunchy hospital story and a sweatshirt in the mail seemed like inadequate compensation for being told you had cancer. There had to be something a little more substantial she could do for the kid. Maybe she could bring the sweatshirt down to the hospital. If Jerry was as stuck on her show as old In-

The-Bag Charley had implied, he would enjoy that. She thought she had a box of the shirts around the apartment someplace, leftovers from a long day at a shopping center that had drawn fewer people than expected. It was enough of a decision to pull her off the bed.

The box was not in the bedroom closet where she expected it to be. It was not in any of the dresser drawers either, and checking those was a major project because she had hung pants and shirts from the dresser knobs and they became dislodged when the drawers were opened. Hands on hips, she scanned the bedroom looking for inspiration, ignoring the fresh pile of clothes on the floor at the base of the dresser. Ah! The hall closet! She remembered that the date at the shopping center had been in the late winter. There, indeed, was the box, under the empty pizza box on which stood her insulated boots. One of the sweatshirts was a child's large, which hopefully would fit a twelve-year-old. She thought for a moment that she should call the business office, then dropped the idea. If Jerry wound up with two shirts, it would hardly break the station.

Now, with the sweatshirt in hand, she felt dissatisfied again. There had to be something more than a crummy sweatshirt. Quad Industries' marketing group had made up some eight-by-ten color photos a while back. Where had those gone? She began going through the stacks of files that sat on and around her desk and coffee table. One of these days, I am going to buy myself a filing cabinet, she thought. She had thought that several hundred times in the past.

She found two sets of photos in a manilla folder in the third pile she tried. The first set had a good picture of her, but Marketing had printed the caption "Life's a bitch and then you die," across the bottom. The layout was designed, supposedly, to appeal to teens, but there was no way she could give that to a child in the hospital. She could cut the caption off, but then the borders would not match and it would look tacky. The second set of pictures had been designed for men over twenty. It showed Acey in her black motorcycle leathers, brass knuckles on one hand and a heavy bike chain in the other. The caption was, "Wanna rumble?" She stared at it for a while. Not perfect, but definitely better than the other one. Maybe Old Souse Charley would have a heart attack when he saw it. She would think of a suitable inscription on the way over.

T R E N T O N ,   N E W   J E R S E Y _____

The Central New Jersey Medical Center, of which the Childrens' Hospital was a part, was actually a sprawling cluster of buildings, interconnected by skywalks, tunnels, and the expedient of putting one structure adjacent to another. It occupied several city blocks, but it had not been designed that way. It had become obvious, in the late seventies, that the Trenton General Hospital building was obsolete. The original plan, as put forward by the hospital, was to replace the old building with a new one. At about the same time, however, the attention of the state legislature had focused on the fact that when patients in the Trenton area needed sophisticated medical care, they went to Philadelphia. This awareness led to a movement to create a first-rate medical center in the Trenton area. Since this movement coincided with the proposal to rebuild Trenton General, politics dictated that the two plans be merged. Trenton General was destined to metamorphose into the Central New Jersey Medical Center, a tertiary care center equipped with the latest technology and staffed by the best physicians. Had some of the more grandiose visions been accepted, the center would have rivaled even the Longwood complex in Boston. To attract the kind of physicians the center needed, the hospital affiliated with a medical school. That gave the staff faculty rank. So, the plans were set, the staff was hired, and the administration was expanded.

Unfortunately, it was easier to approve plans than to find the money to pay for them. At first, the legislators tried to manage by expanding and renovating the old building. When this stopgap measure proved inadequate, they reluctantly approved the new building, but again compromised by reducing the scale of the construction while keeping the old hospital open and connecting the two of them. The development and expansion of the university hospital in New Brunswick, however, threatened to relegate the Trenton center to second-class status. The hospital administration responded by scrambling for whatever funding they could get in an attempt to complete the original plan. The result was a renovated unit here, or a new building there, governed as much by the amount of money available or the whims of the donor, as by the needs of the medical center.

The most recent of these additions was the Childrens' Hospital, now housed in a building of its own. It stood on what had been an open parking lot, joined to the main hospital by an umbilicus of a two-story skywalk that made a dogleg thirty feet above the street connecting two buildings that had been built at angles to each other. The Childrens' Hospital was not, despite its name, an entirely separate hospital. The original plan had called for it to be self-sufficient in all medical departments and services. Money had forced a compromise here as well. The Childrens' Hospital relied on the main hospital for much of the most sophisticated and expensive technology, as well as staff for some medical specialties. This was a dependency and second-class status that irked many of its staff.

The construction of the medical complex had been a major event for the region, although not quite in the manner that had been intended. Women delivered their babies in the main hospital's modern obstetrical suite and the infants were cared for in a brand new nursery that lacked nothing. Unfortunately, the two were in different buildings, separated by about one-third of a mile of corridors and the skywalk. The plans for the Childrens' Hospital had inexplicably omitted sleeping rooms for the physicians on call at night in the hospital. This deficiency had not been appreciated until the building was actually up. Also unknown prior to completion of the main hospital was the fact that the elevators leading to the Operating Room suite were slightly too small to admit a hospital bed. These, and other similar planning gaffes, would probably have remained inside jokes for those who worked or stayed in the complex were it not for the financial shenanigans that had also occurred. There were charges of bid rigging, use of substandard materials, and kickbacks. These had led to the indictment of several city officials, the conviction of two, and the bankruptcy of a construction firm. All of these events had made the medical center a frequent page-one item in the newspapers and had provided staple entertainment for those in the business of hosting radio shows. Probably half the State of New Jersey had either heard or read about Acey Henson's infamous interview with the mayor of Trenton.

Henson: "Would you tell me something about Anthony Mallazzo? We keep hearing that he gave a lot of money to your election campaign."

Mayor Whitehouse: "I wouldn't know how much because I never have anything to do with handling the contributions. It doesn't surprise me, though, because Tony and I are old friends. I'd be surprised if he didn't contribute anything."

Henson: "And the fact that you're old friends and he gave you a lot of money has nothing to do with the fact that his company got the main contract on the medical center, in spite of the fact that neither Tony nor his company has ever had anything to do with building a hospital before this?"

Mayor Whitehouse: "Hey, I don't like what you're implying here. Tony builds buildings. A hospital is just a type of building."

Henson: "A morgue is a type of building too. Do you know the difference?"

Mayor Whitehouse: "Hey! You can go fuck yourself, you fucking little punk. I don't have to take this shit!"

Henson later claimed that the mayor's outburst had taken the station crew by surprise so that they had inadvertently failed to delete it during the broadcast delay. Even though Acey Henson had never actually set foot in the new Childrens' Hospital, this type of association made it feel to her like a place she knew intimately.

She had two primary objectives that morning. Foremost was seeing Jerry, of course. Before she did that, however, she wanted to find this Dr.

Schwartz. She wanted to know a little more about Jerry before she went barging in for a visit.

There was no physicians' directory in the lobby, nor did she waste time looking for one. With a name like Schwartz, she figured, there could be six or eight in just that one building. It seemed likely, though, from Charley's comments that the Schwartz she wanted was a specialist, so she searched for a department to match the problem. When she found it, she was rewarded by a short row of nameplates on the wall, one of which read "Dr. Ezekiel Schwartz."

"Ezekiel," she mused out loud, standing outside the office door. "What in God's name could two parents have been thinking of when they did that to a poor defenseless baby?" She shook her head and pushed the door open.

Dr. Schwartz was not in his office. In fact, aside from a lone secretary the place was deserted. Acey's credentials from WCZY were enough to persuade the secretary to suggest that Dr. Schwartz could probably be found on 4 North. She also threw in a physical description complete enough to have enabled Acey to pick the man out of a lineup.

"You better hurry," she urged Acey. "He's due in clinic, so if you miss him on the floor he'll probably be tied up until mid-afternoon."

Acey assured her that she would hurry. It was always interesting to see what press credentials did to people. She was sure that had she shown up as plain Acey Henson, sans credentials, she would have been offered the choice of waiting until afternoon or an appointment next month.

Schwartz was on the fourth floor, just as Doris had thought. He was standing at the nursing station, draped across it in fact, trying to finish his note for the previous day chronicling the short life and hard times of Diego Aguilar. Acey was certain from halfway down the corridor that the man at the nursing station was the one described by the secretary. That is, he matched the description if one made allowances for how the man would look after an all-night binge. It was not the way she expected an "Ezekiel" to look. Oh well, she thought, full speed ahead.

"Hi," said Acey Henson, "I understand you're Ezie."

Schwartz's face froze. Damn! thought Acey. That line had been a mistake. It had sounded so cute in her head coming up the elevator, but it was obviously a mistake. Her mouth had her in trouble again.

"What do you want?" The tone was not friendly.

"Uh, sorry about that line. I make my living tossing off lines and that one got away from me. I'm Acey Henson from WCZY radio."

"Which is what you should have said first." Schwartz's eyes took in the leather jacket, the hair, and the helmet. His mind decided that he was not up to it, whatever it was. "We already went past the who and reached the what. Who you are is not what you want."

Acey could feel red creeping into her cheeks. She fought for control over her voice. "Okay. I do a show on WCZY. I got a call last night about Jerry Inman. He is one of your patients, I believe."

"That is correct."

"So, I came down here to see him this morning and I would also like to talk to you about him."

"If you want to visit him, you have to clear it with his parents, not with me." Schwartz was already looking back at his chart. "As for the other, I don't discuss my patients with the media. Period."

"Wait a minute. Hold on. I was thinking we could do a show on kids and cancer and build it around Jerry." She had actually thought of if just that moment, but it sounded to her like an excellent idea. There was no point letting Schwartz know that had not been her plan all along.

"I thought I made myself clear," he said, turning wearily around once more. "I don't discuss my patients. I do actually recognize your name and your show and I certainly will not be a party to your using him so you can create a show for your benefit." His voice rose as he spoke.

"Hey! Cooleth thy jets, man. There's no need to put your old *cojones* into an uproar. I'm sure Jerry will enjoy it and I really don't need too much of your time."

"If you haven't met him yet, how can you possibly know if he will enjoy it? Now, the Inmans can do this if they want, it's up to them, but if they ask me I'll tell them that I can't think of a worse idea than letting their kid be exploited like a zoo exhibit on some sensationalist show."

"Now you just wait a goddamn minute! You've never met me before, so how can *you* have the faintest idea what I'm going to do? Or do you just think you're so high and mighty and righteous and pure that you shit vanilla ice cream?"

They stood, almost toe to toe, glaring at each other. Then Schwartz's beeper went off. He looked down to see the number.

"I need to be somewhere else right now," he said. "I don't see any point in continuing this conversation."

The chart note, he decided, was as complete as it would be. He scrawled his signature at the bottom and tossed it on the desk, ignoring Henson's gaze.

Acey stood still, silent and ignored, as Schwartz turned his back on her and left the nursing station. She stood there a moment longer, as if in disbelief. When she looked around, she noticed for the first time that there had been an audience in the form of a black nurse leaning in the doorway to the conference room. The nurse was watching Acey Henson.

"Did you see that?" Acey threw both hands in the air for emphasis. The nurse nodded. "God in Heaven, who does he think he is? I bet he'd never pull an act like that if I was Barbara Walters."

The nurse smiled and it showed in her eyes also. "You never know. Zeke just might. He gets real protective about his kids."

"Zeke? Is that what you call him around here?"

"Yeah, mostly. His family calls him Ezie. He hates it."

"Figures. That's what I get for leading with my mouth."

The nurse smiled again and pushed off from the door frame she had been leaning against. "I wouldn't worry about it. He's actually not such a bad guy, as long as you don't mess with his kids."

"I wasn't planning to 'mess' with any of his kids. I was just hoping to see Jerry Inman and bring him something from the station."

"I know. I heard. What can I say? It was a bad night. They worked all night on a kid and lost him. You really Acey Henson?"

"Last time I looked."

"My name's Dorothy Perkins." She stuck her hand out and Acey shook it. "They had your show on up here last night. Jerry loved it. I heard in Report that he was talking about it all evening, and I know he was still talking about it when he got up this morning. Maybe I can help you."

Acey studied her new ally. Dorothy Perkins was a bit taller than she was, with a fuller, though taut, figure. A short Afro haircut topped a face the color of milk chocolate. The eyes looked sincere.

"Mostly, I'd like to know what he's got and whether I can see him for a few minutes."

"Since his dad called you, I've got no problem with that. What he's got is a hepatocellular carcinoma."

"Which means what? I'm sorry to be dense, but that doesn't mean anything to me."

Perkins chuckled. "No problem. It's a liver cancer. I don't know much more about it than that, I'm afraid. You'd need to ask Schwartz."

"Thanks, but I'll pass. Can I see him?"

"Sure, no problem there either. You really going to do a show around him?"

Acey gave Perkins a sharp look, searching for some hidden agenda. She saw no suggestion of one. "I'd like to," she said. "I'm not sure I can pull it off without Schwartz, though. I need some help there."

"Well, you think on it," Perkins said. "You were right, Jerry would enjoy it. I hope you can come up with something."

Back in her office that afternoon, Acey Henson sat at her desk doodling on a pad of paper. She liked Jerry, he was a nice kid, the sort of mischievous nice kid that she thought kids were supposed to be but rarely were. She wanted to do that show. But how? The problem had gnawed at her from the moment she left the hospital. It was now threatening to destroy her afternoon work schedule. There was no possible way she could brief herself well enough to do a show on that topic, not if she was going to do it in less than a month, and she wanted to do it during that very week. She thought about calling Roger at home, then stopped after she had punched the area code. Roger would agree that the show was a good idea from a programming standpoint, but she knew that without calling him. The background development would still be her job. In fact, a healthy Roger would have told her that she knew her job well enough at this point that she should not need to call him. That was what made her put the phone down. That was how Roger would have handled it in the past and that was how, at work, she wanted to think of Roger. All of which still left her the problem of how to organize the show.

Damn that Schwartz! Why did he have to be such a stuck-up jackass? Briefly, she considered going back to his office, the way a news reporter might, to see if simple persistence would pay off. She discarded the idea because she needed more than a statement, which could sometimes be badgered out of a balky subject; she needed active cooperation. Forget Schwartz.

She had one remaining option. The station employed the services of one Dr. David Whetson. He recorded the Medical Minute segments that the station spliced into the news shows, and he also co-hosted the occasional medically oriented show. She flipped the Rolodex to his name and dialed the office number.

"Hello, Family Medical Associates of Somerset," answered the receptionist on the other end of the call.

"Hi. This is Acey Henson. I'd like to speak with Dr. Whetson."

"I'm sorry. Doctor is seeing patients right now. If you tell me what the problem is, I can have him or one of the other doctors return your call."

Acey sighed. Either there was a new receptionist or this one had a memory deficit. "I said I was Acey Henson, you know, at WCZY. I need to speak with Dr. Whetson on business."

"Hold please." Muzak replaced the receptionist. "I'm sorry, Miss Henson," she said when she returned, "but he is with a patient. He can call you back in about five minutes."

"That would be fine."

Her phone rang barely two minutes after she hung up. "Hi, Acey. Dave Whetson here. What can I do for you?" His voice was a rich baritone that transmitted extremely well.

She outlined the framework of the show she wanted to present. "The thing is, Dave, for this I need a doc for a co-host."

"Hmm. Acey, you mentioned this kid is Zeke Schwartz's patient. I'd use Zeke. He has an excellent reputation, from what I've heard, and with all this focus on building up a major medical center for New Jersey, I'd say he's the main man around here these days."

"There's nobody else you would suggest?"

"Not really. I mean, there are other oncologists around who take care of children, New York and Philly have big centers, but I doubt you're going to get one to come here to talk about one of Schwartz's patients. Is there a problem with him?"

"I've met him. Shall we say that the necessary chemistry just isn't there."

Whetson chuckled. "One of our associates goes down to Trenton a lot. He says that Schwartz does have a reputation for being prickly."

"Drop the 'ly' and you've got it. The man has the charm and personality of an enraged Chihuahua."

Whetson's chuckle turned into a full-fledged laugh. "I don't suppose the well-known Acey Henson could have contributed to this situation by any chance?"

"Well, maybe a bit."

"A bit?"

"All right. Maybe more than a bit. But I won't go further than a thirty-seventy split. The man was a jerk and I can't use him."

Whetson sighed. "What do you want me to tell you, Acey? You asked me for a recommendation about this show and I gave you one. I'm sure there is some way you can work it out."

"Actually, Dave, I have a different idea."

"What?"

"Why don't you come down and do it with me?"

There was a prolonged pause on the other end of the line. Then Whetson said, "Acey, I can't do that."

"Why not? You're a doctor aren't you?"

"Jesus Christ, Acey! I'm a family practitioner. You know that. I tape spots for you on the treatment of athlete's foot or how to detect pinworms. The shows I co-host are like the one I did with you a couple of months ago on why seat belts are important. That's the kind of stuff I do. Not this."

"You could read up on it."

"Have a heart, Acey." From his voice, she could visualize sweat forming on Whetson's forehead. "You're talking about pediatric oncology. That's a weird specialty. I don't know a damn thing about it and I'm not stupid enough to think that I can pass myself off as an expert on it. Hell, if I had a patient like that, I'd refer him to Schwartz and that would be the end of it. If I do this show, I'll make a goddamn fool of myself on the air and that won't be good for my practice. In fact, if I do this show you probably will get Schwartz on the air so he can cut me to pieces in public. Or is that what your twisty little mind was thinking about?"

Acey hastened to reassure him that such was not the case. Whetson could be mollified, but no amount of entreaties could make him change his mind. Finally, she gave up. She quit her doodling also, in favor of a cigarette, and let the smoke trickle out her nostrils while she pondered the situation. Maybe, she thought, she could ignore most of the medical stuff and just stick to the people in the case. People stories always played better than science anyway. Maybe that was the best way to go. If anything, she was even more determined to do the show than before. The contretemps with His Royal Highness the Doctor had only strengthened that intention.

Chapter 9

TRENTON, NEW JERSEY ─────────────────────────

TUMOR BOARD was a title with a grandiose sound to it. At least, Schwartz had thought so back in the days when he was a student. The reality in many ways did not match the image evoked by the name. The Board, which met once a week, did not have a room of its own with the name stenciled on the door. Instead, it met in the Department of Medicine conference room, always assuming that no other group usurped the room and kicked it out, in which case it would convene in a side room off the cafeteria. The Board was also not a real entity in the traditional sense since its members were neither appointed nor elected to their positions. Instead, those physicians involved in caring for children with cancer came as their interest or need dictated. Normally, that group included both Schwartz and Worthington. Three physicians from the Camden area usually drove down and the departments of surgery and radiation therapy at the medical center would send a representative. The meetings were informal; new or unusual cases were presented and discussed. It was designed to be an educational meeting.

There was another side to the meetings, however, one that did fit the name. With few exceptions, there were no standard therapies for children with cancer. Treatment schemes published in textbooks were often obsolete before they were printed. Journals published more up-to-date information, but even these approaches were often no longer the methods of choice. Opinions as to the best treatment varied widely and were sometimes held to with a tenacity inversely proportional to the evidence supporting them. On occasion, violent arguments would break out over what treatment should be offered to a patient, or even if any treatment at all should be recommended. At those times, the fate of a patient could rest with a half-dozen people he had never seen and never would see. Those were the times the Tumor Board reminded Schwartz of the infamous "God Committees" that had parceled out scarce organ transplants. Schwartz made it a point not to yield to peer pressure unless there was actual data, as opposed to weight of numbers, behind an opposing opinion. It had caused Worthington, on more than one occasion, to chide him for being so stiff-necked, especially since he was so reasonable in other forums.

The Tuesday meeting opened quietly with Harvey Gagne from Camden presenting a case of leukemia. Gagne was a general pediatrician who at one time had trained in oncology and, on that basis, handled pediatric oncology patients for an HMO. It had been a routine case, but Gagne had converted it into the "Perils of Pauline" by being too aggressive at the start and then losing his nerve when the situation deteriorated. He presented it with gusto in the apparent belief that he alone had stood between the child and death, blissfully unaware that the potential for the patient's demise had been solely of his making. A year ago Schwartz would have laced into the man without a second thought. He had learned painfully that fighting such battles on every occasion made it more difficult on the cases where it really counted. Although the management of the case had been far from ideal, the outcome seemed no different from what it would have been otherwise. The kid was alive, apparently little worse for the wear; presumably the family was none the wiser. Keep your mouth shut, Zeke, Schwartz told himself.

Jerry was the next case and Schwartz settled back to see how Marienkiewicz fared in presenting it. She handled it rather well, he thought. The case was succinctly presented and all the important facts were there, as were the necessary slides and X-rays. The only rough spot came when Marvin Wu, a Camden oncologist, raised the question of hepatitis.

"He was negative," was Jola's response.

"But how hard did you look?"

The tone was not quite friendly and Jola flushed. Seeing that, Schwartz broke in. "He's negative by all the usual screens and I've sent some tissue off to be checked for viral genes. It will be a while before that comes back, of course, and it does not affect what we are going to do." He thought of mentioning the Pro-Insul, but did not. He had been too tired Monday to start searching for reports so all he knew was the little Mrs. Inman had told him. That was not enough to bring it up here.

Wu did not look interested in contesting the hepatitis issue further, so Schwartz waved for Jola to continue with the case. When she was finished, he flashed her a thumbs-up sign as she took her seat. While Ivory stood up to describe the operation, Schwartz wondered if he might be able to recruit her for one of the fellowship positions when her residency was finished. He liked what he had seen of her work and she seemed to like the kids. That was an important consideration in his field. It was too easy to get angry at the children for not responding to the treatment or for dying, in spite of all your hard work. Thinking about the fellowships made him realize that this Woodward at Meldrum had still not called him back. I should try him again, Zeke thought.

"So, Zeke, what are you going to do with him?"

Gagne's question pulled Schwartz's attention back to the room. He looked around to find everyone looking at him. All the faces wore smug looks that said, "Thank God it's your case and not mine."

Zeke had his reply ready. "I'll give him some interferon and see how that works," he said.

"Why interferon?" That was Dr. Wu again. "Most reports on this disease say Adriamycin has the best response rate. I have the references if you want to see them."

"I've read them," Zeke said, without inquiring which ones Wu had in mind. "The response rates don't translate into living longer and it will make him sick. I grant you, I don't know that interferon will work, but some of the early reports are interesting and I don't know that it won't work. I've been over this with the family yesterday and they are in agreement."

That touched off a predictable argument. One by one, the others lined up in favor of Adriamycin. It was the "standard," such as there was in this rare situation, and to be tried first, never mind that the kids died just as fast with it as without it. Schwartz listened to them, wondering if any of them had analyzed the papers they were citing. In the end, the others had a unanimous opinion. Jerry should get Adriamycin.

"We'll see how he does on interferon," said Zeke Schwartz. "Can we have the next case please?"

Dorothy Perkins stepped out of Jodie's room late on Friday evening and hoped that the rest of the floor had stayed quiet. The child had been hitting her call button all evening, complaining that her incision hurt. The incision looked fine. It had on Perkins's first trip to the room and just as fine on successive trips. The truth was, Perkins knew, that the incision was not the problem. The truth was that her parents had gone home, there was no one to play with, and Dr. Marienkiewicz, who could be induced to sit and tell a story, was not on call. All of that was the problem. Perkins was not surprised. It was only the second day Jodie had been fully awake after almost being dead. So, Dorothy sat with her a while and they made ugly faces at each other and watched television together until, finally, Jodie could snuggle with her teddy bear and fall asleep. Perkins went back to the nursing station and found Zeke Schwartz seated there, writing in a chart.

"Lord in Heaven, Zeke, don't you ever go home? Or are you trying to relive your internship?"

"That's about what it feels like," he answered. He stretched out his arms and legs, one set above the other below the writing surface. "I'm not sure you should talk, though. I thought you worked days this week."

"I did. But, we had two sick calls and no help and a new grad up here, so here I am, working a double. What's your excuse?"

"Not nearly so good. Just swamped and trying to catch up. I am not going to set foot in this place tomorrow."

"Uh-huh. You going to make it to Danny's bar mitzvah?"

"How do you know about that?"

"Gussie called looking for you."

Schwartz buried his head in his hands. When he looked up, he said, "I think I am going to lose it, that's what I'm going to do. Then they can carry me away to some place quiet with thick padding on the walls. What do you think?"

"Fine by me, Zeke. Just don't do it on my shift."

"Thanks, Dorothy, you're about as comforting as an enema." They grinned at each other. "Long as I'm here, is there anything new with my kids?"

"Not really." Perkins dropped into a chair next to him. "Jodie's scared of being alone and scared of the dark. Nothing's changed medically, but she's scared of her shadow now when the place quiets down. I think she needs to see Psych. I've never seen someone come so close to going out and coming back."

"Yeah." Schwartz rubbed his chin. "It makes sense. When I come by she puts on a big show, but I'll bet you're right. I'll see if I can get Funnaro to see her on Monday. Anything with Jerry?"

"No. He's fine. Did you hear about the show Henson did last night?"

"I heard part of it." Schwartz grinned ruefully. "Then I heard it replayed about verbatim when I saw Jerry this afternoon. Did you like it?"

"Loved it. They had somebody down from the station to set it up so Jerry could be on with her like a conference call. So, Jerry was on and his mom, although Charley wasn't here. The Schmidts were here and they got on too. It was nicely done. Real nice. Don't you agree?"

"It was," he said. "I didn't think it would be, but it was." There was a silent moment where they looked at each other before Schwartz spoke again. "I guess I was an asshole on Monday, right?"

"No," said Perkins, "you were a major league asshole on Monday. You were expecting me to tell you something different?"

"Not really." He drummed his pen against the chart. "Any suggestions what I should do about that?"

"I don't know. You were the asshole, not me. What do you want to do about it?"

"I suppose," he said slowly, "I ought to go down there and apologize. That way, if she wants to belt me in the nose, I'll be in range."

"Zeke, you're not thinking of going tonight? You are. Do you realize that show runs until two in the morning?"

"I didn't, but I'm sure I can find something to keep me busy until then. Say, are you using this?" The object he had picked up was a plastic rose that, some time in the past, had fallen from a display and been tucked into a cubbyhole. Perkins shook her head. "In that case," he said, "I'm going to borrow it." He stuck it in his pocket and headed for the stairs.

FLEMINGTON, NEW JERSEY _____

"Hey, Acey, I got a weirdo waiting out here for you." The shout from Pamela Davies stopped Henson just as she was stepping out of the broadcast studio.

"What kind of weirdo?" Acey asked. Pamela Davies was twenty years old and could have passed for fifteen or sixteen. When she had first arrived at the station, fresh from being thrown out of her parents' house, she had brown hair to the middle of her back with bangs over cocker spaniel eyes whose lids always seemed a third closed. More recently, the hair had been crew cut, except for a long pink rattail; there were three earrings in each ear; and there was a fake diamond stud in her nose. She wore Army fatigues three sizes too large for her. She handled the phones and the gofer jobs on the graveyard shift. Pamela's conception of weird sometimes needed explaining.

"I'm not sure," was Pamela's answer. "He's carrying a plastic rose."

"Plastic? My favorite color. How nice!" Pamela grinned in response. "What does he want?" Acey asked.

"To see you. Showed up about twenty minutes ago and said he needed to see you after you went off the air. Didn't say why. You want me to break his fingers and find out? Or should I call the cops?"

Acey smiled at the girl. The image of Pamela Davies, five foot two and maybe ninety-five pounds, breaking someone's fingers was comical. The police were another matter. As far as Acey knew, no one was particularly mad at her this month.

"He's not foaming at the mouth, is he?"

"No."

"Good. What's his name?"

"Don't know. Didn't ask."

Acey sighed. "Okay, I'll go see what he wants. Where did you put him?"

"Firman's office. You sure you want to do this?"

"I think I can handle it, Mom."

The short walk down the hall gave Acey ample time to review a list of all possible males who might appear at the station at two in the morning. It was a short list and none seemed very likely. She wished Pammy would have used a little more common sense in questioning the visitor, but common sense was not one of Pammy's strong points. She turned into Firman's office and came to a dead stop in the doorway. Sitting in the old sidechair, leaning forward with his arms resting on his thighs, was Ezekiel Schwartz. He was indeed holding a red plastic rose.

"I will be dipped in shit," said Acey Henson. "Look what the cat dragged in."

At her words, Schwartz looked up. Seeing her, he stood up. "Ah, Miss Henson," he said, "thank you for coming down." He extended the rose to her. Rather gingerly, she took it.

"Want to tell me what this is about?"

"Ah, yeah." Schwartz's face became progressively redder as he spoke. "I came down here to apologize."

"Meaning?"

"Uh, I, ah . . ." Deprived of anything to hold, Schwartz jammed his hands into the pockets of his jacket and started over. "I mean that I acted like a complete schmuck on Monday. I was wrong and I'm sorry."

Acey cocked her head to one side and looked at him critically. "This is killing you, isn't it?"

"Yes."

"Hmm. Not to look a gift horse in the mouth, or anything, but I am curious. Why the sudden urge to confess?"

"Sure. Reasonable question." It might have been a reasonable question, but Schwartz's discomfort precluded an immediate answer. "Look, is there someplace we can get a cup of coffee and sit down?"

"There's a place we can go a few miles up the road. It's open all night."

"Is it any good?"

"No, but it won't kill you. Just follow me out of the lot."

Contrary to Schwartz's expectations, the diner appeared clean and well kept. Save for a single truck driver at the counter, it was empty. They slipped into a booth on the side away from the trucker.

"Coffee," Schwartz told the waitress. "Heavy on the caffeine."

"Same for me," Acey said. "At this hour, my brain needs a jump start."

The waitress went off for the coffees and neither one seemed anxious to talk before she returned. During the silence, Schwartz took a good look at Acey. He discovered that all he remembered of her from their confrontation in the hospital was the wild hair and the leather jacket. He realized now that she was not as young as he had thought. Her hands told him that. They had seen heavy work in the past. What made her seem so young was the hair and attire and the smooth face dominated by eyes the color of faded denim. It was a very attractive face, he thought. Acey did not notice his inspection because her gaze was off watching the waitress pour the coffee.

After the coffee arrived and after Schwartz had a sip of his, Acey spoke up. "Okay," she said, "I'm listening."

"Right. It's like I said. I got real nasty and pig-headed the other day. It bothers me."

"Happens to us all," Acey said. I ought to know, she thought, but kept that to herself. "I thought you were going to tell me what made you see the light?"

"Right." Schwartz started off slowly but picked up speed as he went along. "I heard part of the show you did last night. Heard part of it and certainly heard all about the rest of it. Everybody really liked it. It was good for the kids, too."

"You didn't think I could do that, did you?"

"No, I didn't." He met her gaze across the table. "I thought you did that stuff where you tear callers apart or make fun of them."

"You mean what they call 'shock radio'?" Schwartz nodded in agreement. "No, I don't do that. I run a talk show and it's a lively one but, as a rule, I don't go yelling and screaming and cursing at people. Actually, I'm not sure I could, even if I wanted to. It's only in the big cities that you have all the creeps crawling out of the woodwork every night. It's still pretty rural out here, and this is where most of my audience is even if you can get the signal in Philly."

"Would you do it if you were in a city?"

Acey took a moment with her coffee before she answered. When she did, her voice was cool and deliberate. "If it was that or not eating, sure. But, given a choice, no. Once you establish a reputation for doing that, there's not much else you can do. I've got other plans."

Schwartz caught the change in tone, from the sarcastic almost mocking lilt she had used before, to serious. He wondered if he was out of bounds. "No offense meant," he said. "I wasn't trying to pry. Well, yes I guess I was, but I was just curious why you do what you do. I've never met anyone who did radio before."

"So, you want to know what makes God's Favorite Space Cadet tick?" That was a good line. An interviewer from some magazine had used it a few months ago. "That's a long story, Dr. Schwartz." Which was exactly what she had told the interviewer.

He winced at the title. "Please, call me Zeke. Or just Schwartz. Just don't call me Ezie."

"Sure. No problem, Zeke. I was your basic Air Force brat, I guess," she said. That, too, was how she had proceeded with the interviewer. "At least, my dad was in the Air Force, one of those MP types, and I was a brat for sure. Anyway, we moved around a lot. I spent a lot of time with the radio or the TV. Used to do shows, or call ballgames, along with the announcers, that sort of thing. Just by myself, of course. Anyway, when I was ten, we were at Holloman Air Force Base, that's in the middle of nowhere near Alamogordo, which is also in the middle of nowhere. While I was there my folks split up. Whether he threw her out, or she walked out, I don't know." Which was true enough, she thought. Of course, it left out all the yelling and screaming. It ignored the fact that Acey spent her time with the radio instead of with other children because she was afraid she might mention "family business" and be punished. It left out the tirades about how the "goddamn kid" was the reason the marriage was not working, or about how the "goddamn kid" was why he drank, or the "goddamn kid" was why he cheated. She was so good at putting out a sanitized, capsule version, just like an answering machine, that it was almost automatic. There were even minor variations in emphasis and detail that she used depending on whether the interviewer was from a magazine that liked to spice a story with a few lurid details, or from a company that might be sympathetic to hiring a hard-luck kid trying to get by on grit. All versions ended with Mom leaving with the "goddamn kid."

A polite cough from Schwartz pulled her back to the present. She realized that she had paused longer than usual at that point. She had let herself dwell on the black eye and the look on Mom's face the day they left. She pulled a cigarette from the pack in her jacket and lit it.

"Uh, look, do you have to smoke that?"

"Yup. I always smoke when I'm nervous."

"*I* make you nervous?"

"No. Now are you going to get nasty and pig-headed again or do you want to hear what I have to say?"

Schwartz opened his mouth and closed it without saying anything.

"Better." She inhaled deeply, turning the tip of the cigarette cherry red, then let out a cloud of smoke. Schwartz fought the urge to cough.

"Does talking about this bother you?" Schwartz asked.

"No," she answered and immediately hoped she had not sounded too curt. An interviewer would not ask her a question like that. "The old brain is just a little tired, that's all."

Acey started to talk again and this time the words flowed along smoothly, interrupted only by brief sips of coffee or drags on her cigarette. She told about moving to El Paso and the gangs there, a tough town to grow up in even if those gangs had not reached the dangerousness of the current ones. It had made her tough and it had made her wild. Her wildness, no doubt, had been a factor in her mother's decision to move east to Hoboken when Acey was fourteen. Moving to the New York area had not been a cure for teenage wildness, especially not when mother had to work. If anything, teenage Acey became even wilder, gone from home two sometimes three weeks at a time, always in trouble at school, sometimes in trouble with the law. Eventually, of course, she turned eighteen. The high school graduated her, thereby getting her out of the principal's hair, and her mother applied the same logic and threw her out of the apartment.

By the time she reached that scene, and quite a scene it had been with her and her mother screaming obscenities across the lobby so loudly that the police were called by neighbors, Acey was surprised to realize how much she had said. It was much more than the canned speech she had set out to give, with more detail and feeling than she would ever let an interviewer see. Certainly, it was much more than she had anticipated saying to a man she had recently contemplated bashing with her motorcycle chain. The only reason she could attribute her volubility to was that Schwartz seemed to be able to sense when she was hesitating or abbreviating and, with a quiet comment or just an expression, could keep her talking. Quickly, Acey reviewed what she had said, decided that she had not said anything she absolutely could not say, and kept going. She talked about bouncing across the country for two years, taking any job she could get, working a while and then moving on. She rattled off quite an array of jobs: dishwasher, truck driver, mechanic ("I figured, if I could hotwire them, I could fix them."), apple picker and so on.

"Anything to make a buck," she said. "Well, almost anything. Tell me, Schwartz, you ever shovel out a chicken coop in ninety degree weather?"

"No."

"It's a unique experience. Made me think about going back to school. I was in Indiana at the time and I was able to get Southern Indiana University to take me. Hey, what do you know? They had a communications major and a student radio station. It was a perfect fit. Gave me a use for all that crazy stuff between El Paso and Indiana, plus I could make money on the side. Got out of school and talked my way into the job at WCZY. The rest," she said with a wave of her hand, "is history."

"Interesting history," Zeke said. "Chicken coops and all. How did you get the name Ace, though? That's an unusual name for a girl."

"My name's not Ace. It's Acey."

"Okay, but where does that come from?"

"My initials. A.C. Acey."

"And what do they stand for?"

"They stand for A and C. God, you're a persistent little bugger, aren't you? You know, I can't believe I've been sitting here telling you the un-abridged version of my life story. I don't usually spill my guts on a first date."

Zeke chuckled. "When I'm not being nasty and pig-headed, I'm actually very easy to talk to. It sort of goes with my job."

"Your job. You take care of kids who have cancer. Right?"

"That's the basic job description, yes."

"Christ. That has got to be the worst job I can think of, and I can think of a lot. I can't think of anyone in their right mind who'd take that job. In fact, I can't think of anyone in their *left* mind who'd do it either. So, why do you do it? Your turn, Doc."

Part of her was interested. Part of her just wanted to change the focus of the conversation, most especially before it led to current and personal questions that would lead to a pass. Not that Schwartz had given any such indication, but that was the way personal conversations usually went.

Zeke reddened a bit under her gaze. "It really isn't like that, you know. I mean, we cure about fifty percent today and when you take care of those kids, that's fifty percent who would not be alive if you weren't there. You really do make a difference. Also, you can't just pull the answers out of a text. A lot of times, you fly by the seat of your pants because nobody *knows* the right answer. I like that. I could never just be a pediatrician and give baby shots all day, or try to treat a cold fast, before it gets better on its own, or say, my voice just dripping intensity, 'Well, Mrs. Jones, we had better discuss starting Billy on the cup today.'"

Acey started giggling as she remembered just how seriously Dr. Whetson discussed those issues. The giggles came close to causing her to slop the coffee into her lap. "Doc, that's terrific," she said. "Are you sure I can't talk you into doing a show? You're a natural."

Looking as though he sensed a trap, Zeke said, "Thanks for the compliment, but I'm still going to pass."

"Why? Come on, Doc, I won't eat you for lunch. I mean, now you know what a pussycat I am."

"Pussycat my left big toes. Really, though, I don't have time. I have a partner who's missing and an associate who might as well be and it's all I can do to keep my head above water."

"I can sympathize. I've got a boss who's missing in action most of the time also."

Schwartz gave her a puzzled look. "I meant that literally," he said. He told her about Wehmer's departure and the shambles it had made of his practice.

"So, why don't you just get somebody else?" she asked.

"It's not so simple. Do you know anything about how universities and medical centers are run?"

Acey shook her head.

"Well, damn few, if any, actually generate the money they need to operate. They all run off outside money—industry, foundations, the government. When I took this job, I was told they had a grant from the federal government to fund it over the next decade. That would pay for salaries, equipment, and so on. It turns out they had the grant for a while before I arrived and they kept coming up short of cash in other places. Nothing huge, just a little here and a little more there because they don't run the place very well. So they would cover it from my grant. By the time I got here, enough money had been burned that I can't hire any Fellows, or expand the clinic, or a whole bunch of things I had planned on. That's why Wehmer left. It's nuts because we wind up paying a hideous amount of money to outside docs to give us some extra coverage, but there's nothing I can do about it. I bitch every time we have a budget meeting, but you can't get what isn't there."

"Doc, maybe I'm dense, but I thought if the government gives you money for one thing and you spend it on something else, you're in trouble."

"No, you're not dense. It's actually illegal. Fact is though, almost every university does it, just not so outrageously, and yes, if we get audited, there will be trouble. But, that almost never happens."

"You could make it happen."

"And what good would that do? The money still isn't there. It wouldn't do my kids a bit of good."

Acey shrugged. "Doc, there's an old saying that nice guys finish last, but the truth of it is that they usually get fucked in the ass before they're finished. However, you're a big boy so you do whatever you like."

Zeke smiled even though she had said it seriously. "You, naturally, would do it differently."

"I'd kick 'em in the balls and let the chips fall where they may," Acey answered. "Of course, you're talking to someone who was arrested when she was fourteen for doing just that."

"And how did that come about?"

"Some damn shopkeeper insisted I gave him a ten when I gave him a twenty. The worst of it was that the police believed him."

"Sounds like you lost."

"Not really. I was out before he was walking straight and he was real nice to me afterward. I guess it's just a question of when it is worth it."

Schwartz stretched his arms and yawned. He had not expected their conversation to last so long. "Yeah," he said, "I guess if I think it's worth it I'll call you. But, in the meantime, someone is always sick and needs attention and I can only stretch so far so, I hope you understand why I don't want to get involved with your show. In fact, I don't see why you are still asking. You got your show and it went well. You didn't need me."

"That's not quite true," Acey said. "Yes, it went well, but that was because I kept it to personal matters. There was nobody to handle substantive questions and we got a lot of them. I'd be willing to bet you would be good at it, just from listening to you talk. Just for example, I had calls from two families who had kids come down with the same thing Jerry has and they had questions about new kinds of treatment. I couldn't do anything except have the office take their names; I didn't even put them on. I . . . what the hell is wrong with you?"

Zeke's face had frozen with a peculiar grimace. "Families from around here?" he asked.

"Yeah, basically. Even with the nighttime bounce, most of our listeners are local."

"And it was the same thing?"

"Yes."

"That's impossible."

"Doc, do me a favor and don't treat me like an idiot. I don't appreciate it." There was an ominous tone in her voice. "I'm a radio announcer; I do the news, too. I may not know what the words mean all the time, but I can read them and pronounce them smoothly. I do recognize them when I hear them. Would you care to tell me why I can't have heard what I heard?"

"I'll go you one better," he said. "I'll give you some figures and then you tell me the reason." He propped one elbow on the table top, unfolding a finger from his fist with each figure he ticked off. "About six thousand kids a year get cancer in this country. It sounds like a big number, but it's not when you think of how big the country is. Most of it is common stuff, like leukemia and brain tumors. Maybe one percent are liver tumors and only a quarter of those are this type. That comes to about fifteen a year in the whole country. Now, would you like to tell me the odds of three cases popping up in a small, rural area?"

"Somewhere between slim and none," she said. It never occurred to her to question his figures. Not the way he had spoken.

"I'd go with none," Schwartz muttered.

"Well, I still heard what I heard," she said stubbornly. "What causes it?"

"Hepatitis, mostly," Schwartz said. He tried to stifle another yawn. "Toxins, sometimes. Sometimes, you never know."

Saying the words seemed to impress them on his tired mind. Three children just did not pop up with a rare liver cancer. No way. The alternative to chance, however, was very unsettling. Of course, he told himself, that was assuming it really was the same cancer, that the kids really were from the same area and that it all happened at about the same time. "That's a lot of assumptions," he mumbled into his coffee cup.

Acey paid no attention to Schwartz's mumbling because the word "toxins" stuck in her mind and set off an alarm. She stubbed out the cigarette she was holding and lit a new one. "When you say 'toxins,' do you mean stuff in the environment?"

"Yes," Schwartz said, "although there have been some odd cancers reported from industrial exposures too. Sometimes, the kind of steroids the jocks use can cause tumors like Jerry's. Now, Jerry is kind of young, but you have kids using that stuff these days. What are you getting at?" That was a dumb question. He knew exactly what she was getting at.

Acey was thinking of the file drawer back in her office. The one marked "Toxic Dump."

"I'm thinking there could be a real interesting story here," she said. "Three rare cancers in one place. We should check around and see."

"Whoa! Hold it right there!" There was real alarm in Schwartz's voice. "Acey, there isn't nearly enough here yet to prove anything. You can't broadcast something like this without more information. Once you do, it's like firing on Fort Sumter."

"Okay," she said. "I'll keep my mouth shut for now. But, what information would you need and if I get it for you will you work with me on this?"

Zeke looked at her. He wished there was some way of knowing if there was another purpose behind her obvious one. He saw an intense young face with luminous eyes. It compelled an answer from him but gave nothing in return. Their short conversation had convinced him that he would have to look into these cases. If the other fathers both turned out to be home builders, or the families lived in homes built with Pro-Insul, he would probably throw up. Acey Henson, no doubt, could be very useful in finding the information he needed. The problem was that it might all come to naught. Could he trust her to be honest if they found nothing, or would she still try for a sensational story? She had been honest once.

"Okay," he said. "The first thing we need is the addresses of those other families, how old the houses are, what the folks do, and when the kids got sick. Also, the names of the doctors who took care of the kids. That should tell us if there is anything to chase after. Can you get that for me?"

"No problem. I told you, I have the phone numbers at the station. I can check this morning."

"Do that. Meet me at my office at noon and we'll see what we've got." So much for my pledge to stay out of the hospital, he thought. Then, he remembered why he had made the pledge. "Christ, it can't be noon. Listen, call the page operator at two and tell her it is urgent. She'll get me and I'll come."

"Sure. Where are you going to be?"

"At a bar mitzvah," Schwartz said with a groan.

Acey grinned. "I can make it later. I don't have to be on the air until six."

"No. Two will be fine, believe me." Schwartz grinned back at her. "I take it this means I'm forgiven?"

"Oh Christ, Doc, you were forgiven when I saw you sitting there like a kicked spaniel holding that silly rose. I'll see you in the afternoon."

She was out in the parking lot before it struck her that he had not even tried to make a pass. "Must be my good luck night," she said to her bike.

Chapter 10

SCHWARTZ PARKED his car in the doctors' lot and walked to the building, fervently hoping that no one, in particular not Dorothy Perkins, noticed him. Most of him wanted to go to sleep. It had been nearly six o'clock by the time he had returned to his apartment earlier that morning. He had gone to bed only to come completely awake no more than an hour later, his mind fixed on those other two children Henson had mentioned. With sleep physically impossible just then, he had gone to his computer and logged onto one of the on-line databases. He had searched for Pro-Insul through the medical databases finding nothing. He had switched tactics then and tried several of the industrial and environmental databases. That gave him a lot of information on insulation efficiency and sales reports, but no hint of any toxic effects. He tried to get at it another way, searching the medical databases again, this time for liver diseases, hoping to pick up a hint of the chemical. Again there was nothing. Frustrated with high technology, he retreated to a time honored approach. He called someone. The someone was Curtis Chang of the National Cancer Institute. Chang was an epidemiologist, a man who studied how diseases spread and who they affect. If there was a family where many relatives had similar types of tumors, Chang was interested and probably knew about it. Similarly, if there was a connection between a chemical and a type of tumor, Chang would know about the cases. Schwartz had worked with him in the past, before he had joined the NCI. He figured he knew Chang well enough to roust him out of bed on a Saturday morning. Chang proved to be awake, in his kitchen eating breakfast.

"It's a little early for consults, isn't it?" he asked.

"True," Zeke replied, "but this is bugging me and it's a quickie."

"Okay, Zeke. What have you got?"

"A twelve-year-old kid with hepatocellular carcinoma, hepatitis negative. I get a history from the family of exposure to an insulating material called Pro-Insul. The father works with it. Have you heard about anything similar?"

"Pro-Insul? Never heard of it. Certainly don't know of any cancers associated with it. Just one kid?"

Zeke thought for a second. If he said three cases to Curtis Chang, it would turn into a federal case faster than he could hang up the phone. "I've just got one kid," he said. "I was hoping you might know something."

"Sorry, Zeke, no. Can I finish my breakfast?"

By the time he had finished with the phone call, it was time to get ready for Danny's bar mitzvah. Tired as he was, he would rather have gone back to bed, but then the family would have taken offense and he did not want to endure that. Fortunately, the page from Henson, at exactly two o'clock, had rescued him just as he felt he was drowning in a sea of *gemütlichkeit*. It was the chatter that he found unendurable. It was the small talk of a room full of small-businessmen and their wives, all of it completely irrelevant to him. It was the same old questions from Aunt Gussie and Uncle Mel and others like them about why he had not become a dermatologist and why he was not wealthy and why he did not take more time off. His explanations, of course, were never believed, because who in that crowd would believe that after doing all that work to become a doctor, he did not want to be a rich dermatologist who played golf two afternoons a week? The reality was that his world was foreign to them, as much as theirs was to him. They were basically nice people, he reminded himself, but he had about as much in common with them as he did with a Tibetan lama. Had he not been expecting Acey's call, he probably would have been praying for a real emergency to occur.

There was light behind the frosted pane of the door leading to the outer office. Either he had forgotten to lock it, or Henson had sweet-talked the security guard into opening it. He pushed it open and found Acey Henson seated in Doris's chair, arms behind her head and boots up on the desk.

"What's up, Doc?" she asked.

"Not me. That's for certain. I'm getting too old to spend my nights off like I did yesterday."

Acey snorted. "I wasn't aware that you did all that much on your night off." She watched as he colored. "What happened, the Missus gave it to you with both barrels anyway?"

"Huh?"

"Missus. Ground Control to Doc, come in Zeke. Try wife. Or aren't you married?"

"Correct on the last," Zeke said. "Well, actually, I was married once, but that was a long, long time ago and far away."

"Doc," Acey said, cocking her head to one side, "you ain't old enough to have a 'long, long time ago.' If you don't want to talk about it, don't worry. It's cool."

Zeke gave a short laugh. "It certainly seems like a 'long, long time ago.' Another epoch maybe."

It had not been memorable. He and Jan had made the mistake of marrying at the end of his first year of medical school. Jan had a certification in elementary education, but what she really wanted was a house in the suburbs, a vacation home in New Hampshire, three or four children and a predictable life. It was an ill-starred union because Zeke was happier in a small apartment, buried in his work to the extent that vacations, and vacation houses, played no part. Once he entered his third year, with night call in the hospital and working hours that never had a definite end, the end of the marriage was not far away. In fact, they had not reached their second anniversary.

"We just grew apart," he said to sum it up. "Once we had gone far enough along our own paths, we just didn't belong together any more. It was a pretty mutual decision."

"Sorry I brought it up," said Acey Henson.

"Wouldn't worry about it. There was no big fight, or anything like that. We didn't have kids and, Lord knows, at that point we didn't own a lot of stuff. I really don't think about it much at all. If you hadn't brought it up, it would not have occurred to me to mention it."

"Hey," she said, "I wasn't trying to make an issue out of it. I'm sure you're basically a real nice guy and I'm sorry it didn't work out and I'm sure there will be someone else."

That brought a sustained laugh from Schwartz. "You and my Aunt Gussie," he said. "I could almost believe you called her up from the station. Listen, Henson, one thing I don't have anymore is too many illusions about myself. I love what I do and my work is what comes first. Always has and I suspect it always will. You've got some idea of the hours I keep. Can you think of a woman crazy enough to be married to me?"

"I can think of plenty," she shot back, "who would be more than glad to marry a doctor who is gone all day and half the night."

"Yeah." Schwartz ran his fingers through his hair, thinking of many of the women at the party he had just left. "Do you know the old Groucho Marx saying? The one that goes something like, I wouldn't want to be a member of any club that would take me?"

Acey grinned and put her feet down on the floor. "Amen to that."

Zeke went to the back of the office where a small coffee machine sat on a shelf. "How about some coffee?"

"Sure."

From the cupboard above the machine he pulled two vacuum sealed pouches, one brown the other orange. "Regular or unleaded?"

"The real stuff, please. I don't know what I'd do without it."

"Sleep, probably," Zeke said. "The nice thing about our coffee, Henson, is that if the caffeine doesn't keep you awake, the pain in your stomach will."

"Thanks for the warning." She watched while he ripped the pouch open and spilled the brown granules into the filter paper. When he said nothing else, she said, "I've got the stuff you asked for, or are you no longer interested?"

Schwartz looked around when she spoke, missed the flange for the filter and almost spilled the coffee. "No, no. I really am interested and thank you for bringing it. Just let me get this brewed. I have a street map in the office to plot these on."

A few minutes and two cups of coffee later, Schwartz unlocked a door in the back wall of the office, which led to his private office.

"You know," Acey said as she walked in, "I always thought you super specialists had offices with wood paneling, deep pile carpet and a wet bar. This looks like basic cellblock."

"Not far wrong. However, it's an office, so I'm not complaining." He moved several piles of charts to one side of his desk and spread out a street map of the counties along the Delaware. "Okay, I've got the Inmans' house marked here. Now, what have you got?"

"Two families. First, the Delgados. They live at 43 Sycamore Drive. It's an older house, more than twenty years. Both parents work in a deli. Thirteen-year-old boy named Mario, got sick in November, died in March. They took him to see a guy named Bernstein at the Childrens' Hospital in Philly." She flipped an index card onto the map. "Bernstein's number is on the card, too."

Schwartz hunted across the map until he found the street. It was a short one, so he just put an "X" in the middle of it.

"That doesn't look too far from the Inmans."

"About three miles," Schwartz said, using thumb and forefinger to compare the distance between the marks to the scale on the side. "Different school district for what it's worth. They split them down this brook, Scheuermann's Run or whatever it is. What about number two?"

"Jimmy Swenson, age ten." She tossed another card on the map. "Dad drives a truck. Mom stays home."

Schwartz picked it up and looked at it. "Acey, this address is in Scranton, Pennsylvania! It's nowhere near here."

Acey laughed out loud. "Easy there, Doc. I know where Scranton is. Give the Ace credit for doing her homework. The Swensons moved to Scranton in January, but Mrs. Swenson's sister still lives around here and, apparently, is a fan of mine. Jimmy got sick in March. A Dr. Mohammed Anwari operated on him in Scranton. Now, before they moved, they lived here." She stuck her finger on the map, a few blocks from the Delgados. "So, they are all kind of close, but, because of the different ages and schools and because the Swensons moved, none of them know about the others."

A sudden worry struck Schwartz as she said that. "What did you tell these people when you called? I mean, how did you get all of this?"

"Easy. I just told them that Dr. Ezekiel Schwartz was investigating a suspicious group of these cancers and that he needed this information to help nail the culprit."

"You did what!?"

She laughed again. "Lighten up, Doc. I just gave them a light touch. No promises, no hints, didn't use your name. I know how to get information without giving myself away."

Schwartz sat back down in the chair with a thump, thinking that association with Acey Henson could be a risk factor for heart disease. Then he stared at the marks on the map. All of the children had lived fairly close together. "Intriguing," was all he said. "I don't suppose you know if either of these two had hepatitis?"

"Doc, what do I look like? A cute young doctor in her little white coat?"

"Sorry. No reason to expect you to know."

"So, what next?" asked Acey.

"First order of business is to make sure all of these tumors are really the same. That's my job. I'll call these two docs and see what kind of information they've got." That, he thought, and find out if the Delgados had their house reinsulated any time recently.

"And what can I do in the meantime?"

"Mostly we need to know what these kids had in common. They didn't go to the same school, but they all lived fairly close to this Scheuermann's Run. Can you see if there is anything funny about this area or this creek? Also, you remember I mentioned steroids. It would be worth knowing if the kids were using them. It occurs to me that you can probably get that sort of information better than I can."

"I can find out. No sweat on the steroids. Give me forty-eight hours and I'll know. As for the creek and the area, I've been putting together information on what has been dumped where for quite a while. If there's a report, I'll have it."

"Good. Let's get our information, put it together and then we shall see what we shall see. Sound reasonable?"

Acey thought so. On a different level, though, she found it odd. In her experience, grown men rarely apologized for their behavior, not unless they were expecting the apology to open doors, specifically bedroom doors. Similarly, busy men, and Schwartz was as busy as any she had known, did not give up free time to do women favors, not unless they were for "favors" in return. In spite of which, Schwartz had not made a pass at her the previous night, nor did he appear to be gearing up for one now. There was not even a wife, a factor which would inhibit a minority of men. She did not think he was gay. Possibly, Schwartz was simply interested enough to want to work with her for the sake of the project. It was an interesting thought, pleasant actually. Other than with Roger, whose interests were obviously different, she had never been completely comfortable working with a man.

"You know, Doc," she said, "something tells me that we're going to make a real good team."

Something in her voice pulled Zeke's eyes away from the map and back to her. He looked a bit puzzled. "I hope so," he said, "but I'm not sure what I've said so far that would tell you that."

"It wasn't anything you said. Just all the things you didn't say." She left him without explaining any further.

After she left, Schwartz sat for a while, staring at the map. Then he sat a while longer, face buried in his hands. What had he gotten himself into? Even without knowing the answer, he could see the ramifications of the information in front of him, just as surely as he knew that Acey Henson could not. Three children in a thinly populated area developed a rare liver tumor, all within several months of each other. Whereas the previous night he had doubted that all of them would have the same cancer, he was now assuming it to be a foregone conclusion. It could not be chance, which implied that it had to be something else. Clusters of cancer cases were nothing new. Anyone who worked in the field had read about them. Schwartz particularly remembered one small town near Boston. There had been twelve cases of leukemia in children diagnosed over a period of a year, with another eight over the next several years. If ever a cluster of cases should have had a cause that had been it, but wells had been dug up and water sampled from one side of the town to the other and nothing had been found. For all Schwartz knew, they were still arguing about it. Most clusters were like that, if not in the numbers involved then in the outcome. Too suspicious to be chance, but no cause ever found. Of course, it did not always end like that. There had been benzene and erythroleukemia and vinyl chloride and an even stranger liver tumor called angiosarcoma. There had also been DES and vaginal cancer in the daughters of the women who had taken it. It could happen and that was what gave Schwartz chills. Two families had heard Acey Henson and called in. How many had not heard the show, or had children who were not sick yet? If something was out there rotting livers, how many sick children might there be when it was all over?

Chapter 11

MORNING RUSH hour traffic meant little to John Lawrence Thigpen, not even the Los Angeles rush hour with its freeways congealed into parking lots and its legions of trapped drivers overloading the local cellular telephone network as they tried to ignore being stuck. It was all unimportant to Thigpen because he set his schedule by the opening bell of the New York Stock Exchange. Since that venerable institution opened three hours ahead of Los Angeles time, most of Thigpen's office was at work very early in the morning. Thigpen came in even earlier, usually one or two hours earlier. He preferred to work on correspondence and routine matters when no one was around. Then, when his secretary arrived, he could dump the whole mass of it on her desk and not need to worry about forgetting to write a stupid letter when the day got busy.

This particular day, he was in even earlier. In truth, he had never really gone home. Instead, he had worked until early evening, then pulled out the travel bag he kept in the office and drove to a nearby hotel. A few hours sleep there, then he was up and back to the office in jeans and a pullover. His suit hung from a hanger by the door. He would put it on before everyone else arrived.

In a way, it was his own doing that he was back at work before dawn, as much his doing as it was Travis Kuhnlein's. He had worked on Kuhnlein for weeks, pushing his idea about Quad Industries. At first, Kuhnlein had not been interested. Quad Industries was a sprawling mess. There were far more attractive companies out there, companies that could be bought, split up and easily sold for a profit. There were no obvious jewels in Quad Industries, no jewels and a lot of junk. It would take too much time and effort to find buyers for all the pieces, which meant that it would tie up a lot of their money. Why, Kuhnlein had asked rhetorically, did Thigpen think nobody had bothered before?

Thigpen had worked for Kuhnlein long enough to know that when an idea was turned down there were two possible courses of action. He could forget it, or he could pull it back, do some more work and present it again in a different setting. Thigpen wanted to keep this particular project alive. Part of him wondered if he did so only to justify the time he had put into sorting out the company. Kuhnlein's opinion was accurate in that respect. The company was a mess. It had proved to be a maze of subsidiaries, some consolidated some not, many with assets whose worth was hard to figure. However, when Thigpen had finished his calculations, he was left with the conclusion that the company's shares were selling for a very cheap price on the New York Stock Exchange. At the stock market value, the price tag for the whole conglomerate was less than a quarter of its sales each year. That price tag was almost the same, or maybe a little less, than the stated value of all the assets Thigpen had been able to account for, but he knew this number was a joke. Land acquired fifty years before was still on the company books at the original value, never mind that some of it was in Orange County, California. No allowance was made for the value of the broadcast licenses. In fact, those radio stations looked as though they could constitute a tidy little business all by themselves. It would not be what Kuhnlein would call a "jewel," but it could be one, perhaps, with John Lawrence Thigpen as its President. That thought, however, did not appear in any of his proposals. What did appear in Thigpen's proposals was that Quad Industries, selling for twenty-eight to thirty dollars a share, was worth between one hundred and one hundred twenty dollars a share. That was what Thigpen was willing to say to Kuhnlein. Deep inside himself, he was sure the estimate was conservative. Eventually, Kuhnlein had bought the idea. Travis Kuhnlein had made himself enormously wealthy so he was, perhaps, entitled to his inordinately high opinion of his own reasoning, but he had worked with Thigpen long enough to know that when Johnny got an idea, there was usually money in it, no matter how screwball it sounded at first.

Once Kuhnlein decided, Thigpen felt like he had been hit by an avalanche. He had found himself with only a few days to prepare a presentation for the men who were going to put their money into the undertaking. That was why Thigpen was at his desk at three o'clock in the morning, making certain that each of the grandees, who would arrive later that morning, had a folder with all the necessary printouts and charts. Thank God for computers, he thought. That was the way Travis Kuhnlein worked, though, and anyone who worked for him had to be willing to cope with the demands. Thigpen had always felt that the rewards were worth it.

So think, Johnny, he told himself. Where are the weak points? Where can this go wrong? What about the numbers, the dollars in the deal? The people who were coming wanted huge profits, obscene profits. Whether it was because they simply wanted profits that big, or because they needed to recoup a previous bungle, they wanted profits beyond what any normal investment would bring. That did not matter to Thigpen. He saw nothing wrong with obscene profits; they separated the winners from the losers and he wanted the same profits. Thigpen knew the dollar projections by heart. There was nothing that anybody would find wrong with them.

At least, the problem was not in those numbers. Thigpen picked up a sheet of paper with a list on it of people and institutions that owned significant amounts of QI. Right on the top line was Meldrum Products, the pharmaceutical company. Some years ago, Meldrum had been paid in QI stock for some corporate deal. Someone would see that, they could hardly *not* see it, and would ask how Thigpen could be sure of taking QI in the face of it. Thigpen had decided to bet that he could talk them into believing that he could deal with the Meldrum stock without giving them any specifics of how he would do it. The money men would probably worry that Thigpen had some privileged information that would land them all in jail, so they would not want the details. Cowards, but the cowardice was a lever Thigpen could use to manipulate them.

The fact was, though, that Thigpen did not have any such information. He wished he did because that Meldrum block really could be a deal-killer. If there was a fight, and Meldrum sided with QI management, the takeover might be impossible. He might not even be able to extract a big greenmail payment. There was a reason, though, that Thigpen had not given up on the idea. A takeover fight would be messy and expensive for QI management, even if they won. If it would buy them a quick peace, QI would probably give up the radio stations. Thigpen was willing to take the stations for himself and let the rest of the deal go, if he had to do it. He could arrange that much financing on his own. Of course, neither Kuhnlein nor the other participants would be too pleased. The hell with that, Thigpen thought. If old Henry the whatever could say that Paris was worth a Mass, then surely a broadcast group was worth a little doublecross. Why not?

TRENTON, NEW JERSEY _____

Clickety-clack! Clickety-clack! The noise filled the air around the nursing station, sounding like a shopping cart gone amok. Every time whatever was making the noise clacked past her, Jola Marienkiewicz found herself losing her train of thought. Normally, a trivial matter, like a little noise, would not have bothered her, but she had spent most of the previous night putting in a seemingly endless series of intravenous lines. Every time she went to lie down on the cot in the resident's office there was a knock at the door accompanied by a nurse with yet another request. Jola had grown accustomed, more or less, to writing orders and notes with a numb mind and eyes that wanted to close, but in that condition it did not take much to distract her.

Clickety-clack! She listened to it again and stopped her pen somewhere in the middle of describing a patient's abdomen. When she focused on the paper again, she began to doubt that the bowel sounds had been decreased in the lower right quadrant. Maybe it had been the lower left. Should she go back and listen again? Damn! In the midst of this confusion, her mind began to wander to thoughts of her apartment. Bobby would be home, he left work promptly at five every day. He was not going to be happy about the state she was in, disheveled and exhausted. He would want dinner, he would probably want to go out, and he would want sex, not surprising since it had been two weeks, maybe three, since the last time. All Jola wanted was to go to sleep.

With an effort, she wrenched her wandering mind back to the note, which was no farther along than it had been five minutes before. Concentrating on the paper was enough to raise sweat on her lip and under her arms. Despite that, she resisted the urge to finish it with a few meaningless lines. This was a Schwartz patient and she wanted the note to look good. She had noticed that most of the house officers were afraid of Zeke Schwartz. They would admire the way he took care of patients, but they were scared of having them on their services. Jola had gotten off to a good start with Schwartz and had begun to accumulate his patients. Schwartz was one attending physician it was worth impressing and Jola badly wanted to impress him.

Clickety-clack! What the hell was that? Finally, she levered herself half-way out of her chair so she could peer over the top of the nursing station. The source of the noise proved to be Jodie's IV pole. The pole looked a bit like an eight foot aluminum coat tree. The central rod was mounted on a metal crosspiece. Under the four ends of the crosspiece were mounted small wheels, similar to those of a shopping cart. Jodie was walking her pole part way down the hall, then running with it to gather speed, and finally hopping on the crosspiece to ride it like a scooter, sailing past the nursing station with the wheels going *clickety-clack*. The glass bottle, half-filled with IV solution and attached to the central line that ran under Jodie's shirt, swayed ominously on its hook atop the pole as Jodie cruised past. For a moment, Jola watched her, mouth agape.

"Jodie, what are you doing?"

"Nothing, Kay Vitch." *Clickety-clack!*

"Well, stop it. You're not supposed to be doing that."

"Why not? Dr. Zeke said my platelets are okay."

This is crazy, Jola thought. Tell a child her blood is clotting properly and she turned a rickety IV pole into a scooter. Jodie started another run past the nursing station only to see Dorothy Perkins step out of a room a little further down the hall. All at once, she jumped off, bringing the pole to a sudden halt. Overbalanced, it tipped to a forty-five degree angle and almost went over, bottle and all, before she could catch hold of it.

"What are you doing?" asked Perkins.

"Nothing."

"Do it somewhere else and don't do it on wheels."

"Okay," said Jodie and turned to walk back up the corridor.

Jola shook her head. "I can hardly believe that kid is up," she said to Perkins, "much less running around like crazy."

"Perkins smiled in return. "Kids are like that. They bounce back real fast. You got to watch it with her, though, Kay Vitch. She's spent so much time around this hospital, she's learned how to manipulate interns real good. She'll drive you crazy if you're not careful."

"Well," said Marienkiewicz, "I can see who carries the weight up here."

"Just as it should be," said Perkins.

Jodie, in fact, had a perfectly good reason for rolling up and down the hall, but it was not one she had any intention of disclosing. She wanted to talk to the boy in the single room across from the nursing station. Jerry Inman was the reason the people from the radio station had been at the hospital, which meant that he was Somebody. That was impressive. Jodie had been keeping an eye on him, as a result, most of the day. She had been watching while Dr. Marienkiewicz had to restart Jerry's IV. Jerry had not cried at all. That was impressive, too, almost as impressive as having the radio station come in. Jodie felt certain of that, having been an expert on IVs before she got her central line. She wanted to do something to get his attention. Coasting up and down the hall on her IV pole seemed like a good way to do it. Sure enough, when she turned back down the hall after Perkins caught her, she could see Jerry looking at her.

She walked over to his doorway and looked in. "Hi," she said, "I'm Jodie."

"I know. They had your folks on the radio, too."

"Yeah. How did you get them to do that?"

"I'm not sure. I think my dad talked to Acey Henson." In truth, Jerry was not sure because nothing had been said on the show, the night Charley first called in, about Acey coming to visit. Charley had been vague when Jerry asked him later and Acey had only said that they had a talk.

"Acey is the lady who does the show?" Jodie asked.

"Yup." Jerry fished the picture Acey had given him out of the drawer in his nightstand and held it out for her. "Do you listen to her show?" When Jodie shook her head, he said, "You ought to. She's pretty crazy. Like riding that pole of yours."

Jodie grinned at the recognition. "I can show you how."

"I can't," Jerry said. He pointed to a tube that emerged from a dressing on the right side of his belly. "I can't walk around with this."

Jodie came over to inspect it. "Does it hurt?"

"Not any more."

"What do you have?"

"Some kind of cancer in my liver," Jerry said.

"I have leukemia," Jodie announced.

Jerry gave her a wary look. He had heard that word in school. "Does that mean you're going to die?"

"No. Dr. Zeke said my chances are fifty-fifty. That's what he told my parents, too. What did they tell you?"

"Nobody said anything like that."

"They're supposed to. Dr. Zeke always does. They're supposed to tell you what your chances are." To herself Jodie wondered if, maybe, Dr. Zeke would not tell if it was really bad.

Jerry had a similar thought and decided he did not want to know if Dr. Schwartz had told anyone else. To change the subject, he said, "How come you don't have any hair?"

"The chemo makes it fall out. Are you going to get chemo?"

"I don't think so."

"Well, you'll know it if you do." With that, Jodie went into a description of what chemo was and how you got it that was probably more detailed than Jolanta Marienkiewicz could have managed. By the time she was done, Jerry still did not know if he was going to get it, but he knew he did not want it.

Eventually, the conversation drifted to things children usually talk about, instead of drugs and hospital procedures that Jodie thought of as good opening gambits. Jodie was a baseball fan, which made her all right in Jerry's eyes. For a Yankee fan, he could forgive all the talk about the nasty things in the hospital. So, they talked about baseball and the Yankees' chances of winning the World Series, which Jodie had to assure him were much less than her "chances." They also talked about parents and where they lived and what they did when they were home. Jerry decided he had found a buddy in the hospital, which was nice. He told her about his Little League team, and how they were doing, and even how they had found a perfect place to go swimming one day when the field was too soaked from an earlier rain to play, but no one had told them not to show up. He started to tell her about this place, where they could swim, blast a boom box as loud as it would go without any adults to object, and even sneak a few beers, when he realized what he was doing and abruptly stopped. Jodie knew something was being hidden and kept asking about it.

"I can't tell you," Jerry insisted. "It's a secret."

"I thought I was going to be your friend."

"You are."

"Then tell me."

"I can't."

"Why not?"

"Because it's only for us, I mean the guys on the teams in my league. That's what we all decided. If you tell somebody else, something horrible happens to you. I mean, I'm not kidding. It's not like I don't want to tell you. I can't."

Jodie considered that for a moment. "You mean somebody told you that and you believed him?" Jerry reddened a bit at that. "Come on! Anyway, I'm your friend. Right?"

"Well, yes, but . . ." Jerry stopped there. He had a feeling that Jodie was going to think he was stupid. He tried to remember who had first said anything about the consequences of talking about that place. He couldn't. They had been going there for a couple of years. "I suppose I can tell you," he said. "But you can't tell anyone, ever. You got to promise."

Jodie was willing to do that. She would never tell anyone about Jerry's place. Jodie was very good at keeping secrets.

Chapter 12

_____

SCHWARTZ SPENT his Sunday breakfast thinking about Jerry Inman. His thoughts were not just about Jerry, they dwelt on two other boys, whom he had never seen but whose names were on the cards Acey had given him. The more he thought about them, the more anxious he became. There was no way he could find out before Monday if all the children truly had the same type of tumor and, without that information, there was no logical reason to do anything further now. His stomach, however, was not logical. He finished his breakfast and pulled the cards with the names and addresses out of his briefcase. He tucked those in his shirt pocket, then went out to his car.

The Delgados lived in Marrville, New Jersey, a small hamlet tucked between two of western New Jersey's rolling hills. The road into Marrville took him across Scheuermann's Run, just south of the town of the same name where the Inmans lived. From the bridge, he could see that Scheuermann's Run was a more substantial stream than he had imagined from looking at the map. Marrville was a three-stoplight town, the three marking the ends and middle of the business center on Main Street. The Delgados lived two blocks away from it. The house was a two-story rectangle with red clapboard siding. The paint around the windows and front door had weathered. Schwartz parked his car in front of the house.

And what, precisely, do I do now? His hospital identification badge was in the glove compartment. He pulled that out and stuffed it in a pants pocket. Do I flash that at her and say, "Just the facts, Ma'am"? He walked to the door feeling like an idiot.

Mrs. Delgado was home and, judging by the background noise, so were two or three children. She had light brown skin with the same weathered appearance as the paint on the door. Straight black hair, streaked with gray, was pulled into a bun at the back of her head. She listened with patience to Schwartz's stammered explanation of his visit, then opened the door and ushered him into the living room. She left him there for a moment while she went back to the kitchen, returning with two cups of tea. After she was seated and each had a few sips, she began to ask questions about what had happened to Mario. Then, she asked Schwartz what she could do for him. There was a standard long list of questions used to investigate possible exposure to environmental toxins. Schwartz had once memorized it, although he could not think of a single instance in which it had yielded an important clue. There were no surprises here either. What he did learn in the course of it, however, was that there had been no insulation added to the Delgado house in the fifteen years they had lived there. There was some new construction going on in the area, but none of it was very close to Marrville. The children played in town, or out on the fields around town, or around the Run. Mrs. Delgado was not too sure exactly where their favorite play areas were. They chatted a while longer and then Schwartz excused himself.

Back in his car, Schwartz sat staring at the card with the Swenson's address in Scranton. It was a long drive away and seemed unlikely to yield much in the way of information. Jerry Inman might possibly have been exposed to Pro-Insul, but Mario Delgado almost certainly had not. Did the Swenson boy matter? Probably not. Any explanation would have to involve a common thread among the three. Right then, Pro-Insul did not seem like the explanation Schwartz was looking for. He drove home with the thought that he would have to find something to keep himself distracted for the remainder of the weekend.

Monday morning found him so emotionally charged that it was all he could do not to bolt straight from bed to the office at six in the morning. Intellectually, he knew it would be useless to do that, but knowing it did not change the way he felt. Getting to work did not immediately defuse him either because there were clinic patients to be seen on Monday morning. Worthington, as usual on Monday, was late, leaving Schwartz to see Worthington's first patient in addition to his own. The steady flow of patients, X-rays, orders, and prescriptions soon convinced Schwartz that he would have no opportunity to sneak upstairs to his office to start making his phone calls. A look at the chalkboard in the clinic office told him that Worthington, with perhaps half as many patients to see, was running late anyway. There would be no help from that quarter. With a sigh, he resigned himself to calling from the clinic office, a crowded room through which a stream of nurses and residents flowed in two directions and where at least three people were always talking at the same time.

He was able to reach Dr. Anwari at his office in Scranton. Yes, of course, Dr. Anwari remembered the Swenson boy. Cases like that were impossible to forget. He had tried to resect the tumor, which had extended into the right and left lobes of the liver, but the bleeding had become uncontrollable and the child had died on the operating table. Schwartz wanted to ask why a surgeon in a community hospital had even attempted the surgery, instead of sending the child to a specialist, but he held his tongue. Criticizing Anwari was not going to help either Jimmy Swenson or Jerry Inman. What it would most likely do was make the man uncooperative, thereby losing the information Schwartz needed. Instead, he said that he was involved in a research project in liver cancer, which was true in a way, and that he was interested in obtaining information on the Swenson case. Yes, Dr. Anwari confirmed, the tumor was a hepatocellular carcinoma. Yes, the pathologist would still have some tissue, although it was probably fixed rather than frozen. No, Dr. Anwari had no idea if the child had had hepatitis. Was that important? No, the child had not been taking steroids. Yes, Dr. Anwari was sure, no steroids had ever been prescribed for the child, so how would he be taking them? Schwartz sighed, thanked him for his time and went back to his clinic.

Two patients later, he tried Dr. Bernstein, who had seen Mario Delgado. This time there was no trouble in obtaining information. Mario Delgado had been an unusual case and had presented to a major teaching hospital. Every study Schwartz knew of had been run, plus a few that were new to him. It was, in fact, the same tumor as Jerry Inman had. Mario Delgado had never had hepatitis. The Philadelphia doctors had looked everywhere, including the DNA of the liver where the virus could sometimes hide from more routine tests.

Over a late lunch in his office, Schwartz pondered his situation. There was no doubt in his mind, he had a small cluster of patients with a very rare cancer. The properly academic thing to do would be to write a paper, he already had enough information to do that. Then he should call the Center for Disease Control in Atlanta, and maybe Curtis Chang as well, and let them worry about why the tumors happened. He could relay all of this activity to Mrs. Inman, who would probably be pleased by the appearance of something being done. In the meanwhile, he could milk the subject for one or two more papers and an appearance at the oncology society annual meeting. He did not want to do that. The CDC, if it did anything more than just add the numbers to its data base, would show up in New Jersey, shovel some dirt or scoop some water into plastic bags, and then mumble something about inconclusive results. A tightness in Schwartz's gut told him that something was very wrong, that there had to be a reason for these cases. Calling in the government was tantamount to giving up, and Schwartz did not want to give up. As he recalled, it had been a physician who had spotted the DES cases. Even in retrospect, they would not have been found by examining the government's database. There was, he decided finally, no need to make an immediate decision. Acey Henson was supposed to be checking to see if there was anything unusual in the area where the boys lived. Schwartz decided that he would wait to see if Henson called back. Then he would make his decision.

The first thought into her head on Sunday morning was how, in God's name, was she going to make good on the promise she had made the previous day? Promise? Hell, it was more like a boast. Sure, no sweat, just give Acey Henson forty-eight hours and she would find out if those kids were using steroids. Christ, how do I get myself into these situations? She groaned and sat up on the side of the bed, the sheet still draped around her.

It was one thing to prove that someone *was* doing something or using something. Find other people involved in the "something," chase them down and then you had it, or at least you had it well enough for broadcast. Proving that someone had *not* done something was an order of magnitude harder, particularly when the "something" was using steroids. Even if everyone Acey knew told her no, that would not prove that the drug had not come from someone Acey did not know. It was always hard to prove you were innocent. Acey remembered that from being a teenager. Why could Schwartz not just test Jerry to see if he had taken any? After all, they did that with athletes all the time. "Hey, Mike, great time in the hundred today; do me a favor and pee in the bottle, will you?" Presumably, Schwartz had a reason. She wished that she had asked him when she was in his office because she did not want to look foolish by calling him up to ask now. So, if you are not going to call him, Acey, stop thinking about it and start doing something about the promise you made.

But, how to do it? Jerry, of course, would know the answer, but would Jerry tell her what he had not told Zeke Schwartz? It was possible. Acey was Jerry's idol, with her picture on his nightstand, while Zeke was the mean, old doctor. Unfortunately, if Jerry said no, she had no way of knowing if he was telling the truth. Even worse, if she talked to Jerry, Schwartz would probably find out and then he would probably have his nose out of joint because it would seem that she was doubting his ability to do his job. That would be bad, although she argued with herself, briefly, that there was no real need to be solicitous about Schwartz's opinion. Forget Jerry for now, she decided. How about his parents? She let out a snort at the thought. Parents never knew anything. Hell, a girl could go through second trimester, some further than that, and the parents would never know. Forget the parents.

If not Jerry and not his parents, who would know? It seemed that the job was doomed to failure. That would be embarrassing. Zeke would think she could not deliver on her promises. The thought made her angry. That was the second time, within a very short stretch of morning, that she had worried about Schwartz's opinion. Why did it matter what Schwartz's, or anyone's, opinion was? What was the matter with her that she was thinking like that?

"Not enough sleep and not enough caffeine," she said to herself. "It's a bad combination."

It was a combination she could do something about, or at least the part about the caffeine. She remembered, at the last moment, to pull on a long jersey before she stepped out of the bedroom. In a moment of compassion for her struggling avocado plant, she had left the shade up in the living room. There was no point in giving the neighbors a free view. It might not be a spectacular view, but there was still no point in giving it away.

Once seated in the kitchen with a cup of coffee, Acey began to feel better. She had a long track record of making foolish promises and then somehow keeping them. She blew on the coffee and remembered the time that she had boasted she could steal the cop car out of the Dunkin' Donuts lot while the cops were inside having coffee. She smiled at the memory. The look on the that policeman's face when she had driven past the window with the lights and siren on had been priceless. By comparison, chasing a few pills would be a piece of cake. By the time she reached the bottom of the mug, she had the outlines of a plan. Jerry's world, at age twelve, was necessarily a small one. If she wanted to know if he had steroids, all she needed to know was who was distributing them locally. As it happened, she had the perfect starting place for the search. The high-school football team.

The idea of starting with the football team had not actually sprung from nothing into her mind, stimulated by a mugful of coffee. The local access channel on the cable network broadcast the high-school games and Acey had the job of providing commentary. That meant she knew a number of the players. Steroids had been a big issue in the county the previous fall, with a good deal of the controversy centering on the football team. The topic had made the Acey Henson show a number of times. Acey knew of several players who were definitely using steroids.

The one she picked as her contact was Ronnie Jankowski, who had just finished his junior year. Acey's information from the fall indicated that Ronnie was the key contact between the supplier and other team members. A telephone call to his home found him there and, two hours later, she met him at the high-school field.

Ronnie played guard, well enough that he would probably play for one of the major colleges in another year. He was a big kid at six-two and two hundred and thirty pounds, some of that bulk having been chemically grown. She had met him during the football season in the course of the steroid debate. Ronnie had been willing enough to talk to her, although cagey about certain names. He had been the source she had tagged "Deep Tackle" on her show. This time, her requests made him defensive.

"Dammit, Acey," he told her, "I don't know what you think you know about me, but you're crazier than anyone thinks if you believe I'm just gonna start handing out names. It was not good around here when you were hitting this on your show and don't hand me that happy horseshit about what I said then. I never thought it would get played up the way it did."

"Hey, Ronnie, cool down! I was careful. I said no names, I used no names. You know that."

"Yeah, but it made a lot of guys uncomfortable. Besides, all the talk got other people digging around. I'm not interested in dealing with that again."

"Ronnie, let's slow down a moment, okay? You're not listening to what I said. If the guys on the team are using them, well, it's your bodies and your balls. Not my problem, I've said my piece. If I wanted to do something to you guys, I could have done it a long time ago and I wouldn't need a whole bunch of new info."

Ronnie turned the implications of that over in his mind. "Okay," he said, "what do you want?"

"I want to find out if a kid named Jerry Inman was using the stuff."

"Jerry Inman?" Ronnie shook his head. "Don't even know the name. He's from this high school?"

"No. He's twelve."

"Twelve?" Ronnie threw his head back and laughed. "Acey, you are a total spaceshot! Where I used to live, down South, you'd get a few kids using the stuff at that age, but not here. Up here, people just don't take sports that serious until high school. You're not gonna find any twelve-year-olds using it around here."

Funny, Acey thought, that is just about what your parents would say about you. Aloud, she said, "How can you be sure?"

"Sure? Christ, why is it so important if this kid is trying to bulk up a little?"

Acey told him.

"Jesus, Acey, you can't get that from steroids."

"I've got a doc who says it's possible. Jerry's a pretty nice little kid. Now, are you going to help?"

Ronnie still looked wary. "If I don't know anything, how can I help?"

"You know who brings the steroids into this area. Unless that has changed from the fall."

Ronnie's face darkened. "No, that hasn't changed. Acey, I'll tell you what, I do know who supplies the steroids that most of the guys use and I think he's the only source around here, but I can't swear to you that this kid of yours isn't getting them someplace else."

"He's twelve, Ronnie. What is he going to do, pedal to Philadelphia on his bike? He'll get it from whoever is close."

"Makes sense. I'll talk to the guy and get back to you. How's that?"

"No good. I talk to him myself."

"Shit! Acey, I can't afford to have you screw me. You do that and I'm in big trouble."

"I've been in big trouble," Acey said. "I would never do that to you."

"I'm still taking a chance. Dammit, I knew you were trouble the first time I met you."

"I haven't been much trouble. So far."

Acey watched silently while the boy thought over that one. She was not going to worry about Ronnie's concerns now. He had put himself into the position he was in.

In the end, he agreed, except that he insisted that nothing could be arranged until the following day. Acey was agreeable to that. It would be her one day off in the week, so she would not be forced to rush back to the station. Quite possibly, she would make her forty-eight-hour deadline.

She met Ronnie the next day, again at the ballfield. From there, she followed his car. The destination surprised her. It was not a gym or a health club, which was what she had expected. Ronnie turned into the parking lot of the Northwest New Jersey Medical Group building and made for the office of Dr. Maurice Stinson, Orthopedics and Sports Medicine.

It was not, however, Dr. Stinson they had come to see, but Jim Flannagan, the nurse-practitioner who worked with him. Acey took one look at Flannagan and wondered if the man was sampling his own wares. The build of his body was barely concealed by the sport shirt he wore. It billowed up from his narrow waist in layers of muscle that grew larger and wider as they moved toward his shoulders. One of his biceps would have been a close match for Acey's thigh. The look on his face was not friendly.

"I don't need trouble here with snoops," he said, "neither does Dr. Stinson. Our training programs are properly supervised and nobody has ever shown any ill effects from any of them. If you're looking to make a wild story out of this, let me give you a piece of advice. Don't. We will sue for slander. I promise you that."

With difficulty Acey swallowed the words she wanted to say. She needed information. Starting a pissing match would cost her the chance to get what she wanted.

"I appreciate the suggestion, but it's not needed," she said, even managing a smile to go with it. "All I need to know is whether a particular kid was on steroids. That's all. I don't need to mention you or your doctor."

Flannagan snorted and leaned back against an exam table. "Normally, I'd wonder how I could know you would keep your word if I talked to you. In this case, though, it's easy. Ronnie said you were asking about some twelve-year-old. We don't deal with any twelve-year-olds, Miss Snoop. Not one. If he's getting it, it ain't from here."

"Who else around here might supply it?"

"Nobody I know."

Acey stared at him. "I'm supposed to believe this?"

Flannagan laughed. "I really don't care if you do. Ronnie asked me to talk to you because you were squeezing him. So, I talked to you. I'm not an idiot. You come around asking about one twelve-year-old, it only makes sense something's wrong with him. Well, he didn't get it here. Now, I hope you're satisfied, but, like I said, you make trouble for us, we'll make a hell of a lot more trouble for you."

"That all depends," Acey said as she stood to leave, "on whether you still have the balls for it. If you know what I mean."

She walked back out to the parking lot with Ronnie, who seemed relieved that the matter was settled. She said nothing to him as he drove off, following on her bike for a few blocks. Then she looped around and came back to the medical building. She walked into Stinson's office suite again, past the few patients in the waiting area. Flannagan was still in his back office where she had left him not long before. She leaned against his doorframe until he looked up from his work.

"What the hell are you doing here!" he exclaimed.

"I thought we should chat privately," she said. "Ronnie's a nice kid, basically, but there are probably things neither one of us wants to say in front of him. You see, I really don't believe you."

"I don't give a fuck whether you believe me or not. Now get out of here, or . . ."

"Or what?" Her voice went hard. "Or maybe you are going to throw me out of here physically? Go ahead. That will make one hell of a story, not to mention the charges. Or maybe you are going to call the police. That should make almost as good a story. Or maybe you will try to throw me out of here and find that you can't."

Flannagan had risen halfway out of his chair and stopped. There was a wild look on Acey's face. Back when she had run with the gangs, most of the boys had been a little afraid of her, even though girls were never admitted as equal members. When she got into one of her wild moods, there was no predicting what she would do.

"Fuckin' coward," she said. "Siddown."

Flannagan sat.

"You want to know what trouble is? Trouble is me telling half the state what I think of you. I know one hell of a lot more about what went on over at that high school than ever came out. If you don't think I can sink you, guess again. You want to dare me?"

Flannagan said nothing.

"I didn't think so. And don't try to threaten me, it doesn't work. Now, was Jerry Inman taking steroids?"

"No. Not from me. Not as far as I know. Dammit, that's no different than I told you before."

"Not true," she said. "This time, I believe you."

Acey might have decided to believe Jim Flannagan, but that did not mean she was willing to discount the possibility that Jerry had been buying the pills from another source. She had the day to herself so, after leaving the clinic, she spent the time hunting down the gym teachers from the high school and the junior high schools and as many students from both as she could find. By nightfall, she had come to the conclusion that she was most unlikely to find any connection between Jerry and the muscle building steroids. It was too easy to find people who knew about the use of the pills in the high school, but no one who knew of younger children taking them. It seemed unlikely that so many people would be so open about the drug use on one hand and deliberately try to conceal it on the other. When she had her fill of finding new people to ask the same old questions and listening to minor variations on the answers, she rode down to Philadelphia and laid the story out for Roger.

Roger was home alone, which meant that it took a long time for the door to be answered. After he let her in, they did not go out to the sun porch. The living room seemed to be as far as Roger had the energy to walk. He lay back against the cushions with his eyes closed while she talked.

His first comment when she finished was, "It sounds reasonable to me."

"Yeah, me too," she said, "but how do I know for sure? It's the same sensation I've had all along."

"You don't have to prove it, Acey. This isn't a court."

"I know how a court works," she said. "I've been there. I know the difference."

"Well, that counts for a lot here. You're a reporter in this. You don't have to prove it, you just need to be reasonably sure."

"Reasonably sure. I am that."

"Good. I'm not saying don't keep your ears open. If things change, you go with it, but right now, the best you can say is that he wasn't using."

Acey wanted to stay, just to visit, but Roger was falling asleep on the couch even while they talked. She pulled a blanket over him and left him on the couch, locking the door on her way out. Then she rode to South Street for a cup of coffee. The day had run well into evening. Noticing that sparked her memory. She had forgotten Schwartz. It would be aggravating, she thought, to have the work done by her deadline only to fail to reach Schwartz. She would just have to hope that he was on call, or working late.

The page operator told her that Schwartz was not on call. Would she care to speak with Dr. Worthington? Acey declined the offer and told the operator to page Schwartz anyway. The phone rang interminably. She resolved to give up on the thirtieth ring and reached twenty-seven when a click on the other end of the line made her ready to be thrilled with her luck.

Unfortunately, it was just the operator to tell her that Dr. Schwartz was not answering. Acey had her try one more time. This time, the operator picked up on the twenty-fifth ring.

"I'm sorry," said the operator, "he still hasn't picked up. Would you like to leave a message?"

"Uh, sure. Can you tell him that I called? My name is Acey Henson and I have some information that he wanted. He can call me at the station tomorrow."

"And is there a number he can reach you at this evening?"

Acey was about to say, "No," but checked herself. She had not eaten lunch and her body was hinting that if she did not eat dinner soon she would regret it. The place she was in would serve as well as any, so she gave the operator the number of the pay phone.

She had not been seated at a table for more than ten minutes when the phone rang. At first, she looked at it askance, thinking, no, it could not be. Some lowlife would undoubtedly emerge from a corner to take a call from a "customer." The phone rang twice more without anyone moving to pick it up. "What the hell," she muttered and grabbed the receiver.

"Hello?"

"Acey?" It was Schwartz on the other end.

"Well, it ain't Barbara Walters," she said. "I said I'd have information for you in forty-eight hours. It's forty-eight hours. I have info. Or, have you forgotten?"

"No, no," he said. She thought he sounded a little defensive, which was all to the good.

"Okay," she said, "how late are you going to be at the hospital? I've got a bit of a drive to get there, or I can come by tomorrow."

"I'm not at the hospital, Acey."

"Huh? Well, where the hell are you? I thought there was a lot of background noise."

"Veterans' Stadium."

"The Vet? What the fuck are you doing there?"

"Watching a ballgame. What else would I be doing here?"

"With your beeper on?" There was no immediate response. "Doc, you're a wonder. A totally screwed up, crazy wonder. Listen, I'm actually in Philly also. Why don't you meet me after the game?"

The words were out of her mouth before she thought about them. Once spoken, she wanted them back. If anything ever sounded like a blatant come on, that line was it. She did not even know if he had gone to the game alone. He might be nutty enough to go on a date with his beeper on. Maybe she had spoken softly enough that he did not hear it.

"If you want, I can leave now," Schwartz said. "The Phillies are down 10 to 1 in the fifth and the only question I've got is whether the Cubs can get twenty hits."

Terrific, she thought. Give a man enough opportunities to make a pass and eventually he will. Why do I do this to myself? Aloud she said, "Give me an hour. I'll meet you at Il Toreador then. It's sort of a local watering hole." She gave him directions and hung up. No matter what else was happening, she did need to eat first.

Il Toreador had begun life in Philadelphia as a theater in the days before shopping malls and multi-screen cinemas. In line with its times, it had been designed to house a large crowd, each individual of which would have an adequate view of the stage. To this end, it had a high vaulted ceiling and a large balcony that swept its wings more than halfway around the circumference of the building. For serious theater, or even burlesque in which it had trafficked, the building was hopelessly outmoded. It could never draw the kind of crowds it would need in order to make money, even if it had not been located next to Chinatown. The owners of the building, being sensible people who took no gratification from being bankrupt patrons of the arts, looked for another way to turn a profit on the building. They converted it into a discotheque.

It was a sound decision. In some ways, the building even looked as if it had been presciently designed with disco in mind. The stage made a superb dance floor. The structure allowed the stage to be illuminated with an ever changing pattern of lights. With the seats torn out, there was plenty of room for onlookers to stand or sit at small tables, both on the main floor and balcony. Even the wings of the balcony, poorly lit and untenanted, were useful for young couples with amorous thoughts and only a minimal need for privacy.

Acey led Schwartz upstairs to the main balcony where she staked out a table near the railing. She indicated that he should wait while she went for drinks. She was back quickly, especially in view of the crowd at the bar, with two large beers. She placed one in front of Schwartz, seated herself and hoisted the other in a toast.

"Here's to it!"

"What?"

"I said, 'Here's to it.' " She drained about half the beer with a long swallow.

"Dammit, Acey, I can barely hear you."

"It is a little loud isn't it?"

That was an understatement. The music emanating from the giant speakers completely enveloped them, the bass rolling right through their bones.

"I thought we were coming to a quiet watering hole to talk," Zeke protested.

"I said 'watering hole.' I never said 'quiet,' " she replied. "Anyway, we can talk. You said it's possible to get cancers like Jerry's from steroids and I told you I would find out if he was taking them." She paused for effect. "Well, he wasn't. I talked to a lot of people who either use them or know people who use them. It's not one hundred percent sure, obviously, but it's as good as you can do."

Schwartz took a sip of his beer. "I'm not surprised," he said.

"Huh? I thought you said something like that was a possibility."

"I did. It was. I had the lab run some studies on Jerry. There are no signs of those steroids in his system."

"Wait a minute! You mean I broke my ass running all around western New Jersey and you just dumped a sample in a machine and already knew the answer? Why didn't you tell me this wasn't necessary?"

"Wait a sec. I didn't say that." Zeke put the beer down, a bit taken aback. "We knew from the start that Jerry was an unlikely user because of his age. Now, the lab tests are good, but they are not perfect and they only detect relatively recent use. When these drugs cause tumors, it's usually after a long period of use. All I can tell is that he hadn't used anything recently. Put that together with the information you found, though, and I'd say it's one hundred percent. Steroids didn't do it."

Mollified, Acey took another swig of her beer. "Okay, cross out steroids. What's next?"

"I don't know." Zeke busied himself with his beer while Acey pulled a cigarette out of her omnipresent pack. The air on the balcony, he decided, was already smoky enough that one more lit cigarette would hardly matter. He waited for her to draw the cigarette to life before he continued. "*Something* is hitting these kids; the knot in my gut tells me that. Unfortunately, that doesn't mean I know what it is. It's like I said the first time we talked about this," he said, "most of the time, there are no answers for these kinds of clusters. No matter how hard you look, you come up with zilch. Not because there are no reasons but because we don't have a clue what to look for. There are just too many things floating around in the environment."

" 'Floating around in the environment,' " she repeated. "You mentioned toxic stuff the other night. Is that what you mean?"

"Yes. In fact, you said you had reports on what had been dumped in various areas. Did you have a chance to look at them?"

"Doc, I've got them, but I haven't gone through them. I've spent my free time chasing overdeveloped jocks, if you know what I mean. I do have the info, though, and I know how to get more if we need it. If there's something floating around, I'll find it."

"Floating!" Zeke gave a harsh laugh. "Those kids did all live around that creek, didn't they?"

"You bet," said Acey Henson. "Now, what do you think?"

"I think it is at least worth looking into."

"Excellent," said Acey with a broad grin. "And even better, it's my job. I've got access to the information and you don't. Say, I like this beat. How about a dance?" She enjoyed watching the surprise on his face.

"Acey, I went to a ballgame tonight, not a dance hall. I'm wearing my hiking boots."

"That doesn't make sense either, Doc. Why would you wear boots to the Vet?"

"Does there have to be a reason? I just did. I can't dance in these; they weigh at least three pounds."

"So? It'll be good for your quads. Come on!"

As she led him through the crowd in front of the dance floor, she wondered what impulse had made her do it. It was as though a part of her wanted him to do something stupid, although she could not think of a reason for that. She was relieved when, after a few dances, Zeke settled for an affectionate hug and went his way with, "Give me a call when you have something." At least, she thought she was relieved. The hug had clearly said, "I like you." She would have been angry had anything else followed the hug. That is, she thought she would have been angry.

Chapter 13

FLEMINGTON, NEW JERSEY _____

ACEY HENSON was entertaining some fantasies when she went to her office the next afternoon. She had no doubt that she would pull open her "Toxic

Dump" drawer and there it would be. "It" would be a report of some chemical dump, forgotten years ago, now leaking toxins into the ground, toxins that had killed two kids and were working on a third.

She would take the report down to the hospital and show it to Schwartz, who would look at it quietly, stroking his chin the way she had noticed he did when he was intent. Then he would say, "These compounds here and here are known to cause hepatocellular carcinoma. That's good work, Acey."

Then she would break the story, he had promised she could, and she would give proper credit where it was due. It would be *her* story the news wires would carry. The networks would want to know who this person was, at a small radio station, who had scooped them on a major toxic waste story. There would be a book. Pulitzer Prize for the book? Maybe. Network show? Definitely.

The dream vanished a few hours later. The file drawer was empty, its contents stacked everywhere around her office. She had been through each report at least twice. There was nothing. Toxic waste had been dumped all across New Jersey during the course of the last few decades, but none of it appeared to have been dumped in the vicinity of Scheuermann's Run.

"Must be the only damn place in the state that isn't toxic," she muttered.

She sat down on the floor next to a stack of her files and smoked a cigarette while she thought about her problem. She could not go back to Schwartz and say that she had been unable to find anything. If she did, he might tell her that it was all just an unlikely coincidence and that she should forget it. Worse, he might call in someone else to do some sort of testing and then it would not be her story anymore. The only way to stay in control of the story was to keep control of the important information.

Could she have missed something? It was possible, although she doubted it. That area was part of WCZY's listening area and she had been doubly careful to check for items of interest to her regular listeners when she had been searching for information for the file. Still, it was possible, in which case she needed to look for material she had missed the first time.

Reaching a decision, she called Eleanor McAfey, her contact at the Environmental Protection Agency in Washington. Eleanor was a colorless individual, Acey had decided on the one occasion they met personally, someone who did little of significance in her own right. She was a person, however, who was both excited and pleased to have a radio personality asking questions about her work, even though, as she impressed upon Acey, her name must never be mentioned publicly, no matter what Acey found. Acey had wondered if there would be a real problem if Eleanor's name became associated with some of the information Acey had, or if Eleanor merely said it in order to make her work seem important. No matter. She had taught Acey what reports were important and how to obtain the ones she wanted.

As usual, Eleanor sounded eager to please as soon as she heard Acey's voice, but this time there was little help forthcoming.

"I gave you the lists of all the sites in that area," McAfey said, "and I saw to it that your requests were processed when they came in. You've already got the information on all the Superfund sites and the RECRA cleanup sites. There aren't any others, not around there."

"Suppose, though," Acey said, "that what I'm looking for isn't classed as a dump site. Suppose somebody had some stuff leak out a few times, or something like that, maybe into the creek. How about that?"

"Anytime someone has a hazardous chemical spill that gets off their site they have to report it to us," Eleanor told her. "You would have those reports."

"What if it wasn't reported?"

"Well, now, if it wasn't reported we wouldn't have anything on it, now would we?"

Acey had to chuckle. "Good answer, dumb question," she said. "Eleanor, I'm sorry, but I really need your help. Where else can I look?"

Acey did not need a picture to know that the other woman liked the feeling of being needed. It was audible in her voice. "Every town has to have what we call a local planning committee. Anybody who stores or handles chemicals has to file information with those committees, what they have, where they store it, what kind of equipment they have and what they plan to do if there is a problem; that sort of thing. You can try looking there. Maybe you'll find something that wasn't reported or that nobody thought needed to be reported. We don't really have the resources here to go around beating the bushes for these things."

Acey thanked her very carefully for her advice. After hanging up, she lit another cigarette to help her plan her next move. Obtaining information from Washington always took time because of the size of the federal bureaucracy; however, obtaining information from a rural town could take even longer because no one might know where it was, in spite of Eleanor's reassurance about local planning committees. She thought back to the previous night, trying to recall if she had given Schwartz the impression that results would be delivered instantaneously. She had not said it in the way she had with the steroid business, but could she have implied it. She decided she had not. Certainly, she had no intention of calling him to ask.

The first problem was finding the right place to call. Jerry Inman lived in Scheuermann's Run, which was north and east of the creek, while the Delgados lived in Marrville on the south side. The former Swenson house was also in Marrville. Perhaps more important, there were more businesses located either around the town of Scheuermann's Run or to the north of it because of where the interstate highway ran. Scheuermann's Run, then, was the logical place to start. Deciding on the location did not, however, tell her who to call. The phone book listed no such creature as a "local planning committee" under the governmental offices. Two calls to the town hall connected her first with the development office and, on her second try, with the zoning office. Finally, after having her call transferred more times than a town that size should have offices, she was able to describe the committee, or what it was supposed to do, to a patient secretary. This individual actually seemed to know what Henson was talking about. The chairman of the local planning committee was, in fact, a police sergeant who worked third shift. Could Miss Henson call back tonight?

Miss Henson could and Miss Henson did, just as soon as she was off the air that night. Police Sergeant Timothy Brackett surprised her by being very accommodating. Acey was welcome to meet him at the station that night if she cared to drive out. She did.

Brackett seemed happy to see her. He was a grizzled man of sixty with a small pot belly who greeted her with the kind of handshake she had become accustomed to while driving a truck in Texas. On the surface, it looked like a greeting between equals, but it was intended to demonstrate that a good ol' boy could reduce any woman's hand to kindling if he so desired. Fortunately for Acey, the heavy outdoor work she had done had left her a sturdy grip. She met pressure with pressure and saw Brackett's eyes widen.

"I am impressed," Brackett said when they released. "I always listen to you talk about what you've done and I always wondered if it was for real. Now I'm sure. Nobody gets a grip like that sitting at a desk."

"You listen to my show?"

"When I can. Best thing on this time of night. When you called, I figured if you were going to come down here, maybe I could get an autograph. I was going to say it's for my daughter, but it's for both of us."

After Acey obliged, she told him again what she was looking for.

"Yeah, I know what you want," Brackett said. "They passed a law saying all companies had to file these emergency plans with whatever town they're in, so they do. The bigger ones do, anyway. Hell, I think Bob's Body Shop down in Marrville is supposed to file one, but he doesn't and you don't seriously think I go chasing after him, do you?" Acey did not. "Yeah. It's a waste of goddamn paper, if you ask me. I haven't the faintest goddamn idea of what to do with them. On top of that, I had to buy a whole new goddamn file cabinet just to store 'em. Come on in back, I'll show you."

The file cabinet held an impressive number of folders. "Is there something in particular you're looking for, or would you just like to look through them?" Brackett asked.

Acey thought about it briefly. "It's probably better if I can browse. By the way, is this stuff supposed to be confidential or restricted?"

"I haven't the faintest goddamn idea," Brackett said. "Nobody ever mentioned. Tell you what. If you find something, you didn't get it here and I never saw you."

"Sounds fine to me."

Acey pulled a chair over to the cabinet and started flipping through the folders. All the folders came with maps showing the location of the business. She discarded all that were not close to Scheuermann's Run, then she started to look at the remaining ones more closely. One of the folders that was in her stack was from Meldrum Products. That one drew her attention, probably because it was a three-ring notebook, the cover embossed with the company logo. Most of the other folders contained only a sheaf of papers held together with a clip. Meldrum, she recalled, had opened a large research and manufacturing plant in the area perhaps four or five years before. The map inside the notebook showed that Scheuermann's Run actually flowed through the grounds of the Meldrum Products plant. That quickened her pulse, but, when she turned to the listing of hazardous chemicals at the facility, the only thing printed there was "None."

So, Meldrum had no hazardous chemicals in the plant, or at least not enough that they had to list them. By all rights she should have put the folder back then, but she did not. Instead, she leafed through it again, front to back, back to front. Lists of names, titles and phone numbers, maps, detailed floor plans, nothing that meant anything. Wait. Maybe there was something. There were two copies of one of the floor plans. She asked Brackett why that was so.

"I couldn't tell you," was his answer. "I got that second one in the mail a few months ago with a note that said I should substitute it for the one in the book. I guess I forgot to chuck the old one."

"They didn't say why they sent you a new one?"

"No."

Acey took the two plans out of the notebook and laid them side by side. The dates on them were different, but otherwise they looked identical.

"I guess they're just supposed to update them on some schedule," Brackett suggested.

"You ever get any other replacements?"

"No."

That tugged at her mind. She set out to scrutinize the plans, checking each feature on the old one against the new one. After about fifteen minutes, she shouted for Brackett.

"Take a look at this," she said, "and tell me if I'm seeing things."

"Look at what?" Brackett asked.

"This." She placed a forefinger on each floor plan. "See, on the old one, there's this connector marked 'W' leading to the storm drain system. It doesn't show at all on the new plan. Otherwise, they are identical. Now, the legend says that all the 'W' lines are for waste water, so it looks like they took something out, doesn't it?"

"That it does," Brackett agreed.

"Any idea what?"

"Haven't the faintest goddamn idea," Brackett said. "I'll tell you who would, though. My cousin Timmy has a company in Somerville. They do a lot of contracting work with the chemical companies and the drug companies, plumbing and that sort of thing. They had a job up at Meldrum late last year, right before the date on this new plan. Maybe he can help you."

Acey's eyes lit up at the suggestion. She eagerly scribbled down the name and address that Brackett gave her.

"I've got a Xerox here," Brackett said. "Do you want a copy of those plans?"

"You bet," said Acey Henson. "I didn't get them here either."

SOMERVILLE, NEW JERSEY _____

Tim Lange was a stout man whose face clearly showed his relationship to Brackett. His office was really no more than a corner of his shop, partially isolated by wooden partitions that did not reach to the roof. Although they blocked out the sight of people moving around on their various errands, they did nothing to diminish the clangor of the equipment or the shouts of the men operating it. Lange seemed to have no trouble concentrating, however. He briefly looked at the copied plans that Acey showed him, then threw his head back and laughed.

"Sure I remember the Meldrum job," he said. "I was wondering when somebody would show up asking about this."

That took Acey by surprise. She had been telling herself, all night and all the way to Somerville, that it would turn out to be nothing, a broken pipe that was taken out instead of replaced or an error in the first plan. The glint in Lange's eye told her otherwise.

"Why would you expect someone to ask about it and what was it?"

Lange laughed again. "What it was was one of the dumbest rigs I've ever seen. Hang on, I keep files on all these jobs." He crossed over to a row of file cabinets set against one of the partitions and rummaged through the drawers. "Ah, here we are. Just wanted to make sure I had the name right. That area on the plan is the manufacturing area for one of their drugs. The plant was designed to be mostly automated but they screwed the design up.

The way it was initially set, their computer was flushing out part of each batch. Stupid. What was even dumber, instead of looking into why his final yields were low, their plant manager just assumed that was all the process would give him and ignored it. I guess their Quality Assurance people caught it eventually. Only took them about three years. We got the contract to fix it."

"That is very interesting," said Acey in what she thought was a polite understatement. "What you didn't tell me, though, is why you were expecting somebody to ask about it."

"Stands to reason," Lange said. "The drug they were flushing out went right into the creek. Now, since my people were working in there, I had them go over all the stuff they used in that area and none of it is supposed to be toxic, but my guess is, even if it was, they'd say it wasn't and who's to know? Anyway, they acted like they had all the answers to everything, in spite of the fact that they screwed up in the first place. I figured, sooner or later, somebody would be asking."

"I take it," Acey said dryly, "that you don't much care to work with Meldrum."

"Damn straight," Lange said. "Bunch of tight assholes in blue suits. God, do you have to yell and scream to get paid. You want to copy that file?"

Chapter 14

TRENTON, NEW JERSEY _____

THE AFTERNOON following her trip to Tim Lange's shop, Acey Henson sat in a chair in Schwartz's office watching him read the report she had copied. Zeke had been surprised that morning when she called to announce her find. He had told her to come by that afternoon, which pleased her because it showed that he was still interested in the story.

"How did you get hold of this?" Zeke asked after he finished reading it.

"I'd rather not go into that," she answered. "Will you take my word for it that the report is authentic?"

Schwartz looked back at the paper. From the expression on his face, Acey knew he was going to rub his chin, even before he moved his hand. It was interesting how quickly one could learn a person's habits.

"I don't doubt it's real," he said.

"Okay, okay, but what do you think about it?" She was sitting on the edge of the seat.

"Interesting." Zeke rubbed his chin again.

"Interesting! I come up with this report and all the man can do is say 'interesting.'"

Zeke put the report down and looked up. "What were you expecting me to do?"

"I figured you would gasp loudly, grab at your chest, fall to the floor and moan softly a few times." Acey got up and glared at him.

It occurred then to Zeke Schwartz that she was serious behind the hyperbole. She very badly wanted him to be impressed. "Dammit, Acey," he said, "I said it was interesting and it is. Quite possibly the most interesting piece of the puzzle so far. Now will you sit down so we can talk about it? If you keep looking at me like that, I likely will fall to the floor moaning."

"Okay." She gave him an exaggerated smile and wink and sat down. "Can you tell me what it is that they dumped into the creek? The report says it wasn't a hazard, and I've checked the hazardous lists, it's not on them, but I don't know whether I should believe it."

Zeke gave her a tight little grin before he spoke. "There's no secret about what it was, most of it at any rate, although there's no reason you should recognize it. The stuff is called Aspergicin. It's a drug we use to treat certain types of serious fungal infections. From this report, it looks like Meldrum was losing part of its product on each batch, with some of the drug winding up in the creek. They don't say precisely what was wrong in the plant design, but I think you can be certain it was unintentional. They sell this stuff for an outrageous price. There's no way they were going to dump it on purpose. In fact, I'd love to have been a fly on the wall when they found out." The thought broadened his grin and made him chuckle.

"Then this is a drug you give people."

"Yup. Jodie Schmidt, that's the other kid whose parents were on your show, she had it. I would say that's the reason she was still around for the show."

"This drug doesn't cause cancer, does it?" Acey was developing a sinking feeling in her stomach, born of the certainty that she had come up with a dud and that Schwartz was just being polite.

"Not that I've ever heard of," Zeke said.

"Then this is useless." Acey stood up. "I'm sorry I wasted your time. It sounded like you were having a busy day."

Zeke looked up, surprised. "Wait a sec. You have to give a guy a chance to finish a thought. I don't talk as fast as you do, Henson."

"What do you mean?"

"For starters, sit your butt back down in the chair for a minute." After she had complied, he went on, "I said I had never heard of Aspergicin being linked to cancer. True enough. However, the drug has only been around a few years and cancers usually take a long time to develop. A long time ago, there was an X-ray dye called Thorotrast in use. Years later, people who had gotten it started turning up with tumors. We are still seeing tumors from that and it hasn't been used in decades. Cigarettes are another good example." Acey had been starting to pull her pack out of her pocket when he said that. She let it slide back into place and pretended there was no link between her action and his comment.

"There are two things to consider," Zeke continued. "First, we usually give Aspergicin for two to three weeks. If you're not cured by then, you're usually in a box anyway. This was leaking for years. If the kids played in the creek a lot, or if it got into the wells, that's a whole different situation. Second, compared to what you could be exposed to in the creek, we give huge doses in the hospital. Sometimes, long exposures to low doses can be very different than brief exposure to high doses. I wouldn't jump to conclusions."

"Fine. I'm not jumping. In fact, I'm sitting here very politely. It sounds like we need to know if the kids play in the creek."

"Yeah." He pushed his hands through his hair. "Sometimes easier said than done. I talked with Mrs. Delgado a while ago and she thought Mario went down along the creek, but I don't think she was very sure of it. Most parents don't have any idea what their kids do, and most of the ones who think they do are wrong."

"Do you think I don't know that, Zeke?"

"Sorry. I'm sure you do. It's just that most people around here don't and I get into a rut. The easiest thing to do is ask Jerry and since he's stashed over in the hospital I can do that when I go on rounds. Which needs to be about now," he said after looking at his watch. "I'd ask you to meet me afterward and we could continue this, but I'm afraid it's likely to take a while."

"That's okay," Acey said, "I have to get over to the station to set up for the news anyway. If you're going to work late, though, you could meet me at the diner after the show."

Zeke agreed, but it was only after Acey left that it dawned on him what he had agreed to. Ezekiel, you're an old fool, he thought. You just said that you would meet her after two in the morning. He sighed. She would probably think that he was going through his second adolescence. He thought about calling the station to cancel, but put the phone down after punching in the first three numbers. He was beginning to enjoy working with Acey Henson. He stuffed his stethoscope into a jacket pocket and headed for the staircase leading to the patient floors.

* * *

Jerry was seventh on Zeke's list of patients to see, not that there was any carved-in-stone order to the list. It was only that he habitually started with the infants and then worked his way around to the older children. Had he thought about his habit, he would have realized that he worked that way because the infant ward was closest to the staircase and, even more important, the conference room on that ward was usually stocked with coffee, peanut butter, and crackers. While sipping a cup of coffee and munching crackers smothered with peanut butter, he could review his patients with the nursing staff. Then, armed with another cup of coffee, he could see his patients, write his notes, and head off to the next ward. As he had told Acey Henson, rounds could take quite a while.

Jerry was talkative when Schwartz arrived, probably because his mother had gone shopping and he was bored. When Zeke asked him what he would like to do at home over the summer, Jerry responded with a day-by-day recital of his Little League schedule.

"God, is that all you do? Play baseball?" Zeke asked him.

"No, but I like playing baseball."

"I figured that. Do you do anything else?"

"Sure. Lotsa stuff."

"Do you go swimming in the creek by your house?"

"Well, most of it's too small," Jerry said. "There's one spot, though, where we can swim. We've got a real awesome place near there, too. I can't tell you about that, though, it's a secret." Jerry said that quickly, as though trying to cover for the fact that he had said anything at all.

"That's okay. I won't tell anyone that you said anything. Who's we?"

"Oh, a lot of guys from around. You know."

"Sounds like it can't be much of a secret if all those people know about it, can it?"

"Well, it's just kids," Jerry said. "Just guys in the league, you know. It's like, if you're on one of the teams it's okay to use it but you can't tell anyone who's not on a team."

"Okay. It's private for your league, then. Do you know all these guys pretty well?"

"Not all," Jerry said. "I mean, I know all the guys from Scheuermann's Run, of course. We've got teams from Marrville in the league too and I don't know a lot of them 'cause they go to a different school."

"Okay. I get it. Do you hang out there a lot?"

"Sure, when it's nice. Unless I'm playing baseball."

Schwartz finished his rounds quickly for him, deciding against a return for more peanut butter and crackers. There were no major clinical problems that evening, so his mind chewed on the problem of Jerry and the creek.

Jerry had definitely been in the creek. Did that mean anything? Would a load of powerful antibiotic do anything except make it a very clean creek? By the time he returned to his office, Schwartz realized that he had no answers for any of his questions.

When he left for the diner late that night, he still had no answers. It was not for lack of trying. He had searched the library for references to Aspergicin and had also gone through the individual issues of a dozen journals for the current year hoping to find some information. There had been none, that is, none that seemed relevant to Jerry. The computer databases were no better. He did notice that Leon Kanzel, who headed the Infectious Disease service both for the Childrens' Hospital and the main hospital, had published extensively on Aspergicin, but by the time he made the connection, it was too late to reach Kanzel at his office. Schwartz considered calling him at home, but he did not. His own curiosity and a post-midnight meeting with a radio announcer did not justify bothering a full professor at home, not as long as Schwartz harbored hopes of achieving tenure. He just hoped that Acey did not think he was an idiot for coming out without much to say.

FLEMINGTON, NEW JERSEY ——————————————

Acey sat in the diner feeling silly. The wall clock, directly across from her, read two-twenty. That, dear fans, is two-twenty in the morning, she thought sourly. She had become so accustomed to working into the night that it might as well have been early evening by the reckoning of her internal clock. However, she knew the rest of the world did not function that way.

What in God's name had put it into her head to ask Schwartz to meet her at the diner after the show? Oh sure, he had agreed, but she should have seen that his mind was focused on the patients he was going to see, not what he was saying. Someone says, I'll meet after work and you say yes, without really thinking about it. At some point, however, he would realize the time that was involved. Then what would he do? There was nothing he could possibly discover that could not wait until tomorrow afternoon.

More than likely, she decided, he would have a good laugh. She could imagine Schwartz bursting out with laughter in the middle of the hospital. Someone would ask him what was so funny and he would say, "This ditzy radio jock asked me to meet her at a diner at two-thirty in the morning. How ridiculous can you get?" Acey could feel her cheeks flush as she viewed the mental image. There was, of course, a logical alternative thought a man could have about a woman who asked him to meet her at two-thirty in the morning. Acey did not want to think about that, which made it very difficult to put the thought out of her head. Those thoughts had been on her mind a good part of the evening. It may have had something to do with the less than inspired show she had given.

So, why was she sitting there, smoking her second cigarette and refilling her coffee cup? One reason was that she had to be there to know if he did not show up. Another was that it would be even more embarrassing if he did show up and she was not there. She was pulling cigarette number three out of the pack when Schwartz walked through the door.

Acey wanted to ask him why he had come and thank him for coming all at the same time. She did neither of those things. What she said was a cool, "Good morning," while hiding her face behind the flare of the lighter and a puff of smoke.

"Good morning, yourself," Zeke said. He slid into the seat opposite to her with a groan. "One of these days they are going to discover that lack of sleep causes senility and then I'll really be cooked."

Is that supposed to make me feel guilty? Acey wondered about it, but did not say it. "Did you come up with anything when you interrogated the prisoner?" she asked.

"What? Oh, Jerry." Schwartz sighed. Then he waved to the waitress to have her bring him a cup of coffee. Once he had it, he repeated his conversation with Jerry.

"And that is the long and the short of it," he said. He had been glad to find her there, waiting for him, and even gladder to find her willing to listen to news that was far from dramatic. "Jerry's been in the creek and I'm up the creek," he concluded.

"Why do you say that?"

"Because it doesn't really lead anywhere." There was frustration in his voice. "Sure, Jerry was in the creek and probably the Delgado boy as well. So what? I don't even know if the stuff can be absorbed through the skin. Nothing in the literature says one way or another. It may even be irrelevant. It's all well-water out there and it could have gotten into that, but I don't know if anyone checked in the past and there is certainly no way to check it now. I still don't even know if it is possible for Aspergicin to do this in the first place. So, I'm stuck."

"Come on, Zeke, don't look so damn glum. At least, now we have the kids in the same place as a chemical that definitely should not have been where it was. That's something."

"Yeah, but it's not really any more than we already had. I just don't feel like I've added anything."

"If you feel that way, I'm a little surprised you bothered to come out here," Acey said.

"I said I would. Being stuck is no reason not to show."

Acey tried to watch his face out of the corners of her eyes as she turned away to blow out some smoke. Schwartz, however, had his coffee cup up and his face was unreadable. Acey had known a great many people who made a big production out of claiming to do whatever it was they had said they would do. Usually, they followed through only if there was no inconvenience involved. Her father came to mind, immediately. She liked the way Schwartz had behaved. Maybe there was a quick way to unstick things.

"You know, Doc, that offer I made to you a while back about coming on the show? It's still open."

Zeke narrowed his eyes at the sudden change in the conversation. "What does that have to do with any of this?"

"I still get calls about the show I did with Jerry. When you do enough of these shows, you can see patterns in how people call in. I'd say there's still a lot of interest out in the community about Jerry. Another show would get a good audience. We could talk about what we are finding, too. Maybe, there will be someone listening who has some information that would help. It happens."

"Say it on the air? Dammit, Acey, that's just what I don't want to do. I'm sure it would generate a lot of interest, more like hysteria I should think. I won't do that. I told you that once."

The moment she saw his reaction, she knew she had made a mistake. Dammit, she had been trying to be helpful! Why was it so difficult to deal with people when you wanted to get along with them?

"Okay. I'm sorry; I shouldn't have said it. Skip this stuff then. We would have plenty to talk about anyway. You'll be a good draw."

Zeke sensed a trap. Once they were actually on the air, it would be hard for him to set boundaries, particularly since Acey was the one who was experienced in guiding talk shows. "I'll think about it," was all he said.

"I put my foot in it, didn't I? My mouth, I mean. I said I was sorry. I keep forgetting that you don't want to stir things up. It's the opposite of what most people would want."

Zeke busied himself with finishing his coffee. "It's okay. Don't sweat it. The fact is, there is an even easier way and I'm an idiot for not thinking of it before now. We know who makes this stuff. Meldrum does. They have to have whatever information there is. I also have a contact there, that is I have the name of a doc who works with their medical group. Worthington put together some arrangement for them to fund a fellowship for us and I'm supposed to talk to this guy, Woodward, about it. I haven't been able to talk to him yet, but I haven't been very persistent either. They don't have to know about Jerry, or that I know about the leak. I should be able to get the information we need. I'll call you at the station as soon as I have something and let you know."

After he left, Acey sat in the booth for a while by herself. There are times to push, she thought, and times not to push. This had been a time not to push and she had almost blown it. Not quite, though. She was glad of that. Actually, she found it amazing that they had been working together this long and Schwartz had not made a move at her. Oddly enough, she thought, just this once she would not have minded if he had.

Acey did not hear from Zeke for the next three days. Granted, he had told her that he would call when he had more information, but by the third day the delay seemed too long. Zeke had been prompt in the past, even when he had little to say; it was a little odd for there not to have been a call, if only to say that there was no further information. It was easy to draw the conclusion that the silence was a by-product of her foolishness at the diner. She brooded about it, unable to devise an appropriate plan to either confirm or deny it. The most direct approach, to page him at the hospital, was unacceptable. It would be easy enough, eight quick numbers on the telephone and a "Dr. Zeke Schwartz, please," when the operator answered, but it was unacceptable. He had said that *he* would call *her*. If she called him . . . She obstinately refused to finish the line of thought on each of the dozen or so times it popped into her head. She knew what it would mean and so would Schwartz.

Brooding about it did not help her disposition. She snarled at Howard with such regularity when she came in to the station in the afternoon that he began to sweat when they crossed paths in the hall. The morning of the third day with no word from Zeke, she called Roger and Jim to say that she could not come to Philadelphia as she had planned. She was in a foul mood and Roger was too fragile for her to risk snapping at an innocuous comment. That night, though, she tore into Pamela Davies after the girl forgot to take down the name, address and phone number of a caller who should have been sent a WCZY sweatshirt. The words were out of her mouth, harsh and clipped, before she had even thought about them and Pammy promptly burst into tears. Acey hugged her and apologized, which soothed Pamela, but did nothing for Acey's feeling of tension.

When she woke on the fourth day, she knew she had to do something. Calling Zeke was still out of the question. What could she possibly say if she did? Fortunately, she conceived of a better plan. She decided to drive over to the hospital and see Jerry. She had called once, after the show, to see how he was doing. It would be perfectly reasonable for her to pay him a visit. If she happened to run into Dr. Schwartz, well, she would not have been looking for him. Anyway, it could be presented that way.

Jerry was in his room with his mother and they both looked glum. Jerry was sad because Jodie had finally healed enough to receive her next treatment and then go home, which left him without a pal. Having everyone say how happy they were that Jodie could go did not help, because he had to pretend to be happy also, even though he was not. Having his mother there should have helped, but did not. She was, in fact, not good company. Added to the strain of spending part of each day in the hospital with Jerry, for the past three days she had come home to find Charley drunk in the house, with no indication that he had ever gone to work. She was aware that, since Jerry had taken sick, Charley had been coming home drunk more often and drunker than usual. She had figured that as long as he went to work, and did not crack up on the way home, there was no point arguing about it, not while Jerry was sick. However, if Charley was just going to lie around drunk, well, that was a different matter. She was not looking forward to the argument. It left her ill-disposed to humor a cranky child.

Given a choice, Acey would have shared their mood. That was not possible. She was the visiting celebrity and she knew the demands that the role made. It would never do to sit down, stare at the wall, and mumble. Instead, she tried to replay some of the better stories from her last few shows. The rendition was not bad, but it lacked her customary sparkle. Jerry pretended to enjoy it and Mrs. Inman pretended to be appreciative.

It was almost a relief to leave the room, although it still left her with the same dilemma she had faced at the station. Going to Schwartz's office was every bit as bad as calling him. After standing in the hallway for some time at a loss, she spotted at the nursing station a stocky young doctor who matched a description Schwartz had given.

"Hi," Acey said, "are you the one they call Kay Vitch?"

Jola looked up from the chart she had in front of her. "I'm not sure who 'they' is. I'm Jo Marienkiewicz."

"Fine by me," Acey said. "Actually, one of 'they' is Zeke Schwartz. I came down to see Jerry and I wanted to ask him how Jerry was doing. Any idea where he might be hiding?"

"He's not in today at all," Jola said. "He called in and left a message that Worthington would be covering for him and only to page him for emergencies. I take care of Jerry on the floor, so maybe I can help."

"Is he sick?"

"No. Actually, Jerry's doing quite nicely. I'm hoping he'll go home in not too long."

Acey bit her lip. The answer had been quite logical, given the way she had phrased her original question. "Glad to hear it. Is it Schwartz who's sick, maybe."

"I have no idea. You could check with his office. They probably have his home number."

That alternative was worse than paging him. The fact that Acey felt as though she was going to explode probably qualified as an emergency, but she did not plan to discuss that with the page operator. Or with Marienkiewicz. Or with Zeke Schwartz.

"I don't need to bother him," she said. "It's not that big a deal." Acey said it while feeling the opposite and hoping that Marienkiewicz was not astute enough to notice.

She left the hospital and drove to WCZY, even though it was early afternoon. There, she found a big note taped to her door.

"Please see me ASAP when you get in. Howard."

"What the fuck?" she yelled at the door. She pulled the note off with a swipe of her hand, gave the door a kick and stomped down the hall to Firman's office.

"Howard, what is this?" She stood in front of him, dangling the note by its tape from her forefinger.

"Ah, I wanted to see you when you got in."

"Yes, Howard, I can read. About what?"

"Who is Zeke?"

Acey's jaw dropped. "What do you mean?"

"I gather you recognize the name."

Acey scrambled to regain her composure. "Yes, I do. What about it?"

Then it was Howard's turn to look uncomfortable as he shifted in his seat. "Look, Acey, what you or any of the other employees here do in your free time is your business, but if you are going to, ah how do I put this, have a liaison with somebody I would appreciate it if you would do it away from the station."

"What!"

Firman's face turned beet red. "The man has called here at least six times in the last two hours looking for you. I know you're sort of a special case around here, but don't you think this is a bit much?"

Acey stared at him for a full minute before answering. "For your information, Zeke is *Doctor* Zeke Schwartz and this is work-related. You can be damned sure I don't hang my private life out where everybody can see it. I think, Howard, that if you had been laid sometime in the past decade you wouldn't be so eager to jump to conclusions about what other people do. So, why don't you take fifty bucks from petty cash and do something about the situation?"

Before he could think of a reply, she was out the door. It was an effort not to run down the corridor but, under the circumstances, that would never do. Once behind her closed door, however, she made a beeline for the telephone.

"Dr. Zeke Schwartz," she said when the page operator answered.

"I'm sorry, Dr. Schwartz is out today. Can I get you Dr. Worthington?"

"No, I need to speak with Dr. Schwartz. He has been trying to reach me."

"Is this an emergency?"

"It is very likely going to be."

"Hold on, please, I'll try to reach him."

It took only five rings before Zeke picked up the line. "Acey?" he said, "Christ, where in hell have you been? I've been trying to reach you."

"Where have I been? The man drops off the face of the earth for three days and he wants to know where I've been." She dropped that line as she realized how it was sounding. "I was at the hospital visiting Jerry. From what I heard, you decided to go on holiday."

"Hardly."

"Okay. What's up?"

"My blood pressure for one." There was no humor in Schwartz's voice. "In fact, I've had it up to my eyeballs. I'm ready to strangle someone."

"Uh, Doc, I get the feeling that there's a bit between three days ago and now that I don't know. Could you fill me in?"

"Yeah, I told you I was going to call Meldrum, right?"

"Right."

"Well, I did. You would think, I am sure, that if you have the name of somebody to speak to and know where he works that it should be a simple matter to talk to him."

"I wouldn't always think that," Acey said, "but I have a feeling that's exactly what you are going to tell me."

"Bingo. I call this Dr. Woodward. He's in a meeting. Fine, I leave my number. I told you I had already tried to reach him about something else. When he didn't call back, I tried again. Dr. Woodward was in a meeting. Same routine. Next morning, still no Dr. Woodward, so I try again. He's not in his office. This time, I figure, I'll take whoever I can get, so I ask if I can talk to somebody about effects of Aspergicin on the liver. They connect me to some woman who wants to know if I had a problem with a patient. I can just see telling this story to some junior assistant flunky. I told her I was just interested in any known effects or problems. She gave me some data and a bunch of references. Turned out that the references were all the basic papers that I already had and all the information was in the package insert anyway. Big help. So, I called back, got the same woman. She connects me to somebody else, who gives me the same information. When I got persistent, she suggested that I call Dr. Kanzel, that's our Infectious Disease Chief here. I told her I'd already done that and that he didn't know. That's when she told me I needed to talk to Woodward. Where's Woodward? In a meeting! You ever hear the Abbott and Costello 'Who's on first?' routine?"

"I invented it," Acey said.

"The way I'm going I could almost believe you," Zeke replied. "Can you believe that she told me the information she gave me was all that they had on Aspergicin?"

"Obviously, you don't."

"Not a chance. There's no way they can spend half a decade getting a drug on the market and have another three years of everybody using it and that's all they know. Which I told her and got some bullshit about federal regulations."

"Sounds like fun," Acey said. "What happened next?"

"Tried again yesterday and went through the same damn routine. All they want to know is if I have a problem with a patient, and the only person, I gather, who is authorized to give any more information than I've already got is this guy Woodward, who's in a meeting. For three days, he's been in a meeting. I got so fed up, I went over there today. What I got was some dummy from their Marketing group who wanted to give me a brochure and a wall chart."

Acey had to fight to keep her laughter from spewing out over the phone. Her effort managed to reduce it to an intermittent giggle that seeped out when she tried to talk. Partly, she was laughing at Schwartz, who was finding being ignored hard to take. She was also laughing at herself for all her needless aggravation. "Welcome to the real world, Doc," she said. "Do you have any other sources of information?"

"Not really, I'm afraid. If it's published, I've got it. Dr. Kanzel, who ought to be the expert, tells me to call Meldrum and Meldrum won't tell me shit. If the stuff hadn't been in the creek, I'd just forget about it, but if it hadn't been in the creek we wouldn't be looking in the first place. As it is, I worry."

"Which leaves us worried, but with nothing to go on. It's a dead end then. You want to write it off as a mystery?" Acey did not and she did not want Schwartz to do so either, but it looked like a logical move from his point of view. If it was going to happen, she wanted him to tell her.

Schwartz did not take her offer. Instead, he asked about a different one. "Acey, you've asked me about coming on your show. Is that offer still good?"

"Sure. What do you have in mind?"

"I've tried all the ways I've ever been taught and we're nowhere, so maybe it's time to try something else. I just want to lay this whole thing out and see what happens. Maybe, when I do, that will rattle Woodward's cage enough for him to talk to me." Schwartz's voice was grim as he said it.

It occurred to Acey that Zeke had a greater capacity for surprising her than anyone else she could remember. "I thought," she said carefully, "that you wanted to keep things quiet. This will stir things up, I promise you that."

"Fuck 'em," said Zeke Schwartz.

Chapter 15

ACEY FELT glorious after they arrived at the broadcast studio. Her pleasure, which showed mostly in her eyes and her brisk gait rather than her infrequent smiles, was only partly due to the fact that she finally had the blockbuster show she so badly wanted. Some of it resulted from simply having Zeke Schwartz in the studio. The hospital, obviously, had been Schwartz's turf; Acey was the interloper. Even the story had belonged more to Zeke than to her. He was the one who understood what was wrong with Jerry, who knew how to sort through the pieces of the puzzle as they turned up. The broadcast studio, though, that belonged to Acey.

Zeke, to some extent, was a mirror of those feelings. His experience of broadcast journalism was limited to a brief statement at a news conference in Boston several years before when he had been involved in treating the son of a sheik. He had never seen the inside of a radio broadcast studio. Consequently, his eyes roved around the room trying to take in all the details. It had the sealed-off, isolated feeling that he had always associated with operating rooms. The walls here, of course, were covered with acoustic tile. Behind the console were two armchairs; he assumed one was for Acey and the other for him. A set of headphones lay on the console in front of each chair. The console itself surprised him. He guessed that somewhere in the recesses of his mind he had developed the image of a talk-show host sitting in front of a telephone equipped with several banks of lines, connecting to one after the other. In fact, there was nothing recognizable as a telephone. Instead, directly in front of the chair he assumed was Acey's there was a nondescript computer monitor, green letters glowing against a black screen. Curious, he asked about it.

"That's how I know what calls I have waiting," Acey said. She had her pack of cigarettes out and was already working on the first one. "The calls don't come in here. Gordy gets them over there." She pointed to the room on the other side of the glass partition.

"Who's Gordy?"

"He's my screener. Couldn't work without him. He gets rid of the drunks, nut cases, and people with one-track minds who call every night wanting to talk about the same bit of obscene trivia that nobody else is interested in. He also blocks out people who are scared to death of the greenhouse effect when we're trying to talk about high-school football with the coach and vice versa. The ones he lets through show up on that screen, with the line, the caller's name, and a blurb about the call. We play it from there."

"How do we do that?" Zeke's uncertainty showed in his voice.

"Well, basically, I do that." Acey's eyes shone behind the cigarette smoke. "I pick the one I want next and put him on the air. Then we talk. There is a few seconds delay built into the machinery so if he starts threatening to cut off your balls, it never gets out of the console."

"Does that happen often?"

"Every now and then. Of course, with me, I get a slightly different type of obscenity. Obviously." She chuckled and blew a smoke ring. "We're getting a little ahead of ourselves, though. First thing, when we go on the air, I do my opening spiel. After that, a quick commercial. Then, back to me. That's when I introduce the topic and you. From there, we'll go into a short discussion of the cancer and the leak and all that good stuff. Let me lead it, especially at first. Ma and Pa and Junior Kettle don't have a real long attention span, so we can't afford quiet monologues. Keep it short, clean, and snappy. You have to have my touch for mania to get away with being long-winded."

Zeke managed a grin in response. "Don't worry. These are the same people I have to explain this kind of stuff to all the time. I know how to do it." What went through his mind as he said it was that he knew very well how to do it, in a quiet room with just him and a family present. Talking at a green line on a monitor with God knew how many people listening was going to be a different order of magnitude. It occurred to him that he had never asked Acey how far the station reached. He crossed his fingers where Acey could not see them and prayed that he would not squeak when it was time to talk.

Acey did not see the fingers, nor guess at his thoughts. She said, "Good. I'll hold you to that. Now, once we've talked for a while, I'll start taking calls and we'll see where it goes. Sometimes, it doesn't go anywhere, but I've got a good feel about this one."

Acey looked at the clock and put on her headset. Then she motioned for Zeke to do the same. A voice said, "Fifteen seconds to air."

"Show time, Doc," said Acey Henson.

The second hand swept past zero and Acey was off like a thoroughbred from the starting gate.

"Good evening, New Jersey! This is Acey Henson, your favorite Ace in Space on WCZY, 990 AM on your radio dial here in Flemington, New Jersey and we're in a pretty tightly wrapped orbit tonight. At least, the orbit is tightly wrapped even if I'm not. We have quite an interesting show for you tonight. You remember, of course, not too long ago we spoke about Jerry Inman, that's the boy down at the medical center with liver cancer, and we had a chance to speak with Jerry and his folks. Well, we've got a follow-up to that story that will knock your socks off, unless, of course, you're not wearing any to start with. Now, we've got to take a quick break here, to bring you a message from Geraldo's Hardware, the perfect tool for any occasion, well almost, and then we'll get on with the story. Hang on now, we'll be right back."

Acey looked around at Zeke while the commercial played. She wore a tight grin; the rest of her body was as taut as her face. Zeke could imagine that if he reached out to touch her, a spark would shoot across to his hand while it was still a foot away.

As the commercial came to an end, Acey picked up her chatter, her eyes still on Zeke. "Now that you've all had a chance to wonder what I'm sitting on up here, other than my broad butt, I'll let you in on it. The kind of cancer Jerry has is pretty rare, but we've learned at WCZY that two other children who lived in the same area have developed the same type of cancer. That should get your attention. It certainly got ours. In case you're wondering if there's some kind of toxic dump involved, I can tell you that there isn't. At least, as far as we know, these kids did not live near any kind of chemical dump. What we did find when we looked around was that the big Meldrum Products plant has had a chemical leak into a stream that the kids played in. Now, this is getting a bit out of my depth, so I have a guest here tonight who does know what he is talking about. That is Dr. Zeke Schwartz from the medical center in Trenton. Dr. Schwartz specializes in taking care of kids with cancer, which makes him one of the nicest people you'd hope to never meet, and, in fact, is taking care of Jerry. Good evening, Dr. Schwartz."

"Good evening, Acey."

"Before we get any further into this, am I correct that Jerry's parents have agreed to let you discuss his case?"

"That is correct, but Jerry is the only one we can discuss. I've had no direct contact with the other families."

"I understand that, but I don't think that limit will cause a problem. One thing that intrigues me is that this is a rare cancer, yet we have three cases, pretty much from the same area. That's a bit much for coincidence, isn't it?"

"No question about it," Zeke said. "We do see suspicious clusters of cancers from time to time, and most of the time we never find a reason for them. Still, this is three cases of the same rare cancer close together. You have to take a close look."

"Right. And what we found when we looked was this leak at the Meldrum plant. Can you tell me something about the chemical?"

"Yes, certainly. It actually is a drug called Aspergicin that we use to treat some types of infection."

"Except, if it's a drug, it shouldn't cause cancer. Should it?"

Zeke began to relax, his earlier apprehension fading. "Of course, it shouldn't, and, as far as I know, there is no evidence that it does. However, it's a relatively new drug and it was in the creek where the kids were and there is no other apparent cause for their cancers. So, I think the situation needs some explanation."

"You're not going as far as to say that this Aspergicin is the cause, then."

"Right. The evidence just isn't there yet, either way."

"Yeah. I guess we could be skating on a slippery slope there. Well, what does Meldrum have to say about all of this?"

"Absolutely nothing. That's another one of the interesting things about this situation. I can't get anybody who knows anything to talk to me."

"I know that feeling. All right, let's leave the Aspergicin for the moment. Can you tell me a little about the cancer and how you treat it?"

With that Acey guided the conversation away from the Aspergicin leak. What had been said so far would be enough to hook the audience. She was quite satisfied with it. They chatted a while longer about liver cancer before Acey broke for a commercial.

"When we come back," she promised, "we'll open the lines and see what you think."

With the minute hand a safe stroke past two, Acey whirled her headset around her forefinger and let out a loud, "Whew! That was pretty intense."

"No joke," said Zeke. His shirt was damp and its collar felt tight in spite of the fact that he had opened the top button and pulled the sides away from his neck. "Is it always like that?"

"Hah! I should wish," answered Acey. I should wish it indeed, she thought. She had figured correctly that people still remembered her first show on Jerry Inman, remembered hearing it or remembered hearing about it. The plugs she had put on the previous few days about this show had clearly served to rekindle those memories. The switchboard had been busy from the start and then, when they had so casually dropped the tidbit about the Aspergicin into the pot, it had been absolutely jammed. She could not remember such a backlog of calls, all on the same topic. Acey had cut everything else out of the planned program, not wanting to break the flow of talk. Had she been able to, she would have dropped commercials as well, but they were sacrosanct. It was possible to play with the timing, but not to forget them. It had not mattered.

"It's actually never like this," she said. "Sometimes, on a slow night, I have to drum up calls with nutty stories, either that or call an 'expert' on something or other whom I know and get him to talk. I'm glad you were willing to stay through the whole show."

"So am I, although I wouldn't want to do it for a living. Damn, you are good at this. I am impressed."

She answered him by turning pink and saying nothing.

"I am not trying to embarrass you," Zeke said, "I meant it. Okay, I'll drop that line. How did I do?"

"Not bad for a beginner," Acey said, finding her voice again. It would never do, she thought, to be overly complimentary. Then, she realized she had already done that when she talked about how unusual the night had been. "I take that back. You did fine, real fine. Hell, if you weren't doing well, you would have known it."

"From the audience, you mean?" Zeke asked.

"Either that, or I would have kicked you in the shins."

"No doubt," Zeke said. "I wonder if that turkey up at Meldrum, Woodward, heard it."

"You never know, I have all kinds of fans." There was a twinkle in her eye as she said that. "Actually, it wouldn't surprise me if he hears about it. We did good."

They laughed and grinned at each other. It felt good. It was the same sensation that came with victory in a sporting match; all the tension had drained out and the body felt at peace. They sat there a bit longer, savoring the feeling. Then Acey pushed her chair back and went for her jacket.

"Tell you what," Acey said as they walked toward the exit to the parking lot, "how about a drink to celebrate?"

"A drink?" Zeke asked. "You mean coffee at the diner?"

"No. A drink drink."

"Sounds good to me. Do you know any place around here that's open at this hour?"

"Nope." She hesitated briefly. "Someone gave me a bottle of Chivas at Christmas. I've been saving it and this seems like a good enough occasion. Are you game?"

Zeke agreed by asking, "Where do you live?"

"Just follow me."

Acey's apartment proved to be in a cluster of two-story brick townhouses set against a wooded lot on the other side of the small town. The complex was quiet when they drove up, so much so that Schwartz was sure they were the only people about. The occasional light from scattered sections of the building was not enough to convince him that anyone else was awake.

They walked up the flight of stairs behind the front door and Schwartz gave a low whistle when they reached the top. "And you complained about my office," he said.

"There's a difference. Your office is open to public viewing," was her reply.

She retreated to the kitchen and busied herself with the contents of a cabinet and the freezer. When she returned, she was carrying a bottle and two cups.

"Chivas Regal in Dixie cups. That's an interesting combination," he said.

"I forgot the dishwasher," she said. "It doesn't affect the taste. Here's to one hell of a show."

She raised her cup, he followed, and they downed the contents.

"You really mean that?"

"I do."

Carefully, she refilled the cups.

"One more," she said. "Dammit, Zeke, but when I first met you, I'd have given any odds that I would have hated your guts forever and the fact is, I like you. So, here's to working with you. It's really been great and I don't say that often or lightly."

He raised his cup to hers. He could hear the change in her voice. It was low now and serious. Her blue eyes looked wider than he ever remembered seeing them before. "It's funny," he said, "but I could say the same and mean every word of it."

They drank and put the cups down and, having done so, ended standing quite close together. Almost shyly, Acey put her hand on his chest, just touching the shirt with the tips of her fingers. She ran them up to his collar, then lightly stroked his jaw. Without saying a word, she turned her face up to his for a kiss.

It started as a gentle kiss, two pairs of lips just lightly brushing each other. They did not pull apart, however, and the kiss soon deepened into one much more intense as she nestled against him. They seemed to linger on it forever, neither one moving, caught up in its spell. Then, Zeke felt her turn slightly away from him and there were two gentle tugs at the front of his shirt. She broke her lips away from his, just a little, to look at him quietly. He looked down to see her holding a fold of his shirt between her thumb and forefinger. While he watched, she repeated the little tug with no more than a flex of her fingers.

"This is a hint, Doc," she said. "Just in case you need me to explain it."

"I can take a hint," he said.

Some time later—a rather long time later it seemed to Zeke Schwartz—he rolled over on his back and let out a long sigh. It sounded like the most appropriate thing to say. He took a wordless mumble from the other side of the bed as an endorsement of his sentiments. It appeared that they had each managed to surprise the other again. They stayed as they were a while longer, he with his arms behind his head, staring at the ceiling, she curled up, just touching his side. Then he got up to look for a towel. Finding one, he walked back into the room to find Acey, head propped up on one hand, watching him.

"What's wrong, Zeke?"

"Nothing. Why?"

"All of a sudden, you went from being really close to being a million miles away. So, I wondered what was wrong."

"I guess wrong is the wrong word. I just think I was a selfish jerk again and maybe I should go."

"Why?" There was puzzlement in her voice.

Schwartz, when he spoke, sounded unhappy. "Because I'm sure that this looks like I did the show just to get a shot at going to bed with you and that's not the way it was. Not at all. But I can see how it looks."

"If it's that kind of appearances you're worried about, you're a bit late," Acey answered with a laugh. "You look embarrassed."

"I think I am."

"Don't be. Zeke, if I didn't want you here, you wouldn't be here. I can't tell you how long it's been since I really wanted to love someone, much less have him spend the night afterward. I want you to stay, if you feel the same way."

"You should know the answer to that," Zeke said, "just from what I was worrying about. You are going to have to move over a bit, though."

Then he had to duck quickly as she flung a pillow at him.

PART
II

There's something happening here,
What it is ain't exactly clear.

<small>FROM "FOR WHAT IT'S WORTH"</small>

<small>BY BUFFALO SPRINGFIELD</small>

Chapter 16

THE HOUSES at Fox Meadow were described in the development company's brochure as spacious, modern, and convenient to New York City. They lived up to that billing. The oldest of them was just three years old and they averaged three thousand square feet of living space. They all came with Jacuzzis in the master bathroom and a real stone hearth for the fireplace. Since the access road to the development led straight to the interstate highway, the occupants were only a little more than an hour from New York, at least when it was not rush hour, in spite of the fact that the houses were within sight of Pennsylvania. That was as about as convenient to the City as a new house was likely to be. One problem with the houses was that the land had been a farm before it had been a development. The houses dotted the flat and open area looking as though they had been dropped from a helicopter. In twenty years, when the saplings and hedges had fully grown, the houses would provide country living for their occupants. Until then, shades and blinds were the only protection against exposing private life to public view, just like in the city most of the dwellers had fled. The other problem was that they were expensive.

Damned expensive thought Dr. Thomas Hart Woodward. He sat in the ground-floor den of his Fox Meadow house and rubbed his temples as he thought of just how expensive they were. Woodward was a tall man, who in his youth had been slender and athletic but now flared instead of tapered at his midsection. He usually wore a coat to hide it, although not when sitting in the big chair at his desk as he was then. He would look down periodically to see if a bulge was visible when he felt his stomach roll over his belt. The hatchet shape of his face was accentuated by a prominent beaked nose. He had a full head of hair, but it had been gray from the time he had finished his residency. Through his partially open blinds he could see the Millers watching television in their family room, although he could not quite make out the program they were watching. Odd family, he thought. Every night he was in the study, he could see them planted in front of that set. Presumably, they sat there from the time they came home to the time they went to sleep. He wondered if they ever did anything else. He also wondered what the Millers might think of his family, if they looked his way as often as he looked theirs. They would see Tom in his study, most nights, Helen watching TV alone with her catalogs and crossword puzzles, the girls upstairs with their competing stereos. Which was odder? He became aware that his mind had drifted and he pulled himself back to his original thought. The house was damned expensive.

The coupon book in front of him on the desk was what prompted the thought, as it did each month when he had to write out the check for the mortgage. There were two more little books just like it, one for each car. He loathed the sight of all three. Behind them was a stack of bills that, as Helen had reminded him over dinner, really needed to be paid. In the past, he had often asked himself why Helen could not have done it. She was perfectly capable of signing her name to a check. She never did, though. He no longer bothered to ask the question. Instead, he looked on the bills as another chore, not strenuous perhaps, but disagreeable. He had thought that this night the totals would come out properly, but that hope was dashed when he opened the Talbot's bill. Dear Lord, he asked silently, how could one woman spend so much on clothing in one month? Of course, it might not have been Helen by herself. Andrea, at age fifteen, was showing signs of inheriting her mother's taste in clothes. Regardless of how it had accumulated, there was no way he could pay it all in one month, which meant that he would have it hanging over his head next month. Of course, the real problem was that the house was so expensive, which brought his thoughts full circle.

Looking back, he had trouble remembering a conscious decision to buy the house. The root of it was that Helen had always pushed for a big house, even when he was a resident and they had lived in a cramped apartment. She had used the occasion of his promotion at Meldrum Products, two and a half years before, to argue again for a larger house. The promotion had not been as big as the house demanded. Certainly not with two teenage daughters whose every word showed that they regarded a car on their seventeenth birthdays as a birthright.

Thinking about money was useless. Once he had seen the Talbot's bill he could not bring himself to write any of the checks. Woodward pushed the checkbook and the bills to one side with a sweep of his hand. One day, more or less, would not make a difference.

The other side of his desk held a small pile of folders he had brought home from work. He looked at them with about as much distaste as the bills. Most of them held promotional materials that he was supposed to review, journal ads and give-away brochures that trumpeted the products of Meldrum's Anti-Infectives Group. He was supposed to read through them to make certain that the marketing whiz who had designed them said nothing incorrect from a medical or scientific point of view. This task actually required a close reading. The Marketing Group looked on competing brands of drugs no differently from the way they would have looked on competing brands of toothpaste. A bar chart showing sixty percent success for the Meldrum product might be labeled as sixty but it would probably look like seventy-five. The solicited opinion of one physician had a way of sounding like incontrovertible fact. The only thing Woodward liked less than reviewing these materials was the meeting to discuss them. The head of the Regulatory Group would be there arguing that the type size for the side effects had to be at least a certain percentage of the type size that set out their claims and, no, you could *not* hide the side effects at the bottom of the page next to an asterisk where the print was almost invisible against the background. The lawyer would be there, too, to make sure that the trademark was used the first time the drug was mentioned in a column of type. That particularly bothered Woodward when he was writing a case for one of the brochures. No one ever put a trademark into a serious medical case report. Fortunately, he did not need to sign his name.

The top folder contained the proofs for a new set of journal ads that Meldrum was scheduling for one of its antibiotics. It was a three-page ad, two facing and one overleaf, an expensive proposition. The facing pages showed, on one side, a picture of an elderly man splayed out in bed and surrounded by tubes and monitors, with a harried doctor standing nearby wearing the expression Woodward termed "I haven't the faintest idea of what is going on" and an anguished family in the background. The caption read, "When you have to be right the first time." The opposite page spelled out how right this drug was in a slew of dire emergencies. Woodward grimaced. It was a pretty decent drug, that was the truth, but actually there was little to distinguish it from several others that were better established. God alone knew if ads like those actually influenced a physician's choice of drugs. Woodward knew that he had never looked at them when he was in practice. He wondered if the increase in sales would pay for the ad campaign. The column of figures with the claims made him groan. He would have to check each one against the package insert and he did not have one at home.

That was enough to make him close the folder without reading any further. It was almost enough to make him wish he was practicing cardiology again. Except, if he was, he would have to worry about malpractice insurance again and in the end would probably not earn any more than he made at Meldrum. He pushed the folder away and consulted his calendar. The meeting was scheduled for nine. If he left home early, he would have enough time to read the material at the office in the morning. He fell asleep in the chair, dreaming that his house had been converted into a clothing store.

The Fates, in the form of Woodward's radiator hose, conspired to prevent him from arriving at work early. A rent opened in the hose in the middle of the highway and stranded him there until a passing policeman spotted him kicking the front tire in angry futility. By the time repairs were effected it was already mid-morning. As he pulled out of the service station, Woodward consoled himself with the thought that even if he had not had a chance to review the materials, he was now so late that he had missed the meeting as well. Matters could be worse.

They were, shortly. His secretary spotted him walking down the hall and raced to intercept him.

"Dr. Woodward, wait a moment, please! You need to see these." She waved several message slips in the air.

"What's the problem, Libby?"

"Mr. Jackson has called three times in the last hour looking for you. He said he needs to see you as soon as you get in."

Woodward paused to consider the implications of this summons. Russell Jackson was Director of Regulatory Affairs at Meldrum's Center for Research. It was his responsibility to ensure that Meldrum Products complied with the full panoply of laws and regulations governing the pharmaceuticals that the Center for Research tested and marketed. Jackson liked to joke that it was his job to keep everyone out of jail. Occasionally, Woodward wondered how much of a joke it was. To have Jackson urgently looking for him did not bode well, and even without the evidence of multiple phone calls, Libby's face told him that it was urgent.

"Tell him I'm on my way," he said. "I just want to drop my briefcase in my office."

By the time he walked across the building to Jackson's office, he had mentally reviewed every phone call, every adverse reaction that he could remember from the past month. It had been quiet, no reason for trouble that he could see. Jackson was sitting at his desk waiting for him with a broad smile that somehow did not involve his eyes.

"Good morning, Tom. Close the door, would you, and have a seat."

Woodward studied the other man trying to divine the problem from his appearance. Russell Jackson was a slightly built man with a receding hairline and wire rim glasses. He was given to wearing dark pinstripe suits, either blue or gray, which made him look like the attorney he was not. Behind the thick lenses his eyes were owl bright. The smile had vanished with the closing of the door and in its place was a mask. Jackson had not risen so high in Meldrum's hierarchy without being able to conceal his thoughts.

"What's the problem, Russ?" Woodward asked.

Jackson leaned back in his chair, but kept his eyes on Woodward. "Do you have any information about liver cancer in patients who have gotten Aspergicin?"

"What? You mean as an adverse reaction?"

A big part of Woodward's job was to keep track of all adverse reactions to any of Meldrum's anti-infective drugs. It did not matter where the information came from—medical studies, phone calls, lawsuits—they all went into Woodward's database. It was then his responsibility to analyze that information and write the necessary reports for the Food and Drug Administration. As Jackson put it, that was Woodward's contribution to keeping them out of jail. Normally, if they needed to know how many reports of a reaction, such as a headache, had been received for a particular drug, Woodward would check his computer and out would pop the answer. For something like this, he did not need the computer.

"Nothing at all," Woodward said.

"Nothing?" Jackson asked. "You're sure? Not during the clinical trials, not since it's been on the market?"

"I'm sure. For God's sake, Russ, that's not the sort of thing I would forget. After all, I monitored the Aspergicin trials before I took this position. If we had a report like that, I'd know about it."

"Good," Jackson said. "Do me a favor, though, and run it through just to make sure."

"No problem. You want to tell me what is going on?"

Jackson sighed, laced his fingers behind his head and swiveled his chair to look out the window. One of the perquisites of being a full director that Woodward envied was an office with a window, to go along with a more expensive desk and a better grade of carpet. Jackson looked out his window long enough for Woodward to begin to dwell on those thoughts. He turned back to look at Woodward when he spoke.

"I took a call from a David Ingraham at the FDA this morning. He's the Consumer Safety Officer for Aspergicin now. I guess some people left a few months ago. Anyway, I didn't recognize the name and I can see you don't either. It doesn't matter. The bottom line is that a radio station out here had some asshole doc from the Childrens' Hospital in Trenton on last night talking about three kids who live along Scheuermann's Run who've got liver cancer. Apparently, he implied that it was due to Aspergicin. Some asshole pharmacist heard it and decided it was his patriotic duty to call the FDA. Ingraham was very upset."

Jackson's speech left Woodward puzzled. It made no sense. "When did these kids get treated with Aspergicin?" he asked.

"They didn't, as far as we know," Jackson answered.

"Then it's ridiculous," Woodward spluttered. "If they never got the drug, what's the connection?"

"That's the interesting part." Jackson gave him a rather frightening smile. "There was a design flaw in the Aspergicin manufacturing area when it was built. Without going into the plumbing details, it leaked a lot of Aspergicin into Scheuermann's Run over the past three years. It never occurred to those damn idiots at the plant to wonder why their yields were low, but that's another story. Fact is, it was in the creek, so at least theoretically, there was exposure."

Woodward could see Scheuermann's Run from Jackson's window. "I never heard about this," he said.

"No reason you should. Aspergicin is not on any list of hazardous chemicals, Hell," he laughed, "it's for human use. No hazard, no anticipated environmental impact, the spill is not reportable. So, it was never reported."

"Then how did this, what's his name, doc find out about it?"

"Schwartz is his name. I have no idea how he heard about it. Knows somebody in the plant, probably. That's not really important. What is important is that I need you to check everything we have on Aspergicin and be ready when the FDA calls back at eleven-thirty. Ingraham is going to have his medical reviewer with him, so I want to have you when the call comes in. Can you do it?"

"No problem," replied Woodward.

After retreating to his office, Woodward noticed that the name Jackson had for the person who had started the furor matched the one on several message slips lying on his desk. Woodward gulped. Some time ago, he remembered, Dr. Philips, who was VP of Medical Affairs, had mentioned that he wanted to help out an old friend at the Trenton medical center. Meldrum funded many programs at the medical center and Philips had promised that Meldrum would arrange to fund a fellowship in a group run by a colleague of his old friend. The colleague's name had been Schwartz, Ezekiel Schwartz.

"I told him you would take care of it when he calls," was the way Philips had broken the news to Woodward.

Unfortunately, that did not mean that Woodward had money in his budget to pay for the fellowship and no one else seemed willing to part with any of theirs. Woodward had initially hoped Schwartz would never call, that he would take it as the kind of off-hand promise that was never meant seriously, which surely it must have been, and that he would forget about it. When Schwartz called, Woodward had elected not to call back, figuring that Schwartz would eventually take the hint. His plan had seemed to work for a while, until Janie mentioned that a Dr. Schwartz had been calling about liver damage in patients treated with Aspergicin and had not been willing to settle for the approved, scripted answer. It was Woodward's job to handle that kind of call, which was one of the reasons his position called for a physician. The problem, from Woodward's point of view, was that if he was talking to Schwartz, the question of the fellowship would come up, and Woodward had no more to say about it than he had weeks before. One of the advantages of having a secretary screen his calls was that he could, if he wished, postpone confrontations like that. Unfortunately, it had been a busy week. He had pushed the messages to one side, where they were hidden by his computer terminal, and had forgotten all about them. Now this Dr. Schwartz was creating an uproar.

On one hand, he felt sick. It was the scared sick feeling when one's stomach knots up. Could he have prevented all of this by a simple return phone call? There was no way of knowing, he tried to tell himself. Anyway, looking at it sensibly, there was no reason to expect the man to go off in such an irrational manner. What finally settled him down was the thought that there was no reason Jackson, or anyone else, needed to know about those calls. He crumpled the slips and dropped them into the waste basket. Then, he took a deep breath and sat down in front of his terminal to find the information that Jackson wanted.

Jackson's call for him arrived at exactly eleven-thirty. Woodward quickly retraced his steps to Jackson's office. Inside, Jackson was seated next to his telephone, which had been switched to function as a speaker phone.

"I've asked Dr. Thomas Woodward of our medical group to join us," Jackson said in the direction of the phone as Woodward walked in. "I have David Ingraham and Dr. Kris Desai on the line," he said, this time to Woodward.

They all exchanged greetings, as much a formality as a way of establishing who was listening at each speaker.

"I've brought Dr. Woodward up to speed on our earlier discussion," Jackson said, "so why don't we start off with some of the questions you have?"

"That would be fine," the voice identified as Ingraham said. To Woodward, his voice sounded young. It did not sound very friendly. "Can you tell me, Dr. Woodward, whether you have any experience with liver cancer in patients who have received Aspergicin?"

"There is none," Woodward said, leaning toward the speaker and trying to sound emphatic and self-assured. Rule number one of talking to the FDA was simple, be direct and do not give any more information than the question asked for. "I've reviewed all of the reports we've submitted back to the approval and also the reports from the clinical trials."

"I see. And is there any information that hasn't been submitted?"

Bastard, Woodward thought. Idiot, too. Does he really think that if I were sitting on a report of a cancer, which by law has to be submitted within fifteen days from the time we hear about it, that I would blithely disclose it to him now? Aloud, he said, "You have everything we've got."

"Hmmm. Okay, I'll accept that. Can you tell me, though, how you explain this business with these children that we heard about?"

At the remark, Jackson's head started to bob around like a dandelion puffball in a breeze. Woodward looked over at him and could see that he was silently mouthing words, but Woodward was unable to decipher them. Seeing Woodward's puzzled appearance, Jackson grabbed a pad, wrote on it and held it in front of the phone.

"Be careful," it said.

You bet, Woodward thought. "I don't see how we can explain it, Mr. Ingraham. At least, not in regard to Aspergicin. As far as we know, none of the children were ever treated with the drug and, given its indications, I doubt that they were."

"I was not suggesting they had been treated with your drug," Ingraham said. His voice was impatient. "There was Aspergicin in the creek they played in and we know it leaked, or was flushed if you will, into the creek over a period of several years. Can you tell me how we can be sure that this exposure is not responsible for those cancers?" His voice, when he finished, was not only impatient, it had an ominous note to it.

Jackson underlined the "Be careful" twice and stuck the pad back under Woodward's nose.

Woodward cleared his throat and started again. "I have been told about the Aspergicin in the creek. However, even if we assume they came in contact with it, the concentration would be almost nothing, much less than we use clinically. Scientifically, it doesn't make much sense that an exposure like this could cause those tumors. In my medical opinion, it isn't an issue."

"Dr. Woodward," said Ingraham, "I don't think you realize just how big an issue it is."

Next to Woodward, the bob and weave of Jackson's head increased sharply in amplitude. Woodward had the sense that he was botching it.

"Maybe I don't see it," Woodward said. "Can you tell me what you find so concerning?"

"Oh Christ!" Ingraham said. "Listen, I've got a half-hysterical pharmacist who called this in and a local office that is ready to go on the warpath. I've got people down here screaming about how this could be on a radio talk show, for God's sake, while we don't know anything about it, and by tomorrow you can bet we'll have one of these ding-a-ling consumer groups petitioning to have the drug pulled and right now you are not giving me any reasons to say that it shouldn't. I would say that we've got maybe twenty-four hours, seventy-two tops, to start putting forward a plan or we are going to lose control of the situation."

Jackson tore off the top page of his pad and started to scribble again. This time, when he held it up, it said, "Don't commit to anything."

I was not planning to, Woodward thought. By this time, the chain of events had his head spinning. The inciting event was so ridiculous, and the reaction to it so overblown, that he was having trouble thinking. In the midst of it, his mind managed to recall that a teacher of his had once said much the same thing about the way the First World War started. He swallowed hard.

Into the silence Woodward left, came the sound of a polite cough. Then they heard Dr. Desai, who had been silent since the introductions. "Am I correct that your human trials with this drug go back a number of years?"

"Yes," answered Woodward. "About seven years now, if you include just the bigger studies."

"And you said that none of these patients developed tumors?"

"I said no liver tumors," Woodward corrected him. "We had a few tumors, of course, but nothing unexpected. Just about what you would find normally in the population we were studying."

"And that's true of these patients right up to now? No liver tumors?"

"Well, wait a moment," Woodward said. "In most of the studies, we only followed the patients for a couple of months past their infection, for a year in the major studies. I can only tell you for that period."

"I see," Desai said. "You know, of course, that it can take years for a tumor to develop after an exposure. So, what you are telling me is that you really don't have any long-term data on whether this drug could cause tumors."

Woodward had the feeling he had walked into a trap. He had to say something, fast. "Now, that's not quite true," he said. Good start, now think of why it is not true. "We ran two animal carcinogenicity studies with daily dosing for two years. That's a lifetime of exposure for rodents. There was no evidence that the drug caused tumors."

"But rats and mice are not humans," Desai replied. In some cases they are, Woodward thought, but then Desai was talking again. "I should think, though, that you could get the human data. Don't you think you could, if you called up your investigators and asked them to check on the current status of these patients?"

Jackson started to wave the message pad. "I might be able to," Woodward said.

"Actually, I think that would be pretty reasonable," Ingraham broke in. "If you can trace the patients from your old studies, and there really are no tumors, and if you survey the physicians who are using your drug to see if any start turning up, I think that could do it. Can we agree on that?"

Woodward knew the answer without looking at Jackson. "We'll have to present it to management."

"Yeah." Woodward could tell that Ingraham was not impressed. "I was quite serious before, Dr. Woodward. If we cannot put a plan in place soon, and I mean very soon, we will be forced to pull the drug. Please keep that in mind."

The threat was crystal clear. Woodward knew that Aspergicin had generated eighty million dollars in sales the year before. Sales was claiming they would bring in a hundred million this year. It was not a super drug, like one of the ulcer medicines, but one hundred million dollars was nothing to sneeze at. The company would not look kindly on the man who cost it one hundred million dollars a year. Woodward had no doubt who the likely scapegoat would be if Ingraham carried out his threat.

"I'm being completely straight with you," he said. "I can't give you a commitment until we meet with management."

"I understand that," Ingraham said while sounding as though he did not. "I need to hear from you by tomorrow morning, though."

"That should not be a problem," Jackson put in. Woodward wondered if the "no commitment" policy extended to Jackson's level.

After the connection was broken, Woodward slumped down in his chair. He felt exhausted. All he could say was, "Jesus Christ."

"Actually," said Jackson, "it didn't go that badly, considering the circumstances. They both sound like they want to work this thing out."

"Can Ingraham really pull the drug?"

"On this evidence?" Jackson frowned. "I really doubt it. Meldrum would fight it in court, that is for sure. That's really not the point, though. In the long run, picking fights with the FDA is a losing proposition. How long does it take to get a New Drug Application approved these days? Two years, if you're lucky and it's an important drug, maybe as long as five otherwise. How long do you think it would take if they go to sleep on it and nitpick you to death over every little thing? You gotta work with them."

"And we're going to do this?"

"I don't know yet. I do have to talk to the VP and he is going to want to talk to as much of the Board as is here. Once everybody buys in, though, we'll meet and decide just how to get it done. I would like to get back to Ingraham today, if at all possible."

In a rather plain office, which seemed furnished mostly in files, David Ingraham was easily as upset as Woodward after the conversation, although for different reasons.

"What did you think of it?" he asked Desai.

The physician shrugged and looked around, although they were the only occupants of Ingraham's office. "You mean the chances of that drug causing those cancers?"

"Yes. You have the medical background. I don't."

"To be honest, I'm inclined to agree with their guy, Woodward. I think it's farfetched."

"But not impossible," Ingraham added. "You seemed to be implying that."

"Nothing is ever impossible," Desai agreed. "I just don't think it's likely."

"Unlikely isn't good enough. We have to be sure." Ingraham drummed his fingers on his desk. "Just look at history here. Look at the drugs that have been approved and then pulled because of problems. Anti-inflammatory agents, for God's sake, which are approved as safe but then one has some fatal allergic reactions and another gives some people kidney failure. A hot new antibiotic is out, for maybe two or three months, and all kinds of problems turn up, including some deaths. These things happen and people forget about all the drugs that are safe. All they want to know is who had the data and when they had the data or when they *could* have had the data and why *we* didn't have it. Each time it happens, there's a bigger stink. Let me tell you, Dr. Desai, if we look at this Meldrum business and say 'no problem' and we're wrong, the stench you smell will be our asses burning over on Capitol Hill."

Desai smiled uncomfortably. Facing hostile congressional committees was not in his job description. "How are we going to build a case that is totally one hundred percent guaranteed to be right?"

"We're not," Ingraham replied. "I'm going to make them do it."

Chapter 17

ZEKE SCHWARTZ woke up and, for a moment, wondered where he was. Then he felt a gentle pressure against his back. Turning over, he saw Acey sleeping next to him. Well, he thought, I was not having a strange dream. He had a memory from college days in the early seventies of waking up in a bed and with a bedmate he did not remember from the night before. He was glad the memory of the previous night was intact. He watched her sleep for a few minutes and thought he could see a faint smile on her lips. The arm with the rose and dagger tatoo lay exposed on the sheet that covered most of the rest of her. That was an odd tatoo for a woman to wear, Zeke thought, although it seemed to suit Acey quite well. If it had not been a wild dream, then it had been a wild reality. Very wild. But nice, too, he reminded himself.

He got out of the bed carefully, so as not to disturb her. His clothes lay in a trail that extended back into the living room. He gathered them up and ducked into the bathroom for a quick shower. He examined himself in the mirror afterward and decided that showing up in yesterday's clothes and a one-day growth would not cause the world to end. That was good, because it was too late to go back to his own apartment.

When he stepped out of the bathroom, Acey was still asleep. He wanted a glass of orange juice, or perhaps a cup of coffee, before he left for the hospital but he could not see waking her over something so trivial. Instead, he went into the kitchen to prospect on his own. He was quickly disappointed. The cupboards were bare, literally. The refrigerator was almost so. A few objects caught Schwartz's eye, but they were not what he wanted. As he closed the refrigerator door, he happened to push aside a cutting board that had been sitting on the counter next to it. Something, he noticed, had been lying under the board. It was a small syringe. Zeke picked it up to take a closer look.

"It's not what you think."

He turned around to find Acey standing in the entrance to the kitchen. She was wearing a long baseball shirt that came to mid-thigh, but nothing else.

"What do you mean, it's not what I think?"

"It's not. I know what you're thinking and it's not. I don't do drugs." Her words were directed as much to the floor as to Zeke. She kept her eyes on a random pattern that a bare big toe was tracing on the tile.

"What?" Schwartz felt his tongue tie up as he tried to switch words in the middle of saying them. She was scared of what he was going to say, he was certain of that. He had never seen Acey look that way before. "Acey," he finally said, "give me enough credit to know an insulin syringe when I see one, especially since I looked in the refrigerator. I wasn't snooping, I just wanted a glass of orange juice and there's not a hell of a lot else in there."

Acey's face was scarlet. "I wish you hadn't found that stuff. I almost never have anyone in here, so I didn't think to put it away better."

"So, I saw it. What's the big deal?" If her blush deepened any further, her hair would have started to redden also.

"Because I didn't need you to see it. I enjoyed last night, Zeke. A lot. I was thinking that maybe this didn't have to be a one-night stand. You following me, Doc?"

"Yeah, as a matter of fact. I've had a similar thought myself. I'm just glad you said something first because with the track record I've got, I would have blown it. However, what does all of that have to do with a vial of insulin in the 'fridge?"

Her reply was terse. "Who wants damaged goods?"

"Oh for God's sake! I can't believe this. Acey, I like you a lot and I've had a wonderful time and this doesn't make the slightest bit of difference. I was hoping we could make something out of this and I still am. Does that take care of it?"

She brought her eyes up to look at him. "I suppose if I had half a brain, I would shut up and take it. But, I can't. I have to be honest. I may be blonde, but I ain't built and I never will be. What you see is what you get, short, swift and slightly shifty."

"I would think, at this point, you would realize that I have a pretty good idea of how you are built." The blush, which had been fading, reappeared, but was accompanied by a little smile.

"You're changing the subject," she said.

"That was the idea." Zeke took a deep breath and decided that trying to explore the original subject before he had to run to work was a poor idea. "I'm sorry I upset you. Truly, I am. I was just hoping to get a bite before I had to go and I didn't want to wake you."

Acey accepted the invitation to ignore the previous comments. "I'm afraid I can't do much about breakfast," she said. "I'm not very domestic."

"Yeah," Zeke sighed. "I'm not either, I guess. How about a cup of coffee?"

"Coffee I can manage."

T R E N T O N ,   N E W   J E R S E Y _____

By the time he reached his office, Schwartz was beginning to feel awake. More awake, in fact, than he had any right to feel after so few hours of sleep. The day had been fortuitously arranged so that he had no patients to see in the morning. It had not been planned that way with the previous night's festivities in mind, but with a view to reducing the pile of notes he had to dictate. It was a chore that Schwartz hated and, busy as he was, it was easy to allow them to accumulate. The only way he had found to deal with the problem was to set aside a morning to deal with that and nothing else. Usually, he growled and moaned when he knew he was coming in to do his notes, but this morning he felt too cheery to bother with the ritual. Unfortunately, his mood did not last past the secretary's desk.

"Zeke, where the hell have you been?" Doris looked flustered. Her usually immaculate desk was a mess and, with her eyes wide, she looked ready to pounce on him as he came through the door.

"I signed out to Barlow last night," he said. "The page operator knows that and I made sure that Barlow knew it too."

"No kidding," Doris shot back. "The page operator told me that several times. I even called your home, but all I got was the answering machine."

Zeke shivered as a chill snaked its way down his spine. Doris was often sarcastic and often used a liberal interpretation of working hours, but she rarely lost her aplomb.

"Did somebody die?" he asked. From his perspective, it was a logical question. The one time he had seen Doris out of control had been when Billy Macrione had a major hemorrhage in front of the clinic desk.

"I haven't the faintest idea," she said. "All I know is that Worthington is on a rampage looking for you. He actually yelled at *me* because I couldn't find you."

In his two and a half years at the medical center, Zeke Schwartz had not once seen Barlow Worthington raise his voice. He had never even heard someone relate a story about such an event happening. Could he have forgotten to give Barlow some crucial piece of information about a patient who went sour overnight? If he had, it still did not occur to him standing there in the morning. Anyway, Barlow himself pulled that sort of stunt regularly. It would be hard for him to be that angry at being on the receiving end for once.

"Is Barlow in the clinic?" he asked. She nodded. "Call down there, then, and tell him I'm in my office. If he's going to rant, at least we can do it in private."

It seemed that Schwartz had barely settled into his chair when Worthington arrived in his office, closing the door with enough force to make Schwartz jump. Doris had not exaggerated. Worthington's face was dark with anger. He glowered at Schwartz from across the room.

"Goddammit, Zeke, what do you think you're doing? Do you want to wreck everything?"

"What was I doing?"

"That radio show!"

"Oh that." It had been in the back of Schwartz's mind that the powers-that-be in the medical center might not care for his airing the case in public. He had not, however, anticipated such a violent reaction from Worthington. "Did you hear the show?" he asked.

"No. Why would I be listening to that station? I did hear all about it today, though, from my friend in Medical Affairs at Meldrum. You must remember, I talked to you about having them fund a fellowship for us? You can be sure he reminded me about it. Do you want to kiss it good-bye?"

"Not particularly, no," Schwartz replied, "but that guy whose name you gave me wouldn't call me back about anything, not the fellowship, not when I wanted information on their damned drug. I've got three kids with the same cancer all living around that creek and that can't be ignored. I didn't say anything that wasn't true or can't be verified."

"Are you going to tell me that you didn't call the FDA and tell them that the drug caused the cancers?"

That brought Schwartz to a halt. For a moment, he just sat and looked at Worthington. "No, I did not," he said finally.

"Well, somebody obviously did, because the FDA landed on Meldrum this morning like a ton of bricks and they think it was you."

"Well, it wasn't. I can't think of a more useless thing to do, anyway. If their idiot, Woodward, will call me, I'll be glad to tell him so. Hell, if he had returned any of my calls in the first place, this probably wouldn't have happened."

At Schwartz's words, Worthington slowly began to transform back into the slightly pudgy grandfather type he usually appeared to be. His voice, too, was much softer when he spoke.

"Maybe there's been a misunderstanding," Worthington said. "I'll have to see if maybe we can all get together and talk." He worked his hands together as though he needed a place to put them. "I really wish you hadn't done it at all, Zeke. It's not very professional. I suppose I should tell you that Ben Ogilvie was also looking for you this morning. I'm sure it's also about this."

"Who is this Ogilvie?"

"Ben Ogilvie?" Worthington's face held a puzzled look. "He's the director of the medical center administration. How can you not know him?"

"More accurately, Barlow, why should I know him? He doesn't see patients and I'm not invited to your budget meetings."

"Never mind that," said Worthington. "I would just appreciate it, if this really is a molehill, that you don't make a mountain out of it now. Okay?"

Schwartz thought that would be fine with him. After Worthington left, he turned his attention to the charts. They formed two stacks, each about a foot and a half high, which Doris had set out on his desk. He pulled a small tape recorder from his desk drawer and popped a cassette into the open slot. The recorder was an extreme of miniaturization, the whole apparatus fitting conveniently in his palm. He had bought it with the idea that it would be easy to carry, which would allow him to dictate his notes on the spot. Unfortunately, in practice he either left it in his desk or, when he remembered to bring it, forgot to use it. He always wrote a note in the charts, but the recorder enabled him to dictate a more complete note that would then be typed by the secretary. The result was supposed to be a legible and complete record that could be put into the patient's file and also mailed to the referring doctor, which would save Schwartz the bother of writing separate letters. It was a nice idea. In reality, he found that it usually took two weeks before he saw the typed notes and then, often as not, they would need many corrections. The delays and corrections meant that, although the typed notes were legible and complete, they were a month or more out of date by the time they were finished. As he did every time he sat down to dictate, he thought that he should change the system to something that worked better. But it had taken Doris months to become accustomed to the present system and the thought of making her learn a new one made him shudder. It was easier to continue the way he was. Schwartz had just pushed the record button when he saw someone standing in the doorway that Worthington had left open.

"Mr. Ogilvie, I presume?"

"Yes. You are Dr. Schwartz?" Unlike the physicians in the hospital, Ogilvie wore a business suit.

Schwartz nodded in response. "I assume you are here about the radio show."

"Yes, partly. Barlow called me this morning, quite upset. He was very concerned about the potential ramifications, especially on our grant arrangements. I've known Barlow Worthington for fifteen years, ever since I came here, and I've never known him to get upset without reason. I assume that this did happen?"

So, it was Barlow who sicced the administration on me, Schwartz thought. Interesting. "The show happened. The FDA didn't. And, as I told Barlow not long ago, I said nothing that wasn't true."

Ogilvie sighed. It was one of those "more in sorrow than in anger" sighs that Schwartz could remember his mother using. "Sometimes the truth is not what counts," Ogilvie said. "Meldrum has contributed millions of dollars to this center. I think we owe it to them to be careful in what we say. The other point I wanted to make is that the person running that show did an extremely nasty hatchet job on this center and the city administration in the recent past. I would hardly choose to give such a person any kind of advantage."

"Yeah, I've heard some of that stuff," Schwartz said. "I've also heard that some of the people involved in that "hatchet job" wound up being convicted, although I suppose that is not the crucial point here either. The fact is, though, she was the key to getting most of the information on these other cases. I mean, what would you suggest that I do?"

"To be blunt, screw her," said Ogilvie.

Briefly, Schwartz considered telling him how literally he had followed that advice, just for the shock effect he was sure it would have on Ogilvie. At the last moment, he decided against it. Instead, he said nothing.

Ogilvie watched him say nothing and decided to take that as an assent. "That isn't the main reason I came by, though," he said.

Schwartz's eyes had drifted back to his charts, but Ogilvie's comment made him look up again. The thought flashed through his mind that they were finally going to restore the funding he had been promised in the beginning. He was quickly disappointed.

"My office received a complaint from the Infectious Disease Group about your use of a restricted drug." Ogilvie recited it formally and with great precision.

Great, Schwartz thought, this is really going to be my day.

"I'm not going to comment on your behavior," Ogilvie continued, "although it might be appropriate for me to do so. The point is that this is not an isolated instance. Utilization Review has flagged your charts before, we both know that. When this complaint came in, we reviewed the case. Jodie Schmidt was the patient."

"I know the case," Schwartz said, "what's the problem? Other than the Aspergicin, I mean."

Ogilvie did not sigh this time. His voice was quite harsh. "We looked through that treatment protocol you are using. A number of the drugs you ordered are not approved for that disease."

Schwartz stared at him, absolutely stared. "What the hell difference does that make? That's what they are used for. And don't think that this is just some crazy scheme that I've dreamed up. Of the programs that have been tested, this one seems to be the best so far. I know it's standard in Boston and, frankly, this is my expertise. Unless I'm wrong, you're not even a physician."

"Frankly, Dr. Schwartz, I don't care what they do in Boston. My not being a physician is equally irrelevant." Ogilvie folded his arms across his chest. "The fact is that is not what those drugs were approved for and because of that the insurance company won't pay for them. They are also very likely not to pay for the whole damn hospitalization. Do you have any idea how much that is?"

"A lot. I couldn't give you the exact numbers, but I'm sure it's a lot."

Ogilvie snorted. "I'm glad to see you are so fiscally aware. Do I need to remind you that your department is a pool of red ink?"

"Now wait just a damn minute," Schwartz retorted. He could feel the heat rising in his face. "If I had the funds I was promised there wouldn't be nearly so much of a shortfall and you know it."

"There would still be red ink," Ogilvie said. "This department is always a drain on the hospital's resources, and I'm not saying that's because of you. It would be true no matter who ran it. We needed the funds in other areas to support groups that do bring in money. It's the only sensible thing to do."

Schwartz pushed his chair away from his desk. "Ogilvie, this is a hospital, and I take care of sick kids. You can't run it like a business."

"I have to run it like a business. Right now, I have to consider what we will do when the insurance sends back the bill on little Miss Schmidt without a check. We can bill the family, of course, but I doubt they are going to cough it up and there's not much I can do about that."

"I suppose not," Schwartz said. "Not after the ruckus when the hospital tried to attach that kid's house two years ago."

"Can we not go into that? The fact remains, we're going to have to eat it and I don't like it."

"Then try adding salt." The anger started to come through in Schwartz's voice. "I'm sorry about the bill, but the kid has to get treated. There's nothing I can do about that."

"Dr. Schwartz, the health of patients is your concern, the fiscal health of this center is mine. Tell me, what kind of chance does this Jodie Schmidt have with your hot new treatment program?"

"The way it looks now, maybe sixty-five, seventy percent."

"So, this is not a guarantee. Right?"

"Absolutely. Never said otherwise."

"Okay. Am I right that there are other regimens that just use drugs approved for this type of leukemia?"

"Yes, some of the older ones."

"And what kind of odds would they give her?"

Schwartz frowned. He did not like the direction the conversation was taking. "Maybe fifty percent," he said. "Maybe a bit less."

Ogilvie pounced on the statement. "Then, the fact of the matter is that she could relapse and die either way, isn't that true?"

"Yes," Schwartz said reluctantly.

"And that could happen anytime during her treatment, couldn't it?"

"Also true. Or afterward, unfortunately."

Ogilvie leaned forward toward Schwartz, pointing at him with his index finger. "So, really, if you switched her to another regimen and she relapsed, it would be impossible to say that it had anything to do with the drugs. Isn't that right?"

"What in hell are you trying to say?"

"That you find something reimbursable to treat her with. After all, if she relapses it could just as easily have happened anyway. You just said that. I trust we understand one another?" With that, Ogilvie shot a glare at Schwartz and left without waiting for Schwartz to say anything further.

At first, Zeke felt like vomiting. Then, he wanted to run down the hall and kick Ogilvie in his fashionably worsted groin. Realizing that he was not going to do that, he wanted to throw something. The recorder was in his hand, so he wound up to heave it at the wall, only to stop with it poised by his head. The recorder was still running. He rewound it and set it to play. There was Ogilvie, quite audibly, making the case for reimbursable drugs. Schwartz did not throw the recorder against the wall. Instead, he popped the cassette out and put it in his pocket.

Chapter 18

SCHEUERMANN'S RUN, NEW JERSEY _____

TOM WOODWARD was not a happy man. It was four-thirty in the afternoon and where he wanted to be was heading toward the parking lot. One of the things he loved about corporate life was that four-thirty was the end of the day, and it was a definite end. Oh, he might spend fifteen or twenty minutes extra to finish up a letter, and sometimes he took work home, but it was always on his terms. There were no patients wandering into the office at five o'clock complaining of chest pain, no calls at two in the morning about problems that had gone on for three days but, thanks to some comment on the Tonight Show, were now an emergency. He liked to think of those things when he had bad days at the office. Except, here it was, the end of the day and Russell Jackson wanted to see him. Woodward distinctly remembered a deadline of "tomorrow morning" in the conversation with Ingraham and Desai. Something must have changed. Woodward was not happy about the possibility.

Jackson was not alone when Woodward entered his office. The man in the other chair was no stranger to Woodward. His name was Patrick Dwyer and the sight of him made Woodward's sphincters tighten at both ends. Dwyer ran Sales and Marketing and not just for the Anti-Infective Group but also for the Cardiovascular Group. Since Meldrum's strength traditionally lay in those two areas, Dwyer presided over an enormous flow of money. For both of those reasons, Dwyer was considered a shoo-in for Vice President in the next year or two and to have a real shot at the top job in about a decade. He had started off "carrying a bag," as did almost all aspirants to high office in Meldrum. He had been an aggressive, outstanding salesman, a start which had launched him along his series of promotions. As a manager, he had retained the "aggressive" and the "outstanding" and added a new sobriquet: ruthless. Pity the salesman reporting to Pat Dwyer who failed to meet his forecast. Fear proved to be an excellent motivator, at least in the short term, and Dwyer's promotions came fast enough so that he had never had to worry about the long term. What showed on paper was that the performance of any Dwyer-led group almost always led the company. Of necessity, he and Woodward had a polite relationship, but that was only for show. Woodward always wondered why the ads Dwyer's group presented seemed to push at the borders of truth and, on occasion, to cross them. It infuriated Woodward that Dwyer would do that, especially when he did it with a drug like Aspergicin that was so obviously effective and had so few side effects. What really left Woodward choked with anger was to hear Dwyer calmly take all the credit for the sales, as though physicians would switch drugs the way they switched gasoline brands and would switch away from Meldrum's drugs were it not for Dwyer and his intrepid sales force.

"Good afternoon, Pat," Woodward said and put a smile on his face.

Dwyer's frame was six foot three, folded into a chair, deeply tanned from the afternoon tennis game with company president he played in place of lunch. He had that "lean and hungry look" first ascribed to Cassius. Woodward thought that he could see fangs amidst the polished white teeth.

"Good to see you, Tom," Dwyer said. His eyes turned to Woodward over a steeple made of his fingers and he looked as though he was really glad to see him.

"Why don't you pull up a chair, Tom?" Jackson suggested. "This may take a while. I spoke to the VP this afternoon and then Ingraham called again. You'll get a copy of my note on that conversation, but the bottom line is that the Board and the FDA have bought into a general plan for dealing with the situation. It is also clear that there is a lot of pressure building up at the FDA. I want to talk to both of you now about some specifics, because Ingraham wants us to call him tomorrow with the details. We'll need to go down there next week to present our proposal at a meeting. You can expect Ingraham, Desai, probably the Director for Anti-Infectives, and someone from Epidemiology. It should be quite manageable. Questions either of you have first?"

Woodward had questions, the first of which was why Patrick Dwyer was in Jackson's office at all. He had no intention of asking any questions, however, until he knew where Dwyer stood. The Sales and Marketing Director had sandbagged him before.

"Okay," Jackson continued, "I think the FDA will be willing to accept that there is no link between Aspergicin and these cancers if we can retrospectively survey seventy-five percent of the patients in our original studies and show no increase in this cancer above what would normally be expected for this population. They also want us to do an annual survey for five years to see if any more of these cancers show up in patients who get Aspergicin. We haven't committed to that one yet; it looks too much like an admission that this could be an effect of the drug. I'm hoping we can avoid it if our retrospective survey is clean. We did commit to do a complete review of the raw data from the animal carcinogenicity studies, just to be sure nothing was missed. Tom, you'll have to coordinate these moves. I'll also need you to pull together a brief report on what we know as of now. It has to be in Washington at least two days before the meeting."

"Is there going to be a labeling change?" That came from Dwyer. Woodward kept his silence.

The "labeling" was really the contents of the package insert. By law, it defined the extent of the claims Meldrum could make for Aspergicin and also spelled out the acknowledged side effects and required precautions. Every advertisement, every representative's sales pitch, had to conform to the contents of this labeling. Any change meant that all the ads, all the promotional give-aways had to be pulled back, changed, and reprinted. It was a lot of effort and it was expensive.

Jackson did not hesitate with his answer. "Absolutely not. Yet. Our position remains that there is no known causal relationship between Aspergicin and these cancers, unless Tom has found something this afternoon that would change it."

Woodward shook his head mutely.

"What do you want my people doing, then?" Dwyer asked.

"Nothing," Jackson shot back. "This is a Regulatory and Medical issue. I want Sales to steer clear of it."

Woodward sensed that Jackson and Dwyer had been disagreeing all afternoon. Normally, well-modulated tones were the rule, even while twisting the knife in an opponent's back.

"I wasn't suggesting that we should be running this, Russ," Dwyer said. His voice was still neutral. "My people are going to be asked about it, though, when they call on the docs. They will need to know what to say."

"Of course." Jackson had his cool back. "Tom can put together a script for them. Any questions that go beyond the script, refer them back to Tom."

"That would be fine," Dwyer said.

The overall exchange made Woodward believe that Dwyer had lost that afternoon's engagement. More important, from Woodward's perspective, it meant that Dwyer had already taken a clear position. He could not easily change that just to score points off Woodward.

"What happens if the data looks bad when we get it?" Woodward asked.

"The data will be whatever it is going to be," Jackson said very carefully. He was looking directly at Dwyer when he said it. "You should both understand that the FDA is going to be hoping, almost as much as we are, that nothing shows up. They're real stirred up now because this took them by surprise, which they hate because it makes them look bad, but they are going to look even worse if there is a real problem."

Dwyer tapped his fingers together. "What I still don't understand," he said completely ignoring Jackson's remarks, "is how this happened in the first place. You said, I believe, that the leak was never reported."

"That's right," Jackson said. "It was not reportable, so none was made. Except internally."

"Then somebody in the plant has a big mouth," Dwyer said. "Have you checked into that?"

"No, Pat, because it isn't worth the effort right now. I talked to Legal, and even if we found that somebody was giving out information, the whistleblower law would probably cover him anyway. Whatever is done is done. It's not important."

The look on Dwyer's face said that this was another point he did not agree with. He kept silent though. That gave Woodward a chance to bring the conversation back to his concerns.

"You mentioned doing retrospective and prospective studies," he said to

Jackson. "The annual survey is actually less trouble, if we have to do it. We can just use Pat's customer list and send out a mailing from here. The retrospective, though, means we are going to have to go to each one of the study sites and pull the patient charts for all the old study patients. That's a lot of work and I just don't have the head count for it. Laurie has a year of monitoring experience, but Jane doesn't and she is pregnant to boot. Laurie can't cover all the sites herself, not even if we had a year to do it."

"I agree," Jackson said, "but even if we had time to train people, we don't have the budget to hire for this. What we can do is use the clinical study monitors to check the sites and report back. They're in the field anyway and we should be able to do this quickly. We'll give you a Senior Clinical Research Associate to coordinate it. I've got someone in mind who should do a good job for you."

"Who?"

"MLD."

Woodward looked puzzled, then irritated because Jackson was laughing at him. "What does MLD mean, other than minimum lethal dose?"

Jackson seemed to be enjoying Woodward's irritation. "From what I understand, that is the nickname she has picked up. However, her real name is Maureen Lynne Delahanty. She's in Oregon right now, but I sent a fax to her hotel. She can take the redeye back and meet with you tomorrow morning."

"And why do they call her MLD?"

"You'll find out." Jackson chuckled again.

PORTLAND, OREGON _____

The doctor's waiting room was full, so Maureen Delahanty stood, leaning against a wall with her briefcase between her feet, trying to interest herself in a copy of Sports Illustrated that was three months old. There was nothing in it that she wanted to know, and did not already know, but she read the articles anyway. They were more interesting than looking around the waiting room. Seen one waiting room seen them all, was Delahanty's motto, and there was nothing about this one to change her mind. She was, conservatively, a good two decades removed from the youngest of the patients who filled the room and probably four from the average. The patients were largely women, all of whom had short white hair and wrinkled pale white skin—well almost all, there was one black. Some had canes, one had a walker, most had support stockings. They were as much general issue as the waiting room itself, which was furnished with rows of fake wood chairs and wallpaper that would have been better suited to a cheap motel. Maureen Delahanty ignored all of it. She just occupied her patch of wall and floor until the receptionist called her name. Then she picked up her briefcase, brushed a few strands of coal black hair behind her shoulders, and marched to the door leading to the examination rooms and doctors' offices.

Delahanty cut an impressive figure. She was easily five foot eleven, even wearing flat shoes. There was bulk on that frame too, wide through the hips and even wider through the chest. She wore a long patterned dress that she believed created the visual impression of a tapering at the waist although, in truth, her midsection was straight and solid down to the point where her hips began. Her face sported freckles on a sunburn, thin lips pressed into a straight line and a snub nose above which brown eyes focused solely on the office door at the end of the corridor. The receptionist had tried to meet her in the doorway but she scuttled off to the side as Delahanty went past.

Dr. Donald Madagen was Delahanty's target; his office was the last one along the corridor. She had spent five weeks without success trying to secure an appointment with him. Always, Madagen had been too busy, or conveniently out of the office. Ultimately, she had managed to squeeze some time out of the secretary by dint of coming to Portland and doing her insisting in the waiting room. The problem was that Madagen was conducting a study for Meldrum Products and, although he was enrolling patients as planned, his casebooks were a mess. The longer he ducked her, the longer it was before she could have her forms corrected. She would not have minded so much had there not been so many to correct.

Donald Madagen was sharp featured, with graying hair combed sideways over a large pink bald spot. He wore wire rimmed glasses. He greeted her by standing behind his desk and they exchanged pleasantries neither one meant seriously.

When they were seated, Delahanty opened her briefcase and withdrew a stack of forms four inches thick. Each one was actually a triplicate form. Yellow stickers along the edges festooned the pile. She reached over the desk and placed them on top of the chart Madagen had open there.

"What's this?" he asked.

"These," she said, "are the corrections that have been accumulating since I saw you last, about three months according to my calendar." Her voice was surprisingly girlish in view of the body it came from. "This is what I have been calling your office about for the last month. I've written on the stickers what the problem is for each page. You need to make the corrections, just a line through the old one, and initial and date the new ones."

"I've done clinical studies before," he said brusquely. "I know how it's done. I don't have time to go through all this now."

Delahanty smiled and blinked. "I can't take these pages back for data entry until it's done. The stuff I've flagged either has missing entries or the entries don't match the patient charts. You need to sign these pages at the bottom, too."

"Maureen, you see how busy I am. I told you I don't have time. I thought," he said, "you said you were bringing the check."

Which, thought Delahanty, is the only reason I got an appointment to see the good doctor. Madagen had enrolled half of the patients for which he had contracted. That contract specified a third of the money up front, a third after half the patients were entered and the remainder at completion. At twenty-two hundred dollars a patient, it was a considerable sum.

"I've got it," Delahanty said. She opened the briefcase again and took out a white envelope. She held it out in the air in front of him so he could read the name and address through the glassine window. Madagen reached for it, only to have Delahanty pull it back a little so that his hand missed. In a reflex action, he reached again and almost sprawled across the top of his desk before he realized how ridiculous he looked.

"Dammit, Maureen, what are you doing?"

"It's simple, Dr. Madagen," she said in the same tone she had used to say hello, "you want your check, I want my data. So, you take care of the corrections, I'll take care of the forms and leave you the check. Otherwise, I'm going to sit here and tear it into fifty pieces."

"You can't do that!" Madagen's flush went from his cheeks to his bald spot. "I'll call your boss right now. I'll have you fired!"

"Go right ahead. Do you need the number? Dave is as sick of waiting for these forms as I am. He knows all about this." Actually, Dave knew nothing about it, but that did not bother Delahanty at all. She knew when she had people intimidated. In fact, Madagen made no move for the phone.

"Okay," she said, still in the same tone of voice, "let's get started." The check went back into the briefcase and her index finger came to rest on the top sheet in front of Madagen. "The first one is patient 103. You wrote that her white count was normal, but the value is actually outside the range you provided for your laboratory. You need to change it to abnormal and indicate whether you think it is clinically significant."

Madagen looked at patient 103's form and then sagged back in his chair. "Look, this is going to take quite a while. You know what needs to be fixed, hell, you've got it all written out. Why don't you just make the corrections? You can use my initials. It'll make it easier for both of us."

Delahanty froze him with a stare that would have given a barroom brawler pause. "The monitor, which is me, does not write on the case record forms. Ever. You know that. You're the only one who's allowed to do it. If I do it with your initials, it's called fraud."

Please God, she said silently to herself, do not let him sit there and tell me that it was okay with the monitor he worked with before because, if he does, there is going to be no end of shit. Fortunately, either her stare or the mention of fraud took the starch out of Madagen. Unsurprisingly, he was late for his next appointment.

She was silent after she left Madagen's office, saying only the minimum words necessary to call a taxicab and then nothing while waiting for the cab or in response to the driver's chatter. The papers were safely back in her briefcase, all the problems resolved. There were no longer any errors or omissions to make Meldrum's Data Review throw up their hands and run in circles. Nothing to cause the computer to spit out a correction slip that meant she had to take the pages back into the field and fix them. Those were the things that slowed down data entry, which then delayed the data analysis, which in turn delayed the reports and which, if there were enough delays, could let someone else market a drug first and cost Meldrum Products a whole lot of money. It was rare for many corrections, if any at all, to be needed on pages brought back by Maureen Delahanty. That was what made her such a good monitor.

Partly, that skill came from attention to detail and a good understanding of the studies she monitored. Maureen Delahanty had been an intensive care nurse for several years before joining Meldrum. That training accounted for her knowledge. She knew the diseases and the drugs as well as most of the physicians. Part of her talent for monitoring also came from the fact that she enjoyed browbeating doctors. Her years as a nurse accounted for that attitude as well. She hated cleaning up after them, taking their orders when they did not know what they were doing, trying to tell them what orders they ought to be giving, and then standing by while they took all the credit for the work that she had been breaking her back doing. She had quit after seven years when an intern, scarcely two weeks out of medical school, handed her the famous "I am the doctor and you are the nurse" line while she was trying to give him some desperately needed advice. As she recalled, the patient had survived the aftermath of that doctor's decision, but it had taken several people working all night to accomplish the feat. The following morning she had walked down to the nursing office and told them what they could do with their job.

Industry was better. The docs were hired by the company to treat patients in the company's studies and it was her job to see that they did it the way the company wanted. It was a role she could enjoy, even if it was a pain to have to sit down and make certain that every damn thing the doctor wrote in the company's case book could be documented somewhere in the patient's chart. The only physicians that she had to be subordinate to were the company docs in charge of the studies and she paid little heed to them. Hacks they were, most of them, who could never make it as real doctors.

Unfortunately, hacks or not, they had a great deal to say about how the Clinical Development departments were run at Meldrum. Before she had been there long, everyone knew that Maureen Delahanty had an Attitude. That was why, good as she was, she was still a Senior Clinical Research Associate rather than a manager. It was also, she suspected, why she was monitoring this stupid trial of a me-too heart drug, which, even if it managed to win approval in Washington, would never capture more than a few percent of the market. I ought to be working on the high tech drugs, she thought bitterly. Possibly, telling Dr. Waggoner at that study review that he did not have the faintest idea of what was going on had not been such a good idea, especially since the Vice President of Clinical Research had been there. It had been true, and it had served Waggoner right, but it had also led to this horrible site in Portland.

The University, where Madagen had his office, perched high up on a cliff overlooking the city. In some ways, it clung to the cliff rather than perched on it. The hospital was the only building Delahanty had seen where the basement was on the ground floor while the main entrance, on the other side of the building, had to be on the ninth floor. Nothing was close by and everything was uphill, a combination she loathed from the day she first saw the place. There was, of course, a fantastic view from that cliff, that is, there was a fantastic view if the sky was clear. That had happened for a total of one day since Delahanty had been coming to Portland. Were it not for that day, she would not have even known the view existed. Normally, the skies were gray and threatening to rain, if it was not actually raining. If I wanted to live in a drizzle, she thought, I would have joined a British firm.

Back at the hotel, the red light on her telephone was flashing. It was not, however, a telephone message, but a fax waiting for her at the front desk. Puzzled, she tore aside the cover sheet while she was standing at the counter. The letter was brief. She was directed to fly back to New Jersey that night—a ticket would be waiting at the airport—and report to a Dr. Tom Woodward in the morning. That was a bitch, she thought, an all-night flight and then straight in to work. Normally, the company turned a blind eye if people took a half day off after a night flight. The name Woodward was a puzzle, too. She vaguely recalled that he worked with the Anti-Infective group. Delahanty worked for Cardiovascular. Since the directors of those two groups were barely on speaking terms, relations between the personnel were frigidly civil, at best. They did not work together. Then, she noticed that the letter was from Russell Jackson, not from her manager. Since when did the boss of Regulatory Affairs send a letter to a CRA?

"Excuse me, Miss," the desk clerk asked, "is everything okay?"

"Nope," she said. "A certain something appears to have hit the fan. Which is why they called me." She smiled as she said the last.

SCHEUERMANN'S RUN, NEW JERSEY _____

Woodward spent the earliest part of the next morning wondering what this "Minimum Lethal Dose" person might be like. Normally, he enjoyed working with the CRAs. They tended to be young and, more often than not, female. A reasonable proportion of them were pretty. Although unofficial company policy mandated suits or dresses as stodgy as the clothes the men wore, Woodward still found them easy on his eyes. His appreciation of them did not imply that Woodward had ever said, done, or even hinted at anything approaching indiscretion. He had never even considered it, although whether his restraint stemmed from loyalty or cowardice was unclear even to him. At most, he daydreamed a little. He just enjoyed being around the young women, with their chatter of boyfriends and first cars and their drive to prove themselves in their first, or sometimes second, job. They often made him wonder if his daughters, who seemed to be drifting in no particular direction, could ever develop into such energetic young women.

He realized with a start that someone was standing in his doorway and that the person had to be Maureen Delahanty. With a twinge of regret, he disengaged from his daydream. She was obviously not the perky young girl he had been conjuring up in his mind. Instead, her face wore a scowl that clearly said she had needed to change planes at O'Hare at five o'clock in the morning.

"I'm Delahanty," she said, sticking out a hand.

Woodward reached across his desk to take it. Her hand, he noted, was almost the size of his own. He indicated one of the chairs placed in front of his desk. She settled into it and placed her briefcase on the other.

"Got a fax yesterday, told me to report to you today. It's today. I'm reporting."

The abrupt delivery took Woodward aback. Now I know where the nickname comes from, he thought.

"What do you know about what's going on?" he asked.

"Only that I had to take one of those damned flights I can never sleep on and that I'm here expecting you to tell me something that will make it seem worthwhile."

She had assessed Woodward in that first minute and found him wanting. It was not the handshake alone that did it. She had shaken hands with too many salesmen to put any credence in a firm grip as a guide to character. It was simply that the rest of Woodward seemed as soft as his handshake, a little stooped, a little weak. She was not impressed. She rarely was when it came to physicians.

"I suppose I should start from the beginning," Woodward said. At first, he hesitated over how much to tell her. Then, he realized that Acey Henson was broadcasting the story across their part of the state. He might as well tell Delahanty all of it. When he finished, she caught his eye and said, "What do you think? Did the Aspergicin cause the cancers?"

"No way," Woodward answered. "Not a chance. I've been through the data here and I don't believe it."

"So, you think the story is a crock?"

"Absolutely."

"And we're going through this rigmarole to keep the FDA quiet, so they can look like they are on their toes and making us do something?"

"Basically."

"So," and suddenly her voice changed and became quite harsh, "what happens if I bring back something that says it's not a crock? What then?"

Woodward met her eyes straight on. He even had a little grin on his face. "The data is what the data is," he said quietly, giving her the same answer Jackson had given him. "Let's just you and I hope to God it's good."

"That's fine by me," she said. Silently she was hoping that she would not have to find out if Woodward was as good as his word. "Tell me one other thing. This guy Schwartz. You said he is supposed to know his stuff, but it doesn't sound like he thinks it is a crock. What's his stake in this?"

"He's an academic, Delahanty," Woodward said, "and he's still fairly young. I don't know if you know how that game works. He'll milk some papers out of this, I'm sure. Publications are what an academic needs to get promoted. He also gets his name in public, which academics don't usually get. That kind of recognition is also good for the career, never mind that it comes out of our hide."

"An asshole, then," she said. "All right, how do we do this?"

In response, Woodward pulled a three-ring binder from his bookshelf and put it out on the desk. "I've put together a list of all the physicians who were investigators for Aspergicin. This book also has the patient numbers and initials of every patient they treated. The highlighted names are the biggest investigators. If we just hit those, and ignore the small fry with a couple of patients here and there, we can do it. The CRAs from Anti-Infectives can hit the sites, get the docs to pull the charts and send the information back here. You need to manage them so that it gets done as fast as possible and you get the data pulled together as it comes in. One of the people from Computer Services is setting up a database for you. If there are problems at a site, you may need to go and clean it up. Then, we'll see what we get."

Delahanty did not move. "What you're describing is a manager's job," she said.

"I don't have a manager's slot," said Woodward. "Just a very temporary position for a Senior CRA."

She turned it over in her mind for a minute. It really did not matter what they called it, the job description was that of a manager. If she did it, the company would have to acknowledge at her next review that she was doing a manager's job. It would be hard for them not to give her a promotion, especially if she did one hell of a job on it.

"So, you got a temporary Senior CRA," she said. "You got phone numbers in that book?"

The morning soon began to show signs of turning into the Red Queen's treadmill. Having finished his talk with Delahanty, Woodward needed to find some place for her to work. He had naively assumed that Jackson had arranged it when he had transferred her, but that was not the case. Finding room was easier said than done in a company that had experienced five years of unbroken growth. He eventually secured a room that had been designed as a small conference room and was only one floor removed from his office. Delahanty at once pointed out that the room lacked a telephone. Since her job, as Woodward had outlined it, depended on a telephone, one had to be installed. Delahanty lacked the authority to order a phone installed, so Woodward had to write out the work order. Unfortunately, Delahanty needed the phone that day, not next week, which was when Systems Services offered to put it in. Woodward lacked the authority to order them to change their priority list. That meant he needed his supervisor to co-sign the work order. Since his supervisor's secretary insisted there was no free time on the schedule, Woodward had to walk over to the man's office, wait for the door to open between meetings, stick the work order on the desk and wait while it was signed. Then, returning to his own office, he found one of the boys from the Document Room wheeling a cart up to his door.

"What is this all about?" he asked.

"Got a request to deliver you a copy of these," was the reply. "Can you sign here for them, please?"

"These" turned out to be the animal carcinogenicity studies. There were two in all, one of mice and one of rats, describing the occurrence of tumors in animals who received, for two years, either a placebo or different doses of Aspergicin. Each study consisted of six volumes, each volume being, in accordance with federal regulations, no more than two inches thick. Woodward groaned as he flipped through the pages of one of the volumes seeing page after page of tables that described everything from how much the animals ate over two years to what each of their organs looked like at the end of that time. Woodward had a suspicion that the Washington bureaucrats spent more time measuring the distance between the covers than they did looking at the material in between. He had just settled back at his desk, resigned to plowing through the volumes, when Dwyer showed up.

Woodward usually had the same enthusiasm for a visit from Pat Dwyer as a Russian from a generation ago might have had for his local KGB agent. The events of the past day made Woodward even more uneasy.

"Hi, Tom. Got a moment?"

"Sure, Pat. Have a seat."

Dwyer seated himself in front of Woodward's desk and fixed him with an unblinking gaze. Woodward found that gaze one of Dwyer's most disconcerting habits.

"Tom, I came by because I just need to chat with you unofficially. Just you, me and the wall."

Woodward wished he had a hidden tape recorder handy. Whenever Dwyer used that phrase, some plot was being hatched. No matter how careful Woodward tried to be, no matter how he watched his words, he always came out looking suspect to his associates and no better off for his discomfort.

"Tom, you told Jackson that you don't believe Aspergicin could be connected to these kids, right?" Woodward nodded. "You don't know what's going on though." Dwyer said it as a statement of fact, not a question.

"Right. I mean, we may never know what happened, but the idea about Aspergicin doesn't make sense. Once we get this survey done, I think that will be obvious." He stopped there because Dwyer was holding up a hand.

"Yes," said Dwyer rubbing his chin. "Look, Tom, medical analysis is all very well, and I'd be the last person to try and tell you the right or wrong of something medically, but sometimes I think people forget this is a business and it runs by the same rules as any other business."

"What do you mean?" Woodward asked.

"Simple. Aspergicin competes against several other products, and rather successfully. We've been increasing our market share steadily since launch. Good news for us, bad news for our competition. Now, who are our competitors?" Dwyer ticked off four names on his fingers. Then he repeated one of them. "You probably aren't aware of it, but these guys play real hardball, quite dirty. I'm not saying anything secret, everybody in the industry knows it, at least on the Sales side. Have a bad adverse reaction with a product? Docs get mailings about it. File an NDA that competes with one of their main drugs? People turn up with odd questions, things you would swear were not public knowledge. Now, nobody has ever proved anything illegal, but it gets quite dirty just the same."

"What are you getting at?" Woodward asked again.

"Just this. How much do you really know about those cases Dr. Schwartz reported? How real are they?"

"Good God!" Woodward exploded. "Are you suggesting that someone paid Schwartz to make this whole thing up, just to improve their competitive position?"

"Absolutely not. I never said that." Dwyer's voice was sharp. "I am suggesting that you look at the facts. Actually, I doubt Schwartz is making anything up and I think that kid down at the medical center has to be real. But, even Schwartz admits that he has only seen that one kid. The other two, as I understand it, are already dead. The information was supplied to him. How convenient! How carefully did he check it out? After all, Dr. Schwartz is looking to make a name for himself just like everyone else. Then, there is this leak, which nobody outside this company should have known about, and that information lands in young Dr. Schwartz's hands right alongside the other info so he can put two and two together. What does that say to you?"

To Woodward, it said paranoid, but one did not call Pat Dwyer paranoid. Not to his face. Not unless there was another job offer waiting.

What Woodward said was, "It sounds rather unlikely."

"As unlikely as Aspergicin causing those cancers?"

Dwyer had him there. What was it, he tried to remember, Sherlock Holmes had said about the impossible?

"I assume you're telling me this because there is something you would like me to do."

"Certainly," Dwyer said. "I'd like you to see how much info Schwartz really has, where it came from. Talk to him. See if you can find out what is going on. You can do that, can't you?"

"That is within my discretion," Woodward said carefully. "He doesn't have to agree to see me, however."

"You can try, though."

"Yes, but it will have to wait until after the FDA meeting, though. There is just too much to do before then."

"No problem," said Dwyer. "I quite understand."

Chapter 19

WOODWARD HATED confrontations. He avoided them as much as possible at home, which he supposed was why he could never control the Talbot's bill and why his daughters stayed out late when he told them not to do so. He also avoided confrontations at work when he could, which was one of the reasons he no longer saw patients. Unfortunately, going to see Schwartz, he was certain, was going to lead to a confrontation. He did not see any way to avoid it. Of course, he could have told Dwyer no, but arguing with Dwyer was a bad idea. He had hoped that Jackson would veto the planned visit when they discussed it. To his chagrin, Jackson had liked the idea; in fact, he had insisted that Woodward arrange the meeting before they went to Washington.

"We need background on these cases before we meet with the FDA anyway," Jackson had said. "Going to see Schwartz personally may be the best way to do it. It will give you a chance to give him some positive strokes while you are getting the info. Just make sure you don't give him anything. None of our data goes out, that has to be clear." How that last command could be coupled with giving Schwartz "positive strokes" Woodward was uncertain.

Woodward figured that had he told Jackson that the visit to Schwartz had been Dwyer's idea, Jackson's response might have been very different. However, as matters stood, Jackson was praising Woodward's initiative, which Woodward hated to lose. Perhaps more important, word of that would probably have found its way back to Dwyer, who would then consider Woodward to have abused his confidence. Woodward did not want to deal with the situation that would result.

There had remained the forlorn hope that Schwartz would refuse to see him until after the FDA meeting, if not forever, but Libby had no trouble scheduling the appointment. It occurred to Woodward as he drove down to the medical center that if he had made the call to Schwartz's office he could have found a way to make the meeting impossible. Libby had made the call, however, because Woodward did not want to take the chance of having

Schwartz answer the telephone himself, thereby starting a conversation Woodward did not really want to have. Life could be very complex.

Schwartz had ambivalent feelings about the call from Woodward's office, which Doris relayed to him. Had he taken the call himself, he thought he would have refused to see the man, so frustrated had he been over his previous attempts to reach Woodward. Doris had taken the call though, and Woodward had the magic "MD" after his name, and the matter was presented as pressing, so the appointment was made without consulting him. Anyway, there was still the matter of the fellowship that Worthington kept holding out.

"For God's sake," Worthington said when Schwartz brought up his second, or third, thoughts on the issue, "see the man and be polite. I spoke with my friend again and I think we can still salvage the situation. Just make sure you're sorry about the fuss and make real clear that you didn't bring the FDA into this."

"Barlow, how sorry am I supposed to be? I mean, if I hadn't made a fuss, I wouldn't be seeing Woodward and we wouldn't be getting anywhere anyway."

"Now you don't know that, so let's not jump to conclusions. Dammit, Zeke, for once can't you be a little political?"

"I can try."

Schwartz was in the hospital when Woodward arrived at the office, but Doris assured Woodward that she would page him right away. Woodward hoped that the return call would say that Dr. Schwartz had an emergency and could Dr. Woodward come back another day? There was to be no such luck. Schwartz said that he would be right there.

The office did not impress Woodward. He spent the time waiting for Schwartz studying a collage of photos of children from the clinic that had been tacked to the bulletin board. About fifteen minutes later, the door opened behind him.

Schwartz walked into his office to see Woodward turning around to meet him. "Zeke Schwartz," he said by way of introduction, extending his hand at the same time.

"Dr. Tom Woodward," Woodward replied.

They stood a moment, sizing each other up, Schwartz in his white coat over slacks with multiple creases and Woodward in his dark blue suit. Neither assessment was very favorable.

"Why don't we go inside?" Schwartz asked.

After they had settled into his back office and closed the door, Schwartz continued. "Your secretary said that you needed to talk to me about the hepatocellular cancer cases."

Woodward might have hoped that Schwartz would have said more, provided some start to the conversation, but it did not happen. Schwartz delivered his opening statement and stopped. He looked at Woodward from behind his desk in a way that asked, "Are you going to waste my time?" although he did not actually say that.

Bereft of an easy opening, Woodward could only clear his throat and launch into the speech he had planned during his drive.

"What you may not know," he said, "is that we do investigate any reports of reactions to our drugs. Now, even though this isn't the usual kind of case—I mean we know those kids were never actually given Aspergicin— the implication has been made that they were exposed to it in the creek, so we are going to look into it." Woodward thought that was a good introduction. He sounded like a good citizen, going a bit beyond what he was actually required to do.

"I was quite careful not to say that there was a direct relationship," Schwartz said.

"We need to do this anyway."

"Yeah. I'm told that the FDA jumped to conclusions. I'm sorry about that. I certainly didn't intend it that way."

"Not an issue," Woodward said, while thinking that it was precisely the issue. What he wanted to do, instead of being bland and polite, was to jump up and grab Schwartz by the collar and scream in his face that Schwartz had no idea of how the industry and the government worked and that fools who stuck their noses into that business for piddly personal gain had no conception of the forces they could unleash. Woodward neither did nor said any of that. He needed Schwartz's cooperation and telling the man off would spoil the opportunity. He could also have apologized for not returning Schwartz's earlier phone calls, but he figured that unless Schwartz brought up the subject, he would not mention it.

Schwartz, for his part, had merely made the ritual apology that Worthington had indicated would be necessary. He hated doing it in the same way he hated apologizing in general, and hated it even more when he did not feel in the wrong. He consoled himself with the thought that if this meeting brought him more information about Jerry, even if it told him what was *not* wrong with Jerry, then it would be worth the trouble.

"Okay, Dr. Woodward," Schwartz said, "tell me what I can do for you."

"Basically," Woodward said, "I need whatever information you have available on those three cases, particularly regarding medical history and pathology reports, hepatitis status and other laboratory findings. That way, I can file a complete report."

Schwartz thumbed through a set of folders on the right hand side of his desk and pulled one out. "I have a pretty complete summary on Jerry Inman, that's my patient here. Doris can make copies for you if you like. I have some notes and a Path report on the one from Philly. I'm afraid all I have from Scranton are the notes I made on my conversation with the doc. He's a surgeon at a community hospital, so I don't have all the details I'd like."

"I see," Woodward said. "If he's a surgeon all the way out in Scranton, though, how did the case get to you? Is he someone you know well?"

Schwartz frowned at the questions, which caused Woodward to inwardly curse himself for having listened to Dwyer. After a pause, though, Schwartz answered. "I don't know him at all," he said. "In fact, I've never met the doc from Philly either, although I know his name. I found out about the cases because the families called WCZY after the first show that Henson did. She passed the names to me."

"I see," said Woodward again as Schwartz passed the papers across the desk. "How sure are you that these tumors are the same?"

Schwartz frowned at the comment. "I'm as sure as I can be. The kid in Philly was at CHOP and I talked to the pathologist. They're competent. The one from Scranton, well, I can't be that sure. On the other hand, the findings on the slides are not exactly subtle."

"That one in Scranton hasn't been reviewed by anyone else, has it?"

"Not that I know of," Schwartz said, "but even excluding that, you have two solid cases, and I wouldn't exclude it."

"No other potential causes for the tumors?"

"None that I know of. Again, the information from Scranton is sketchy, but certainly on the other two there was no evidence of hepatitis."

"No other chemical exposure?"

"Again, not that I know of."

"But you can't be sure, I take it."

"Look, Dr. Woodward," Schwartz snapped, "how sure is sure? These kids had no history of other exposures, their parents didn't work in any industry that might have led to an exposure and there is no evidence of anything else in the area where they lived. If you want me to swear that there are no toxic dumps that we don't know about and that the kids could not have gotten into something we don't know about, of course I can't do that. That is a lot like me asking you to swear that this can't be some unknown reaction to Aspergicin that you've never seen before. Or can you do that?"

Woodward had the abrupt sensation that he had been placed on the defensive. "No," he said, "I can't do that."

"Hnnh. I do take it that you haven't seen this in Aspergicin treated patients."

"That is correct."

"No liver tumors at all, no cirrhosis, nothing like that."

"No."

"How many patients did you test the drug in?"

"You mean during our trials?"

"Yes."

"About fifteen hundred."

"Fifteen hundred." Zeke repeated the number and turned it over in his mind. "If this was a really rare event, then, say one in a hundred thousand, you probably wouldn't have seen it."

"Yes, but wait," Woodward protested, "that was just during the trials. The drug's been on the market for a couple of years, which means many thousands of patients have been treated. We still have no such report."

"That doesn't necessarily prove anything," said Schwartz, holding up his hand. "Suppose a doc treats some druggie who's had hepatitis and the guy comes up with a liver tumor. He'll blame the hepatitis so he won't make anything out of it."

"You'd call it the hepatitis too," Woodward replied.

"True, but that's not the point. What I mean is, a tumor here and a tumor there, well that happens. You won't hear about it."

"We hear about more than you might think," Woodward said, thinking that there was no very good way for Schwartz to respond. "In any event, we're going to do a complete review of all the patients who got Aspergicin during the trials. That will give us a complete series of patients over several years. If there is 'a tumor here and a tumor there' we will see it."

"Except that it is still a relatively small series of patients and if this is a rare event you could still miss it entirely."

Woodward began to feel flustered. First Schwartz had said that he did not mean to imply that Aspergicin had caused the tumors, now he seemed to be arguing that it had. He groped for a good rebuttal.

"If it is such a rare event, Dr. Schwartz," he said rather testily, "how do we get three cases among boys whose only exposure, if you can call it that, was to a little leak in a creek?"

"I don't know." Zeke was becoming irritated as well. He had worked through the line of reasoning often enough on his own and knew that it ended in a question mark. "It would be very interesting to see the data from your survey when you collect it."

The statement sent up warning signals for Woodward. Jackson had been very specific on just that point. No data was to be given out. Even without that instruction, Woodward thought that he would be very unlikely to give his raw data to the opportunist who had caused the problem in the first place.

"Let me assure you, Dr. Schwartz," he said, "that when we have the data and analyzed it we will file it with the FDA and we will also publish it."

Woodward might have sounded a trifle pompous as he said it. Schwartz raised on eyebrow.

"Are you an oncologist, Dr. Woodward?"

"No. I was trained in Cardiology. Why?"

"Because this is an oncological problem. I would think that you would want someone in the field to work on it. If you want to publish it, I would be willing to collaborate with you on it."

Zeke had intended the offer as an olive branch. Unfortunately, Woodward had his own preconceived notions of Schwartz's motivations.

"Dr. Schwartz, this is an issue of patient safety. Meldrum will do whatever is necessary to ensure that physicians have the necessary information to take care of their patients. This is not a vehicle for generating publications."

Woodward should have stopped after his second sentence. He knew it and he regretted that last sentence as soon as he had said it. It just seemed to pop out of its own volition.

Zeke exploded. "The purpose of a doctor is to take care of sick patients. Period. Publications be damned. Of course, I don't know what you would know about that since all you seem to do is shuffle paper and spout the company line just like an old time apparatchik. I would like to know just what it is that you think you contribute to taking care of people."

Woodward was not supposed to start an argument with Schwartz. He knew that just the way he knew that he should not have made the crack about publications. Schwartz's angry remarks, however, cut too deeply to ignore.

"I have a good deal more to do with it than you think," Woodward said. "Anything new in medicine comes from us in the industry, not from you. Oh sure, you may have a great idea, but we are the ones who make it practical for people to use. The only tools you have are the ones we give you."

"Oh really? I buy tools from an idiot at Sears. He only thinks he knows how to use them."

They glared at each other across Schwartz's desk. Although neither one had raised his voice, the feeling in each one's tone was clearly audible. Suddenly, in the tense silence, Woodward realized the degree to which he had lost control of the situation. It was almost as though someone else, not him, had been making those statements. The feeling made his hands go cold and his stomach cramp. He had visions of Schwartz complaining that Meldrum was trying to belittle him or put him down, although Woodward tried to tell himself that the odds of that happening were almost nil. It was, however, definitely time to end the conversation, before something worse happened.

"Dr. Schwartz, I don't see any point in continuing this. I have the information I need and I do thank you for that. I'll be glad to send you a reprint when the study is published, but I am not going to release any unpublished data. There is simply no possibility of that." He gathered the papers together and put them in his briefcase. "Now, could you direct me to the bathroom?"

"Sure," said Zeke. "There's one down the hall on the left as you come out of the office. It's marked 'Gentlemen,' but it's okay if you use it."

SCHEUERMANN'S RUN, NEW JERSEY _____

Although it was, perhaps, the last thing Woodward would have wanted, the first person he saw the day following his visit to Zeke Schwartz proved to be Patrick Dwyer. Woodward had figured that Dwyer would look for him and he had planned to avoid him. Knowing that Dwyer always came to work early, Woodward had arrived a few minutes late. That way there was no chance of Dwyer cornering him in a nearly empty building and every chance that Dwyer would be caught up in a meeting. What Woodward wanted was an opportunity to speak with Jackson. That way, he would have a chance to paint Schwartz as a truculent opportunist, just in case Schwartz was sufficiently angered by their argument to cause further trouble. It would also let Jackson decide what, if anything, should be done next. Unfortunately, it was Jackson who was tied up in an early meeting, while Dwyer had apparently been waiting for Woodward's arrival. Woodward barely had time to discover that Jackson was unavailable before Dwyer stuck his head into the office doorway.

"Hi Tom, are you busy or do you have a moment?"

"Sure, come on in," Woodward said, while wondering what would happen if he told Dwyer to get lost. Nothing would happen immediately, he was certain of that, and Dwyer probably would leave with the same nonchalant air he had on arrival. Unfortunately, Woodward thought it likely that something unpleasant would happen in the future.

Dwyer closed the door and settled into a chair before continuing. "I was just wondering how it went with Dr. Schwartz yesterday," he said.

The question, like Dwyer's appearance, was no surprise. With a little sigh, Woodward accepted the inevitable.

"It went about as well as could be expected," he said. "This Dr. Schwartz turns out to be very difficult to deal with."

The only change in Dwyer's expression was a raising of his eyebrows. "Did he cooperate though? Did he give you the information that you needed?"

"Yes. Eventually."

"And the cases?"

"The one at the medical center is well documented, but we figured that anyway. Of the other two, one came from Philadelphia and that one seems to be fairly well documented also. I'd say the diagnosis is definite. The last one, though, was done in a community hospital. There really isn't much supporting data."

"So there are only two real cases. Not three."

"Well, the third one may be real."

"But you don't know for sure."

"No."

"Then there are two real ones. Did Schwartz say how he got onto these cases?"

"Through the radio station."

"Acey Henson again." Dwyer said it almost dreamily. "How interesting. It really does make you wonder what is going on, doesn't it?"

"How so?"

"Oh, come on, Tom. She has the info on the leak *and* she is the one who provides Schwartz with the cases. Probably would be worth looking into Schwartz too, from what you just told me. You have to wonder if he really knows what is going on. Do you think he would keep at it if he did?"

Woodward almost lost the thread of the conversation before he realized that Dwyer was back to his theory of conspiracy orchestrated by a competitor. He remembered Schwartz's comments about industry and had to grin in spite of himself.

"From what I saw of Dr. Schwartz, I can't see him cooperating with any company on anything. I doubt he'd take kindly to being used."

"Interesting."

"What are you planning on doing?" Woodward demanded, suddenly anxious.

"Doing?" Dwyer asked, his eyebrows going up again. Then he gave Woodward a beatific smile. "The only thing I'm going to do is advise our reps to avoid Dr. Schwartz. After all, all I do is sell drugs." He paused for a moment. "You know, I think I'd appreciate it if you didn't mention this conversation to Mr. Jackson. You probably remember that he asked me to stay out of this investigation."

Chapter 20

WOODWARD ALWAYS hated going to Washington for meetings with the FDA. National Airport was claustrophobic and the traffic afterward was a nightmare. At times, it took as long to drive from the airport to the FDA building on Parklawn as it did to fly to Washington in the first place. On this particular day, in spite of the importance of the trip, Woodward's mind was elsewhere and the protracted journey simply gave his mind more time to run in distracted circles. Woodward had a habit, one which might have been thought ridiculous had he ever mentioned it to anyone. He routinely kept count of the number of condoms in the medicine cabinet in his house. This morning, there had been one fewer than the last time he had checked. He knew that he and Helen had not used one in that interval, which raised a series of uncomfortable thoughts in his head. Could Helen be cheating on him? It seemed impossible, but he was certain that he would not have been the first person to feel that way. He could ask her, of course, but that would precipitate a row and he would have to tell her how he had gotten the idea in the first place. He had no stomach for that kind of scene. In any case, it might not have been Helen. Andrea had been tending to stay out late and she was the right age for such things to happen. He had not confronted her either. After all, confronting her would be unlikely to stop her from having sex, if that was what was happening, and if she was going to do it he supposed it was better that she was taking a condom. Anyway, he thought, he might have misremembered the count. If that were true, he was best off keeping his mouth shut, as he had done. On the other hand, maybe he should have exploded. Those thoughts effectively kept him from thinking about the meeting.

Part of him was grateful for the distraction because the FDA meetings were something Woodward preferred to do without. Jackson was always there and Jackson monitored the flow of conversation with the fervor of a commissar. Woe betide the unwary Meldrum physician, or other Meldrum representative, whose inadvertent comment opened up a new line of FDA questioning and delayed the progress of a Meldrum drug. Woodward's stomach would tie itself into a knot from the moment the blocky Parklawn tower came into view and would not relax until they were on the plane leaving National Airport and Jackson had indicated that he was satisfied. Yes, the routine meetings were bad enough. This meeting was far worse because the fate of Aspergicin was so clearly at stake. A mistake in this meeting could have devastating results.

All of the dreadful possibilities left Woodward feeling grateful that it would be Dr. Phillips who made the presentation at the meeting. Normally, Woodward would have felt slighted that he was not permitted to present Meldrum's position. This time it was okay. It would not be Woodward's fault if the presentation was botched. He had even gone so far as to suggest to Jackson that his, Woodward's, presence was not really necessary. Unfortunately, Jackson had not agreed with that argument: Woodward knew the available clinical data better than anyone else. If there was a question Phillips could not answer, he would look to Woodward for help. Otherwise, of course, Woodward was to keep his mouth shut. That suited Woodward quite well on a day where he was mostly thinking that he should have said *something* before he left home.

They arrived at the Parklawn building twenty minutes early, the traffic having been unusually forgiving. The building was impressive, a large tower of offices, the lobby done in marble and metal, a suitable edifice for the body that regulated pharmaceuticals in the richest country on earth. It usually reminded Woodward of a court building. A crack Jackson had made when they were boarding the plane about keeping out of the dungeons under Parklawn rose unbidden in his mind. He swallowed hard and tried to get rid of the image the comment created.

Once they were upstairs the grandeur began to wear thin. Most of the furnishings looked old and often more appropriate to a public high school than a seat of government. One of the bulletin boards in the hallway had seen so much use that there seemed to be more holes than cork, even though the dates on some of the notices were two years old. The hall itself was in need of a fresh coat of paint.

They found the assigned conference room without difficulty. It was a large room with windows looking out into the gray and rainy Washington day. In the middle of the room four large, rectangular, metal tables, the kind with the fake wood top, had been pushed together to form a large conference table. Chairs were set all around the table and more chairs ringed the perimeter of the room.

Jackson surveyed the scene with distaste. "We were told this was going to be a small meeting," he said. The unhappiness in his voice was evident.

"It still could be," Woodward suggested. "Maybe this room was set up for something else."

"Fat chance," said Jackson. He walked around the table to the side under the windows and put his briefcase on the table in front of one of the chairs there. "Damned if I'll sit with my back to a door here. Normally, I'd want to intersperse us with the Agency people, but looking at this, I'd rather we all sit together."

They were there for perhaps five minutes when a man opened the door and looked in. He had sandy hair, long enough to fall into his eyes when he leaned forward, and a moustache of the same color that drooped over his upper lip. His white shirt was open at the collar.

"Ah!" he said, spotting the trio at the far side of the room. "You're from Meldrum?"

"Yes. I'm Russell Jackson."

"Good! Glad to meet you. I'm Dave Ingraham," he said and walked around the table to shake Jackson's hand.

Jackson introduced Woodward and Phillips. Then he said, "I thought this was going to be a small meeting to get an agreement on how we are going to proceed."

Ingraham grimaced. "That was the original idea. Unfortunately, you know, you've created quite a fuss here. Aspergicin was a 1-A drug that got fast-tracked and, as you know, there was a lot of discussion about the number of patients required for the trials and the length of follow-up that would be needed. Now, well," he gave a wry grin, "a lot of people want to be involved."

"Great," said Jackson.

"Hey," Ingraham said, "just doing our duty, protecting the public. Right?" The grin broadened a bit.

"Of course," Jackson murmured.

"Well, I just wanted to check and make sure you were here." Ingraham looked at his watch. "We've got some other meetings running late this morning, but I imagine people will be here in about ten minutes."

After Ingraham left, Woodward muttered, "Hypocritical bastard."

"Maybe," Jackson said. "Maybe not. Some of them believe it. Others, well, the way to become a star at the FDA is to find something that prompts a full audit and if you find something that leads to an actual prosecution, then you're a real hero."

"That's very comforting," Woodward said. "Everybody is looking to score the same way they did with thalidomide."

"Not exactly," Jackson said.

In fact, the FDA was much older than thalidomide. It had been formed shortly after the turn of the century, although at that time its authority was limited to making sure products were accurately labeled. It took a disaster in the thirties to change that. It happened when the makers of one of the first antibiotics, sulfanilamide, were searching for a way to make the drug into an elixir so that it would be easier to take. It was a difficult problem because the drug stubbornly refused to dissolve in most liquids that were used for such purposes. Finally, a chemist at the company found a solvent that solved the problem. The company bottled the sulfanilamide elixir and distributed it. Unfortunately, the miracle solvent was ethylene glycol, a major component of anti-freeze and, as it turned out, a deadly poison. Hundreds of people were dead before all of the elixir was recovered. That led to the Food, Drug and Cosmetic Act of 1938, which required products to be tested for safety before they were marketed. Thalidomide had come much later, a disaster that did not happen in the United States because the marketing application was delayed so long at the FDA that the reports of birth defects in Europe surfaced before approval was granted in the United States. That episode, the amendments to the Act, and the additional regulations it spawned led to an atmosphere in which the safe decision was always to wait for more data, or to just say no. This tendency was reinforced by repeated attacks on the FDA's competence every time a problem was found with a marketed drug. That led, just as inevitably, to the screams of special interest groups that more people were dying from the lack of drugs, often available in Europe, than had ever been harmed by defective drugs on the market. In response, particularly after the AIDS epidemic hit, there had been some loosening of the requirements for approval. Aspergicin had been one of the beneficiaries of these changes. The people at the FDA were not going to be very happy if a drug that they had helped to move quickly through the system caused them to look as though they had not been sufficiently vigilant.

The Meldrum group's privacy did not last long. Soon Ingraham was back, this time at the head of a small group of people. They were followed by a trickle of additional people and the trickle quickly turned into a stream, until it was clear that the large number of chairs placed around the room was insufficient. It was going to be standing room only.

"Jesus," Jackson muttered under his breath, "everybody wants to see a public hanging."

Most of the people who crowded into the room were just that, spectators, who had found some pretext for watching. They neither introduced themselves nor did Ingraham introduce them to the Meldrum trio. Ingraham did introduce a number of people who would participate in the meeting. Even that abbreviated list was long enough that Woodward was glad to see Jackson writing down their names and titles. He doubted that he would remember all of them when the meeting was over. There was Dr. Desai, of course, whom Woodward remembered from the telephone conversation. He was a short, somewhat plump man with light brown skin and jet black hair. There was Dr. Elizabeth Jessup, a gaunt woman who was Director of the Division. They were followed by Phil Greenwood and Bill Jones, who were introduced as physicians from the Center for Disease Control. They were an oddly matched pair, Greenwood being fat, blond, and seemingly not out of his twenties, while Jones was a tall black man with salt-and-pepper hair. Then there was Michael Turner from the FDA's Epidemiology group and beyond him a chemist and a pharmacologist and a few others whom Woodward forgot immediately after they were introduced.

Finally, everyone was seated, at least those who could be seated, and the meeting began. Ingraham opened it by thanking Woodward, Phillips, and Jackson for coming (as if they had a choice), and then asked Phillips to proceed with his presentation. Phillips began with a brief recapitulation of the events, making it clear that no one at Meldrum had any reason to suspect the existence of any of the cases prior to Acey Henson's broadcast. He then told of Woodward's investigation of the reports, noting that only two of the cases could be considered adequately documented. He offered to review what they considered as adequate documentation, and it looked as though Greenwood and Jones wanted to hear it, but Turner waved it off.

"I think we can accept that there are two cases," he said. "You will submit the documentation later?"

"With our report," Phillips said.

Woodward let out a small sigh of relief. Internally, he was almost certain that Schwartz had been correct in his insistence that the third case was genuine, but the documentation was not there and that mattered with the FDA. It was always easier to argue that two cases were just unfortunate coincidence than three cases, regardless of the facts. Looking at the faces of Greenwood and Jones, he felt that the point was not lost on them.

Meanwhile, Phillips proceeded to review the data from Meldrum's studies and then their estimates of the number of people treated with Aspergicin since its approval. Through it all, he returned to one principal point. There had never been a case of liver cancer reported in an Aspergicin treated patient.

Desai spoke up as Phillips concluded. "I believe we discussed this on the telephone. Your patients were all treated and followed for only a relatively short period of time. These children may well have had prolonged multiple exposures that began several years ago."

"We understand that," said Phillips. "That is one reason we have proposed to retrospectively survey our study patients. Although the duration of treatment, that is if you will, the exposure, was relatively short, they received higher doses, systemically I might add, than these children could possibly have been exposed to."

Someone, Woodward thought it was the person introduced as the pharmacologist, spoke up from across the room. "I would assume," he said, "that someone has checked to see if this stuff is absorbed across the skin?"

"Ah, yes. It is," Phillips said. "At one time we had actually planned a topical formulation, but we never did any studies with it."

Across the table from Phillips, Greenwood looked as though he was being restrained by an invisible hand while Phillips was speaking. As soon as Phillips finished, he burst out with, "Dr. Phillips, was there any evidence of liver damage at all, of any kind, in your patients?"

"What sort of liver damage?"

"Well, specifically, I was thinking of cirrhosis, which can be a precursor to this cancer, or even just abnormal liver function tests."

Phillips looked over to Woodward, who responded to his cue. "There were no cases of cirrhosis that I am aware of, although I would want to check our records to be sure. As for the liver function tests, yes, about three-tenths of a percent of the patients had abnormal values that came back to normal after treatment. That's in our labeling."

"But you haven't followed these patients any further, have you?"

"We will in our survey."

Greenwood was shaking his head. "But you are not proposing to do any investigation. All you are going to do is check on their status. That will only find patients who have progressed to the point of being obviously sick. I don't think you can tell me that your drug is not liver toxic and I don't see that you are going to find out."

"What are you suggesting?" Phillips asked.

"I would think that if you talked to your investigators, just two or three, they could take a series of consecutive patients who either had Aspergicin two to three years ago or who were just treated, and do liver biopsies on them. That would tell us if there is liver toxicity, particularly pre-cancerous, with this drug."

Phillips should have been the one to respond to the CDC physician. That was how Jackson had planned the strategy for the meeting. Unfortunately, the proposal was so ludicrous that Phillips opened his mouth but nothing came out. It was as though he was stuck.

It gave Woodward time to decide that something needed to be said and then the opportunity to burst out with it. "You can't be serious!" he shouted.

"Why not?" asked Greenwood. "You really don't know if there are changes in the livers of your patients."

"Dammit, there is no evidence of liver damage! A liver biopsy is an invasive procedure. It's not something you have in the morning before you go to the office."

Greenwood slapped his palm against the tabletop. "Thank you Dr.

Woodward," he said sarcastically, "I went to four years of medical school, too. For all I know, you are setting up your patients to die of liver cancer five years from now."

Woodward's eyes goggled and an angry reply was rising in his throat when Jackson kicked him sharply across the shins. Instead of shouting back at Greenwood, he gave a loud cough. At the last moment, he realized where he was and did not reach for the leg. The kick had been cleverly delivered; no visible movement of Jackson's upper body gave away what had occurred.

Woodward gave Jackson a look of pure anger. Leaning close, he hissed in Jackson's ear, "Dammit, this is nuts! He can't ask us to just stick a group of people in the liver. Not on this data."

Jackson, without changing expression, turned to reply, whispering behind his hand. "I know that, Tom. So does Jessup. Just let him talk. If we take it to our investigators, they won't do it, and even if they would, the Institutional Review Boards won't approve it. So let him talk. We have enough enemies in this room without starting a personal vendetta."

It might have ended there, an angry outburst and nothing more, but Greenwood was not content to stop. He used the opportunity afforded by Jackson squelching Woodward to turn his attention back to Phillips. He wagged his finger at Phillips to embellish his comments.

"I do not find your data reassuring at all, Doctor. All you can show me is that two children who had long-term exposure to low amounts of Aspergicin have developed liver cancer. The fact that you give, in comparison, huge doses to patients does not reassure me because you really don't know that it is safe. All you know is that for the short period you have followed patients there are no overt signs of trouble. I said it to Dr. Woodward and I will say it again. You may be killing people with that drug and you can't tell me that you know different."

That was too much for Phillips who shot to his feet, face flushed red. "That is a very serious accusation you are making *Doctor* Greenwood," he shouted. "Serious and totally wrong."

Phillips was practically shaking with his anger. Fortunately, the arrangement of the tables put Greenwood two table widths away from Phillips and therefore out of reach. Regardless, Jackson had a grip on Phillips's coattail as though he wanted to ensure that Phillips did not launch himself across the table at Greenwood's throat. That seemed important because Greenwood was also rising out of his chair, closing the distance between them, his index finger still pointed at Phillips's nose.

"All right! We can do without the theatrics. Now sit *down,* gentlemen." The flat, hard voice silenced the commotion that was building in the room.

Phillips and Greenwood both dropped back into their seats. Woodward looked around and saw that the source of the voice was Elizabeth Jessup.

Jessup continued talking in a voice that brooked no interruption. "There are some important issues here and I do not want to lose sight of them. Now, there were a small percentage of patients who had altered liver function studies. Your report also noted two patients who had very marked elevations of liver enzymes although I am inclined to agree that the data do not favor an association with the drug. Nevertheless, there is a great deal of data that we do not have and I do not find it useful to sit here speculating about what the data we do not have might show if we had it. We need to decide what data can reasonably be obtained and how best to obtain it."

Woodward was impressed by the ease with which Jessup took over the meeting when it threatened to get out of hand. Then, he noticed something else. Jessup had made a point of saying, at the beginning of the meeting, that she had not had a chance to read Woodward's summary. That was the reason she used for having Phillips recapitulate everything. Yet no one in the room had mentioned those two patients before. They were in the report, of course, Woodward could not have left them out. They were not prominently discussed in the report, however, because Woodward had been unable to definitively account for the findings. Jessup had read the report, then, and quite carefully, too. Why had she concealed it? Was she looking for an inconsistency, a contradiction that would tell her that Meldrum's reports could not be relied upon? Woodward wondered about that. It certainly told him something about Jessup, but what did she want? There were three types of people who served in the agency, given that the FDA was chronically strapped for funds and unable to pay competitive salaries. The large majority were mediocrities, content to be civil service bureaucrats. The capable minority was divided into two groups. There were those who enjoyed the power of their position. For them, the ability to thwart even large multinational companies was compensation enough for the low pay. The last and smallest group were truly dedicated to the job. They believed in the mission of the agency and in what they were doing. The first two groups were easy to deal with. It was clear what they wanted and usually clear how to give it to them. It was the last group that posed the hardest problems. They wanted to do what was right and sometimes it was difficult to figure out just what that was. What was Jessup after?

While Woodward was pondering Jessup's motivations, Phillips had recovered his composure. "I think a reviewer would conclude that there was no potential benefit to a patient for submitting to a liver biopsy that would offset the risk of the procedure. Now, we can take this proposal to our investigators, but don't be surprised if that is the answer we get back."

Gee, that was a good idea, he was saying to Greenwood. Probably would have told us what we want. Just damn unfortunate we cannot do it. Not our fault, you understand, it is the docs and the review boards that will not buy it. It was soothing. It was reasonable. It was nauseating.

Greenwood eventually subsided, although in the end it took a comment by Jessup to the effect that Phillips's points were well taken to quiet him completely. Greenwood might have shut up, but the look in his eyes remained unfriendly. Woodward wished he could have overheard the comments Greenwood periodically whispered into the ear of Dr. Bill Jones. Clearly, Meldrum Products did not have a friend at the CDC. Still, as Woodward thought about the situation, he could not see that it mattered a great deal. Turner, the FDA's epidemiologist, seemed to make a point of taking positions opposed to the pair from the CDC. That tended to put him in agreement with Phillips. It was the FDA's position that Woodward really worried about. They were the ones with the power to make his life miserable. If the FDA epidemiologist was happy with what Phillips was saying then, as far as Woodward was concerned, the CDC could scream all they wanted. There was nothing they could do. As for Turner, his only real concern seemed to be that any cases of liver disease Meldrum found be reported on the proper forms. If that was all it took to keep him happy, Woodward would be glad to oblige.

The meeting soon settled down to a discussion of the data that Woodward would collect and the period of time that would be allotted to complete the project. The final result, perhaps not surprisingly, was quite similar to the proposal Jackson had given Ingraham over the telephone. When the meeting ended, Woodward noticed that Jessup lingered, just long enough that she walked out the door with him and Jackson. In the conference room, Woodward had marked her as a tall woman, who would have been good-looking had she not been so thin. Up close, he could see the dark hollows under her eyes. The lines of fatigue on her face were only partially hidden by makeup.

"Hi, Russ," she said. Her voice held none of the iron Woodward had heard during the meeting. It just sounded tired.

"Good to see you again, Elizabeth," Jackson answered. "The circumstances could be better, I suppose. How are you doing?"

The corners of her mouth twitched upward. "About the same. Head count is not enough and we can't even fill that. Budget's down again, but the workload is up. You figure it. You're not helping matters any."

"It wasn't exactly our idea."

"I know."

Jackson seemed to notice for the first time that Woodward was standing next to him. "By the way, Elizabeth, this is Tom Woodward. He'll be handling the studies we agreed on."

They shook hands, which Woodward expected to be perfunctory, but was not. Jessup turned back to Jackson and there was not even the hint of a smile on her face.

"Russ," she said, "I need that retrospective by October. I know we didn't set a date in there, but that's when I need it."

Jackson looked at Woodward, an eyebrow raised.

"We can certainly try," Woodward said. "I mean, I won't know for sure how possible it is until we start checking the sites."

Jessup took a quick look over her shoulder at the thinning group of people. "Let me be blunt," she said. Her voice had gone cold and hard again and her face matched it. "We need to have your report by October. Not 'maybe by October.' Not, 'as soon as we can.' By October."

"Why the urgency?" Jackson's voice was as mild and as soft as he could make it.

"Senator Barcellini is going to hold hearings in October. You don't need to be a psychic to know that Aspergicin is going to be high on his agenda. If I have your report by then and if it shows what we both expect it to show, then I think we're okay. Lord knows, there are enough other things for him to go after. But, if he can get his teeth into this, I don't know where it will go. It's got all the ingredients—environmental problems, dying kids—for a real *cause célèbre*. Of course, I shouldn't need to tell you that. Or have you given up listening to the radio?"

Jackson winced. "I never listen to the talk shows. They never have anything good on."

Jessup smiled at him. "No, I suppose they don't." With that, she turned and walked off down the hall, leaving them standing by the conference room.

Jackson was not quite ready to go, however. He touched Woodward's arm and motioned him down the hall, away from where any other people were standing.

"What you did in there almost cost us a great deal. You can't do that sort of thing, Tom." His voice was low and inaudible three feet away, but harsh nonetheless. "That's not acceptable behavior and you have to know it."

The rebuke stung Woodward. "You mean I'm supposed to sit there and just listen to that bullshit?"

"Yes."

"Oh, for Chrissakes, Russ! I mean, can you believe that bit about medical school? Maybe he has gone to med school but I doubt he's ever taken care of a patient."

"Probably not, but that's not the point. You can't let your medical sensibilities be offended."

"But the man is an idiot."

"Not everybody in there was, however. Jessup for one is not. You noticed, didn't you, how it ended? The thing is, if you kick and scream enough, someone is going to figure that you really do have something to hide, or, even worse, you'll get them into an us-versus-them pissing match, which almost happened. Then, we'll never get anywhere. As it is, well, you saw how the FDA epidemiologist reacted."

"You mean Turner?"

"Right. All that is happening is that the CDC is looking to score points off the FDA by picking up an association first, one the FDA missed. Turner's not going to be eager to let that happen. He would rather play it our way, at least as long as the data looks good. And you heard what Jessup said. It's not always about medicine down here? Understand?"

Woodward had plenty of time on the return trip to contemplate what Jackson had said. It gave him a whole new perspective on what it meant to deal with the government. It also gave him plenty of time to wish that he had chosen to make his stand over the Talbot's bill and not over Greenwood's stupid proposal.

Chapter 21

TRENTON, NEW JERSEY _____

"Hello, Acey?"

"Yes, hello Dan. You're on the air. My little monitor here says you're calling from Valley Forge. Is that true?"

"Absolutely true, Acey."

"Valley Forge, huh? Now that, as they used to say, is far out. Almost as far out as my orbit. I didn't think our signal went that far."

There was an audible chuckle from Dan. "It doesn't always, Acey. Some nights it comes through fine, sometimes not at all. Usually it's there, but a little fuzzy."

"Sounds like me. What's on your mind, Dan?"

"Well, first I just wanted to say that I really like your show, Acey. I started listening to you when I lived in New Jersey and when I moved out here a year ago I kept listening."

"Thank you, Dan, it's great to have loyal fans. Don't move any further, though, I don't want to lose audience share."

"*I'm not planning on it. What I really wanted to talk about though was those kids with cancer. I mean, they're talking about it on the shows here, too, but I heard that you, like they say, broke it first. I wanted to know if you really did and, I figured, if it was, you would be the person to talk to.*"

"*Okay, Dan, one question at a time. The answer to the first part is yes. We did break it first here on WCZY. Whether that makes me the expert is another question. What do you want to know?*"

"*I wanted to know if you thought that drug did it. I mean they give that stuff to people, don't they?*"

"*They sure do, Dan. Now, whether that's what caused this mess I don't know, but the facts are that Meldrum had a leak where it wasn't supposed to and right now they won't say anything to anybody. All of which is about as effective as a sixth grader who's leaked in his pants in class and thinks that if he keeps his mouth shut nobody will notice.*"

"*I like that way of putting it, Acey.*"

"*Thought you would. Now you tell me, what do you think ought to be done?*"

"*For starters, I think those families ought to sue the pants off Meldrum.*"

"*I believe there are going to be some lawsuits, although I don't think any have actually been filed yet.*"

"*Well, I hope they do. You know, that's about the only way you can really get these companies' attention. Otherwise, they just ignore you. One of the talk show hosts here has been saying that people ought to get together and boycott Meldrum's stuff until they close that plant and take the drug off the market.*"

"*What do you think? Do you agree with that?*"

"*I think so.*"

"*Even though nobody's really sure yet? The doctors I've talked to tell me that it's an important drug to have.*"

"*So they say now. I mean, would you want your dad to get it?*"

This time the chuckle came from Acey. "*I assume you haven't met my old man because I could take that in two very different ways.*"

Dan's laugh joined hers. "*Okay, but you know what I meant.*"

"*Yeah, and the answer is I don't know.*"

"*Well, can we vote on it? That's something you do that I really like and they don't do it around here.*"

"*Sounds reasonable to me. Give us a sec to set it up here. Dan, thank you for calling, I got to move along here. This is Acey Henson on WCZY, 990 AM asking you to call 1-900-GO-WCZY 1 if you would give Aspergicin to a loved one and 1-900-GO-WCZY 2 if you wouldn't and let's see how Meldrum makes out. Each call is fifty cents.*"

From the results, George McGovern had more support in 1972.

THE CHILDRENS' Hospital had its own Emergency Room. It was a block from the Medical Center's main Emergency Room and was very much like a kid brother; it had all the same features only smaller. In addition to having fewer rooms, it had fewer doctors and nurses, children as a rule being neither as sick as adults nor as likely to wreak havoc on their own bodies, which was not to imply that the Emergency Room was not busy. The flow of traffic, however, was not constant. It moved in time to a set of specific rhythms. Eleven o'clock on a Sunday evening meant that it was beginning to quiet down. Traffic on a summer Sunday was usually fairly steady until then, unlike the winter when a flood tide of patients would appear a magic thirty minutes after the last football game ended when whatever was ailing Junior suddenly became an emergency.

This particular eleven o'clock meant to Jolanta Marienkiewicz that it was almost time to leave. Schedules for the physicians in the Emergency Room were arranged so that the coverage would be greatest at those predictable times of peak flow. After midnight on Sunday, one person was sufficient. Jola checked her watch. Fifty-eight minutes to go. She looked over at the greaseboard by the main desk, saw no room numbers under the "Waiting" column and breathed a sigh of relief. Whenever a patient was brought back to be seen, the charge nurse would write the room number in that column. The first physician free was supposed to see that patient. No new numbers meant no new patients to see, at least not right then. If she was lucky, it would stay that way for another fifty-six minutes. She could, if she wanted, stroll out front to the waiting room and see if anyone was there, but she did not have that much energy. She slid, or slumped, into a chair at the large desk shared by the doctors and nurses. It was, she thought, the first time she had sat down in three or four hours.

Jola flipped through the pages on her clipboard that listed her ongoing work. There was not too much left. There was the six-year-old with asthma in room five, who she could tell from experience was not going to be able to go home. Unfortunately, she also knew from experience that if she admitted him right now, the people on the floor would moan and groan that she had not tried hard enough to keep him out of the hospital. So, she would listen to his chest again in ten minutes and he would still be tight and wheezy so she would give him one more hit of medication and wait another fifteen minutes. That one more hit would bring him to the magic number of doses that was considered "trying hard enough" so that, when he was still tight and wheezy afterward and she sent him upstairs, the floor intern would be unable to bitch. She had learned that lesson often enough. The thought occurred to her that if she stalled just a bit more, she would be able to leave and then it would be the night doc who would have to call upstairs with the admission. The family had already been in the Emergency Room the whole evening, what difference would another twenty minutes make? Unfortunately, Tony C. was the night doc and Jola knew perfectly well that he would look at the kid and send him home. That would not make the child any less tight and wheezy, however. Without a doubt the boy would bounce right back to the Emergency Room in the morning and have to be admitted then. The only difference was that Tony C. would not have to make the call upstairs. Tony was quite popular with the house staff for keeping their nights as quiet as possible. Jola shook her head. She would play the game with the meds because she was tired of being called a softie and a sieve, but that was as far as she would go. It would make as much sense to the family as anything else they had endured. The only other sheet left on her clipboard held no problems: an infant with a cold and a little dehydration who had drunk the electrolyte solution greedily and now needed only to urinate in order to convince everyone that he was ready to go home.

Fifty minutes to go. With just a little luck she would go home on time. It was like an electric shock then, when she looked up and saw another number on the board. She did not recall seeing the charge nurse walk back with anyone, but the number was there regardless, a big purple "3U."

A confusing mix of feelings kept her in her seat. She *did* need to check on the asthmatic. If she got up and walked around to the other side of the horseshoe of rooms she could simply have never seen the number. On the other hand, the "U" after the number meant urgent. She looked around for the other house officers. Tony C. was nowhere to be seen. He might be with a patient, but Jola doubted it. Tony had a talent for being elsewhere. The Senior Resident, Eric Rosenbloom, was sitting with a sandwich in the nook behind the main desk that served as a kitchen. He was a hatchet-faced toothpick with, it seemed, enough gold at neck and wrists to drown him in a swimming pool. She could ask Rosenbloom; he had to stay all night anyway. Any request to Rosenbloom, however, was invariably followed by a whining inquisition into why he should be the one to do it. She remembered Zeke Schwartz turning on him once during rounds and calling him a marvelous excuse for anti-Semitism. Jola wished she could use a line like that. Zeke was obviously Jewish, even if Jola did not think of him that way, and he was also an Attending Physician so he could make comments like that. Jola was neither. She found it easier to avoid Rosenbloom. She ought to see the kid in room three.

Still she hesitated. She had seen more "U's" than anyone else during the course of the evening. It was not fair. Then she shrugged and got up. Nothing was fair. A line from an old television game show ran through her head. "What have we got for you, Jolanta Marienkiewicz, behind door number three?" She pulled the sheet from the bracket by the door. It was Jodie Schmidt.

It was a good thing she had the sheet with Jodie's name on it because otherwise she never would have recognized the child in the room. Jodie was wearing her wig, which she never did in the hospital, and the cap of dark curls that framed her face made her look like a different person entirely.

Jodie had no such problems. "Hey, it's Dr. Kay Vitch!" she said and held her hand up for a high five.

That introduction was enough for Jola to decide that there was no immediate problem. The whole story, when she asked for it, was brief. Jodie felt fine; her parents thought she was acting fine. However, she had felt warm at home and her temperature was 101° F. The Schmidts had not forgotten. They simply put her in the car and drove to the hospital.

"Do I have to stay, Kay Vitch?"

"Probably." Jola said it reluctantly. She knew when Jodie had last been treated and that made it likely there would be very few white cells in the blood count she was sending off. It did not matter that Jodie felt fine or looked fine for that matter. Schwartz was very strict about hospitalizing his kids when they had fever and low white counts. Having seen what had happened to Jodie at the beginning of the summer, Jola had little trouble accepting the doctrine. However, it meant she would have to call upstairs and endure the griping of the floor doc who would complain that the kid looked perfectly healthy and did not need to be in the hospital. She would also have to endure another round of "that Polack sieve will admit anything," and never mind that Zeke Schwartz would castrate the house officer who sent Jodie home with a fever and no white cells.

Jodie was not happy either. "Are you sure I have to stay?"

"Well, we can wait for your counts to come back from the lab, but I'd say the odds are pretty high. What's wrong, sport? It's not like this is anything new."

"I know that. But, my mom is going over to see Mrs. Inman tomorrow and Jerry promised he'd show me this place he's got."

"I don't get it. You can see this place the next time she goes." Mrs. Schmidt and Ellen Inman were both active in a local support group. They were an unlikely looking team but they had become friends the night of Acey Henson's show and had worked together ever since.

"I don't know. Jerry said he'd show me tomorrow. He didn't say anything about another time."

"Well, what's so special about this place?"

"That's a secret," Jodie said. "I can't tell."

"Oh." Jola looked up to see Mr. Schmidt grinning at the earnestness of the conversation between his daughter and the doctor. She grinned back and said she would return when she had the lab report.

She had taken only two steps outside the room when one of the nurses appeared around the far corner of the corridor. "Jo!" she yelled, "we need you in the Trauma Room. Now!" The Emergency Room nurses had seen, at one time or another, almost everything there was to see. When they yelled, it behooved one to move.

The scene that greeted her in the Trauma Room as she ran through the door was Bedlam. The center of it, lying on a table under operating room lights, was a young black man, seventeen years give or take a couple. He had been stripped of his clothes and was covered with his blood, of which there was a great deal. The staff was arrayed around him, Tony C. pumping on his chest, Rosenbloom trying to start an IV, an anesthesiologist at the head giving oxygen and a bevy of nurses pulling out equipment and setting it up. What struck Jola the most was the din.

"Give him some albumin!" shouted the anesthesiologist.

"I need normal saline on this line," said Rosenbloom.

"Albumin," said the anesthesiologist.

"Dammit, the line's out," said Rosenbloom.

"Can you give him some epi and bicarb?" asked Tony to no one in particular.

"We need the EKG on," said Rosenbloom.

"Forget the EKG, I need that line," said the anesthesiologist.

"Goddammit! Which one of you is in charge and what do you want first?" screamed the charge nurse.

It was not obvious.

Tony looked up and saw Jola at the door. "Jo, nice of you to join us. Could you come up here and pump him a bit?"

She looked daggers at him, but it was a poor time to start an argument. Instead, she moved to take Tony's place at the bedside.

"What happened?" she asked as they changed places.

"Beaten and shot. God knows what else. A friend brought him in here instead of the main ER."

She stood there and pumped for all she was worth, hand heels jammed into the youth's sternum, while everyone swirled around her. Tony would order one drug, Rosenbloom something else and the surgeon, when he arrived, something else again. The charge nurse again asked for the person in charge, but she did not get an answer, only more orders. Jola could make no sense out of what was happening and she doubted the nurse could either. It was not the way she remembered Schwartz running a code. It struck her that none of them really knew what to do. That made her go cold with fear, but she could not think of what to do either. Instead, they just floundered along, the way a chicken will after its head has been chopped off, and the blood, staining the sheets and puddling on the floor, continued to drip. Finally, someone decided, or possibly a consensus developed, that their efforts were futile. The frantic motion stopped. Tony watched the EKG trace a flat line for a minute and then snapped it off.

"That's it," he said. "Show's over, folks."

Jola walked out of the room with a heart as heavy as her feet. She looked for Tony so she could sign out her patients, but he said that he had to finish up "this business." She could sign out if she wanted, but the patients would have to wait until he got around to them. It was late enough, and she was tired enough, that she was willing to ask Rosenbloom, but by the time she looked for him he had gone upstairs. In the end, she did the work herself. The asthmatic was admitted, with the floor protesting that if she had given him his last med when he *should* have had it, she *could* have sent him home. Of course, that was nothing compared to the reaction when the intern upstairs found he would have to admit what seemed to be a perfectly healthy Jodie at one-thirty in the morning.

LOS ANGELES, CALIFORNIA _____

The spreadsheet that Thigpen was staring at on the screen of his computer had the look of a corporate financial statement. It was not, however, a breakdown of a potential target company nor did it represent one of the companies Kuhnlein's group had acquired and still owned. In fact, it was not the picture of a company at all. It represented Thigpen's best estimates about the holdings of his older brother, William. It was mirrored by another spreadsheet that portrayed Thigpen's own holdings.

These were not files that Thigpen would ever store in the computer in his office. There were too many nosy individuals and some of them were very facile with computers. Thigpen kept the files on a disk that usually stayed in his apartment. He had brought it to work because he was nearing a decision point on Quad Industries and he hoped the numbers would give him some inspiration.

At the moment, all they were producing was a scowl on his face. His figures on William were about one month out of date. They were a bit unreliable to begin with since they were assembled from a mixture of things he knew, things that William's brokers and bankers should not have told him and guesses based on things William said. Being a month out of date added to the uncertainty. Despite these problems, the spreadsheet presented a detailed picture of William's property, stocks, bonds, and cash. The companion spreadsheet, which showed Thigpen's own holdings, was, of course, exact.

The two Thigpen boys had started out with identical inheritances. The sole difference was that William was two years older, which meant he received his trust fund two years before John Lawrence. That gave William two extra years to play with the money while John Lawrence was hobbled by the trust department of the bank. That had resulted, according to Thigpen's figures, in a significant deficit vis-à-vis William. In addition, William had those two extra years of working. Since William had become an investment banker, he earned good money and, since he had managed to keep his job when the boom ended, he still earned good money. Through all the years John Lawrence had tallied his money and his brother's money, William had remained on top. John Lawrence had closed the gap recently, thanks to his success with Kuhnlein, but William was still winning.

Now, however, that could change. If John Lawrence could close the Quad Industries deal, he would be an *owner*. He would own a real company, not just some Mom and Pop drugstore that anyone could aspire to own. That would even the score with William, he thought. For all William's money, he would still be a hired hand. Even better, if John Lawrence could actually manage to take over Quad Industries, not just bite off the radio stations, he would beat William and be an owner too. That was why he sat there looking at the spreadsheet comparison. It gave him inspiration.

He needed the inspiration. Under United States law, once someone owned more than five percent of a public company, he had to declare that fact and state what his intentions were toward the company. There was, of course, a grace period of ten days within which the filing with the Securities and Exchange Commission would have to be made, but ultimately, it would have to be done. Thigpen and his partnership had quietly built up a 4.9% stake in Quad Industries. That had taken a lot of money and there were limits as to how long Thigpen could tie it up in a stock that would not go up on its own. So, he had to do something. Should he go ahead and bid for the whole company before he had to declare his position? He did not need to do that. He could buy more stock, go over the limit and then either make his bid or try to force Quad Industries to restructure in some way that gave him the radio stations. So much depended on what Meldrum would do because of that damn block they held. Much also depended on whether he could convince the Wall Street pundits that his bid was "serious." If they said so, the speculators would rush to buy Quad Industries stock and they, in turn, would be happy to sell it to him. The pundits, though, would be trying to guess Meldrum's position too.

The agony was that once he went public there would be no turning back. Since he had been less than candid with Kuhnlein and his other partners about his motives, he was more nervous than usual. He had gone through the ritual with the spreadsheets every day for the past week to quiet the butterflies in his stomach.

"Which is all well and good," he said to his computer, "but it would probably be better if you did your homework."

His homework involved knowing all there was to know about what his target company was doing. This was not nearly as onerous as it sounded. Thigpen subscribed to a database that contained the contents of several major newspapers as well as all the financial publications and the wire service releases. The computer was programmed to scan for and store any information relating to a list of companies Thigpen typed in. He merely had to check the file and see what had accumulated. There was not much there, a smattering of news on companies Thigpen was only peripherally interested in at the moment. Those could wait. There was nothing on Quad Industries. There was, however, a news bulletin on Meldrum Products. Thigpen had put that company on his list because of its relationship to Quad Industries, so he read that bulletin before looking at any of the others.

The item had come from the Associated Press, which meant it was only a brief paragraph. Apparently, Meldrum had dumped some chemical into a river and now some kids in the area were turning up with a rare liver cancer. Tough break, he thought. The back of his mind wondered idly if it would be worth selling Meldrum stock short. He dismissed that thought: the Quad Industries project needed his full attention. It was almost by chance, then, in the instant before he erased the bulletin, that he noticed the call letters of the radio station credited with carrying the story. WCZY. Dear God, he thought, that is Howard's station. In the same instant, another thought shot through his head. That station is owned by Quad Industries!

Possibilities rapidly began to take shape in his head. He had met the current CEO of Meldrum Products in the past. There was a reasonable chance that he could get through on a telephone call, always assuming the man was not out of the country or something equally unfortunate. It was extremely unlikely that anyone at Meldrum Products would realize that WCZY had anything to do with Quad Industries, not with the way that company was organized, but the fact could be pointed out. The result should be fun.

Give me a lever and I will move the world, Archimedes is reputed to have said. Thigpen rejoiced in having found the lever that, he believed, would roll all of Quad Industries right into his lap.

Chapter 22

THE HEADQUARTERS of Quad Industries occupied five floors of one of mid-Manhattan's gleaming towers. Some might have wondered about the location because, of all the many and varied companies owned by Quad Industries, not one was located within the New York metropolitan area. Some might have wondered, but others would have noted that Richard Ames, the CEO of Quad Industries, made his home in Scarsdale, in Westchester county. They might still be surprised that the headquarters of a giant corporation would be selected on the basis of the CEO's commute, but then few of them would know Richard Ames or his relationship to the company.

Ames had run Quad Industries for nearly eighteen years, having succeeded old Harry Penrose, who was the son of the original founder. The company was not even called Quad Industries back then; it was still Penrose Foods and Packing. It was a rather humdrum name for a humdrum business, but it was a very good business when it came to making money. Ames and the company owed their subsequent fortunes to his shrewdness in recognizing that Penrose Foods and Packing made far more money than was needed to sustain the company. There were obvious limits on how much money could be reinvested into a business like Penrose, and Ames, owning few of the company's shares at that time, had no intention of paying out the money as dividends. Instead, he used the money to buy other companies. For a while, it seemed that if a company was for sale, Richard Ames was buying it. Thanks either to luck or skill, depending upon the allegiance of the observer, the companies that Ames bought also generated profits. All that money, combined with the hard times of the mid-seventies and again in the early eighties, allowed Ames to expand Penrose even further. Quad Industries was finally born in 1982, when the management of a defense electronics firm bought by Ames told him that they thought the Pentagon would have trouble awarding contracts to a company called Penrose Foods and Packing. Ames obliged with a special shareholders meeting, the name was changed, and indeed the military business picked up. Whether this was more a tribute to the insight of management or a commentary on Pentagon practices is, perhaps, best left unresolved.

All of the above history left Ames, with his title of CEO and seat on the Board of Directors, as absolute ruler of a huge business empire. True, Harry Penrose was still Chairman of the Board, but that was really an honorary position given out of deference to the old man's status as founder's son. Harry Penrose had rarely, if ever, opposed Ames from the day Ames took control and, now in his eighty-third year, was unlikely to do so in the future.

It was the future, though, and not the history that preoccupied most Quad Industries executives. Ames was sixty-four. The company by-laws specified that officers retired at sixty-five. Most insiders were betting that Ames would force a change in those by-laws to permit him to stay on, despite rumors that he no longer had such a good grasp of the business. There were very few, at any rate, who believed that Ames would willingly hand over control of his empire. That did not mean that he lacked a designated successor. He had one. Over eighteen years, he had had many of them. A wag had once commented that Ames changed heirs apparent the way most men changed underwear. A reporter from Forbes magazine had once asked Ames during an interview what he thought of the analogy. Ames had replied that it made sense because, after a few good farts, most men liked to change their shorts. He had followed the comment by daring the magazine to quote him. To no one's surprise, they did, whereupon the nameplate outside the heir apparent's office changed yet again.

If everyone else in Quad Industries was thinking about the future, on this morning Ames was thinking about the present. He had just been chewed out over the telephone and the chewing had gone on for a good twenty minutes. Ames was not accustomed to that kind of treatment. Unfortunately, the caller had been the CEO of Meldrum Products. Several years before, Meldrum had wanted to dispose of a national drugstore chain that it owned in order to concentrate on drugs, which were more profitable. Ames had swapped Quad Industries stock for the drugstore business, which left Meldrum as Quad Industries largest shareholder. Consequently, if the Meldrum CEO wanted to chew out Ames, well, Ames had to sit and take it. It had never happened when Keeler was CEO of Meldrum Products because Keeler and Ames were close friends, but Keeler had retired the year before. The current CEO was a young Turk for whom Ames was rapidly developing a serious dislike. Having to listen to the man squawk put Ames in a foul mood and it was fortunate that no one was in his office to see it.

Ames did not cut a prepossessing figure in the best of times. He was largely bald, with only a fringe of black hair above his ears and neck. He lacked sufficient height to properly distribute his weight (God help the man who called him short or, worse, fat). When he was angry, as he was now, his eyebrows drew together and jutted forward like those of New Hampshire's Old Man of the Mountains.

As he usually did when he was angry, he told his secretary to have Jim Morrison come to his office. Ames was momentarily taken aback when she told him that Morrison was already on his way. Could that shit at Meldrum have called Morrison too?

"Goddammit, Jim," he said the moment Morrison stepped through the door, "what do you know about what's going on at Meldrum?"

Since Meldrum Products was not the reason Morrison had been coming to Ames's office, he stopped for a moment to think. Jim Morrison was the current President of Quad Industries, which meant he was Ames's heir apparent, the title of Prince being out of fashion in corporate circles. He had lasted longer than anyone else in that job and his longevity was largely due to caution and careful consideration at times like these. Certainly, no one had ever suggested that Morrison owed his job to toadying Ames. Most people simply felt that Morrison was a dour and stubborn Scot who would endure anything in the service of his ambition. Privately, Morrison drank a lot of Maalox.

"I'm afraid I don't know anything about Meldrum, Dick," he said finally.

Ames was Dick, or Dickie, to his friends and acquaints. Many of the former and almost all of the latter also called him the Big Dick if they were assured of privacy and a discreet audience.

"You don't?" shot back Ames. "Well, you're about to." Wrapped up in his own anger, Ames forgot to ask why Morrison had been coming to see him in the first place.

Morrison noted the omission as well, but made no move to correct it. When Ames was wound up about something his focus tended to narrow to that topic alone. For a similar reason, Morrison did not bother asking about what had happened at Meldrum. He knew he would hear about it shortly. He was correct.

"For twenty minutes, I had to sit and listen to that damned snot over at Meldrum give it to me about one of our radio announcers," Ames said.

"Which station?"

"WCZY in New Jersey. They are actually located fairly close to the big Meldrum plant there."

"And what did he do?"

"She. What did she do, you mean? He was quite clear that it was 'she.' Apparently, Meldrum had a spill into some creek. This bitch picked it up and is making a big thing of that and a couple of cancer cases in the area. Meldrum is sure the whole thing is bogus, but she keeps hammering it on the air and it's starting to get a lot of play."

"If it's bogus why can't they refute it?"

"I gather they can't exactly prove their position, so it just keeps going and getting worse."

"So, Meldrum is pissed at us?"

"Basically."

Morrison's jaw tightened, although Ames did not notice. "I think," Morrison said, "we should talk about this." He held up several sheets of paper that he had brought with him.

"What's that about?"

"A 13-D filing," Morrison said. "Somebody has bought five percent of Quad Industries. Five point three percent to be exact. The shares are held by a group calling itself Mirage Partners. They sent a letter, signed by someone named John Lawrence Thigpen."

"That's one of Kuhnlein's pet jackals," Ames said. "I doubt he's gone out on his own, so you can assume Kuhnlein is running the show, whether his name is there or not. Did he say anything interesting?"

"The usual blather about 'undervalued assets' and how we should consider either selling out or restructuring to 'maximize values.' " Morrison put added emphasis on the last two words. Mentally, he told himself that there was a lot of truth to the blather, but since he wanted to run a company rather than retire, he did not voice that opinion.

Ames just gave a nasty laugh and said, "Just tell him to go diddle himself. The company is not for sale."

Morrison's face tightened up a bit more. When Ames was preoccupied he would hear what was said but he would not necessarily be listening to it. Making Ames listen to things he was not interested in at the moment was an art that had become more difficult with passing years.

"Dick, a week ago, even a day ago, I would have said the same thing, but now I wonder. Don't you think it's a bit odd that this happens just as we have a nasty incident with Meldrum?"

Ames's eyes narrowed. "What do you mean?"

"Well, normally I'd say Thigpen would have a tough time convincing anybody that he has a chance because of the Meldrum block. But, it's no secret that Meldrum hasn't been happy with so much cash tied up in our stock ever since they changed management last year. Get them pissed enough, and they might sell it, or vote against management, which would be just as bad. Hell, if the Street even thinks they might sell, the arbs will own half our shares in no time. And, then, we better check our own parachutes."

"You think this is a setup?" Ames hissed.

"Maybe. Maybe Thigpen caught the news and decided to bet that this could blow our relationship with Meldrum. Maybe he bought the radio jock to set it up that way. Maybe a little of both. Does it matter?"

"Not really. Setup or not, we have to make sure that block stays with us."

"We can't buy them out, Dick. I mean, I'll run the numbers to be sure, but I don't see any way we could swing it. You just can't pick up the phone and call Drexel anymore."

"Yeah. Well, as long as they don't do anything with it or the proxy, it doesn't matter, so the first thing we need to do is stop this radio bullshit. At least, things won't get any worse."

"What would you like me to do, Dick?"

"Get hold of the station manager at WCZY. Spell it out to him in easy to understand words that these shows have to stop and make sure he doesn't go blabbing the reason why. Also, tell him to send that announcer of his up here so I can talk to her myself. We need her to help us back out of this mess. After you've done that, dig Bob out of his finance meeting and bring him up here. Even if we can't buy out Meldrum, we should be able to put together a package that will screw the dear Mr. Thigpen."

FLEMINGTON, NEW JERSEY ───────────────────────────

Acey Henson had barely walked through her office door that afternoon, she had not even had time to put down her helmet, when she felt a hand grab a hold of her arm. Turning around, she saw Larry Forster, the comptroller.

"Can it wait, Larry?" she asked. "If I'm over budget, I won't be any more over budget in five minutes after I've taken my coat off and had a cigarette."

"It's not about budget," Forster said, "at least not that I know. Howard said he wanted to see you as soon as you came in."

Acey sighed. "All right. What's bothering El Rotundo now?"

Forster shook his head. "I have no idea. He got a call from corporate this morning that started it. Go see him, please, and make life more pleasant for everybody else."

Much as Firman had insisted on seeing Acey the moment she arrived, he was not happy to see her seated across from his desk. The phone call he had received from Morrison explained that, of course. Firman had never expected to receive a more direct message from Jim Morrison than the President's letter in the Quad Industries annual report. To have the President of Quad Industries call him on the phone and personally berate him for damaging the company's interest with his programming left Firman sick to his stomach and fearing for his job. Henson had turned out to be at the bottom of it, which was no surprise, although the particular issue corporate was upset over was. Although he might have been pleased at the prospect of Acey Henson being taken down a peg or two, this matter had the feel of something worse. Corporate might fire her. That would undoubtedly serve Acey Henson right, but it would leave a big hole in Firman's schedule. It would also cause programming troubles with Bannerman still out. Firman had no idea how he could handle both problems on short notice, which could also put his job in jeopardy even if he survived whatever it was that Henson had done. From the moment he had hung up the phone, Firman had closed his door and brooded at his desk, except for frequent trips to the bathroom where he brooded in front of the urinal. Station personnel who had ventured to disturb him at either site were swiftly and scatologically dismissed.

"Howard, the moment I showed up, I was told I had to see you instantaneously, with no time even to piss. I've been sitting here for three minutes and you haven't said a thing. What gives?"

With a jolt Firman realized that he had wandered off into the same thoughts he had been having all day, in spite of the fact that Henson was in his office.

"Corporate is pissed at you," he said. "Really pissed."

He had the immediate satisfaction of seeing her taken by surprise. That was definite. There was no missing the reddening of those cheeks. She hid it quickly, making a production out of extracting and starting a cigarette, but it had been there. No matter what else happened, Firman had the satisfaction of jarring Acey Henson.

"You want to tell me what they're pissed about?" By the time Acey spoke, her tone acknowledged neither surprise nor concern.

"Absolutely," Firman said. He was feeling a bit more relaxed now. "It's this toxic leak thing you've been pushing. It's got headquarters in an absolute uproar and they want it stopped."

For a second time in a very short while, Acey was taken by surprise. This time it was not visible, between the smoke and the reaction to Firman's first statement she had clamped a mask over her features. Inside, though, she felt turmoil. If anything, she would have thought that a careless remark, a bit too risqué or taken personally by the wrong someone, would be the cause of trouble in the corporate hierarchy.

"Howard, that's impossible. I've been real careful about what I say and how I say it, so it isn't my mouth, and this story is playing real well. Christ, it's getting picked up all over."

"Acey, it's not impossible. I just had the President of Quad Industries on the phone telling me how very possible it is. They don't like it."

"Want to tell me why?"

"I don't know why! Morrison didn't go into that."

"Probably some stupid misunderstanding," she muttered.

"Hah! Well, if it is, you'll have the perfect opportunity to correct it." Acey gave him a sharp look as he said it and Firman felt pleased. For once, he could let someone else argue with her. "Mr. Richard Ames wants to talk to you personally about this. Do you know who Ames is? He's the CEO of Quad Industries and a member of the Board. He wants to see you in his office today, just as soon as you can get there."

"Today? No chance! Howard, I have to do the news at six and I've got preparation to do. There's no way I can be in New York and still do all of it."

Firman was grinning. He finally had an opportunity to tell Acey Henson exactly what she was going to do, and she could not bluster her way around it because it had not been Firman's decision in the first place.

"So, you won't do it all. You're just filling in for Bannerman on news anyway. We can easily fill in for you. Acey Henson can be 'out on assignment' this evening. If I have to, I'm sure I can pull Wally or Harris to cover your show for tonight, too. But, the bottom line is this: Morrison said you don't go on the air until you straighten this out with Ames. This is coming from corporate, not from me, so there's no point arguing about it here."

"You're certainly right about that, Howard." Her voice was grim as she stood up. "You find subs for me tonight but, let me tell you, it's going to be tonight only. I'll see you back here tomorrow and I'll give you eight to five it'll be business as usual."

Acey left Firman's office and headed straight for her bike in the parking lot. There were probably things in her office that she should look at or take with her, she knew that, but just at that moment, she did not care. Her helmet was one of those things. She did not care about that either. She did not know quite what to make of the way she felt, although vomiting seemed like a distinct possibility. She kicked the Harley into life and pulled out onto the road.

She did not head directly for New York. Simple arithmetic told her that, short of discovering teleportation, she had no chance of salvaging her schedule. That being the case, she discovered that what she wanted to do was go to her apartment first. The feeling was intense, if not entirely rational, so she told herself that she could take some satisfaction in making Mr. Richard Ames wait until the end of the afternoon for his precious meeting.

The apartment felt safe and comfortable, which made her loathe to leave. Just for that reason, instead of settling into a chair she forced herself to change clothes, dressing with precision to suit her mood, which was now leaning toward combative. When she was done, she checked her watch. If she left now, she would be at the offices of Quad Industries well before the end of the afternoon. It was too early. She would rather make Ames wait. There would be just enough time, she decided, to go to the medical center first. She reached Schwartz's office feeling as though she would burst if she did not talk to him. Unfortunately, there was no one in the office except Doris.

"Hi," said Acey in a tone that was a little more brusque than she intended, "I'm looking for Zeke."

"Dr. Schwartz is not in the office right now," was the reply.

"I can see that. Can you tell me where he is?"

"He's in the hospital seeing patients."

"Zeke is always in the hospital seeing patients. Do you know where he is in the hospital?"

"No, I'm sorry, I don't. Would you like to leave a message?"

"Can you page him?"

"Is this urgent?"

Acey was not in the mood for conversations that went nowhere. She fixed the secretary with a look that said that if Doris considered her health important, the matter was urgent. The look apparently registered far better than any words because Doris, without saying anything either, picked up the phone and dialed the page operator.

When the phone rang, Acey snatched it up. "Hi, Zeke, this is Acey. I need to talk to you."

"Acey? Where are you?"

"In your office. Right where you dialed, remember? This is important. Can you come down?"

"I'll be right there."

Schwartz arrived a few minutes after he hung up, puffing noticeably. "What's the story?" he asked. "You sounded really concerned."

"Maybe I am. Can we talk in back?"

She followed him into his back office and closed the door while he sat down.

"When I got to the station today, I was told to stop the liver cancer story," she said.

Zeke's eyebrows went up and his jaw went down. "Who said to do that?"

"Quad Industries. That's the company that owns the company that owns the station. They want me to stop it and I can't go on the air tonight because I've got to go to New York to talk to them about it."

"It was that bald?" Zeke asked. "Management just called up the station and told them to have you shut down the story and go up to New York for a conference?"

"Yep. That's the way Howard told it, and I'm inclined to believe him. I heard Howard was in the bathroom five or six times an hour before I got there. It's a pretty reliable indicator; excitement always gets his kidneys in an uproar."

"This is crazy."

"I didn't say it was sane."

Zeke stroked his chin with his right hand. "No idea why, though? I mean, I'm getting shit over it down here, but I know why. The way they carry on about academic and intellectual purity, you would think this was Harvard, but this should be money in the bank for your company."

"So I would think, too," Acey said. "I haven't a clue, Doc. Quad Industries owns a lot of companies but Meldrum Products isn't one of them. I can't think of a link between the two, although, if there is, maybe I'll find out this afternoon. The dude I'm supposed to see is the CEO."

Zeke's eyebrows went back up in amazement. "You're going to see the CEO looking like that?" he asked. His voice slid most of the way up an octave as the words came out.

"And what is wrong with the way I look?"

Zeke wondered where to start. The outfit Acey had pulled together included leather pants, which tucked into high leather boots, laced to mid-calf, all in black. A matching jacket covered her torso and she wore fingerless gloves, also in black.

"Acey, if this guy is a CEO, he's going to be middle-aged and stuffy. Do you really think he is going to listen to you seriously if you show up looking like that?"

"Hey, I like leather. If he doesn't, that's his problem, not mine. Any other complaints, Mr. Picky? Excuse me, Dr. Picky." She planted herself in a defiant pose in front of his desk.

"The hair is a bit much, too." Zeke considered that a mild understatement. On top, where it was cropped short, the hairs stood stiffly at attention. The hair on the side, where it was cut longer, was swept back away from her face and equally rigid. A burst of bright blue edged with pink colored the sweep of hair.

"What about my hair is too much?" asked Acey Henson.

"Jesus Christ, Henson! If I had as much stiffener in my prick as you've got in your hair, I could wear out four of you in one night and then hang my towel on it while I shaved in the morning."

That brought a smile, which produced dimples and a little softening of Acey's face. "It might be fun to see you try," she said, "although I would suggest using something other than mousse. Are you on call tonight?"

"Unfortunately, yes."

"Too bad. You're actually cute for a physician, especially when you're horny. I guess I'll see you tomorrow, though."

NEW YORK, NEW YORK _____

Acey found the building that housed Quad Industries to be intimidating. She found that sensation peculiar. She had roamed around New York for much of her adolescence and it had never intimidated her then, so she did not have the excuse of a farm girl from North Dakota who walked down the streets with her neck hyperextended because she could not believe how far up those buildings went. The sensation was there, however. She had become aware of it while she was standing at the guard desk in the lobby, all cold marble and brass with an array of Big Brother's own television screens behind the desk. The guard stared at her while she signed the visitor's register. When he inspected her entry—name, company and destination—the stare turned to a scowl. He had her wait in front of the desk while he called upstairs to Quad Industries to verify that this unlikely looking person was there to see Mr. Ames. The guard still looked unconvinced after he hung up, but he pushed forward a visitor's badge and directed her to the elevators.

"All right," she muttered to herself in front of the elevator, "the guard doesn't think I belong where I'm going. So what?"

When Acey had run around New York years before, there had been plenty of places she did not belong. That had never bothered her. Acey Henson did as Acey Henson pleased, that was how she had always lived and anyone who was troubled by that did not have to like it. So it was odd that, now, when she actually belonged in the building, she felt as though she would be thrown out the moment she was recognized. Even worse, it bothered her.

Where had that come from, she wondered. It took her only a moment to fasten on a reason. Zeke Schwartz was the reason. He had put it into her head and she was being stupid enough to pay attention to his opinions. I wish I had never stopped at the hospital, she thought. I wish I had never let him apologize to me. I wish I had never talked to him in the first place. Those thoughts repeated in her head all the way up the elevator.

The feelings did not go away when she entered the Quad Industries office suite. If anything, they intensified. The secretary looked down at her the way an aristocrat in Dickens's London might have looked at a beggar. Acey could tell herself that the feeling was crazy, but that did not make it go away. The secretary did nothing but answer the phones and type other people's letters, so Acey told herself, but she still felt inferior. The secretary was probably still paying for the dress she was wearing; Acey knew she could have bought it outright, but she still felt poor. Maybe Schwartz had a point about the clothes, but damn him for bringing it up. She pulled out a cigarette and reached for her lighter.

"I'm sorry Miss Henson, this is a no smoking area," the secretary said.

"What?"

"It's company policy. There is no smoking in any of the offices."

The secretary's smile seemed smug to Acey, just like the teacher's pet who would report her for some stupid mistake.

"No problem," Acey said and tossed the pack onto the desk. "Why don't you check these with the guns and other deadly weapons. I'll pick them up when I come out."

The secretary just smiled again, this time without parting her lips, and ignored the comment. I bet you are a real airhead, Acey said to herself as the secretary escorted her to Ames's office. The cigarettes remained back on the secretary's desk.

She did not have to wait long outside Ames's door. Initially, she was glad of that because she was feeling more and more edgy and she was afraid that she was losing control of herself. The longer she waited, the more likely that was to happen. When she saw the office, though, she changed her mind. That office had been designed with intimidation in mind. It was a long rectangle set into a corner of the building, with Ames's desk tucked into the outside corner. The walls behind the desk were glass, giving a majestic view of the cityscape on both sides. They also let in a lot of light, which made it difficult to look at the person behind the desk. The desk was not really a desk; it was a massive table of gray stone and metal without drawers of any kind. The man behind the desk did not need drawers. No computer screen was evident anywhere in the room. The man behind the desk had subordinates to tell him what was in the computers.

Richard Ames sat behind the desk writing on a sheet of paper. That sheet and a small file folder to its right were the only objects on the desk. He did not get up when she entered; he did not even look up when she sat down in front of the desk. Acey assumed that the studied indifference was intended to emphasize who was in charge. She found it irritating and a challenge. She fought to suppress that sensation. Her control was fragile enough without further problems. When Ames finally finished with his paper and looked up, his eyes seemed to focus somewhere around the back of her head.

"You are Miss Henson?" he asked.

"That's correct."

Ames did not introduce himself, nor did he offer to shake hands. "It was my understanding that you would be here much earlier this afternoon. Is there some reason you are so late?"

Acey shrugged. She wished that she had a cigarette. Rules against smoking or not, at least she could have held it. Unfortunately, her pack was back on Miss Airhead's desk with no immediate means of retrieving it. Ames's eyes shifted to fasten on hers.

"I was told to be here this afternoon. No specific time was mentioned." She found herself chafing under his gaze as though it were a wrestling hold.

"Next time," he said, "I think it would be advisable for you to check details like that in advance. But, that's what this is all about isn't it? Checking details?" He opened the file folder and made a study of the top page. The contents of the folder had nothing to do with Acey Henson, but she had no way of knowing that. "This story you've been pushing about the leak at the Meldrum plant, why don't you tell me how you see it from our point of view."

"You mean from WCZY or Quad Industries?"

"Same thing."

"Well, it's been very good." Acey wanted a snappier line. Ames was giving her, she thought, one opportunity to sell him on the story, but her brain seemed to lack its usual edge. "It's holding the audience very well and it's had a positive impact on our advertising sales." Maybe, she thought after she said it, a better response would have been just to say that it is one hell of a story. It would have sounded more natural. On the other hand, though, she felt Ames would want to hear about audience and sales.

Ames said nothing right away. Instead, he reached down into the wastebasket under his desk and pulled out a newspaper clipping. He tossed it onto the desk in front of her. "Have you seen this?" he asked. "It's from a Pittsburgh paper. Your signal doesn't go nearly that far, so this is all secondary stuff."

Acey leaned forward to pick it up. It was a short article. The headline read, "Local radio host calls for boycott of Meldrum Products."

"Did you see it?" Ames asked again.

"No," Acey answered. "I don't usually check Pittsburgh papers."

"Ah, yes," Ames said softly, "this matter of checking details again." In fact, Ames had not seen the article either. One of Morrison's people had found it when they were looking for props Ames could use for his meeting. He had placed it in the wastebasket so that he could make a show of pulling it out. He had never bothered to read it.

"What do you think of that, Miss Henson?" he asked.

"I think it's stupid," Acey said. "I had a caller mention something like this going on in Valley Forge, so I guess it's spreading around. If it starts turning up on the syndicated shows, I guess you could hear it anywhere. The idea is ridiculous, though. You can't switch drugs like you can gasoline."

"*You* think it's stupid. People can come to grief over stupid things, even when they are right. But you haven't considered that. Which brings me to the story itself. How carefully did you check out those details?"

"Very carefully, I think."

"You think. Obviously, you do not think!" His voice suddenly cracked out like a shot and his hand slapped down on the desk top. "This is a totally irresponsible piece of reporting. You do not know that this leak is responsible for these events, but you have tied us to that position. You have also associated us with this stupid boycott. You are leaving us with our ass hanging out. I will not have you jeopardize this company. I want this story stopped," he demanded, "and I want it done now."

Acey, at first, did not know what to say. Anyone with a moment to reflect would realize that a great many stories had been floated on even less substantial grounds, but the whole point of Ames's outburst had been to make it difficult to think about the statement. Ames had a great deal of practice with the technique. It was effective.

"Are we being sued," she asked.

"If we are, and you're needed, you'll hear about it then," Ames said. "Right now, I want this business stopped. Is that clear? You put a stop to it and you do whatever is necessary to disassociate us from it."

"That's not quite so easy," Acey said. "It's not just a story, like on the news. This is a talk show. People call in to talk about it and they're calling other shows, too. I can't just turn it off."

"Of course you can," Ames snapped. "You control who gets on and where the talk goes. Shut it off."

"Even if I could, doing it could ruin the show."

"That may be the price you have to pay."

"Now wait just a minute . . ." Acey started to say.

"No." Ames cut her off. "I've told you what is to be done and you will do what I tell you. Or else. I can have you off the air like that." He snapped his fingers.

It was the "or else" that caused something else to snap. Something inside Acey. That had been her father's favorite phrase. He had used it on her and on her mother and often had followed it with a concrete example of what "or else" could be. After they had moved out, her mother had taken over using it on her, at least until she had grown up. Those two words made the anger well up inside her until it swamped all the feelings she had been contending with since she had left the station.

"Well, the thing of it is, Mr. Ames, that you can't just yank me off the air right now." There was a distinct change in her tone. Ames noticed it too. "If you do, you have to know that I'll wind up on another station faster than you can shit and I'll just have that much more to talk about. You think that will stop the story or 'disassociate' you? Bullshit! All you'll get is a big investigation into your 'cover-up' of this Meldrum leak. If the story bothers you now, it'll really bother you then. So, you can't really shut me up. The best you can do is have me do what I'm doing, which is at least responsible, and I won't have to be 'responsible' if you can me. So, I'm going to assume that I'm still on the air with no restrictions. Am I right?"

Ames pressed his lips into a thin line. "Your analysis is correct, Miss Henson, but only to a point. You are correct that I would prefer not to see this turned into a public vendetta. That would hardly be in the company's interest. However, you must realize that your threat is valid only as long as this remains a hot story. The glare of publicity does not last forever and neither does your contract. My memory lasts far longer. I think you should consider that before you sacrifice the future for a brief present. What do you say to that, Miss Henson?"

Acey stood up. "Go fuck a duck. It ought to fit just about right."

Jim Morrison, having carefully coached the secretaries, knew exactly when Acey Henson left. He waited an additional ten minutes, then went up to Ames's office. He found Ames at his desk, brooding over the New York skyline.

"How did it go?" Morrison asked.

"Badly."

When there was no further comment, Morrison tried again. "How badly?"

"In plain English, she told me to go fuck a duck."

It took Morrison a moment to realize that Ames was being literal. "That doesn't sound good," he said.

"You're very perceptive," Ames snapped. Then, wearily, "Sit down, Jim, and let's figure out what has to be done."

Morrison settled into the same chair Acey had just vacated. "Did you try to buy her off?" he asked.

"No," Ames answered. "You have to see her, Jim; she's a weird character. It just didn't seem like she would go for it. I tried to order her off it. I already told you how that went. At least, I'm glad I didn't try to reason with her. If I'd told her the whole situation, I bet she'd broadcast that over the whole state too."

"She'll know soon enough," Morrison said. "After all, this stuff isn't secret."

Ames smiled. "True. However, Jim, not everyone reads SEC filings in the john."

Morrison did not smile in return. "If this takeover gets rolling, it'll be in the papers. She reads those, I'm sure."

"And then, at least, we never ordered her to stop for that reason."

Morrison hid his frown behind a hand. He would bet that anyone could be bought if only one were willing to spend the time necessary to figure out what the price was. Ames no longer had that kind of patience.

"What would you like to do now?" Morrison asked.

"What I'd like to do is drop her out this window," Ames replied. "More realistically, I'm thinking I should just bite the bullet and have her fired."

"Don't do it," Morrison said sharply, sharp enough to make Ames look around at him. "I can just see her on some national show telling how she was forced off the air to cover up the Meldrum leak. Meldrum is our biggest shareholder. The press will make it out that Meldrum engineered her ouster. You can bet on that. That will mean no end of trouble for Meldrum, which is just more trouble for us. The cure is worse than the disease."

Ames smiled again. "That's just about what she told me, minus the Meldrum info, right before she told me what to do with a duck. Even not knowing that, she was betting that pulling her off the air would cause more trouble than it's worth."

"She's right."

"That doesn't help, Jim. If this bullshit is allowed to go on, we are likely to lose the Meldrum block. Isn't there some other way of shutting her up?"

Morrison was privately thinking that, as far as Meldrum was concerned, the damage was probably already done, and whatever more Acey Henson might say would not matter. It might be more useful to assume the Meldrum block gone and look at the options that were left. Ames did not want to hear that just yet. He wanted to hear how to turn Acey Henson off. Morrison tried to oblige.

"Maybe there's another way to do this. That original show of hers, the one that got this started, had a physician on it. He was the one who really made the connection between the leak and these cancers. More precisely, I think he's the reason this was taken so seriously."

"What are you thinking?"

"Well, if he were to do a public about-face on this, come out and say everything has been blown out of proportion, that might quiet it down."

Ames swiveled away from the window view to face Morrison. "Do you honestly think that getting this MD to get up and say 'never mind' is really going to stop this lunacy?"

"No, of course not," Morrison answered. "That's not the point, though. If this guy reverses himself, says he goofed, overreacted, whatever, it knocks the props out from under that radio jock. They both look like fools and people stop paying attention to them. Sure, this mess will continue to grind on, but it removes us as irritants to Meldrum and that's the only important issue we need to consider." In his own mind, Morrison was not nearly as certain as he sounded, but that did not matter either. From his perspective the only important issue was pulling Ames's focus away from the Meldrum block, which Morrison was ready to give up as lost, so they could concentrate on the measures necessary to repel Thigpen.

Ames considered the plan for a few minutes. Then he asked Morrison, "Do you know this guy?"

"No," Morrison said, "but I do know some people in Trenton I can talk to. There are a number of favors I can call in."

Ames grunted. "Do you think it will work?"

"One chance in four or five, I would guess."

"Worth a shot, then."

Morrison allowed himself a little smile. He could tell from Ames's face that now he would have an opportunity to discuss their important business. "I think," Morrison said, "that this would be a good time to go over some of the options Bob's group has laid out. They could be useful, even if we do hang on to the Meldrum block."

PHILADELPHIA, PENNSYLVANIA _____

"You said what!" Bannerman's voice rose into a shriek; it lacked the strength for a real shout. He sat forward on the couch, the greatest degree of animation he had shown the entire evening.

Acey grinned at him. It was a rather smug grin. She was feeling pleased with herself. She repeated the end of her story with relish.

"Jesus Christ!" Bannerman pulled his bathrobe tightly across his chest. "I cannot believe you told the chief executive officer of a Fortune 500 company to do it with a duck. This is not what you would call a good career move, Acey."

In return, she laughed. "Come on Roger. The man was planning to can me after this is over anyway. Telling him off changes nothing. Am I right, Jimmy?"

Jim was seated in a wicker chair across the coffee table from where Acey perched at the front of an identical chair. The chairs flanked the couch where Roger slouched. Jim did not reply immediately, so Acey just continued to look at him while he thought. In contrast to Roger's bathrobe, he was neatly dressed in slacks and a rugby shirt and held a cup of tea on his lap. Acey recalled that, before Roger started to feel ill, she had thought they made a cute couple. Of course, Jim was still cute, but that was a rather silly train of thought. No one had ever said life would be simple.

Eventually, Jim put his cup down on the glass table top. "If we assume that there is some reason that Ames does not want to be publicly associated with stopping the Meldrum story, then I agree with you."

"Safe assumption," Acey said. "Have you ever heard of somebody like Ames calling a show host in to chew her out? Of course not. Hell, even if I had done something actionable, I'd get reamed out by Legal, not by him. I would think that if I managed to do something so egregious as to get him this pissed, he'd just fire me on the spot, or have Howard do it, more likely. Since he didn't, he can't. What I would love to know is what Mr. Dickhead Ames is so afraid of."

"I suspect it's just as well you don't," Jim said. "If you find out, I wouldn't talk about it and I would't talk about him trying to shut you up. The moment you do that, he no longer has anything to lose by firing you."

He broke off when he noticed that Roger was lying back against the cushions of the couch, large beads of sweat standing out on his forehead. "You feeling okay, Rog?" he asked. "Maybe we should bring you up to bed."

"Yeah," Acey agreed. "Enough excitement for one evening. Anyway, I thought you told me you were taking those pills."

"I am," Bannerman said irritably. "I even get up in the middle of the goddamn night to take those pills. Much good they're doing me."

"Well, are you sure you got the real ones?" she asked. "I mean, are you sure they didn't stick you in one of those stupid trials where they flip a coin to see if you get the sugar pills?"

"Goddammit, Acey! It's not funny!"

"Easy, Rog, easy," Jim said. Then turning to Acey, he said, "It's not possible. They can't just 'stick' you in a trial. Trust me on this, even if I wasn't the youngest person to make partner at the firm."

"I believe you," she said. "I was just trying to, oh, never mind. I should just watch what I say, as usual. C'mon, Rog, we'll give you a hand getting upstairs."

TRENTON, NEW JERSEY ————————————————————————

When Zeke Schwartz's beeper went off at nine o'clock the following morning, he was sitting at the nurses' station on 4 North trying to calm down. He had already been there for a half hour because the pump controlling the flow of an intravenous line, which had been programmed to push a certain amount of fluid through the line each hour, had failed. The electronics inside it had not recognized that the pump was turning futilely and continued to tally the fluid its chip thought had been administered. None of the floor personnel during the night had bothered to look at the actual bag of fluid, which was just as full in the morning as it had been the previous night. All of which left Schwartz having to explain to the parents why their child was not going home for another day. He was not happy.

His first thought when he saw the beeper flashing an outside number was that one of his patients was headed for the Emergency Room. That would fit the way the day had started. It turned out, however, to be a Dr. Charles DiPietro, who identified himself as being a member of the State Medical Board.

"I wanted to talk to you, Dr. Schwartz, about that patient of yours you discussed on the radio show. Jerry Inman is his name, I think."

"That's the patient," Zeke said. "What's on your mind?"

"I found it very upsetting," DiPietro said, "as did a number of other people here. I have to tell you that I think that was an extremely unprofessional thing you did."

"I'm sorry you feel that way," Zeke said, "but I believed that everything I said was true and I still do."

"I am not trying to question that," DiPietro said. "The issue is that it was very exploitative of your patient and his family, especially since, as you acknowledged, you can't prove anything."

"Excuse me," Zeke said, his voice hardening, "the show was fully discussed with the family beforehand."

"To reply to that, I would point out that it is easy to mislead a patient. I cannot believe that the family is well served by becoming the focus of regional gossip, which is what the result of your action has been."

"What are you trying to imply?"

"That you need to get this family back out of the limelight," DiPietro stated. "Whether that means apologizing for creating a tempest in a teapot or doing something else to damp some of this speculation I don't know, but you need to do something."

"Dr. DiPietro, to put it bluntly, on what grounds are you sticking your nose into my case?"

"Do I need to remind you, Dr. Schwartz, that this Board licenses physicians in New Jersey?"

" 'This Board,' " Zeke said, emphasizing his words, "is going to buy a whole lot more trouble than it bargained for if it tries any monkey business with my license."

"You're not being very helpful, Dr. Schwartz," said DiPietro.

"I'm not trying to be," Zeke said, and hung up.

He stared at the receiver after it was back in the cradle. That was pretty stupid, Zeke, he told himself. Certainly, this DiPietro was a jerk who had no business involving himself with the Inmans, but there were better ways to have handled him. Almost any way would have been better than blowing up. So, why did I do it? Because I am pissed that no one cared enough to make certain that this kid was getting his fluid, or even cared enough to wonder that the bag was still full. Because all someone cared about was writing down what the pump read and never mind what was really happening. That sort of attitude can kill people. DiPietro just called at the wrong time.

"Oh well," Zeke muttered, "even if he hates my guts, there's not a whole lot he can really do."

It was not one of his more accurate prognostications.

Chapter 23

THE MEAL was exquisite, thin slices of tender duck arranged on the plate to resemble a duck, crisp beans and asparagus arrayed around the duck like bulrushes, and a delicate brown sauce that held just a hint of wine. The elegant table setting was worthy of the food—sterling silver utensils and china plates with an elaborate blue pattern swirling around the circumference. Despite the elaborate show and the quality of the cuisine, Ben Ogilvie was not enjoying his dinner. He sighed a little as he cut the last slice of his duck. He was not really tasting it at all and that was a shame because it was not often that he had such a meal. Unfortunately, given the mood of the evening, it would have been just as well if Pat Dwyer had taken him to the Ground Round instead of northern New Jersey's best known French restaurant.

The mood had been sour from the start. He had met Dwyer at the outer door, the two men having arrived almost simultaneously from separate parking lots. Normally, Dwyer presented a hearty hail-fellow-well-met attitude but it was conspicuously absent from his greeting. His face was pinched and closed, his words guarded. Ogilvie had not had a successful career in hospital administration without developing a politician's knack for judging people. Just that first glimpse was enough to make him wonder if he should find a pretext for canceling the dinner. He did not do it, though. The dinner had been long planned and the restaurant beyond the sort of indulgence Ogilvie usually allowed himself, so they went in and were seated. The dining area was cramped, with just a few small tables, which put them close together. Ogilvie ordered wine quickly, thinking that it might loosen some of the tension he saw in Dwyer's face. It did not do that, but it did seem to loosen Dwyer's tongue.

Ogilvie found out quickly what was bothering Dwyer. It was Aspergicin. Specifically, it was what the current news was doing to Aspergicin and what it might do in the future. Dwyer might hide some of the words he really wanted to say behind phrases like "adversely impact sales," but the jargon did not hide the angry, clipped way the words were uttered.

"It would be amazing, really, if it were not so unfortunate," Dwyer said. "Some impact on Aspergicin, of course, was inevitable, but we never would have expected the magnitude. Now, I'm hearing that some hospitals are actually getting letters demanding they not use any of our products. Now, nobody has actually dropped a Meldrum Products drug from their formulary that I know of, but if this continues it could quite possibly adversely impact our overall sales too."

There was that phrase again. It made Ogilvie acutely uncomfortable. His hands were cold, his face was hot and his collar felt far too tight. He felt that way because it seemed likely that Dwyer attached to Ogilvie some of the blame for what had befallen Aspergicin, the drug on which Dwyer had pinned his forecasts and hopes of further advancement. It seemed that way since it had been Dr. Ezekiel Schwartz who had precipitated the problem and since Zeke did, in a remote way, work for Ben Ogilvie. For a moment, Ogilvie considered pointing out that, unlike a corporate executive, he had very little control over what the hospital physicians said publicly. He decided against it because Dwyer had been selling to physicians and hospitals his entire adult life and obviously knew how medical hierarchies worked. There was no point further upsetting the man by telling him what he already knew. Still, Ogilvie would have liked some way to deflect the criticism.

Ostensibly, the dinner had been designed as a sales meeting. That is, Dwyer was going to wine and dine the head of a major medical center and try to convince him to have the hospital order Meldrum products. If that had been the only agenda for the evening, Ogilvie would not have cared about Dwyer's mood. He would have had a good dinner, at company expense, and worried not at all. However, the relationship between the medical center and Meldrum was not quite as simple as that of customer and salesman. A great many Meldrum dollars went into the medical center. The large bronze plaque outside the center's new surgical suite proclaimed to all that it had been built by the generosity of Meldrum Products. The same theme repeated itself, on a smaller scale, throughout the center. The medical center could ill afford to alienate the source of those funds and Ogilvie knew it.

"Look, Pat," he finally said, having decided that it would be best to force the problem into the open, "I can understand how difficult a time this is for you, but I don't see how you can put the blame for what happened onto the medical center."

Dwyer looked up at Ogilvie from the apple confection that had been brought as dessert. "I don't recall saying that it was your fault. If I did, I would like to apologize."

"Well, you didn't exactly say it in so many words." Mentally, Ogilvie cursed himself for having overstated his case. Now, he felt defensive. "You did rather imply responsibility though. I mean, my point is that we had nothing to do with the spill and most of this brouhaha is because this damn Acey Henson has kept bashing the issue on the air. We've had our own run-ins with her in the past, so I know how bad it can be."

Dwyer pushed himself away from his dessert, which put more space between himself and Ogilvie than the tiny table permitted. Then he ran his fingers through the hair just over his ears and finally clasped his hands behind his head. "Forgive me if I implied any direct responsibility," he said. "Let's be honest, though, shall we, Ben? The main reason everyone took this Henson seriously is because your Dr. Schwartz lent a certain respectability to her position. He is, I have heard, well respected, something of an authority even. Without him, she's just another crazy, and we get them all the time, if not always on the air. This whole business could have been properly handled and put to bed by now, but because Schwartz is involved everybody thinks there has to be something to the story. That keeps everybody, from the FDA to the newspapers, poking around and that keeps the story in play. That's what is so frustrating. We know there's nothing to it, but try to prove that to everyone's satisfaction under these conditions . . ." He let the phrase hang and shook his head.

"I see your point," Ogilvie said, "but I don't see that there is much I can do about it."

"No, I rather doubt it. Although, you know, I just had a thought." Ogilvie doubted that Dwyer had just had the thought. He wondered if Dwyer had been working toward that moment the entire evening. "You mentioned that you had experience with Henson," Dwyer went on. "Does Schwartz know what kind of a crazy he's dealing with?"

"I've discussed it with him. Zeke is not terribly receptive to suggestions." If that question was Dwyer's contribution to the situation, Ogilvie thought it sadly lacking. "Is there something you would like me to do?" he asked.

"No, no, definitely not," Dwyer said quickly. "Under the circumstances, I would not want even the appearance of any pressure coming from Meldrum. I'm sure you understand what I mean. We have enough to deal with without that."

Ogilvie was fairly certain that he knew exactly what Dwyer meant. He was equally convinced that Dwyer's meaning had nothing to do with the fortunes of the New York Yankees, although that was the only topic Dwyer seemed interested in for the remainder of the meal.

Ogilvie was still thinking about that dinner when he reached his office the next morning. Dwyer obviously wanted something from him. Ogilvie had also decided that what Dwyer wanted was for Schwartz to drop his association with Henson, at the least to quit supporting her and preferably to repudiate his earlier position. Dwyer also wanted it accomplished without even a hint that the idea had come from Meldrum. The dilemma then, as Ogilvie saw it, was whether to do Dwyer a favor and if so how to do it.

The first question was easy to answer. If he refused, the flow of Meldrum dollars could easily dry up. Dwyer had the power to do that, even if he had not been so crass as to point it out over dinner. That was the potential danger. The potential reward was that if he did the favor, Dwyer would then owe him one. That gratitude could lead to bigger grants. The arguments were heavily in favor of helping Dwyer. The problem was, how? A direct appeal to Zeke was probably futile. He had already tried that approach in the Jodie Schmidt case. Ogilvie winced as he thought of the bill the center would have to absorb. No, Zeke Schwartz was unlikely to listen to logic.

Sitting at his desk staring off into space did not bring a solution to the problem. It would be, Ogilvie decided, better not to think about it for a while. Maybe his perspective would change. It would be better to think about something he enjoyed.

As it happened, he had set aside most of the morning to experiment with the new computer system. The project had been his brainchild, one of which he was very proud. The system linked several other computer systems within the hospital, allowing a review of patient admissions, consultations by different services, medications ordered and laboratory tests ordered. Ogilvie was certain that the patterns that emerged from the information would show him where money could be saved. The system would also allow him to ask "what if" questions. He could change the frequency of a type of consultation, for example, and see what it would do to the medical center's finances. The "what if" questions were one of the best things about computers. He played with it for a while, looking at graphs for the last three months, three years and ten years, which was as far back as records had been entered. The work was going slowly, because his mind was not really focused on what he was doing, when the idea suddenly popped into his head. It was so simple, so obvious, that it left him staring open-mouthed at the screen. Computers were great for "what if" questions.

Well, what if? Feverishly, he started typing a query into the machine. Up came lists of names and medical record numbers. A few more keystrokes and the screen held billing information by department. Ogilvie leaned back and blew out a big gust of air. The idea would work. It would give him a way to help Dwyer. Even better, it would prick the balloon of the pompous Dr. Schwartz. That, in itself, made it worth the effort. It had always irritated Ogilvie the way Schwartz made a virtue out of his ignorance of the economic realities the hospital faced. Schwartz could and did stand there, self-righteous asshole that he was, claiming to care only about his patients, while he made Ogilvie look like a heel for pointing out the limits to what could be done. Of course, Ogilvie assured himself, if Schwartz and his kind had their way, the hospital would run out of money in a very short time. No doubt, they would blame that on Ogilvie, too. In thinking about Schwartz, Ben Ogilvie had almost completely forgotten about Dwyer. He resented the way Schwartz acted and this seemed like a perfect opportunity to redress the balance. Welcome to the muck, Dr. Schwartz!

Schwartz was sitting at his desk writing, when Ogilvie appeared in his doorway. Ogilvie said nothing, at first, which entailed several minutes of watching Schwartz write, before Schwartz looked up. Zeke discovered a queasy sensation building in his stomach when he saw Ogilvie. His first assumption was that this was going to be a replay of their previous conversation. Zeke had grown no fonder, in the interval, of basing his medical judgment on the hospital's budget. Had there been a back door, he would have used it. Not having one, he simply sat there. It was only when Ogilvie did not speak immediately that Zeke noticed that Ogilvie was carrying a briefcase. Oh God, Zeke thought, I bet he's rounded up every one of my admissions for the last month.
"Good morning," said Ogilvie.
"Good morning," said Zeke Schwartz.
The conversation briefly stalled there. Ogilvie cleared his throat and asked, "Do you have a minute?"
"I guess so," Zeke answered, "you're standing in my exit. What can I do for you?"
Ogilvie flushed. Just then, he wished he had not been so stern with Schwartz over the Schmidt case. It was not that he had any doubt of being justified in his position; it was only that he needed Schwartz to listen to what he was going to say. The look on Schwartz's face could not be mistaken for sweet reason. It would be a shame to waste such a good idea because the man was unable to receive a business reprimand without taking it personally.
With that in mind, Ogilvie started by saying, "This has nothing to do

with our last conversation." He was gratified to see Schwartz relax a bit in his chair.

"What is it then?"

"I wanted to talk to you about this business with WCZY."

Zeke frowned. "As I recall, that was part of our last conversation." He leaned forward on his elbows, twirling his pen between his fingers.

"This is different," Ogilvie said. "Maybe I can't convince you that I'm concerned about your reputation, although I am, but I'm sure you'll believe that I'm concerned about the hospital's reputation. Right now that's in jeopardy. Both of them. You've let yourself be used by a nut case, a real lunatic, and if you don't put a stop to it, you and all of us are going to be a national laughingstock."

Schwartz sighed. "Ben, I know you have reason to dislike Henson and I'm not going to argue about it with you. I'm not sure that's reason to call someone a lunatic."

"That has nothing to do with why I called her a lunatic," Ogilvie said, his voice rising. "She *is* a lunatic. I don't mean that figuratively. She's an honest-to-God crazy."

"How do you know that?" Schwartz asked.

"She's been hospitalized here several times," was Ogilvie's answer.

"So what?" Schwartz gave a sharp laugh and pushed himself back from the desk. "This isn't a psych hospital and the woman has diabetes. So what if she's been hospitalized?"

For an instant, the response unsettled Ogilvie and he did not answer as smoothly as he had planned. How could Schwartz know that Acey Henson had diabetes? Just how much could a good doctor tell about a person just by looking at him or her? It was an unsettling thought, particularly with Schwartz gazing intently at him. He coughed lightly to cover his hesitation, then went on.

"The 'so what,' " Ogilvie said, "is that our computer system can cross-check the billing from different departments, in this case psychiatry and social services, against the dates of admission." He opened his briefcase and pulled out two folders so thick that he could barely reach around them with his hand. He dropped them on Schwartz's desk with a slap that sounded like a pistol shot. "Our system only goes back ten years, but that was long enough, it turned out, to get the lead. I strongly suggest that you take a look at these notes and see just what you've teamed up with. Then, maybe you'll realize why you need to extricate yourself from this situation before everyone gets a good look at her."

Schwartz looked at the folders without saying anything. They were light tan manilla folders with a simple metal clasp to hold their contents in place. Each one was about three inches thick. The edges of the folders showed long usage. They were crumpled and frayed, gray from uncounted hands. The label on the top folder, in black Magic Marker, read "Henson, Alice Catherine, Volume 3 of 4." The bottom one said "Volume 4 of 4."

"Those are her hospital charts," Schwartz said.

"The last two volumes," Ogilvie agreed.

"Those are confidential."

"Yeah." Ogilvie actually grinned. "They're restricted to hospital personnel and what are we, if not hospital personnel?"

"You're not a physician," Schwartz protested.

"True," replied Ogilvie. "That's why I signed them out to you."

"Christ, Ogilvie, I don't have any legitimate reason to have them either."

Ogilvie's grin took on a nasty aspect, particularly around his eyes. "That's a good point to keep in mind while you decide what to do, especially since they are signed out to you. You really should read those notes, Dr. Schwartz. I'm sure you won't need anyone to tell you what they mean. I'm sorry to be so blunt about it, but you don't take hints very well."

As he left the office, Ogilvie decided that he did not feel sorry at all.

FLEMINGTON, NEW JERSEY _____

Zeke intended, after Ogilvie walked out, to simply ignore the matter. He had no intention of reading the charts and there was plenty of other work to do. Making that decision, however, was easier than keeping it. The next several hours proved to be unproductive. He could not keep his mind on what he was trying to do. When he found that he had been sitting in the laboratory for fifteen minutes with a slide on the microscope but had never looked at it, he gave up. He called the page operator and told her that he would be out of the hospital and to call him only for emergencies. He told Doris the same thing. Then he stuffed the charts into a plastic grocery bag and headed for his car. He pulled into the WCZY parking lot only twenty minutes later, quite a feat in midday traffic. It was a typical East Coast summer day, which is to say hot and humid, but his sweat was only partially due to the weather.

He stuck his head in the front office and said to no one in particular, "Has Acey come in yet?"

"A little while ago," said a man he did not recognize. "Is she expecting you?"

"No. I'm Schwartz. It's about the show."

That produced recognition. "Why don't you just go on back, then," the man said. "If the door's closed, pound on it."

The exchange left Zeke relieved. In his driving urgency to leave the hospital, he had neglected to call the station first. The door was indeed closed, so he took the advice and knocked. There was no response, so he knocked louder. He was wondering whether she might have gone to the bathroom when he heard a chair scrape inside. He knocked again.

"Christ on a stick! Come in already." It was Acey's voice. Once he was through the door, she gave him a rather disinterested "Hello."

She was, in fact, so intent on what she was doing that Zeke could have been forgiven for thinking that they were not in the same room. Acey had several of the day's newspapers open, blanketing her desk, file cabinets and part of the floor. She had a pair of scissors in her hand and was busy clipping a story here and one there from the open papers. The clippings went into the background file that she kept for her show. Her disregard was actually, in part, intentional. The threat Ames had made the previous day had scared her, something she had hidden from Roger and Jim with her bravado. She had almost hidden it from herself, but not quite. By the time she had left Philadelphia, she had wanted to talk with Zeke, but not at the price of being interrupted by his damn beeper. So, she had smothered the feeling overnight and was dealing with it that afternoon by concentrating solely on possible storylines for her show. She was no longer in a mood to discuss Ames or QI. In fact, she was again irritated at Zeke for having made her upset about her clothes.

"Acey, I said I needed to talk to you," Zeke said for the second time. "I'm not saying it for practice."

"No, I wouldn't think so," she said without looking at him. "Zeke, I can't now. I missed a goddamn day's work yesterday and I was behind before that happened."

On another day, Schwartz would have taken the rejection at face value and left. The internal pressure that had brought him to the studio, however, was not going to go away until he spoke to her and he knew it.

"I really need to talk now, Acey," he said.

"I can't, Zeke. Maybe I'm not saving a life, but I am busy." She might have been a little curt. Turning to clip an article put most of her back to Schwartz and might have reinforced the impression.

"Dammit," he said, "will you listen to me for a goddamn five minutes, Alice Catherine Henson?"

That got her attention! At the name, her back stiffened, the movement swept the paper she was cutting off the file cabinet and the pages fluttered in disarray to the floor. When she turned around, her mouth was as wide as her eyes.

"Where did you find that?"

Zeke was glad he had closed the door behind him, although it was doubtful that the walls completely muffled the noise.

"That's what I needed to talk to you about," he said. "These were dropped off in my office this morning." He pulled the two volumes from the plastic bag and set them down on the *Washington Post*, which was spread across the top of stacked file boxes.

Acey looked at them but did not touch them. With a little flip, she tossed her scissors on top of them.

"How did you get those?" There was no longer any fire in her voice. It was flat and dull.

Schwartz told her the story of his conversation with Ogilvie, omitting none of the man's comments. "It seems to me that Ogilvie has every intention of getting nasty," he concluded. "So, I figured, if he's going to try and use these, you ought to know what's in them. That's why I brought them."

"Yeah, sure." She picked up the cover of Volume 3 with thumb and forefinger, sending the scissors clattering to the floor. "I know what's in here. I read it all a long time ago. What do you think about it?"

"I didn't read it," he said. "I just brought them. That's all."

"I don't believe you." She fished a cigarette out of a pack on her desk, lit it, sucked it fiercely to life and blew a cloud of smoke into the air between them.

Zeke felt the grayness swirl around him and he could feel his eyes begin to sting. Acey's office was small by itself. As it filled with smoke, it seemed to shrink, all four walls closing in around them. His eyes fastened onto the glowing tip in front of her face.

"Could you put that out?" he asked.

"No."

"Dammit, why not? I feel like I'm choking in here."

"Then go outside. I want it."

"What the hell for?" Zeke could feel his anger rising to meet what he heard in her voice. "Just what do you need it for?" he demanded again. "You know you have diabetes and you have to know damned well that those make it worse."

"Oh, save it for your clinic," she snapped back.

"I don't need to save it for my clinic. I take care of kids, remember? And that has nothing to do with it. You shouldn't be smoking."

"Will you stop treating me like one of your goddamn patients!"

"I am not treating you like one of my goddamn patients!"

"The hell you're not! Why are you bugging me about this?"

"Because I care about you!" The words shot out of his mouth without thought, much the same as his earlier comments. He had not thought at all about what he was saying from the moment Acey had said she did not believe him.

Acey closed the distance between them until they were almost toe to toe.

She glared at him out of blue eyes gone stone cold. She inhaled deeply on the cigarette while she scanned his face.

"Hah!" she exclaimed, exhaling and blowing the smoke in his face. Schwartz let out an explosive cough and doubled over rubbing his eyes. When he straightened up, with his back against the door, he saw that she had turned around and walked back to her desk. From there, she whirled around to face him again.

"I said I didn't believe you. I don't. It's bullshit. I can't believe anyone would sit there and not look, not even you. After all, it makes such interesting reading. Shit, I was a pretty screwed-up kid from a screwed-up family and I wouldn't believe I had any problems. So, periodically, I wouldn't take the insulin, 'you know there's nothing wrong with me,' I'd say, that's the whole routine, and they'd cart me off, semicomatose, to the hospital. I'm sure I fried a few brain cells that way. I was certainly wild when I woke up. They all had a good time writing about it. It's all true, too."

"I told you I didn't look at any of it."

"And I said bullshit. Did you like the one in Volume 4 where I woke up and told the intern I was going to break the IV bottle and cut his balls off with it if he didn't let me go home. Do you have any idea what it's like to have your hands and feet tied to the bed rails while the social worker reads you what she's writing? I doubt it. Then, there's Volume 3. Half of that's about my miscarriage. You must have loved that."

"Miscarriage?"

The question halted her rapid fire speech. She crushed out the remainder of her cigarette and lit another one. She looked carefully at the surprised expression on Zeke's face.

"Son of a bitch! You really didn't read through them, did you? There's no way you could have missed that fiasco. I will be damned."

"I told you I didn't."

Acey shook her head and sat back against the edge of her desk. It was as though she had been looking for something to prove Schwartz was telling the truth and now she had it. No one reading her chart could have missed that episode and no one who had read it could have looked as stupefied as Schwartz when she mentioned it. The anger was gone and so was the energy she needed to hold herself up. Her arms and legs now seemed to hang from their sockets. She inhaled and let the smoke trickle out her nostrils.

"I didn't believe you," she said, "couldn't believe you, didn't want to believe you. What's funny, is that, all of a sudden, I don't mind you knowing about it, any of it. I did have a miscarriage. Hell, I was a fifteen-year-old punk who wasn't going to listen to anybody and was going to do whatever I damn well felt like. So, I did and got myself knocked up, a real gristlehead move if there ever was one. I guess it was the only time I can say that having diabetes did anything that worked out well. I was out of control, my sugar was out of control, and I just bounced in and out of the hospital. I lost the kid, no surprise really, and probably for the best." She laughed, but it sounded forced. "I mean, having me for a mother wouldn't be too great, would it? Bad enough now. Back then, forget it! I've always wondered, though. No, cut that." From across the room, Zeke could see the shiver that gripped her torso. It passed in a moment, along with the sad look on her face, but he remembered it for a long time.

"I'm sorry to hear it," Zeke said. "It can't have been easy dealing with all that."

"It wasn't. I was just a crazy fucked-up kid, Doc, and maybe the only difference today is that I don't let it show so much, but, in case you're worried, I'm not psychotic. Even the four tight-asshole shrinks I saw at one time or another never said that."

"I never thought it," Zeke said. "I think I know enough not to need a chart for that. What the hell, I mean, we're all a little crazy in our own way. Look at me. I've got to be as nutty as you, it's just not the explosive kind of nutty."

Acey grinned at him. She planted her hands on the desk alongside her hips and pushed up so that her body hung, suspended from her shoulders, an inch clear of the desk, while she waved her legs in the air. "You are pretty weird, Doc. I knew that from the moment we met." She settled herself onto the desktop crumpling the *Star-Ledger* in the process. "Now, do you mind if I smoke?"

"No," he lied, and grinned along with her because she knew he was lying. "I still need to talk to you about those charts, though. Ogilvie didn't make a scene in my office for no reason. I'm sure he's planning to spread that stuff around if you don't quiet down."

"Possibly," Acey said. "Let me tell you about my meeting with Dickhead Ames yesterday." She was brief, but complete.

"Damn," was the first word out of Schwartz's mouth. "You know, when this first started I thought that maybe there could be some connection between Aspergicin and these kids, but I knew it wasn't real likely. When I look at the science of it, a causal connection doesn't make sense. But then, you look at all of this crap that's happening." His voice trailed off.

"And you have to wonder," she finished for him. "Yeah."

"So, what are you going to do?" he asked.

"Me?" Acey leaned back on the desk and laughed at the ceiling. "I just finished figuring out tonight's show."

"But what about that stuff?" Schwartz pointed at the chart.

"But nothing. Zeke, what am I? I'm a radio personality with a reputation for being bizarre and maybe a bit crazy. I'm not going to be appointed

Secretary of State. That shit, well it's personal, but other than that, it's no big deal. Hell, it's quite the thing these days for stars to hang their dirty laundry out in public. Publish that and my audience share will probably go up. The question is, what are you going to do? Can you stand the heat?"

"Huh?"

Acey laughed again, her good humor totally restored. "Sometimes you say the dearest things when you don't say anything. Your weasel, Ogilvie, isn't shooting at me. He's after you. You're my expert and he wants you to jump ship. He's not warning you to get out of the way because they're going after me, hell no! He's threatening to ruin your reputation, not mine; mine's too hard to ruin. After all, guys like Ogilvie are mostly politicians. Having those charts on the desk, what would he do in your place? He'd check it out, of course. Once you do that, whether you want to drop me or not, Ogilvie has you because if it gets out that you went through the charts, you got problems. After all, it's well known that I can be pretty vicious." She chuckled as she said it. "The one thing he'd never expect is that you'd come here with them. Politically, that would be crazy because, like I said, who would trust themselves to vicious little me?"

Zeke let out a laugh of his own. "What can I say? Bedfellows make strange politics."

"Cute, Doc. Not very good, but cute. But, seriously, you tell me. What do you want me to do?"

"Knock yourself out," said Zeke Schwartz. Then, looking at his watch, "I've got to get back and make rounds."

"Good evening, New Jersey! This is Acey Henson, your favorite Ace in Space and I'm back in orbit after a highly unusual night on the ground. And before you take that thought any further, I had my feet on the ground, not my back. Anyway, it's been an interesting day. Hell, interesting! Lord, Almighty, you wouldn't believe where my medical records turned up today and it seems that they got there because of this discussion we've been having about the Meldrum leak. Well, they're sitting here with me now, as is Ted Cromartie from the Law School at the University of Pennsylvania and he's going to have something to say about the way those records got here. Then we'll get our lines open and see what you think of all this, since most of us have some medical records somewhere. Who knows, maybe we'll read an excerpt or two, although I'll tell you in advance, they don't write down the juiciest parts.

Jola was concentrating so hard on the note she was trying to write that she almost jumped off her stool when Zeke Schwartz said, "Good evening."

"Not yet, I hope," she said and looked at her watch for confirmation. It was, indeed, just past four-thirty.

"I suppose not," Schwartz said. "Well, good afternoon, then."

"Sure," Jola said. "What can I do for you?"

"Nothing. I just wanted to let you know that Jerry is going home this evening. You've spent a lot of time with that family. I thought you might like to stop by before they leave."

"Thanks, I'll try. What time are they going?"

"Mrs. Inman said around six," Schwartz replied. "Are you on tonight?"

"No, thank God. I'm just trying to finish up down here. I promised Bobby we'd go out for dinner." She saw no need to mention that he had been groaning for the last week about how he had been reduced to going to McDonald's for dinner. "I should be able to swing by for a quick hello once I've signed out here."

"Good. Jerry will like that and Mrs. Inman will appreciate it even if she doesn't show it. You did a real nice job with Jerry when you were up there last month, not just handling the medicine but working with the family."

Jola blushed. "Thanks," was the only word she could manage.

"My pleasure," said Schwartz. "Have a good evening and enjoy that dinner."

The blush lasted for a few minutes after Schwartz left. Compliments were rare in the hospital. The hospital staff—and it did not seem to matter whether it was an attending, a resident or even a nurse—were quick to point out mistakes and shortcomings. It sometimes seemed to Jola that those were the only kind of comments an intern ever heard. This was nice. She was still thinking about it when she was interrupted again, this time by the Chief Resident. For a moment, she thought that Schwartz had spoken to him about her work but she was quickly disabused.

"How's it going, Jo?" he asked.

"Pretty well. Trying to get ready to sign out."

"Yeah. Look, Jo, we've got a little problem here. Maggie on 4 North had to go home sick a little while ago and she's on call tonight. You're up for sick call. I know it's not great to get hit for sick call this late in the day, but there's not much I can do about it."

Jola's mouth hung open. "I'm signing out in fifteen minutes," she protested. "We're supposed to know by noon if we have to take sick call."

"I know that," the Chief Resident said. "I can't help it that Maggie started feeling sick this afternoon."

"She always feels sick when she's on call."

"That's inappropriate," the Chief Resident snapped. "Is there some reason you cannot take call?"

Jola decided that he would take a dim view of a dinner date as a reason to avoid call. "No," she said.

"Good. They are expecting you for sign-out at five."

"Five! I still have to finish here."

The Chief Resident just shrugged. "I saw Schwartz when I came into the ER," he said. "Is he bringing someone in?"

The change of topic told Jola that the subject of sick call was closed. "Not that I know of," she said.

"Good. We're tight for beds tonight. Incidentally, you'll just have one open on 4 North when Jerry Inman goes home. That should give you a quiet night."

That is not the point, she thought to herself as he left. She looked at her watch again. There was no way she could possibly be on the floor by five. At least, if she called home right away, Bobby would not be home yet. That way, she could leave a message on the answering machine and avoid having to explain the situation.

It was actually twenty after five before she reached the conference room on 4 North. Gathered there were Tony C., one other intern, two medical students and the Senior Resident, who turned out to be Rosenbloom. None of them looked very happy.

"Nice of you to come by, Jo," he said. "We've been sitting here for twenty minutes."

At the sarcasm in his voice, she felt herself go hot. "I had to finish in the ER," she said. "If there was a problem, you could have beeped me."

"We did," Rosenbloom said.

Jola felt even worse. Her beeper had gone off, she had not answered it and, in her rush, had forgotten about it. "I'm sorry," she said. "I just found out about this a half hour ago."

"Oh, come on, Jo, Maggie went home at least two hours ago, which is when I spoke to the Chief Resident."

Jola simply looked at him and said nothing.

"Okay, okay," Rosenbloom said. "This is just wasting more time. Let's get to it."

Evening rounds consisted of walking around the floor, going room to room. At each room, they would stop and review the status of the two patients inside. Since Jola knew none of the recent information about any of the patients, she wanted some detail about how they were doing and what she was expected to do that night. That put her in conflict again with Rosenbloom, who was interested in the briefest possible reports. The tension rose as they went around the floor and the hour grew later. Rounds took so long that by the time they reached Jerry's room, the Inmans had already come and gone. That bothered Jola. She also worried that Schwartz would hear that she had not come as she had promised. It annoyed her that Rosenbloom was openly grateful for one less patient to see.

When rounds finally dragged to an end, the house staff and medical students headed for the elevators. Jola watched them go from a short distance down the hall, fists clenched at her sides. Just as the doors opened, Tony glanced back at her and detached himself from the group to walk back.

"What's eating you, Jo?" he asked. "I mean, sure it sucks to get hit for sick call right at the end of the day but, shit, it could happen to any of us. Probably will."

"Sure. Tony, how sick was Maggie?"

Immediately, he looked wary. "No idea," he said. "I wasn't on the floor. Rosenbloom saw her, said she could go. Is that why you're pissed?"

"That's not it," she said.

"What then? You're looking like you need a doctor instead of being one."

"Isn't it obvious?" Jola snapped. "It's not bad enough I've got to take sick call for a ditz who probably isn't really sick, but I had work in the ER to finish and all Rosenbloom can do is bitch and moan that rounds are late and they are taking too long. Dammit, I'm sorry if they were long but I don't know the floor."

Tony sighed and put a hand on her shoulder. "Look at it from their point of view, Jo. It was five o'clock. They all want to go home."

"Well, that's all well and swell but I still had work downstairs before I could come up. What do they expect me to do about that?"

"Turf it off," Tony said, "just like we all do. Christ, ninety-eight percent of those kids don't belong in the ER anyway. Whatever they've got could be handled at home or, at most, in the private's office. The best place for them is OTD, as in out the door. You greet 'em and street 'em, sayonara Charley and adios muchachos. It doesn't take that much time."

"Yeah, sure. And what about the two percent who are really sick?"

"If they're that sick, they'll come back."

"I can't do that, Tony."

"Well, you should. What do you think, that you're being a hero putting in a whole bunch of extra time? You're not, you know."

"I'm not trying to be a hero, Tony," she said softly. "I just want to be a good doc."

"Yeah. But look at you. If you're like this now, what are you going to be like in February?"

"I don't know." Her voice was almost inaudible.

"I do. Fried to a crisp. It ain't worth it. Shit, none of these people appreciate it. Spend as much time as you like, they'll still turn around and sue your ass if something happens they don't like. You want to slave thirty-six hours over some kid? Make a mistake and they'll still crucify you, no matter how much you sweated. It ain't worth it. It's a job, Jo, that's all. You put in your time, pick up your check, such as it is, and get the hell out of here as soon as you can. That's the way to do it."

Jola shook herself, as though she had a shiver, and, in the process, dislodged Tony's hand. "Tony," she asked, "why did you become a doc?"

"Seemed like a good idea at the time." He smiled. "More precisely, that way my grandmother keeps me in her will."

"Jesus."

Tony seemed to ignore her reaction. "Jo, I worry about you, sometimes. I really do. Keep this up and you won't even make it to February, don't even think about June. Look, I'll tell you what. We're both off Saturday. Why don't I pick you up in the afternoon and we'll have a pleasant evening and forget about this place?"

"Tony, did you forget something? I have a fiancé I'd like to spend Saturday with."

"That's a point." He smiled again. "Well, the offer is good anytime you just want to get away and talk." He gave her arm a little squeeze before he left.

Jola waited until the elevator doors closed behind him before she went back to the nursing station. It was going to be a long night.

PART
III

Give me a moral man who insists on doing the right thing all the time, and I will show you a tangle which an angel couldn't get out of.

FROM "THE ONCE AND FUTURE KING"

BY T.H. WHITE

Chapter 24

EARLY SEPTEMBER in the hills of New Jersey was normally a time of ambivalence for children. The weather was usually pleasant, still warm enough to run around out of doors without a jacket but without the sauna conditions that prevailed in August. It was the perfect kind of weather for outdoor games. Unfortunately, with the passing of Labor Day also came the beginning of the school year, which blocked out the best time of the day.

Normally, Jerry would have shared those mixed feelings. This particular September, however, he was almost eager to return to school. He had felt much better during August, especially after they let him go home, even though he hated having to go to the doctor so often for shots. He even felt well enough to go back to the baseball league. Unfortunately, while the baseball team let him come to the games and wear his uniform and sit on the bench, they would not let him play. That was fine for a while, but Jerry soon felt that he could swing a bat or run to first base as well as any of them. His coach would not agree. The other kids would not let him play in the pick-up games either. He took his protest to Dr. Schwartz during a clinic visit and Schwartz said it was fine for him to play, but his mother said, "I'd just as soon he didn't." At other times, he would have turned to his father for help against his mother, but Charley was not around much and, during that particular clinic visit, although he was there he said nothing. That was the end of the matter as far as Jerry playing baseball. That was why Jerry was anxious for school to start. He could sit in class and be no different than anybody else. He was sure they would not let him play in the soccer league either, but if he went to school nobody would notice if he skipped soccer.

Soon after school began, however, Jerry's condition began to slowly deteriorate. This was not something he noticed. It was not even something his parents noticed. It was a gradual change and Jerry, for the most part, felt the same from one day to the next. His parents saw nothing because Ellen Inman was trying not to pay attention and Charley was mostly drunk by the time he came home. It was a teacher who, toward the end of the month, noticed that Jerry was thinner than he had been at the beginning of school and too tired at the end of the day to keep up with the class.

The teacher was young and, of course, she knew that one of the children in her class was suffering from cancer. Although she had been provided with this information, no one had told her what to expect of such a child. Seeing Jerry's fatigue raised the concern in her mind that one afternoon he would simply put his head down on the desk and die of an acute attack of cancer, the way such children often did in the movies. After a week of worrying about it, she spent a sleepless night and resolved to call the Inmans the next day.

Ellen Inman took the call calmly, much to the surprise of the young teacher. "It's the shots Jerry's taking that make him tired," Mrs. Inman said. "That's not too unusual and we don't worry about it."

"Are you sure?" asked the teacher. "He's really pooped at the end of the day."

"He's fine at home," said Mrs. Inman. "I'm sure it's just the shots."

"Well, okay," the teacher responded, "but he was taking the shots, wasn't he, when school started. He wasn't tired then."

"He was sometimes. I will mention it to the doctor though." Ellen Inman thanked the teacher for her concern, because it was really nice that she had bothered to call, and hung up the phone. She did not call Schwartz right away.

The delay was not really intentional. Ellen Inman believed that Jerry was tired because of his shots. She refused to allow herself to believe anything else. She had too many other problems for Jerry to be sick again. Charley had lost his job. She had suspected that for a while and finally proved it one day when she found him at Milardo's Bar and Grill in the middle of the day. The confrontation had been loud and heated, Charley having denied it at first. Luckily, the owner of the bar knew them both and declined to charge them for the broken glassware. That was all the luck she had out of it, however. She had thought that by confronting Charley over the issue of his job, he would feel compelled to find another one, from shame if nothing else. That did not happen. With his joblessness out in the open, Charley seemed to feel free to sit home and drink, as opposed to going out as though he was going to work. That exasperated Mrs. Inman. Without a job, they had no insurance. She told Mrs. Schmidt about the situation, in spite of having been raised to keep family problems private. Mrs. Schmidt was sympathetic, even to the point of offering to have the parents' group raise money for Jerry. Ellen Inman turned that down. She had also been raised never to take charity and she was not going to start now. Jerry simply could not be sick again, she told herself. Anyway, she figured, they had an appointment to see Schwartz the last week of the month. Maybe if Jerry stayed home and rested for a day or two, he would feel better by then.

Jerry did not feel any better by the time they were due to see Dr. Schwartz. Ellen Inman thought that he did, but that was only because she had convinced herself of it. The truth was, Jerry was exhausted.

In the actual event, Ellen Inman's perception of Jerry's energy turned out not to be very important. Jerry had lost most of the weight he had regained the previous month and, as soon as Schwartz saw that on the clinic sheet, he was looking for trouble, protestations that Jerry seemed fine notwithstanding. The question Schwartz had to answer was, where was the trouble? The logical place to look was the liver, which was where it had all started. There was not much to see. Jerry's eyes had gone back to being white right after his surgery and they had stayed that way. The portion of his liver that remained to him was still functioning. His belly, where the surgery had been done, was hard to examine, all the suturing left hard ridges and lumps under the surface scar. Schwartz was used to the lumps and bumps, though. They did not feel any different than on the last occasion he had examined Jerry. None of that was reassuring, not when the child was losing weight. Schwartz drew some blood and sent Jerry off for an X-ray of his chest. All of that had been planned for the visit anyway, so Schwartz was able to temporarily postpone discussing his worries. One or more of those studies might answer all the questions. Then, he tried to forget about all of it while he saw his next patient. Scarcely had he finished seeing that child, however, when his beeper rang. The person on the other end of the call was the radiologist.

"Zeke," he said, "I'm looking at a chest film on a kid of yours named Jerry Inman."

"Yeah. What have you got?"

"Nothing good, I'm afraid. Multiple metastases in both lung fields. All new since the last film."

"Shit. I'll be right down."

The walk down the corridor was futile. The film looked just as the radiologist had described it. There was new tumor growing in both of Jerry's lungs.

"Damn." Schwartz jammed his fists down into the pockets of his jacket. "That's one hell of a fast relapse."

"How long since his surgery?" asked the radiologist.

"About two months."

The radiologist let out a whistle. "Tough luck."

"No shit," said Zeke Schwartz.

When he returned to the clinic, he took Ellen Inman into one of the examining rooms, leaving Jerry playing with the Pacman in the waiting room.

"I'm afraid the tumor is growing back," Schwartz said. He wished, just as he always wished, that there was some way of saying it without actually saying it. That was never possible, of course, so he said it as gently as he could knowing that the words would strike harder than most physical blows.

Ellen Inman's face did not change, although tears built up at the corners of her eyes. She turned down the proffered Kleenex and wiped the tears away with her fingers. "Damn," she said. She took a long breath, let it out and said, "Damn," again. "I knew this was going to happen," she said. "Can you treat him again?"

"Not with the interferon. That's already failed. There's no point in giving it any more."

"But there are other drugs. You said so."

"That's right. We talked about some of them when Jerry first got sick."

"Can you give him one of those?"

"Of course."

"What happens if you don't treat him?"

"The tumor will keep growing and it will kill him."

"Those people and their damn plant." The words were said softly, but not so softly that Schwartz could not hear them. A shudder went through Ellen Inman's body. "How long?"

"That's hard to say. Judging by how fast it came back, I don't think very long. Weeks maybe."

"And one of those other drugs could cure him?"

"Unfortunately, I don't think so." Schwartz looked carefully at Mrs. Inman, trying to gauge what she was ready to hear. "We can make it go away again, maybe, but it will come back again. That's the nature of these things."

"But maybe one of those drugs could keep it away for a while?"

"It's possible, although I have to tell you, the odds aren't very good."

"If they aren't zero, I want to take it. If there's any chance at all, even if it's not for a cure, I want it for him."

"I can do that."

"Okay." She took another deep breath. "Look, Dr. Schwartz, does Jerry have to be in the hospital right now? I mean, I'm going to have some trouble paying for it." She stopped short of saying why.

"Actually, no," Schwartz replied. "There's no reason he has to be in right now. I'd like him to be able to spend as much time at home as he can, so we'll use a regimen that shouldn't require him to come into the hospital."

"Thank you." She took a Kleenex then and blew her nose. "Dr. Schwartz, is that plant up there what's killing my kid? Are you sure?"

"I'm not sure," Schwartz said. "I wish I was."

Ellen Inman seemed not to hear him. "I don't want them to get away with it," she said. "I don't want that at all."

* * *

Jerry was going to be the lead topic of discussion at the Tumor Board. Zeke knew that and knew there was no way of dodging it, so he listed Jerry as the first case. Might as well get it over with, he thought. The "it" would include not only the discussion of the case, which might be fairly brief because there was little that could be said, but also all the slightly veiled barbs. The interferon had obviously failed, and failed rather fast too, so now certain people would have the opportunity to say, "I told you so," and make other reproving comments about Zeke's management of the case. It made no difference that the result would have been the same had Zeke yielded to their treatment suggestions in the first place. They would just shrug and claim that at least the child would have had the "first-line" treatment. Zeke thought sourly that it did a patient no good to say, "Cheer up, at least you're dying the way the literature says you should." There were always some, though, who could be counted on to start an argument and it only became worse if they sensed that the presenting physician was beginning to squirm under their attack. It was for that reason that Zeke planned to present the case himself. If potshots were to be taken, they would have to be aimed directly at him rather than some poor house officer sent up to the front of the room as a sacrifice.

Attendance was quite good, Zeke noted when he arrived for the meeting. He wondered if that was chance or due to the possibility of seeing Zeke Schwartz eat crow. No matter. He was not going to give them the pleasure of seeing him hesitate. He walked directly to the head of the table, handed out the attendance sheet for everyone to sign and launched into his presentation while the paper was still making its way around the table. It was a concise description of Jerry's course from his first arrival at the hospital to the present day, including a summary of the discussion at the first Tumor Board. There were no extra words, but nothing was left out either. If someone had wanted to teach a medical student how to present a case, it would have made a good model. Zeke ended with Jerry's most recent chest X-ray projected on the screen. The normally black lung fields looked as though they had been pelted with tiny snowballs, each one a focus of spreading tumor.

"That's where we stand now," Schwartz said. "My personal feeling is that no purpose is served by pushing more therapy, not in this tumor at this stage, but the family wants to try something and there is no reason that we can't. Comments please?"

"I guess the interferon was a flop," said Dr. Gagne.

"I'd say that shows an uncanny grasp of the obvious," Schwartz retorted.

There was complete silence in the room after that. Schwartz kept his eyes on Gagne. Go ahead, Schwartz seemed to be saying to the others, but first, tell me which one of you will not make a mistake or have a good decision turn out bad, before I forget about today. From the silence, it was clear they were thinking the same thing.

Gagne shifted uncomfortably in his seat. "We could have tried the Adriamycin first."

"Which would have done about as well as it always does in these cases," Schwartz said, "which is lousy. Is anybody interested in discussing the further management of this case?"

"The best advice I could give would be not to buy any long-playing records," said Dr. Wu.

The gallows humor broke the tension and brought a grim smile to Schwartz's face. "Okay," he said. "Any treatment options besides that?"

The options, once they began to discuss them, were few in number. In a short period of time, the group had concluded that Jerry should get the Adriamycin he did not receive the first time around.

"Zeke, I know you were opposed to this the last time we talked," Worthington said, "but it is very reasonable as a second-line option."

"As good as anything else," Schwartz said, "which is to say, not much. However, among the possibilities we have, I agree with you. In fact, I've already told Mrs. Inman that this is what we are going to do."

Agreeing that it represented the best of a bad set of choices did not mean that Zeke was happy about it. He was not. Jerry was being treated because there was something available to treat him with and doing it made his parents and the other physicians feel better. Zeke did not delude himself that it was likely to make Jerry feel better. Jerry was not unique, either, a fact that also made Zeke unhappy. It was one thing for a fifty-year-old man to listen to all the possibilities and say that he wanted to be treated even when there was no chance. Zeke himself was not sure how he would decide if he was the one listening to the death sentence. It was not Jerry's decision, though. It had been his parents' decision, more exactly it had been Mrs. Inman's decision. The situation gnawed at him, the way most things did when he had no control over them. It made him grumpy on rounds, which he took out on the house staff. It made him toss half a perfectly good pizza into the trash at his apartment. Mostly, it kept him from concentrating on anything until it was late enough to drive over to see Acey. Once at her apartment, he recounted the events of the day and his displeasure with them. She listened, without saying anything, until he had finished and she had her cigarette lit.

"I guess I'm dense," she said. "What's wrong with trying?"

"Because this stuff isn't like taking two Tylenol. If I give him enough of a dose to have any chance of affecting the tumor, I'll probably make him sick. There's too much bad that can happen and not enough good."

"Then why don't you just say no?"

"Because I can't. Well, that's not exactly right. I could, of course. But Mrs. Inman isn't ready for that. I spent a lot of time talking to her. She can't deal with the idea of not doing something. Not yet."

"But maybe he'll be lucky. It could happen, couldn't it? I mean, maybe it would be a miracle, but miracles happen occasionally, don't they?"

Zeke sighed. "Acey, have you ever heard of chi-chi?"

"Chi-chi? That was a golfer, right?" When she saw Zeke was not smiling, she said, "No, I haven't."

"Okay. I don't know where it came from, originally, but it's basically from a story about three English missionaries who are captured by savages. They are tied up and thrown into a hut and then the chief of the tribe comes in. He walks over to the first man and says, 'Englishman! You have a choice. Death or chi-chi.' Given that choice, the missionary naturally chose chi-chi. So, they carried him out of the hut and down to the river where they cut him apart, just a little piece at a time, and then drowned him so that he died horribly. Then the chief went back to the hut and said to the second man, 'You have a choice. Death or chi-chi.' Well, he knew the first man hadn't come back, but given the choice, he too chose chi-chi. Whereupon, they carried him out to the village square where they flayed him alive and staked him out in the sun so that he died horribly, too. Again the chief returned to the hut and this time confronted the last man. 'You have a choice,' he said again. 'Death or chi-chi.' The last man thought about it. Neither of his companions had returned, and he had heard the second man's screams, so he had a fairly clear idea of the choice in front of him. Summoning up all of his courage, he looked the chief in the eye and declared, 'I choose death!' For a moment, the chief was taken aback; he didn't know what to say. But then, he smiled and rubbed his hands together and said, 'All right. Death it is. But first, a little chi-chi!' Sometimes, Acey, treating people is like chi-chi. You're not allowed to die without it."

"Doc, that's sick!" The ash on Acey's cigarette had grown to half its length and scattered when she thumped the kitchen table with her hand.

"I didn't say it wasn't sick. That's just the way it is sometimes. You wind up doing what is possible instead of what is best."

"The way you tell it, this doesn't sound like a new insight."

"It's not. Anybody who cares about what he's doing knows when he hits one of those times. You learn to make the best of bad situations. I've just never felt like talking about it with anybody before."

Acey flushed and hid it behind smoke. "You know," she said, "now that I think about it, maybe I could use that story of yours on the show, I mean, the basic joke is old, but I've never seen it twisted that way before."

"Try it Henson, and I'll strangle you on the air. Is there some particular reason why I can't pay you a compliment without you trying to wiggle out of it or make me angry?"

Acey blew smoke. "Compliments and me don't mix. When I get one, I look for reasons. God, don't look so serious! I'm not going to use it on the show. Listen, maybe I can't take a compliment, but I can give a massage and you look like you could use one. Why don't you come to bed and I'll cure what ails you?"

Chapter 25

FLEMINGTON, NEW JERSEY _____

ACEY FELT exhausted after her show the following night. She left the studio and stopped at the door to her office. Her shoulders sagged as though she was carrying a sixty pound pack rather than her battered leather jacket. From the doorway, she could see the stack of work she had left on her desk. Earlier that evening, she had left it there with the foolish idea in her head of tackling it after the show. No way. It was too much to deal with at two in the morning.

The admission brought an automatic mental protest. Nothing was too much for Acey Henson, a voice asserted somewhere in the back of her head. The voice, however, could not move her to action. It was more of an empty ritual, left over from the times when it had been true. There was too much to do and she knew it. There were even times, of late, when she wished that Ames would finally go ahead and fire her, simply so that she would no longer be faced with more work than she could do.

"Bit off more than you could chew," she murmured. "What the hell, I make a living off clichés." It had been fine for a while, back when she had figured that Roger would be better in a week or two. She had been able to tell herself that she could do anything for a week or two or three. Roger, however, had not come back in any number of weeks. Acey had been forced to the realization that he was never coming back. He might linger a while longer, a miserable shadow of the person she fought to remember, but he would never come back to work. Even Howard, she believed, had come to that conclusion, although what Howard thought the reason might be she could only guess. Howard, who had never bothered to make the effort to pierce Acey's deception about the illness, proved equally unwilling to force the issue of Roger's return. Howard was content to avoid the problem, leave Roger on the payroll, leave his office empty. It had occurred to Acey that it was Acey who was making it possible for Howard to duck his responsibilities. She was covering for Roger, doing Roger's job, and that meant that Howard did not need to do anything. Unfortunately, that meant that Acey had to do her show, Roger's regular work, and all of Howard's work that was routinely left for Roger. She was running out of steam. She was afraid that the fatigue was beginning to creep into her show. Her customary verve was lacking. If that went on, her ratings would suffer with predictable dire consequences. Still, the only way out was to stop covering for Roger and that was unthinkable to her. To do that was the same as yelling, "I give up!" Acey would sooner slit her wrists. True, another job might come along, as she had told Roger, but one had not materialized so far. The only other escape would be when Roger finally died. She had no idea of when that might happen. Zeke might, but she had not asked him.

"I'll be damned if I'm going to root for someone to die," she said into the doorway. If she asked Zeke when Roger might die, he might think that she was anticipating it.

Thinking of Zeke made her shake her head. There was another complication in her life. She liked what she had with him, even if she was not sure what it was. Zeke, certainly, had never put a tag on it. Was it an affair, a relationship, or something else? What was it supposed to be? Zeke liked what he did, worked hard at it, and seemed to find it perfectly natural that she did the same. Their time for each other was worked around each schedule, even at the expense of sleep. When Acey thought about it, she found it equally reassuring and troubling. She thought she liked the arrangement, but she wondered if she could expect it to continue. She was more than a little scared that it would not.

"Christ," she said in the direction of her desk, "it's not as though I'm a damned virgin with a crush on the teacher."

Acey shook her head again, trying to clear it. She had lived with uncertainty most of her life. Only in the last two years had she been able to settle into a comfortable routine. Now Zeke and Roger were threatening to bounce her out of it. She found that the prospect upset her. Stability was too comfortable.

"All of this," she said, "is neither getting my work done nor getting me rest."

She realized with a start that she had been speaking out loud and looked around to see if anyone might have overheard. She could not recall how much she had said and how much she had only thought. There was no one in sight, not surprising for the middle of the night. Even if someone had heard, so what? There were advantages to being considered weird.

To hell with work! To hell with the schedule and most especially, to hell with the advertising budget. They would still be there when she came back. Carefully, she pulled the door closed, giving the knob a habitual twist to check the lock.

The night air was cool and moist. Usually, it picked up her spirits, but not this night. It was a clear night, with a myriad stars overhead and no moon, just the kind of night she loved to stare out into. Acey felt too tired for stargazing. She undid the chain on her motorcycle and then looked back at the WCZY building, mostly out of relief at leaving. As she did, something caught her attention. There was something wrong with the building. It took a moment before she could decide what it was. When she recognized it, her breath came in small, rapid gulps. There was light in her office, not the light of the desk lamp or overhead light. It was a dim light, as though the corridor light was coming through an open door. Acey had closed that door. She knew she had. She waited for the overhead light to go on, someone searching for the schedule, or a paper, or something left in the office. It did not go on. Someone was in her office, in the dark, and wanted it that way. All of a sudden, Acey was not weary any more.

Carefully, she wrapped the chain around her right hand, leaving about ten inches and the padlock dangling free from her fist. Then she walked back into the building. Inside, the corridor was silent and empty. Normally, Acey's stride down the corridor announced her presence to anyone within earshot, but she could move quietly when she wanted. She glided along with only an occasional scuff, no louder than the sound of her breathing.

She came to a stop at the open door to her office and flattened herself against the wall. From inside, she could hear a shuffle of feet followed by the squeak of a file cabinet drawer. Someone was definitely in her office. Acey fought to control her breathing, which was becoming rapid and deep. If it sounded as loud to others as it did in her ears, it would give her away. It might have been smart to back away from the door at that point and call the police, but she did not. Acey Henson had never called the police in her entire life, except, that is, for names they did not appreciate.

Ever so cautiously, she eased her face to the edge of the door jamb. In the office, she could see someone at her filing cabinet. Fortunately, the person's back was to the door. It was a rather small someone, she thought. Then, recognition sank in. It was Pamela.

Casually, Acey reached her arm through the door and flipped the light switch on. "Is there something you're looking for?" she asked.

At the light and the words, Pamela gave a shriek. She hopped in the air, spun around and then lost her footing, tumbling back against the file cabinet, which gave out a hollow thump. Her face flashed red, then white. No words came out.

Acey looked at the girl with a puzzled frown. She could easily think of reasons for Pamela to be in her office, but few of them involved the file cabinet and in no case was there a reason for her to be there with the light out. Pamela's performance on being found did not suggest a legitimate errand.

"I'd like to know what you were doing," Acey said. "In fact, I'm expecting a careful and totally original explanation."

The explanation was not forthcoming, at least, not right away. Instead, Pam sagged back against the file cabinet and started to cry.

"Tears won't do it, Pammy," Acey said. The only thing they did was to convince her that something was wrong.

Acey stepped completely into the office and closed the door behind her. "I'm waiting," she said.

"I didn't want to," Pam whispered amidst her tears.

"Didn't want to what?"

"I didn't want to do it."

"That tells me nothing." There was an edge in Acey's voice.

"I can't! You'll fire me if I tell you," Pam wailed.

"Maybe. However, I can assure you that's nothing compared to what I'll do to you if you don't tell me."

Pam looked up and caught sight of the chain for the first time. "Oh, God," she said. "You wouldn't."

"Don't ever bet your life on what I would or wouldn't do. Now. What happened?"

With a sniffle, Pam slid down to the floor and folded herself into a ball, hugging her knees to her chin. When she spoke, the words barely escaped from the circle she drew around her body with her arms.

"Jason made me do it," she said.

"Who is Jason?"

"My boyfriend."

"Huh. I didn't know you had a boyfriend. What's the story here? Tell me a little bit about this Jason."

"I met him about three weeks ago." Pam stopped there, but started again when she saw Acey's face. "I was at a bar in Somerville and I saw this guy. He was just gorgeous, you know, I mean he looked like someone in those posters at Jack La Lanne. I was just looking at him and then he looked back at me. And then he came over to talk to me. It was so great."

"I'll bet," Acey said. "Tell me something about this kid other than his chest."

Pam flushed. "Jason's not a kid," she said. "He's twenty-eight. He's a salesman, you know, like office supplies. He has his own condo in Bridgewater. That was great. I mean, you know I don't get along with my folks so he said I could move in with him. It was so great. I mean, damn it Acey, look at me!" She flung her arms out wide. Tears were rolling down her cheeks. "I don't look like much and here's this terrific guy who wants me and loves me."

"Can we hold the hormones for a moment, please?" Acey's voice was more acerbic than, perhaps, she had intended. "If it was so damn terrific, how did it get to this?"

Pam sniffled a bit and wiped at her tears before picking up her story. "A few days ago, Jase came home and told me he had a problem. He didn't say what it was, just he had a problem with some guys. I figured it was money. I told him he could have my paycheck if it would help, but he said it wouldn't. But, then, he said that he thought there was something I could get for him that would help."

"And what was that?"

"Jase said if I could get him the information you found about that Meldrum leak, that would help."

Acey stared at the girl without saying anything. Meldrum and Aspergicin again! But why would anyone squeeze little Pammy Davies to find Acey's information on the leak, especially since it was all public now anyway? Briefly, she thought of Ames at QI, then dropped the idea. If Ames wanted her information, he could easily have called her and demanded to see it. Another thought came on the heels of the first. Maybe there was more information and someone thought she had it. Acey decided to wait on that question. The answer was not obvious and she doubted that Pam knew.

"Okay," Acey said, "Jason wanted to do something with the material I got on Meldrum. Why did you say yes? He can't be that good a lay that you'd do something like this."

Pam went scarlet and started to cry again. "I didn't say yes," she insisted.

"That's odd," Acey said. "I could swear I found you digging through my file cabinet."

"Yes, but I didn't want to!"

"Then why?"

"Do I have to tell you?"

"Yes." Acey's tone brooked no further argument.

"All right," Pam said. "Look, Jase and I would get high a lot, or Jase would get me high. It was nice. Everything felt so good. When I told Jase that I didn't want to do it, get your file I mean, he said that I had to. If I didn't, I would be betraying him, that's what he said, when he was already in trouble. If I did that to him, he was going to get even. He'd tell the station about my getting high and then you'd can me for sure."

"Swell guy you found. What kind of stuff were you doing?"

"Nothing major. Just pot and some blow."

"Shit. Pammy, you're damn lucky all he's got you doing is rifling my filing cabinet."

Pam looked down at her feet. "So, what are you going to do to me?"

"I ain't going to do nothing," Acey said. "Not yet anyway. I do have something that I want you to do."

"What?"

"Were you just going to bring this back to his place?"

"Yes. He said if I found it, I should call him and then come straight to the condo."

"Hmm." Acey's eyebrows knit together while she thought it over. "I don't think we want to do that. Instead, I want you to call him, tell him you've got it but you're too scared to go back to his place. Tell him you'll meet him by the Speedway. Do you know this area?" Pam nodded as Acey sketched out the location. "Good. Now the question is, will you do it?"

"What's going to happen?"

"Nothing that shouldn't happen," Acey answered. "He's just using you, you know. It's nothing more than that."

That was easy for Acey Henson to say. Easy for Acey Henson, who had absorbed enough lumps and abuses in her life to look, automatically, for ulterior motives behind even the kindest words. It would be a lot harder, Acey knew, for Pam, who had probably never before had anyone treat her as important or tell her that she was pretty. It was going to be a close thing, Acey thought, whether Pam held to her fantasy that this Jason cared for her. Acey watched the girl closely. A tear rolled out the corner of Pam's eyes and her lip quivered when she tried to talk.

"I'll do it, Acey," she said in a voice that was little more than a whisper.

"Good."

"Acey, what are you going to do afterward? I mean, you know, about me."

"You ever get high at work?" Acey asked.

Pam shook her head, no.

"Then, as far as I'm concerned, you can stay here and keep working for me. But," and Acey's voice turned harsh, "you're going to quit using as of tonight. If I find out you're using, or if you lie to me, I'm telling you right now, I don't believe in counselors, I don't believe in social workers, and I don't believe in any touchy-feely therapy bullshit. Cross me on this and I'll beat you to a pulp and then I'll fire what's left. Clear?" She snapped the heavy chain taut between her two hands in case added emphasis was needed.

Pam nodded a silent yes.

"Say it."

"I'll do it," said Pam.

The phone call went well, with Acey using the station's equipment to listen in. Pam's voice was literally shaking with terror. Whether the terror was induced by the thought of bringing the documents to Jason or by Acey was an even bet, but it was irrelevant to Acey's purpose. Jason had no trouble believing that the girl telephoning him was verging on hysteria. He readily agreed to meet Pam at the Speedway. In fact, Acey thought, there was even relief in his voice that Pam was going to meet him. The way she sounded, it would have been easy to believe that she would throw the folder in a ditch and run away.

The Speedway lay adjacent to Route 31 on the outskirts of the town. On many summer nights, it would be thronged with people cheering the stock car races, but at this hour it was dark and deserted. The tall pines around the Speedway and the many small buildings by the track created pools of shadow darker even than the rest of the night. That was the feature that decided Acey on the location.

They left Pam's car out in plain sight while Acey wheeled her bike into the shadows where it would be invisible almost until it was stumbled over. Then, she hid herself the same way.

The waiting was always the worst of any undertaking for Acey. Whether she was out with a gang as a teenager or waiting to go on the air, waiting gave her time to think. That was dangerous. Was Jason coming alone? There was no way of knowing the answer. It seemed reasonable. After all, he had originally expected Pam to come to his condo. There would be no reason to have henchmen there and it would probably be difficult to find any at three in the morning. Would he be armed? Good chance, Acey thought, which meant there was some risk of getting hurt. She tried to put that out of her mind. This would not be the first time she had been in a desperate fight. Pam was another matter, but the girl had to learn about the world sooner or later. Experience was mostly a matter of surviving your mistakes.

The sound of footsteps brought her alert. She had chosen her vantage point well. She had a clear view of a figure detach itself from the night and walk over to where Pam was waiting. All was as it should be. Jason would have to walk past Acey on his way back to his car. Acey could not hear the conversation between the two of them, but there was not much of it. She saw Jason take the folder and start to turn away. Pam tried to move back to him, but he turned and shoved her roughly to the ground. Acey held her breath, wondering if disaster would strike. It did not. Jason just stood over the fallen girl and gave a short laugh. Then he turned away again.

Jason never saw the heavy motorcycle chain as it came whistling out of the night. He had no inkling of anything wrong until it whipped into his face. The stunning blow knocked him off his feet. Before he could regain his feet, the chain smashed down on his head again and again. He rolled on the ground but the lashing chain followed him. Heavy boots thudded into his ribs and some of them cracked. He moaned, remembered his gun and tried to draw it. The gun was no longer in its holster. Acey had it. She put a knee between his shoulder blades, grasped a handful of hair and pulled his head back to touch the muzzle of the revolver.

"Do you understand what is going to happen if you don't talk to me?" she asked.

The reply was incoherent.

"I asked you a question, motherfucker, I won't ask again. You're useless if you don't talk."

"Yes! I can. Don't shoot! God, don't shoot!"

"Give me a reason not to. Why did you want the documents on Meldrum?"

"I was hired to get 'em. That's all I know. Honest!"

"Hired by who?"

"Guy at Meldrum," Jason answered.

"Who?" Acey shot back. "I want the name!"

"Dwyer. A guy named Pat Dwyer. That's all I know!"

Acey shoved his face down into the dirt and stood over him. "This is a lucky day for you, Jason. You're going to live. If you want to keep living, I suggest you be careful what you say. You cause me trouble and, well, I know people who'll find you. When they do, it won't be a halfway job."

She stepped away and saw that Jason was making no effort to rise. His hands were paddling at the ground and his breathing seemed labored. She walked over to where Pam was sitting, soundlessly, on the ground. "Okay, Pammy, show's over and it's time to go home. I'll have him taken care of. Now, I guess, you know something about the way I grew up."

SCHEUERMANN'S RUN, NEW JERSEY

Later that morning, Pat Dwyer walked into his office at the Meldrum plant. As was his habit, he put his briefcase down on his desk and, before he sat down, he punched the code into his telephone to check his messages. The synthetic voice from the phone told him there were four. The first three had come from salesmen on the West Coast in the early evening. They were routine; he did not even need to take notes. When the machine told him that the last call had come at four-thirty in the morning, his eyebrows went up. Calls at that hour were very unusual.

The tape, when it began to play, held a muffled woman's voice. "Mr.

Dwyer," it said, "Jason has an urgent message for you. Call him ASAP at 555-1548." There was nothing else.

At Jason's name, Dwyer looked up and realized that his office door was open. He walked over to it and looked outside. It was still early, most of the staff had not yet arrived and there did not seem to be anyone who could have heard the message. He closed the door, walked back to his desk and dialed the number.

The phone was picked up and a voice on the other end greeted him with, "Good morning, Medical Intensive Care Unit."

Chapter 26

FLEMINGTON, NEW JERSEY _____

"I FIND it hard to believe that Meldrum tried to burglarize your office." Zeke Schwartz was sitting on the floor of Acey's living room next to the couch, the couch being piled high with file folders. One arm rested on the top of some of them.

"Believe it," Acey replied. "It's true."

She was seated in the armchair, a cigarette in one hand and a cup of coffee in the other. She took a sip of the coffee, made a face and dumped the contents of the cup into the avocado's pot. "Re-microwaving this stuff doesn't work," she muttered.

"You're going to kill that plant."

"Haven't yet."

Zeke looked away from the plant and thought about what Acey had told him. It still seemed incredible. Such things did not happen outside of Hollywood movies, paperback books or the government.

"Do you know who's responsible?"

"A guy name of Pat Dwyer. I checked him out. He's in charge of Sales and Marketing at Meldrum. Supposedly, he's quite a hotshot."

"Stupid move if you ask me," Zeke said. "What could he get that's worth the risk? I mean, now you really have some ammunition to use."

Acey shook her head. "Not really, I don't."

"Why not? This whole thing stinks and has from the start. It's just one stone wall after another and it makes me wonder what the truth is. Anyway, you could call it Meldrumgate, or Druggate, or Leakgate, or something like that."

Acey did not laugh. "Zeke, please shut up and leave the catchy slogans to me. You're not very good at it. But I can't do it anyway."

"Why not? As I recall, I was the only one holding you back when this got started. Now I'm not."

"True. The problem is that they used Pammy to get at my stuff. There's no way I can do the story without blowing her away also. I don't want to do that. She's just a kid and she's no worse than I was at her age. If she learns from this, she can still do okay, but not if I make a public case of it." That was the truth of it, Acey thought. All kids do dumb things. If you did not have parents who could and would bail you out when you made a mistake, then you had to hope that your mistakes did not do lasting damage. Pam had come perilously close to the line. If Acey gave her a shove, she would go over.

"I have a feeling I shouldn't ask why it would cause her so much trouble," Zeke said.

"Very accurate feeling."

"Okay. I've caused enough trouble of my own with this Aspergicin business without dragging someone else into it." Zeke leaned back a little and had to interrupt what he was saying because in moving, he dislodged some of the files his arm had rested on. With a convulsive grab he managed to catch most of them but one folder skittered away and papers cascaded across the floor.

"Zeke, you're messing up my filing system."

"Sorry. I figured you wouldn't notice. Here, I'll get them."

He leaned forward to reach for the papers, but Acey stopped him.

"Leave it for now," she said. "You were going to say something else, I think, before you got clumsy."

Zeke looked blank for a minute, trying to recall what had been in his mind. Then he snapped his fingers.

"I have it. I actually said it a little earlier. Why would someone at Meldrum do this? It doesn't make sense. We've already told the deep dark secret, so why take the risk of rifling your files?"

Acey had a glint in her eye as she spoke. "Precisely the question I asked myself when I caught Pammy. Why? Suppose there is more to this leak than has come out? Put yourself in their place. Has nasty Acey Henson shot her wad or does she have the rest of the story ready to go? Things like that can change a person's strategy."

Zeke looked puzzled. "What else could there be?" he asked. "They know I've seen the material you have. If there was some kind of further information about the drug, I would have said something a long time ago. It does not take a genius to figure that out."

"Something else about the leak, then," Acey suggested. "Maybe not something medical."

"I can't think of what that could be and I really doubt this Dwyer is going to tell you."

"Dwyer may not," said Acey. "However, I can think of somebody who might."

"Who?"

"The same guy who gave me the first report."

SOMERVILLE, NEW JERSEY ————————————————————————

They met in Tim Lange's Somerville office three days later in the afternoon. Lange had been a little evasive when Acey had tried to arrange the meeting. For all his cheerful desire at their first meeting to give Meldrum the trouble he thought it deserved, the events of the summer had shaken him. It was, he explained to Acey, a lot like the morning after a wild party. The hangover made you wonder if it had been worth it and it certainly made you think twice about repeating it. Seeing the Meldrum story splashed across the front pages and on the evening news, with all the accompanying talk of lawsuits and congressional hearings, made him fearful that someone would pinpoint Tim Lange as the source of the leak, so to speak, about Meldrum's leak. If that happened, he figured that no company larger than a corner drugstore would be interested in his services. Acey had eventually worn down his resistance, but the sight of her in his office, all leather and hard edges, was making him regret giving in. The added presence of Zeke Schwartz, another central figure in the Meldrum drama, only increased his unease. In reality, Schwartz was as uneasy as Lange, although for a different reason. Being out of the hospital during the day made him feel guilty, a bit like cutting school. Lange read only the look of impatience on Schwartz's face and read it to mean that the man was going to pressure him to say things he would regret later.

It was for that reason that Lange did not even give them an opportunity to speak before he disclaimed any ability to help them. "It's like I told you on the phone," he said. "I don't see what good it's going to do going over this Meldrum business again. I gave you everything I had and I'm starting to wish I hadn't. I can't afford to get mixed up in this. I had no idea what that damn spill did."

A number of uncomplimentary thoughts passed through Acey's mind as she listened to Lange. Most of the companions of her youth had very clear views of people who tried to back out when trouble started. It made no difference that many of those companions were in jail or dead. That was the way Acey had grown up and that was the way she still felt. That she kept all of those feelings from rising to the surface was a tribute to what she had learned over the past three years. Roger had taught her to keep her real goals foremost in her mind and not to give in to distractions. She did not say what she thought.

Instead, she said, "I understand just how you feel, Tim. In fact, that's why this conversation is necessary."

Lange motioned for her to continue, his face indicating that he did not believe a word she said.

"The fact is, Tim, that someone tried to steal my file on the Meldrum case."

Lange went pale behind his desk. Suddenly, he grabbed a stapler from the desktop and flung it across the room. It smashed into the opposite wall with a clatter that echoed in the office.

"Goddammit! I don't need this!"

"Cool down, Tim," Acey said. "She had kept both hands in the pockets of her jacket and had not moved an inch. "Nobody got anything, so you're in no trouble at all. And, like I said, we understand your position. That's what this is about."

"I don't see how that makes sense." Lange held his body stiffly, as though he expected to be physically attacked.

Acey nodded her head toward Schwartz, who took up the conversation. "The logical reason for this is that there is more to the leak than has come out and Meldrum is trying to find out whether we know about it. It can't be something medical, so it has to have something to do with the actual leak."

"And suppose," Lange growled, "that it is nothing more complicated than wanting to find out who set them up?"

Acey shrugged, bringing her hands out of the pockets. "I doubt it. They couldn't exactly do anything with the information they got that way."

"I'm not so sure I agree with you," Lange said.

Acey shrugged again. "You don't have to if you don't want to. However, I still think that the best chance for you to stay out of the limelight is if we know what else they may be looking for, if there is anything else. That will save a whole lot of poking around, which could lead God knows where."

"Yeah, right," Lange said sourly. "I'm starting to think that meeting you may be the low point of my life."

"Funny, my father used to say much the same thing."

"And what if I tell you there is nothing more to it?"

"I don't know," Acey said. "Is that the way it is?"

"I don't know!" Lange threw his arms up in the air and started pacing behind his desk. "I don't know what to make of this damn business any-more. When we took that job it just seemed like a typical fuck-up. I wasn't even surprised that Meldrum tried to keep everything so hush-hush. Who needs publicity? I can understand that, whether it's toxic or not. I mean, what do I care if they kill a few fish? But this business with kids with cancer. Christ, I didn't think it was going to cause something like that."

"Meaning," Zeke put in, "that if you had known you would have kept your mouth shut?"

Lange flushed. "I didn't say that."

"Then what difference does it make? We'd all be in the same situation we are now anyway. Look, I take care of these kids. I need to know what is going on."

Lange looked uncomfortable. He could hardly say that he wished the kids would die without involving him. Instead, he said, "They're saying there's going to be a congressional investigation."

"Maybe," Acey said. "But, if Barcellini does start calling people, he'll call you anyway because you are in the records as having fixed the leak. That doesn't mean anyone needs to know that the original information came from you, unless, of course, you want to be a hero on the national news." She almost gagged on the last part of the sentence. Flattery always beat threats, Roger had said, but it tasted worse in her mouth.

"A broke hero is still broke," Lange countered. "Besides, I'm not sure there is any info beyond what I gave you, at least not that I have. I just don't know. It's always the same with these corporate people, they always think they know everything about their process and that you couldn't possibly understand it, even if they were willing to tell you more than the bare minimum to do the job, and you have to fight even for that, and never mind that they had to call you to fix their fuck-up in the first place. Sure, it's a fancy place they've got with all their automation, but I don't know why they are so damned concerned you might see something. Hell, I've seen other plants for antibiotics and one fermentation process is a lot like any other."

Lange's rambling monologue was interrupted by a loud snap of Schwartz's fingers. Both Acey and Lange turned to look at him. "Fermenta-tion!" he said. "Maybe that's the point."

"How so?" Acey asked.

"Because that's the way a number of antibiotics are made, even today. They are natural products of some bacteria or fungus. Penicillin is a perfect example. A lot of them are chemically modified afterward, but the basic molecule comes from a bug. You just grow a batch of whatever the bug is and purify the antibiotic. I remember that Aspergicin is made that way, too, because they had to modify the genes of the bacteria that makes it to get it to make enough."

"Which leads you where?"

Schwartz turned his attention to Lange. "Do you know if the stuff that Meldrum spilled was just Aspergicin or could it have been the crude mix, bugs and all?"

"They said it was just Aspergicin," Lange said.

"But could it have been the crude, whether they said it or not?"

"I don't know. Maybe. Why?"

"I wonder if that bacteria can live in the creek," Zeke said to no one in particular.

Unfortunately, that one insight was all that their detective work yielded. Tim Lange did not know whether the Aspergicin producing bacteria had gone into the creek. They might have been able to deduce that from plans of the plant and Lange's knowledge of the repair job, but Lange showed a remarkable lack of interest in doing any further work. He no longer had plans of the plant. When Acey offered to bring him copies of the plans from the village office, he declined. Acey considered trying to bully him, but did not. It would not be enough to simply have Lange look at the plans. They would have needed Lange's understanding of the layout and of the repair job in order to deduce the components of the spill, if indeed it could have been done at all. Without Lange's active cooperation, it was hopeless.

The result was that Schwartz did not know if the bacteria had gone into the creek nor if, having done so, they could have lived there. Presumably, he thought, somebody at Meldrum Products knew the answers to those questions, but he doubted that anyone would tell him if he called. In his mind, he could only wonder if, perhaps, there had been quite a bit more Aspergicin in the creek than the amount spilled from the plant because, if the bugs could live in the creek, they would go on producing Aspergicin. Even if he had the answers to those questions, however, he still did not know if Aspergicin, in any amount, could have caused Jerry's cancer. It was frustrating.

Acey found that the question of "bugs in the creek" made an interesting show. She had a telephone interview, pre-arranged of course, with Zeke during which they talked about how antibiotics were made. Then she floated the question. Could the bacteria have been in the creek? That show brought almost as great a response as her original show on Jerry. The fact that Meldrum's bacteria had been genetically altered, even if only to increase their production of Aspergicin, made the discussion even more intense. A good many callers, it seemed, were more concerned about the genetics of the bacteria than they were over the amount of Aspergicin in the creek. There were proposals to boil all tap water before using it, just in case the "gene-engineered bugs" could have contaminated the municipal water. Then, there was concern that boiling might not kill genetically engineered bacteria and there was a run on bottled water at the stores. In spite of the fact that the Meldrum plant was a long way from any population center, there were demonstrations in front of the gate for a week, accompanied by television news teams. Acey reported on the television newscasts of the demonstrations that had been sparked by her show and found that interest in the story compounded daily. She half-expected to receive a call from Richard Ames, but one never came. When it came to the Meldrum story, Ames was clearly going to do nothing as long as the story was playing and Acey stayed away from any link between Meldrum and QI.

The shows and demonstrations and newscasts had other effects beyond boosting Acey's ratings. Meldrum, naturally, was forced to issue an angry denial. No, there had been no bacteria in the creek and, even if there were, they could not have lived there. That was reported on the news too, but no one in the towns near Scheuermann's Run believed it. Not surprisingly, the news percolated to Washington where, once again, Dan Ingraham at the FDA was taken by surprise by developments with Aspergicin. No, he told reporters, the FDA had no knowledge of Aspergicin bacteria in the creek. Unfortunately, he could not say that the FDA knew the bacteria had *not* been in the creek. Ingraham had no information about that at all.

Ingraham made that point rather emphatically in a phone call to Russ Jackson. That call came as soon as Ingraham was able to escape to his office after being grilled by the Deputy Director over why he did not have the information. As Ingraham explained it to Jackson, he had to have that information as soon as possible because Jessup would have to testify at Barcellini's hearings and the question would undoubtedly arise there as well. In fact, there was the possibility that Barcellini would question the Commissioner about it, so they absolutely had to have the information.

Jackson, unfortunately, did not know the answer. That was because the manufacturing records did not make it clear what had gone into the creek. Everyone on the manufacturing team was certain that only Aspergicin was involved, not the bacteria, but nobody could prove it. Jackson had been aware of this situation from the time he had reviewed the records the day after Acey Henson's infamous broadcast. He had never mentioned the ambiguity to the FDA on the time-honored principle that one gave the regulatory authorities precisely what they asked for, and nothing else. Neither Ingraham nor anyone else at the FDA had ever asked Jackson if anything but Aspergicin had leaked, so Jackson had been content to leave well enough alone. If the question occurred to the FDA, he had figured, he would deal with it when it arose. Unfortunately, that infernal Henson had popped the question on the air (how could she have figured it out?) and now Ingraham had been surprised again. Jackson paid for Ingraham's surprise in a thirty minute phone call that ended with him promising to study the creek below the plant to ensure that none of the Aspergicin bacteria could be found there.

Jackson then called Woodward to tell him about the new twist in the case. It would be necessary to add the results of the study of the creek to the report Woodward was preparing on the Aspergicin study patients.

"I don't expect much trouble from this," Jackson said. "First of all, I don't think the bacteria could live in the creek, so I doubt we'll find anything there. Second, and probably more important, as long as you don't find any evidence of trouble with the patients, it probably doesn't matter what we find in the creek."

"Except," Woodward said, "for the public hysteria we'll have to deal with."

"They're hysterical anyway," Jackson replied. "Or have you found some way of driving into the parking lot that doesn't involve going through the main gate?"

Woodward grimaced. "I know. Isn't there some way we can get rid of them?"

"No. Remember freedom of assembly and all that? Don't worry. The story is just about played out on TV, I think, and once the cameras go, the pickets will get bored and quit. More to the point, how is the study going?"

"So far, so good," Woodward said, "but I'll feel a lot better when it's done with."

"So will I," Jackson said. "Are we going to make our October deadline?"

"I hope so. We're working at it."

"That's not good enough," Jackson said. "We must have it done, especially now. That's why I got you Delahanty. Push her. She'll see that it gets done."

"I'll do that," Woodward replied.

Pat Dwyer was in the room as well since he would need to instruct his sales force in how to answer questions. "You've been rather quiet, Pat," Jackson said. "No questions?"

"Nope. I think it's pretty clear what we have to say. I think also that maybe now you believe me when I tell you somebody in the plant is giving out information."

Jackson sighed. "You may well be right, Pat, but like I said before, that doesn't change what we have to do. I notice you're not clamoring for an investigation this time either."

"Nope," was all Dwyer said. Thus far, Jason's name had not surfaced in any of the stories, but Dwyer's enthusiasm for private investigators had been dampened. The source of Henson's data would have to go unknown,

unless someone else was willing to take chances with his career. Dwyer
figured there would be other opportunities to influence events, opportunities that would let him use the leverage his position afforded. He saw no
reason to discuss that with either Woodward or Jackson.

Thigpen sat in a booth at Maury's and tried to avoid looking at his watch.
Normally, Maury's was a favorite haunt of his. They served real food,
prime rib and Idaho potatoes, instead of bits and pieces of things stuck on a
plate like a child's collage, that passed for a meal at so many of the trendy
restaurants. They also ran the air-conditioning high so that the leather of
the booth was cool against his skin, a little touch he always appreciated
when the Santa Ana was blowing. Unfortunately, he had not come for a
quiet dinner. He was planning on dinner, yes, but he was also there for
business. Thigpen was no stranger to conducting business over dinner, or
any other meal for that matter. This time, however, he was in a restaurant
because his business could not be conducted at the office, and that made
him nervous. Who might see him at Maury's? Well, so what if someone did?
He had chosen Maury's partly because it was not unusual for him to be
there. What remark might be overheard, though? He looked at his watch
while telling himself that he was being paranoid. The person he was meeting was female. All anyone would see, even those who knew him, was
Johnny Thigpen having dinner with a young lady, a common enough event.
All that anyone would do would be to wink and maybe say, "Hey Johnny,
hope you close this deal before you catch something."
    In fact, his "date" arrived precisely on time. As she walked over to the
table, Thigpen stood up to greet Marilyn Glennoch. In an area famed for
beautiful women, Thigpen thought her outstanding. Tall and in her mid-
thirties, she moved with a grace that befitted the highly ranked tennis player
she had been. She wore a navy suit, calculated to set off shoulder-length
blonde hair and green eyes, and a white shirt, open at the collar to emphasize her tan. It did not matter that her hair was brown at the roots, or if the
eyes were green courtesy of Bausch and Lomb. Marilyn always took his
breath away.
    "Hi Johnny." She gave him a man's handshake and eased into the booth
opposite him. "What's it to be? Dinner first, or business?"
    That was typical Glennoch, straight to the point.
    "Business, I think." Thigpen was too wound up to try a dinner of incon-
sequential chitchat.
    Glennoch smiled broadly, the cat that was about to swallow the canary.

"So, this QI deal is really going to go through." The smile became even broader. "Most people think you're just looking to be bought off and that includes some pretty sharp people."

"That may happen," Thigpen conceded. Then he had to stop as the waiter came by.

In the interlude, Glennoch's face went from smile to puzzled frown. "You don't sound very certain."

"I'm not."

"If it's that up in the air, Johnny, I guess I don't understand this meeting."

Thigpen wanted to smile at her bafflement, but figured she would not appreciate it. He could understand her position. Marilyn Glennoch was an executive recruiter or, in blunter language, a headhunter. She ran her own firm these past five years, although Thigpen had known her since she was an associate with somebody he had forgotten. Glennoch had established a reputation for efficiency in finding people to fit jobs and for reorganizing the managements of companies that had been sold. Her reputation also included a considerable amount of whispering about her methods. Scuttlebut had it that she had found a candidate for one long-vacant position by bedding the man and using the opportunity to talk him into looking at the job. That, of course, was just talk, although Thigpen had reason to know she could be wild in bed when she wanted to be. What was fact was that those eyes, whatever their real color, could turn hard and cold when money was at stake.

"The attempt is real, Marilyn," he said. "What I can't tell you is whether the whole deal will go through. Ames is a tough old bastard and he has good lawyers. We got a stroke of luck a while back, though. Meldrum Products had a toxic spill and a couple of kids turned up with cancer; you've probably heard about it. Well, it got picked up by a QI station and Meldrum, of course, is a big QI shareholder and there you have it. The leverage is priceless. I still can't be positive the whole deal will work, but there will be at least one spin-off, no matter how the rest of it comes out. That's where I want to start."

"Okay. What's the spin-off?"

"QI's radio stations. Sold as a group they make an attractive property."

"Who's the buyer?"

"Me."

At first, Thigpen thought she had inhaled one of the ice cubes in her drink. She had not. She had simply halted, with her lips on the glass and two wings of blonde hair touching the glass on either side. Eventually, she put the glass down.

"You are buying the broadcast group?"

Her question had nothing to do with how Thigpen was going to buy the stations. The man knew how to find money. She was simply surprised that he was doing it.

"I am definitely doing it," he said. "The plan, if the takeover works, calls for spinning them off as a separate group. Even if Ames beats us off, he'll have to sell some things. I'm in a position to see that the stations go and, either way, I'm in a position to get them."

"Johnny, it sounds grand, but, frankly, you don't know shit about the media business."

"So what? In fact, that's why we're talking tonight. I need to know, in advance, the minimum management structure I'll need. I need to identify the people already in place that I have to keep and people I need to attract. Which is where you come in."

"Johnny, you've never had a line position in your life. You've always been staff."

"True. Figure that into the personnel requirements."

"Fees?"

Thigpen had to smile. Marilyn could get a lot of mileage out of a single word.

"Flat fee for the consultation on the organization. When the deal closes, contingency for the open positions."

He saw her eyes narrow. Under the terms he was offering, she would be paid for finding candidates only if the candidates actually took the jobs. When they had worked on other Kuhnlein takeovers, Glennoch had always been on retainer, where she was paid just for looking for the candidates, regardless of whether they signed on.

"Kuhnlein doesn't know about this." She said it as a fact, not a question.

"Not the part about me reserving the broadcast group for myself."

"You're playing with fire, Johnny, but you don't need me to tell you that." She drummed her fingers on the table and looked past his head for a brief moment. "You'll see that I get all the contracts for other open slots on this deal and the outplacement for QI people you let go?"

"I can do that."

"Then it's a deal. What are you having for dinner?"

Chapter 27

DELAHANTY WAS fuming on the inside, although she did her best to keep it from showing. When she had first set out to collect the information for Woodward's report on the original Aspergicin patients, she had nightmares for two weeks straight. She was going to need to coordinate the activities of several monitors she had never met and was going to need to make them cadge information out of even more physicians whom she had never met. It was a daunting prospect, although the prospect of a promotion, dangling just visible in front of her, provided the impetus she needed whenever the work seemed too difficult. For all the possible problems, though, the project had gone smoothly. The data were flowing in from the study centers around the country that she had targeted as having the greatest yield of patients.

And now this. Of all the potential obstacles to her project that she had imagined, the biggest, most serious, had been unexpected. Even more aggravating, it had cropped up practically in her own backyard, in Trenton. Dr. Leon Kanzel had been one of Meldrum's major investigators. He had participated in the comparative studies of Aspergicin and he had also conducted an open treatment study of his own near the end of the drug's development. That last study had included a number of children, which had made Woodward emphasize it as a crucial component of their review. Considering that Kanzel was a long-time Meldrum investigator, and that the hospital was right down the highway, Delahanty had decided that it was the perfect place to send Laurie, Woodward's inexperienced underling. At first, everything went well and Delahanty had congratulated herself on finding a way to make Laurie productive. The patients from the comparative studies were reviewed quickly and the data entered into Delahanty's growing database. When Laurie moved on to the patients in the open study, however, she bogged down.

At first, Delahanty was convinced that Laurie was the problem. Kanzel's open study had been run after everyone was already convinced that Aspergicin worked. The study was really just a mechanism to increase the number of patients treated with the drug before it was formally approved. Consequently, the records were skimpy, compared to the thick logs collected in the comparative studies, and there had been no plan to keep track of the patients after their treatment ended. Delahanty assumed that, without a detailed case record to guide her, Laurie was lost. She spent a couple of weeks trying to squeeze more performance out of Laurie but then gave up. Although Delahanty knew that the biggest part of a manager's job was seeing that subordinates did theirs, she also knew her chance of promotion depended on completing the project on time. She was damned if she would let it founder on Laurie's limitations. One day, she simply told Laurie to watch the phones, and off she went to Trenton.

In short order, it became clear that Laurie was not the problem. It was Kanzel. That put Delahanty into Woodward's office and not in a good mood.

"I just can't get at it," she told Woodward. "It's almost impossible to see the man. Now, granted, he's the head of Infectious Disease there, but he has had time before. Now, he's on service, or working on some other project and he's not interested. When I did catch up with him, he told me that dredging through the records of the comparative study patients was a generous enough allocation of his time to this project. When I told him that if I could just get to the records, I could probably do it without taking much of his time at all, he told me, and I quote, that no follow-up records were made for the open study patients, he did not have their charts, and he was damned if he was going to waste his time trying to find them."

"That doesn't sound good, Maureen."

"Dammit, Tom, I know that. If it sounded good, I wouldn't need to be here telling you about it. I think the best thing we can do is to back off for a bit, get out of his face. Kanzel will be off service next month, maybe he'll be more receptive then."

Woodward leaned back in his chair. He did not look happy. "Can't do that. You know the deadline on this thing. End of October. I need those patients."

Delahanty made a face. "I don't see how I am going to get them."

"Have you tried the study coordinator?" Woodward asked.

Delahanty's face stayed in its frown. "Of course I did. The one who did these studies is long gone, no surprise really. Kanzel has a study going now, but it's not a Meldrum drug, so we're not the ones paying for the coordinator and he's not willing to give us her time. Of course," Delahanty went on, "if we could come up with some bucks, maybe that will change his tune. Money can do wonderful things, you know."

"Can't do it," Woodward said. "I just don't have the budget. It's not just Kanzel, you see. If we pay him for finding this stuff, then we're going to have all the other docs holding out for cash, too. I can't do that."

"Why not, Tom? If the story is that we get fucked if we don't get this project done, why can't the company come up with the money?"

"Because I was told we had to do it with the resources we have," Woodward replied.

Delahanty thought that was a delicate way of saying he lacked the guts to go back to Jackson, or whoever was in charge, and ask for more money. God forbid you should look inefficient, she thought.

"Okay, what do you want me to do?" she asked.

"Keep trying," Woodward said. "We need that data and we need to be done by the end of October."

Thanks for nothing, Delahanty thought as she left his office. I hate you for this, Woodward, I really do. When I get this done, you damn well better put me in for that promotion.

She went up to her office and slammed the door. Then she sat at her desk and scowled. She could not find the data because Kanzel would not cooperate and all Woodward could do was tell her that she had to do it. Forget Woodward. Forget Kanzel, too. Think, Maureen, she told herself. You are an ICU nurse. It is not as though you need to have some jerk doc hold your hand while you read a chart.

The primary stumbling block to her pursuit of the records was that in the case record forms Meldrum had identified each patient only by initials and a number. There was no way to take that information into the hospital and find the hospital records of the patients without Kanzel's help. Or was there? Delahanty went to the files and pulled out a copy of the original protocol and forms for Kanzel's study. Then she smiled.

For many studies, Meldrum did keep a record of the full names, addresses and hospital numbers of the patients. The information did not show up in any of the files Delahanty had because no copies of the original were made. The sheets were stored, locked in the vault, against the possibility that some catastrophic side effect of a drug would be discovered that would make it necessary to find all the people who had taken it. A blank copy of that page, however, was included with the file copy of the other forms and its presence told Delahanty that the information existed. Delahanty had never heard of one of those confidential lists being used, but the present situation seemed, to her, an adequate emergency. She had no intention of calling the patients herself, the company would take a very dim view of that, but the information might give her a way to find the records without the good graces of Dr. Kanzel.

Back she went to the hospital, now armed with a list of names and medical record numbers. Her first stop was the admitting office, where she sweet-talked a clerk into letting her see the inpatient and clinic lists. Anyone who had been treated with Aspergicin had once been very ill. It was a reasonable assumption that many of them would still have regular contact with the hospital. Lo and behold, one Charles J. Foster, age sixteen, had been admitted to the pediatric division that day. He had been CJF, patient 507, age twelve in Kanzel's open study.

Once she had that, she went straight to the floor, her heart pounding. What she was doing was at least irregular. If someone questioned her, or called the company, there might be trouble. The floor seemed devoid of activity just then, with the exception of a tired-looking woman attired in green scrubs, sitting at the nursing station, writing in a chart. Delahanty walked up to the station unnoticed by the woman. Seeing her continue to write, Delahanty leaned over the top and said, "Excuse me."

Jolanta Marienkiewicz looked up with a start to see a large woman, possibly a few years her senior, suspended almost over her head. She had not heard anyone walk up. That was not too surprising because Marienkiewicz had been on call the previous night. It had been a busy one, so much so that she had not had the opportunity to even lie down, much less sleep. By the end of the following day, it was thirty-five hours since she had last been to bed. By all rights, she should already have gone home but the clinic schedule had left her as the only physician on the floor when a boy arrived to be admitted for surgery the next day. She had wanted to leave him for the on-call person that evening, but the boy's mother had made a fuss, and Jola could hardly blame her, so she had taken the history, done the physical and was trying to keep her eyes focused on the page in order to write a note she hoped was coherent. She did not want another problem.

"Excuse me?" Marienkiewicz said back.

"That was my line," said Delahanty. "I'm looking for one of the physicians who works on this floor."

"You've found one. I'm Dr. Jo Marienkiewicz." If there was a wary look in her eyes it was because she was praying that this was not the mother of another child who would have to be seen and admitted that very second.

Delahanty saw the expression but assumed the demands for explanations would be coming from Marienkiewicz. "I'm Delahanty, Maureen Delahanty," she said to head off those questions, "I'm a monitor for Meldrum Products. I need to get some follow-up information on a patient from one of our studies."

Not another mother! Marienkiewicz thought. Immediately, Delahanty was downgraded from a menace to an annoyance.

"Miss Delahanty, I'm sorry, but there are no clinical study patients on this floor right now. Perhaps on 6 West?" The last was said hopefully because, right on the heels of her relief that Delahanty was not a mother with an admission in tow, came the concern that a patient was supposed to be admitted on some crazy study protocol that would have her spend the next hour half exsanguinating the kid and the hour after that figuring out where to send all the blood. Where were Humphreys and Sanchez? Clinic ought to be over by now. She turned back to the chart hoping that Delahanty would disappear and discovered that she had written slantwise across two lines.

Delahanty did not disappear. Instead, she chuckled. "I should have been more precise," she said. "This patient was in a study about four years ago. We're doing some long-term follow-up on this group and I was told he'd been admitted here. Kid name of Charles J. Foster."

Marienkiewicz held up the plastic binder in which she had been writing. "Charles J. Foster," she said. "I just admitted him. But your information is still wrong. He's here for elective surgery for some trouble from a car wreck a few years ago. He's never been in a study."

Delahanty glanced at her notes. "Charles J. Foster, medical record number 36-8892-054?"

"That's right," Marienkiewicz said.

"Well, he was treated with Aspergicin when it was an investigational agent four years ago for an infection that occurred during his hospitalization after a car wreck. Same wreck, I'm sure. The data will be in the old chart." She indicated a cart behind the desk where a large number of folders were stacked. "I don't need the old chart, though. Just a brief interval history from then to now and his current condition."

Marienkiewicz, of course, knew precisely where the information from previous admissions would be and resented being spoken to as though she was a first year student, and a dull one at that. She was tempted to throw the notebook at Delahanty's head, let her take what she wanted and forget the matter.

Instead, with deliberate sarcasm in her voice, she said, "Contrary to popular belief, Miss Delahanty, we do check a patient's history. This child did not get an experimental drug." With that, she made a show of slamming the notebook to the desktop and shoving her chair backward as she stood up. Then she walked over to the cart where she found Charles J. Foster's old chart and brought it back to the desk.

"Okay," she said, "here we are. April 12 four years ago. Admitted through the ER after MVA. Here's the discharge summary. Plenty of drugs, but no Aspergicin, experimental or otherwise."

Delahanty frowned and took hold of the chart. Quickly, she leafed through the pages of daily progress notes that were placed after the summary. Then, "Ah! Here we are." In the progress notes was a copy of her case record form page with notations about the Aspergicin doses. "Whoever did this summary wasn't too careful," she said, "although, I admit, a four month hospitalization is a lot to dig through. Well, you know what they say. 'Seek and ye shall find.' "

Marienkiewicz turned bright red. This infernal woman was making fun of her. She wanted to cry and suddenly had to fight the urge in order to prevent it from happening.

"What is going on out here?"

Marienkiewicz turned around to find Dorothy Perkins behind her. The nurse had come through the corner conference room, drawn by the noise made when Marienkiewicz had begun slamming book and chair around. Now Perkins stood with her arms folded, glowering at both of them. Marienkiewicz could say nothing. She felt that, if she opened her mouth, tears would start to flow from her eyes.

"I would still like to know what is going on," Perkins said. "I know what it sounds like is going on. It sounds like a barroom brawl, but that can't be true, can it, because this is a children's hospital. Right?"

"I'm sorry about the noise," Delahanty apologized. "There was some confusion about a patient in one of the Aspergicin studies. I think we've cleared it up."

"Aspergicin? Who's getting Aspergicin?"

"Nobody," said Marienkiewicz, finding her voice. "It was Charley Foster, four years ago in one of the experimental studies."

Neither she nor Delahanty were prepared for what happened next because Perkins shot back, "Bullshit! I took care of Charley Foster four years ago. He didn't get Aspergicin."

"It's in the chart," Marienkiewicz said.

"Kay Vitch," replied Perkins, "I don't care. I took care of Charley every day I was here for the four months he was here. That mother of his was here every day, too, and let me tell you, you couldn't give that kid Tylenol without her going up one side of you and down the other wanting to know why and who ordered it and could it hurt him. No way in hell she would have signed for anything experimental and even if she did, there's no way I'd forget. If it's in the chart, the chart is screwed up."

Perkins's comment made little impression on Marienkiewicz. She really did not care, right then, whether Charles J. Foster had or had not been given Aspergicin four years ago, or whether his mother would have had a screaming fit over it. None of it was important because, right that instant, Charley Foster did not have to be given anything at all. The only thing important to her was finishing her note so that she could sign out and go home. Her feet ached, as did her legs behind the knees, from too much standing. She had been wanting to brush her teeth for the last eight hours. Those were the problems she wanted to attend to and this silly argument about a four-year-old chart was standing in her way. Again, she felt like crying.

For Delahanty, however, Perkins's comment was as welcome as a kick in the stomach. She had been all set to gloss over the summary. Hell, the notes were in the chart. It would not have been the first time a house officer had been sloppy about details. Except, this feisty, little, black nurse had barged in and claimed that it had never happened. Which was right? Dear God who watches over clinical monitors, she thought, do not let there be a problem with the charts. Not now. Not when she had to do all this work. What should she do about it? She did not want to talk to Kanzel or even Woodward until she knew more. Perkins might have taken a vacation and forgotten that she had been away, something peculiar might have happened to this one chart. There might not be a problem. Delahanty wished she could be certain of that.

As politely as possible, she said, "Look, Dr. Marienkiewicz, I think we have a problem here about this documentation."

"Why? Does getting the Aspergicin have anything to do with whether he can go to the OR tomorrow?"

"No."

"Then *we* don't have a problem."

"Dammit, wait a second. Your chart says he got the drug, the nurse here says he didn't, at least not that she knows." Perkins glared at that remark, but said nothing. "I've got a whole list of people in this study. What do I say about their charts?"

It occurred to Delahanty that her original plan of surreptitiously accessing the charts was not going to work. If, God forbid, there was a problem with the records, she would need to scrupulously document every move she made and she would have to stay completely within the rules. She was not even certain how she could make her present position legitimate. She could hardly take any more chances.

"Marienkiewicz, I need some help getting to these charts."

Jola's mouth dropped open at the effrontery. "You want me to pull the records? Are you crazy? I'm an intern here. I can imagine what they'll say if they find me pulling charts so a company can look for mistakes."

"Then can you tell me the name of somebody who knows about this drug who would do it?" Delahanty asked.

That was when Perkins decided to speak up again. "Zeke could," she said.

Marienkiewicz looked at her for a minute, then nodded her head. "Yeah, I'd agree with that. You want somebody to ask; I'd ask Zeke Schwartz."

Zeke Schwartz! Not the name Delahanty wanted to hear. She felt the walls closing in while her promotion receded into the distance. Zeke

Schwartz was the asshole who had caused the whole problem. Now she, Maureen Delahanty, was going to ask him for help in investigating a problem with Meldrum's records. That would not play very well back at the company. Unfortunately, she had to have answers and she needed them quickly. Neither Perkins nor Marienkiewicz seemed disposed to proffer another name. Oh well, she thought, no one at Meldrum needed to know what she was doing until it was over.

"Fine," she said, "can you introduce me to him?"

"Not tonight. I'm pooped. I've got to go home."

"When then? This is important."

"Dammit, Delahanty, it's four years old. Christ, meet me here after morning rounds. Say ten."

Finally, they left her in peace, Delahanty back to her company, Perkins off to answer a beeping IV pump. Marienkiewicz sat down again with her chart. She glanced at her watch and saw it was late, well past normal for sign-out. She lifted the phone to have Humphreys and Sanchez paged. Just then, she remembered. She had promised Bobby yesterday morning, absolutely promised, that she would come home early after her call day. God, she had promised to make a roast for dinner! Sitting there, phone in hand looking at her watch, she knew she had no hope of even being home at dinner time, much less fixing anything more elaborate than a frozen dinner in the microwave. She put the phone down and buried her head in her hands. The tears rolled past her fingers and smudged the ink in Charley Foster's chart.

TRENTON, NEW JERSEY _____

Marienkiewicz finally went home, too late for dinner. There was no one in the apartment when she reached it. There was not one of Bobby's notes either, the ones that told her he had been reduced by hunger to eating at McDonald's. He usually left them on the kitchen table, although sometimes they were posted on the refrigerator. There was nothing in either location. She assumed that he had become tired of writing them. In spite of the way those notes annoyed her, not finding one was even worse. She sat down on the living room sofa for a minute and woke there, in much the same position, at six in the morning.

The apartment looked unchanged from the time she had come home. The light was still on in the kitchen; the table was still bare. The bed in their bedroom was unmade, but that was the way they usually left it. There was no sign that Bobby had been in the apartment any time that night. That finding gave her a sick feeling in the pit of her stomach.

It was an effort to drag herself to the bathroom and turn on the shower. While she let the hot water sluice over her, she tried to replay the previous afternoon in her mind, primarily to assure herself that there had been no way for her to have come home any earlier. In the process, she remembered her conversation with Delahanty, at which point she froze when the import of the conversation struck her. A hospital chart fudged? That had to have been the implication of Delahanty's words. The idea was most unpleasant. She had ignored it at the time, handling the conversation the way she would a dislodged IV, a problem to be resolved as quickly and with as little effort as possible. Thinking about it in the shower, it was as though she was hearing the words for the first time. She dressed quickly and hurried to the hospital. Bobby, for the moment, was forgotten.

She was distracted all through rounds, which earned her several uncomplimentary remarks from the Senior. Once free of them, she found it impossible to concentrate on her work but, fortunately, it was nearly ten o'clock by then. Delahanty arrived precisely on time, looking much the same as she had the previous day, with the sole exception of a differently patterned dress. It was in sharp contrast to Marienkiewicz who was haggard, with hair that had been washed and combed but little else.

"Pleasant evening?" asked Delahanty.

Fuck you, thought Marienkiewicz. She said, "I slept well, which was all I planned."

"Good." Delahanty smiled. "What's the story with Schwartz?"

"I was just waiting for you." Marienkiewicz picked up the telephone and paged Schwartz. Three minutes later, the phone rang. "Hi, Zeke," she said, "this is Jo Marienkiewicz. I need to speak to you as soon as possible. It's rather important." She listened to the reply, then put the phone down. Turning to Delahanty, she said, "Okay, let's go."

It was a grim, initially silent triumvirate that convened in Schwartz's office a few minutes later. Marienkiewicz found her mind oscillating between Bobby's absence and Charley Foster's chart. She doubted that any good would come of either one. Delahanty kept her eyes on Schwartz, trying to divine his thoughts from his face. The attempt was a failure, she thought, which only heightened her anxiety. Five times she cursed herself for having agreed to meet with Schwartz, a man whose name was taking even more verbal abuse at the company than the FDA. She consoled herself, or tried to, with the thought that she had no choice. She could not have taken Charley Foster's chart to Woodward and insisted that he investigate Kanzel's study. That would have meant explaining how she had the chart in the first place. Anyway, she did not trust Woodward that much. If there was really a problem, there would be less temptation for Woodward to bury it if she had a lot more information than she did now. So, there she was, in the same room as Schwartz, Meldrum Products's version of the Great Satan.

Schwartz looked irritated, if not actually Satanic. He had a full schedule of patients in his clinic. His eight-thirty quickie, a child supposedly in just to have his blood counts checked, had looked a little sick at the desk and proved to be far sicker than he looked. Arranging the evaluation for the regrowing tumor Schwartz suspected had taken time, as had talking to the anguished mother. He had yet to see his second patient when Marienkiewicz's page had sounded. Most of the patients, Schwartz knew, were tolerant of delays in the clinic; unforeseen problems were frequent enough that the official appointment schedule was more fantasy than reality. They would not, however, wait patiently forever. Schwartz's "What's the problem, Jo?" was curt.

The question was enough to yank Marienkiewicz's mind completely away from Bobby. Schwartz had taken a leading role in making the nickname "Kay Vitch" stick to her. It was unusual for him to use her real name unless there was trouble. She tried to tell herself that the presence of a stranger was responsible for the formality.

Introducing Delahanty did not improve Schwartz's demeanor. Meldrum Products was not a happy topic for him. Both Marienkiewicz and Delahanty could see that. Jola stumbled over her words a little as she rushed to move from Delahanty to the problem with Charley Foster's chart. As she recounted the story, she feared that it would sound trivial, that Schwartz would chew her out in front of Delahanty for wasting his time. When she finished, though, all he said was, "Let me see the chart." He spent only a few minutes looking through it. When he was done, he sat back and ran his hands through his hair, leaving the chart on his desk.

"Generally," he said, "when Dorothy tells you that something is so or not so, it is the way she says. This hospital segregates the nursing notes and clips them in behind the doctor's progress notes. There is no mention of Aspergicin in those notes, and there would have to be since it was experimental at the time. Likewise, although there is a Xeroxed order sheet for Aspergicin, it doesn't appear in the nursing medication record. So, Charley Foster never got Aspergicin and his chart was doctored to make it look like he had. Would you care to tell me what is going on, Miss Delahanty?"

"I wish I knew." Her throat seemed to close up at that point. She had to swallow hard to push the next sentence out. "We're trying to do long-term follow-up of the patients in the Aspergicin studies." She decided that mentioning the reason was not needed. "There were three studies conducted here, all by Dr. Kanzel. We had no problem checking all the patients in the first two. Dr. Kanzel was not helpful about getting the charts for the patients in the last study. This was the first one I could find."

Schwartz's voice was grim. "Are you telling me that the Chief of Infectious Disease at this hospital forged patient records for a clinical trial?"

"I didn't say that!" Delahanty said those words as fast as she could.

"Yeah." Schwartz looked at his watch and sighed. "I've told you what I think. Is there something else you want me to do?"

"Yes," said Delahanty. "I told you that Dr. Kanzel would not get the charts for me. I need someone to pull the charts so I can review them and I'm going to need an attending physician to vouch for what I find."

"You already have the right to examine those records," Schwartz replied. "Why don't you have your people tell Kanzel to produce all the records for an audit?"

Delahanty winced. "Not on the basis of one chart I can't. Aspergicin is a pretty sensitive subject right now. I'd need more evidence before I did anything like that."

"And why come to me?" Schwartz asked. "I can't believe Meldrum Products is asking me to look into their studies."

"Meldrum Products isn't asking. I am."

"Let me translate this," Schwartz said. "You don't trust your people to do anything about this unless you put a stick of dynamite up their ass."

Delahanty flushed. "I didn't say that either."

"Okay. But tell me, what happens if we do this and it's not just one patient, it's a whole bunch of them?"

"The data is what the data is," Delahanty said. "If I lay it out for them, they'll play it straight. I'm sure of that."

"All right. I'll tell you what. I'll pull the charts for you. I don't have time to sit here and sift through them with you, though. I am also not willing to let you have them by yourself. I want you both to go through them, pull any ones that look fishy and let me see them. Then, we'll see where that takes us. Okay?"

They both nodded.

"There's just one thing," Delahanty added. "I can't afford to have this broadcast on the radio, if you know what I mean."

"Delahanty," said Schwartz, "I'm an oncologist, not an idiot."

Chapter 28

THE BOARDROOM at Meldrum Research was not a place that Tom Woodward frequented. It was up on the top floor of the complex, right next to the President's office, another location he had little need to visit. The fact that the boardroom existed at all was an indication of the importance of Meldrum Research within the company as a whole. Strictly speaking, Meldrum Research was nothing more than a subsidiary of Meldrum Products. It had no outside stockholders, nor had it ever, and its president reported to the president at Meldrum Products corporate headquarters. Consequently, there was no absolute need for Meldrum Research to have a boardroom or, for that matter, a Board of Directors. However, research was what kept a pharmaceutical company alive. The money disposed of by Meldrum Research and the money the sales of its products generated was so great that, in many ways, the headquarters of Meldrum Research was even more important than the corporate headquarters of Meldrum Products. The research unit, therefore, had its own Board, albeit composed entirely of Meldrum Products people, and a boardroom for them to meet in. The decor of the boardroom reflected the importance of Meldrum Research. The carpet was thick. The walls were hung with original abstract oils that cost many thousands of dollars and surrounded a table made of a massive slab of wood that had probably cost more than the paintings.

Woodward had previously been in the boardroom on two occasions. The first had been when the project research staff had been called there to receive bonuses the day Aspergicin had been approved. The second had been to listen to Pat Dwyer's initial presentation on Aspergicin to the Regional Sales directors. Woodward could imagine no reason for him to be summoned to the boardroom other than a catastrophe. With all the problems Aspergicin was now having, he could only surmise that a catastrophe was indeed approaching when the notice landed on his desk at 9:30 in the morning. "Meeting in the Boardroom at 11:30," it said. "Lunch will be served."

By the time he had taken the elevator to the top and walked over to the boardroom entrance, his mind had had plenty of opportunity to amplify that theme. His mouth was dry and his palms damp when he opened the door. What he saw on the other side did nothing to reassure him. Arrayed around the table he saw Tim Bennett, Chief Counsel for Meldrum Products, Bartlett Janeway, Vice President of Operations, Jackson and his boss Ernest Whitcomb, Vice President of Regulatory Affairs, and, ominous as always, Pat Dwyer. As Woodward took a seat, Gary Majors, the President of Meldrum Research, walked in. Concentrated in that room were almost all the people who counted at Meldrum Research. They were a monotonous-looking collection, all in dark blue or gray with differences only in the ties that crossed the starched white shirts. There was not a woman, not a tinted skin, not a Jew, among them and probably never would be. The sight was enough to make Woodward lose his appetite, which was not much to begin with as the food at upper management meetings seemed to be chosen in the same way as the art: if it was rich then it had to be good. The food always gave Woodward gas.

Majors opened the meeting with a brief statement. "The purpose of this meeting is to review our position on Aspergicin in view of the rapidly developing hysteria over the incident in Scheuermann's Run. Mr. Bennett?"

"Thank you. I just would like to mention that although no lawsuits have been filed in regard to this leak, it is only a matter of time until such action is taken. I expect this to be true regardless of whether a convincing link between Aspergicin and these cancers is demonstrated. I bring this up to remind all of you that your records, memoranda, notes and whatever are potentially subject to subpoena."

Bennett stopped there, but Woodward knew the sentence he had left unspoken. If there is anything fishy, anything at all, in your office, get rid of it now! A quick look around the table told Woodward that everyone else had heard that sentence too.

"Thank you Mr. Bennett," Majors said. "I should note that minutes of this meeting will be kept and distributed for approval later."

Woodward translated that as meaning: Watch what you say. This one is on the record.

Then Majors spoke again. "Mr. Jackson?"

Jackson proceeded to give a careful account of events starting from the discovery of the leak to Acey Henson's infamous radio show. He was interrupted midway by Bennett.

"Am I correct," the lawyer asked, "that at no time during this period did that leak constitute a reportable event under federal or state regulations?"

"That is correct," Jackson said. Jackson, of course, had said that before and this was not the first time Bennett had heard it. This time, however, was for the record and Jackson spent some time detailing why the event did not fall under any of the chemical spill rules. Listening to the recital, Woodward realized why he had not seen Jackson the previous day. The man had been rehearsing!

Jackson proceeded to outline their dealings with the FDA and the agreement at which they had arrived. He finished by saying simply, "That is where we stand today."

"So," Majors said slowly, "Dr. Woodward, are you convinced that these cases of cancer are real?"

Woodward's eyes and mouth opened as though he had been hit with a cattle prod. He looked quickly from Majors to Dwyer and back again. There was no doubt in his mind that Dwyer had planted that question with Majors. It made him thankful for the day he had confronted Schwartz, unpleasant as it had been.

"Based on what I saw, they're real," he said, and hoped he had not appeared hesitant.

"Real cases," Bennett said, "but no documented connection to Aspergicin?"

"Also correct."

"Hmm." The lawyer slumped back in his chair and folded his hands across his belt. "Dr. Woodward, I understand that you have not yet completed your study, but a substantial percentage of the work has been done. Correct?"

"Yes."

"Any similar cases?"

"Not so far."

"I see. Tell me, Dr. Woodward, in your professional, medical opinion, is there any connection between Aspergicin and these cancers?"

Suddenly, Woodward felt like he was on the witness stand. He had been deposed once, and later called to testify, in a colleague's malpractice case. It had been similarly unpleasant. His throat clamped shut and he could only hope the other sphincter would behave the same way. He was going to have to give Bennett an answer and never mind that he had made the same statements before. This time it was official. If sometime later it all went sour, Bennett would point at the record and say, "Well, we did have our medical expert investigate. How could I know he was wrong?" Once that happened, Woodward would be lucky to find work at a Doc-In-The-Box. He wished that the study were truly done, wished that, at a minimum, Delahanty had the rest of Kanzel's patients finished.

"I see no reason to believe that Aspergicin had anything to do with those cancers," Woodward said, "based, that is, on the data I have to date."

Always hedge as best you can, he told himself. The only problem was, in this case, that he had precious little room for hedging. Management clearly wanted a definitive, on-the-record statement from their medical expert, which was him. If he waffled too much, his career would be doomed just as surely as it would if he were wrong. It was one of those situations in which even taking night call again did not seem so bad. There was a slight frown on Bennett's face when Woodward tacked on his qualifier. The lawyer would have preferred that he left it off. Bennett's reply made it clear why.

"We learned yesterday that a group called the Community of Concerned Scientists is going to file a petition today with the FDA to have Aspergicin removed from the market."

Dwyer spoke up then, as if on cue. "Based on what Dr. Woodward has said, that makes no sense. There are no grounds for it."

"I agree," said Bennett. "I see no reason to believe the FDA will grant the petition. I am also going to suggest that we do not yield to the pressure being applied to have us voluntarily remove the drug from the market. Were we to do so, it might well be construed as an admission that Aspergicin is responsible. Given Dr. Woodward's opinion, that would be unwise. In some respects, we are in a rather difficult position because we are in the right. If Aspergicin were responsible, we could cry *mea culpa,* make a public act of contrition and work out a deal that would limit the damage. Unfortunately, it is rather difficult to prove innocence and that there should be no damages at all."

"Which brings us to how we should proceed," Majors said. He spent the next forty-five minutes detailing the strategy Meldrum would follow. They would resist, vigorously, any attempts to bar Aspergicin from the market. That would be Bennett's job. Equally, they would oppose any suggestion to alter the labeling of Aspergicin, the fine print in the ads and the package inserts that warned physicians about potential complications, unless Woodward turned up new evidence. Jackson, of course, had that responsibility. Woodward was to finish his study as soon as possible, not only because the FDA wanted the data but because Dwyer's salesmen needed to have quick, definite answers for the doctors and pharmacists to whom they sold the drug.

"I want to make it clear, though," Majors said, "that this is to be done quietly, without publicity. There will be no ads, no press releases, no publications. Just get the report to the FDA and act as though the case is closed. We will not add any fuel to the fire."

Dwyer chimed in then, and Woodward was struck by how pleasant the man's voice was in the presence of rank. "It would be helpful, though, after the report has been filed if we could have one of our investigators present the results at one of the scientific meetings. The work, obviously, is Dr. Woodward's, but, in terms of keeping things as quiet as possible, it would be better if someone not associated with the company presented the study."

There was a murmur of agreement around the table. In fact, any physician who was recruited to make such a presentation would be unaffiliated with the company only in that he would be Dr. Whoever from the University of Wherever rather than from Meldrum Products. The physician would come from the list of investigators that Meldrum used for its studies and would have been taking Meldrum's coin for years. Dwyer then proceeded to suggest a couple of names. That impelled Woodward to join the conversation for the first time since Bennett's interrogation.

"I wouldn't," he said. "At least, I wouldn't use them. They've presented so much of the Aspergicin data and they've given talks at so many hospitals to support our sales force that they have too visible a stake in this."

"Okay," Dwyer said agreeably, "who would you suggest?"

"I don't know, right off the top of my head. I'd like to look into it. Besides, I'd like to at least have all the data in-house before I start recruiting someone."

He thought he had dodged it, for the moment anyway, but Jackson chose that moment to ask, "What about this Dr. Kanzel? From your investigator list, he has a large number of patients."

"That's a good thought," Dwyer said. "He's local, so the choice makes sense, he's an opinion leader in the medical community and he hasn't presented for us before."

"There's just one problem there," Woodward said. "Getting the data from him on that big open study of his has been like pulling teeth. I'm not sure I want to depend on him."

Dwyer chuckled. "He's not getting paid for this is he?"

"No."

"Well, that's probably all there is to it. Pick a big meeting held someplace nice, say Hawaii, or Snowbird this winter, if he skis. Let him bring his family out. You'll probably find that you get your data a whole lot quicker too."

"I don't have the budget for that." Of course Woodward thought, remarks could be edited from the minutes for some people.

"No problem," Dwyer replied, "this is all within labeling, so it's legal if I use Marketing funds. Right?" Bennett and Jackson both nodded.

Woodward still felt uneasy, but he also felt trapped. Kanzel seemed such a logical choice. The whole strategy the group had evolved seemed so logical. Woodward, however, was keenly aware that the entire edifice was constructed on the assurance of one Dr. Thomas Hart Woodward that Aspergicin had nothing whatever to do with hepatocellular carcinoma.

"Nice job," Dwyer patted him on the back when the meeting broke up.

"Thanks," Woodward said mechanically. He was sweating worse when he left the boardroom than when he went in.

Woodward followed Jackson down to the latter's office and made it clear, by hanging around the doorway, that he wanted to speak to Jackson. After a few minutes, Jackson asked him to come in and tell him what was on his mind.

"It doesn't make sense to me," was what Woodward said after the door was closed.

"What doesn't?"

"This whole strategy!" he exploded. "This whole 'file the report and forget it' idea and maybe we'll pay some doc to put up a poster at an Infectious Disease meeting. Dammit, we didn't do anything wrong! Why not go public? We've got our animal data, we've got all our human data. Soon, I'll have this report too. Put it in the papers, put out a statement, have a news conference. Just sending the report to the FDA and slipping something into a meeting won't make this issue go away."

Jackson sighed and turned his chair to look out the window. "Tom, the only people who count as far as these data are concerned are the FDA. We need to convince them. No one else."

"But we're right! Why let the public bullshit go on? You heard the way Bennett was talking in there. There are going to be God knows how many lawsuits out of this the way we're going right now."

"Undoubtedly," said Jackson. "You heard Bennett. If we were guilty, we do a public penance and hope for the best. But, we're not, or so you tell me. Tom, lawsuits may or may not be filed; judgments may or may not be rendered; but the facts of the case have *no* bearing *whatever* on whether any of that occurs. That's just the way the system works."

"We could try."

Jackson shook his head. "It would probably be futile. Besides, there's more to it here than that."

"What?"

"I probably shouldn't tell you this, but I will. Just remember, you never heard it. You've heard of Edward Buford?" Woodward nodded. "Yeah. He's Majors's boss and he reports to the CEO at corporate. Everybody, including him, thought he was going to get the CEO job. The Board pulled a surprise though, and he didn't. He was a big supporter of that deal where Meldrum got the Quad Industries stock. That may have had something to do with his not getting the job, because our new CEO didn't favor it. All of which makes Buford a rather uncomfortable subordinate to have around. Now, here comes this mess at Meldrum Research, a unit for which Buford is responsible. The CEO says to Buford, 'Keep a lid on it. No publicity.' Buford turns around and tells Majors to keep it quiet. I'm simplifying, of course, but that's the essence of it. Now, it won't stay quiet, not this type of case, and Majors knows it as well as you do. Buford, I'm sure, does too. So, Majors is doing everything Buford asks, and doing it meticulously. That way, when it blows up, it will be all on Buford, not Majors. The CEO will just roll over on Buford. The charge will be either that he made a mistake by not going public, or he made a mistake by being unable to keep it quiet. It doesn't matter. The CEO just needs a good excuse. It might be enough to can Buford. Majors might get his job, if he can show that he did just what Buford asked for so Buford can't lay the blame off on him. It's just a chess game."

"Christ. While they're playing chess, the company could get creamed."

Jackson shrugged. "As long as the data say we are right, what's important is who wins at corporate headquarters."

"And what happens if, when the rest of the data comes in, it's different and we have a problem?"

Jackson turned back to face him. "Tom," he said without a blink, "don't be wrong."

TRENTON, NEW JERSEY _____

The review of Dr. Kanzel's patients went slowly. It was agonizingly slow for Marienkiewicz who was not used to the kind of review Delahanty was conducting. It was even slow for Delahanty. She had done many chart reviews, but none quite like this. A fair number of the patients were simply dead. They had entered the study ill with AIDS or cancer and four years was just too long to expect them to have survived. Their records, consequently, had long since been sent to a warehouse. Under other circumstances, Delahanty would have been satisfied with a note from the physician saying they had died of their pre-study disease, but that was no good here. She had to prove, beyond any doubt, that the patients had been treated with Aspergicin. That meant that the records had to be exhumed from the warehouse. Every now and then she worried that some officious clerk would wonder why there was such need for the records of dead patients, but no such inquiry was made. Schwartz requisitioned the charts and no one questioned him.

Once the charts arrived, they formed a pile in one corner of Schwartz's office. Pile was perhaps too weak a word. They formed a mountain. Some patients had charts comprising ten or fifteen or more thick volumes. Simply finding the correct place in the chart to look for the Aspergicin study could be a chore. Once located, the detective work began. All the medication sheets, all the order sheets had to be checked to see if Aspergicin had truly been given.

The patients seemed to fall into three classes. There were a substantial number, about one-third of the total, for whom the records were all in order. The charts held the proper orders and medicine sign-offs; there were notes about the patient's progress on the study; there was an informed consent. Those were, in some ways, the hardest to review because Delahanty insisted on checking every detail, comparing every entry on her copy of the case record form to an original entry in the chart. That insistence led to several clashes with Marienkiewicz, starting with the first chart they pulled when Marienkiewicz despaired of finding the original laboratory report of a blood culture.

"It's mentioned in the progress note," she protested. "You have the result there. Why do we need the lab slip?"

Delahanty snapped back, "Because doctors' notes frequently have the same utility as the people who write them, which is to say none."

Marienkiewicz looked at her, face hot and furious. "Just what do you have against doctors, Delahanty? Or is it me?"

Delahanty never looked up from the chart she was reading. "I've got nothing against you, or doctors for that matter. It's just an observation I've made. More than once. Do we have that lab slip yet?"

Eventually, they found it. Even when they had corroborated all the information from the study, they were still not finished with a patient. Each one who had been treated had to be followed down to the last time he or she had been seen. Delahanty had not forgotten the original purpose of the review.

In addition to the pile of patients whose data was verified, two other piles of charts were growing. One had charts like Charley Foster's. They had varying amounts of information from the Aspergicin study, but in all cases the crucial evidence that the drug had actually been given was missing. Then, there were the majority of the charts, which had no evidence at all that the patient had received Aspergicin or, in some cases, even had the disease that supposedly was being treated.

"I don't understand it," Marienkiewicz said one day as the pile of phony records grew higher. "Why bother to put fake material in the charts of only some patients? I mean, some of them are fixed up so well you could easily take them for real, just like Foster's in fact, if Perkins hadn't said something. But these others," she tossed aside the chart she had been holding, "one look and you know it's fake. Why bother with only some of them?"

"Because the study wasn't monitored closely," Delahanty explained. "Normally, when I monitor a study I'm there every one to two months, depending on the study, and I check everything in every record. This wasn't an important study, though. All we got out of it was some supportive data about the drug. Obviously, the monitor didn't check every record. Probably, he was lazy about it, too. He knew nobody was looking too closely. So, when he came out, instead of picking patients at random, which he should have done if he wasn't going to check them all, he let Kanzel hand him a sample. My guess is that if Kanzel didn't have enough real ones on hand, he dummied up a few. Everybody stayed happy. Too bad the data is important now."

"Yeah."

Delahanty did not pick up the chart she had started to reach for. "What are you so down in the mouth about? It's my headache, not yours, except for the time you're spending."

"I don't mind the time," Marienkiewicz said, "at least not now. I did when we started, I guess, but not anymore."

"I noticed you got more available since we started. But if it's not that, then why do you look so glum all the time? Your guy being an ass?"

Marienkiewicz shuddered. She did not want to talk about Bobby at all. Anyway, he was not the reason.

"You wouldn't understand, Delahanty," she said. "Not the way you feel about docs."

Delahanty threw the chart back on the floor. "Try me."

Marienkiewicz did not answer immediately. Instead, she made a production of taking her glasses off and wiping them. "I've wanted to be a doc for as long as I can remember," she said, "all the way back to when I was a little kid. I think it's just about the finest thing a person can be, and I don't care what you think. This, this mess," she indicated the charts with a wave of her hand, "is horrible, just horrible. It's like I've been betrayed. It's eating me up. I've got to get to the bottom of it."

"Marienkiewicz," Delahanty said, "take it easy. It's a job. That's all it is. You do your work; you go home. That's all there is. It's just a job."

"Not to me."

"Then, I think you've got yourself a bit of a problem here," said Delahanty.

That was not the only problem that Marienkiewicz had. An intern's schedule normally made only the barest allowance for sleeping and eating and none for extra-curricular activities. In order to find the time for the chart review, she began to skip some of the teaching conferences that were held for the house staff. That drew the attention of the Chief Resident.

"Jo, can I talk to you for a minute?" he said one day, stopping her in the hall.

"Sure."

"Listen, Jo, don't take this the wrong way. I mean, it's not as though we take attendance at conferences or anything, but I've noticed that you've almost stopped going to them. Is something wrong?"

"No, not a thing. I'm just busy, that's all."

The Chief Resident looked thoughtful. "Jo, if you're feeling swamped, it's okay to ask for help. We can reassign some of your patients if you need to lighten up. I mean, you wouldn't be the first intern who got overloaded."

"Thanks, but that's okay. I can handle my patients."

"Well, I'm glad to hear that, but the teaching conferences are important for your education. I can understand missing them now and again, things come up on the floor, but not all the time. If your patients are keeping you that busy maybe you should give up a couple of them."

"It's not my patients," she said. "I've been working on a research project with Zeke Schwartz."

That was close enough to the truth for her to say it with a straight face. She did not think that telling the whole truth—that she was investigating fraud in a hospital study—would be a good idea. She still had trouble believing it herself. The Chief Resident frowned at her response.

"Jo, research is a fine thing for house staff to become involved with, don't get me wrong, but you can't let it interfere with your primary responsibility. Right now, that is learning enough medicine to take care of patients properly. Schwartz of all people ought to realize that. Now, you've had a rough couple of rotations and I don't think it's a good idea for you to let this get in your way. If this research keeps taking excessive amounts of your time, I can have a talk with Schwartz myself. Okay?"

She left that meeting somewhat unnerved, wondering what Schwartz would say if the Chief Resident pursued the matter. As far as she could tell, though, he never did. Schwartz never said anything about it, nor did the Chief Resident bring it up again, although he continued to monitor her absences. Given a choice, she would have preferred to solve the problem by spending her evenings working on the project. Her relationship with Bobby had reached a point where she did not care if she saw him when she went home in the evening. Delahanty, unfortunately, was not interested in working evenings. Finally, the chore was finished. It remained only to review the results with Schwartz, to obtain his agreement to the conclusions. Schwartz, as Marienkiewicz expected, said he would meet them "after rounds." She enjoyed telling Delahanty that this meant some time after five-thirty, but more likely after six. Delahanty glowered at that, but she had no choice. She needed Schwartz.

That evening meeting began with even more tension than their first one. Delahanty, in particular, was more nervous than at any time since nursing school. She could not be sure how Schwartz would react and she could not write a script for him to follow. If he went crazy, he might ruin everything: their Aspergicin review, probably the drug itself and certainly her promotion. Tersely she gave the totals of those patients who had really been treated with Aspergicin and those whose records had been faked, then handed him a list that put each individual listed as having participated in the study into one of the groups.

Schwartz studied the lists for a few minutes, chin in the palm of one hand. The delay was more to put his thoughts in order than to try and absorb everything on the page. He knew from conversations with Marienkiewicz what the conclusion would be even if he had not known the actual tally until that moment.

Finally, he spoke up and said, "Kay Vitch, do you agree with this list? Patient by patient?"

"Yes," was all she had to say.

"Well." Zeke tilted his chair back almost to the point of tipping over and put his hands behind his head. "Delahanty, life sure sucks, doesn't it?"

Delahanty, startled by the comment and by the grim smile on Schwartz's face, said nothing.

Schwartz did not wait for her. "Tell me, Delahanty," he said, "you guys ran this study, or sort of ran it. Do you have any idea why this happened? I mean, Kanzel is established. He's chief of the division, well known in the field. He's not the sort of person I would expect this from."

Delahanty shifted uncomfortably in her seat. "I don't know for sure, but I can guess."

"Go ahead."

"This wasn't an elaborate study and Meldrum wasn't willing to pay that much per patient. In the file, I saw a bunch of letters between Kanzel and our research group arguing over the price. He wanted two to three times what we were willing to pay, although he finally agreed to what we offered."

"And then just inflated the number of patients to make the total match what he wanted," Zeke finished for her. "Cute. Jo told me what you said about how he got it past the monitor. I wonder if he has done this before."

"The other Aspergicin studies checked out I told you," Delahanty said quietly.

"I wasn't necessarily referring to your studies," Schwartz said. "This place does a lot of clinical studies. Kanzel is in charge of Infectious Diseases, not just for adult medicine in the main hospital, but also in the Children's Hospital." He saw Marienkiewicz swallow hard while Delahanty just looked straight ahead.

"What are you planning to do with this information, Dr. Schwartz," Delahanty asked.

"Do with it?" he repeated. "I'll have to take it up with the administration here. I imagine we're all going to have a rather unpleasant session with Kanzel. I'm somewhat more interested in what you're going to do."

"Much the same as you, I guess."

"And then what?"

"And then the shit hits the fan."

"Cute, Delahanty, but not very specific." Schwartz's voice was harsh. "The more things that happen, the more I become uncomfortable with this drug. Finding out that the data on a large chunk of your patients were falsified does not reassure me that your company knows what it's talking about when it comes to the safety of Aspergicin."

Delahanty flushed. "Dammit, Dr. Schwartz, I can't tell you precisely what will happen because I *can't*. You don't think these decisions are going to be made by me, do you? I doubt they'll even be made by my boss. But I told you when we started that if the data was there, it would be acted on. A company can't sit on something like this. It would be suicide. You have to trust me on that."

"You understand that I won't permit this to be sat on?"

"Dammit, don't threaten me, Schwartz. I thought we had a deal here. You help me get the data and I'll see that it's followed through. I've done my part so far and I'll keep doing it, but you go on the air with this and the first thing that will happen is I'll get fired."

"Delahanty, if you're so damned scared that I'm going to run down to WCZY with this, why did you come to me in the first place?"

"It didn't look like I had a choice," she retorted. "Now, will you give me time?"

"I'll give you time," Schwartz said.

Chapter 29

TRENTON, NEW JERSEY

"HEY, ZEKE! Don't disappear." Perkins's shout brought Schwartz to a halt just before he vanished into the stairwell. He let the door close without going through it and turned around.

"What's up?" he asked.

"That's what I was going to ask you," she said. "Why is Jerry Inman coming in today?"

Schwartz's face turned somber at the question. "Nutrition mostly. His mom says he's not eating and he's losing weight again." He shrugged. "I figured we'll bring him in and get some calories into him, hyper-al if nothing else. Mostly, though, he's in to give Ellen some respite. She's been calling just about every day now, and really sounds like she's had it. She could use a few days break. Just don't put that on the admitting sheet. I'm in enough trouble with Utilization Review as it is."

Perkins nodded. "That fits. Did you know he was here already?"

"No." Schwartz looked surprised.

"Well, he is. Mrs. Inman brought him up and split as soon as the paperwork was done. Jerry's not too happy about it. Won't talk, won't cooperate. Won't do anything, for that matter. Can't say as I blame him, since I doubt I'd enjoy being dropped off like the laundry, but there it is. You think you could talk to him?"

Jerry was sitting on his bed when Schwartz walked into the room. Jerry's arms were folded across his chest; his eyes seemed to be focused somewhere between the end of the bed and the blank television screen. His features were set in what was supposed to be a stern and stubborn gaze but actually looked more like a pout, especially around the mouth. He did not acknowledge Schwartz's entry, even the focal point of his gaze did not shift. He might as well have been a stone.

He would, however, have been a very thin stone. In fact, thin would have been a generous description. Jerry had been thin when Zeke first met him. After the surgery and the interferon treatment he had put on some weight so that he looked like a normally thin boy. Now he looked emaciated, with hollowed cheeks and a concavity between shoulder and elbow where the biceps should have bulged. It was amazing, Zeke thought, how fast the body could melt when it was being eaten away from the inside. Jerry was not really even sitting on his own. The head of his bed had been cranked up almost to the vertical, and he was leaning with his back against it. Zeke came over to the bedside and put his hand on the railing, all with no sign of recognition from Jerry.

"Hi," said Schwartz. There was no response. He tried again, with the same result.

"*Guten tag,*" said Schwartz. "*Wie geht's?*"

Jerry's eyes flicked over to Schwartz, then back to that point in mid-air. There was no other response.

"*Sprechen Sie Deutsch?*"

"This time, Jerry turned his head and focused on Zeke. "What?" The word came out slowly, as if pulled.

"Would you rather speak English?"

"What was that?"

"German. I said 'Good day' and asked you what was going on. That's about my entire knowledge of German, so I'm hoping you'd rather speak English."

"That's stupid," Jerry said. "I don't speak German."

"Yeah, I know. From what I heard, you were speaking mostly 'angry' a little while ago and nobody understood that either. Maybe if we just speak plain, old English, you could tell me what the problem is."

"Sure," Jerry said. "I hate this." He turned away to look at the blank television.

Zeke sighed. "Kiddo, if you liked it, you'd be nuts. Then I'd have to call a psychiatrist."

"Well, why do I have to be here? Why can't I go home?"

"Because you're not eating and you're having trouble just getting around the house. Your mom wants us to give her some help taking care of you and see if you can get some strength back." It was close to what he had told Perkins and just as close to the truth. There was no point telling a sick child that his mother, grown weary of trying to manage a drunk husband and an invalid child, had temporarily solved the problem by throwing one out and stashing the other in the hospital.

"I'm plenty strong," Jerry said. "I get around just fine."

"That's not what I'm hearing," Schwartz said. "Incidently," he said pointing to the nasal prongs lying on the pillow, "the oxygen works better when you wear it."

"I don't like it."

"Suit yourself, but you will feel better if you wear it." He did not push any more than that. Jerry would probably put it on, just as soon as he was out of the room.

"How come my mom left?"

"I don't really know." I could guess, he thought. Ellen Inman was devoting most of the time and energy that she had to finding ways to battle Meldrum Products for having done this to Jerry. And that, he thought, is almost certainly my fault for having stirred up the controversy in the first place. Even if Aspergicin was the cause, and Schwartz still put the 'if' in the sentence even mentally, even if that were true, there would be time to settle with Meldrum later. Jerry needed his mother now. Maybe it was Zeke's fault, or maybe, just as likely, Meldrum was only an excuse, a reason for Ellen Inman to get away from Jerry and the hospital and all the problems they represented. If it had not been Meldrum, it would have been something else. Jerry could have used his father, too, but Charley was hopeless. That had nothing at all to do with Meldrum.

"Would you like something on the tube?" Zeke asked.

"No."

"Yeah. Listen, Jerry, I have to make rounds and see the other kids, but I can come back for a while afterward and we can talk."

"Nah, that's okay."

"No talk, huh? Well, I can come back and we can play poker."

The corners of Jerry's mouth twitched up in the first smile of any kind Zeke had seen in a while. "I'll beat you," he said.

"Probably."

Jerry was in the hospital for a week and went home only marginally better than when he had come in. Mrs. Inman had gained a week of not having to care for him, which had been valuable enough that she wanted to extend it, but Schwartz put his foot down at that. Jerry needed to be home as much as possible. Schwartz was running out of things he could do and Jerry asked to go home every day. He lasted a week at home before Mrs. Inman brought him back to the clinic. In that week, all the small gains of the week before had been lost and then some more. Where, on his last admission, Jerry had been silent out of stubborn anger, this time he was silent from exhaustion, eyes dull rather than defiant. He was no better the next day.

On the following night, Zeke was in his apartment pulling on his boots when the phone rang. He cocked one eye at it and debated whether to answer it. He had planned to drive to Acey's apartment, take a nap, and then meet her when she returned home from the station. It was a typical rendezvous. He was off and so was his beeper. In that situation, to have the phone ring in the middle of the evening was a ninety percent chance of bad news and a ten percent chance of someone trying to sell him something. The phone rang again. He cursed softly. Had he not decided to change his clothes, he would have been out the door and in his car before the first ring. At the third ring, he cursed again and picked up the receiver.

"Hello, Dr. Schwartz?" said a female voice.

"Speaking."

"Good. This is Marie on 4 North. I'm really sorry to bother you at home."

"Not a problem. What's wrong?"

"Jerry is not doing very well. Dr. Marienkiewicz thought you should be called."

Zeke paused to consider the statement. "Not doing too well" was a phrase that covered a lot of possibilities. When coupled with an evening call to the home of the attending physician, who was not covering that night, it meant "terrible."

"What happened?" he asked.

"We're not sure. Septic maybe. His blood pressure is down and he's hypoxic. We've got him on forty percent oxygen, but his lips still look cyanotic. Dr. Marienkiewicz just sent a blood gas, but we don't have the results yet."

Schwartz did not really need them. Between his disease and the drugs that had been used to try to treat it, Jerry was rather anemic. It was a characteristic of blood that the less oxygen it carried, the darker it looked, which is what gave the bluish cast to the lips of people who had trouble breathing. The visible color effect, however, depended on how many red blood cells were present. For someone as anemic as Jerry to be cyanotic, he had to be very short of oxygen.

"What else are they doing?" Schwartz asked.

"I think they're going to try to move him to the ICU."

That also made sense. Schwartz had a sequence of questions and ideas building in his head, but the telephone was a poor way of putting them into effect. "I'll be right in," he said.

Before he left, he placed a call to the radio station. There, he left a message with Pam explaining the situation. Then he called Acey's apartment and left a similar message on the answering machine in case the first one became lost in the lumberyard of Pam's mind.

When he reached the hospital, he went first to the ICU, assuming that the transfer would have happened during the time it would have taken him to drive in. When he reached the unit, however, Jerry was not there. The nurses told him that they were expecting the transfer, but for some reason it had not happened. The reason that occurred to Zeke's mind was that matters had come unstuck on 4 North, which sent him racing for the staircase.

His first step into the hallway confirmed his fears. There was a crowd in Jerry's room and the crash cart was parked and open just inside the door. The scene inside was predictable. Jerry was stretched out on the bed at the center of a swirl of activity. Schwartz recognized one of the anesthesiology fellows at the head of the bed bagging oxygen into a plastic endotracheal tube. One of the senior residents stood over the EKG machine calling out orders while a team of nurses moved to carry them out and Jo Marienkiewicz pumped on Jerry's chest. Schwartz moved over to the EKG to stand behind the senior resident, whose name he remembered was Dave Osborn. It took only a few minutes for Osborn to update him on the situation, which was very bad indeed.

"What are you planning," Schwartz asked after Osborn had finished.

"I was thinking we'd try one more round of meds," Osborn said. "What's his prognosis if we pull him through somehow?"

"Nil for the long term," Schwartz said, keeping his field of view centered on Jerry and the EKG strip. "Not much in the short term either."

"Do you want to go one more round?"

"Sure, one more is fine. If you don't get something back after that, though," he pointed at the EKG strip, "I'd call it."

Osborn nodded and called out the orders. Then they watched the EKG strip as the drugs were given. It remained the same, a basically flat line, broken occasionally by a broad bump as the heart gave a useless twitch.

"All right, let's try to live better electrically one more time," Osborn said.

In response, Marienkiewicz pulled the paddles off the defibrillator, spread some gel on Jerry's chest and pushed the paddles down into the gel.

"Off!" she cried.

Everyone stepped clear of the bedside. She pulled the trigger. There was a loud click. The needle gauge on the defibrillator jumped and so did Jerry's body. Immediately afterward, Schwartz and Osborn peered at the EKG to see what it traced on the strip. There was no change.

"Damn," Zeke said. Then he turned to Osborn and said, "That's it, I'm afraid." Then in a louder voice, he called out, "I'm afraid we've got no response. I'm calling it. Thank you, everybody, for your help."

An eerie silence descended on the room where, until that moment, there had been so much commotion. Schwartz shut off the EKG with a loud snap. The nurses stopped the intravenous drips and began to disconnect them. Jola Marienkiewicz stood still next to Jerry looking at her hands, which seemed poised to go back to compressing his chest.

"Jo," Schwartz said, "has anyone called his parents?"

It seemed to take a moment for the question to register in her mind. Then she snapped out of her daze.

"Yes. I had them called a little while ago. They should be on their way in."

"Good. Thank you. I'll speak to them when they get here." He lightly touched the arm of one of the nurses standing near him to get her attention. "Can your people handle the clean-up here?" he asked. "Good. See if you can clear the parents' lounge for the Inmans when they get here. I'll take care of the final note."

Zeke took Jerry's chart out to the nursing station where he sat down and opened it to the last page of the progress notes. Whenever there was a death, whoever was in charge had to write a final note to document how and why it happened. When he looked up to order his thoughts, he saw Marienkiewicz standing by the desk looking at him. Her face held a glassy gaze, as though someone had struck her between the eyes.

"Are you okay?" he asked her.

"I don't think so." Jola shook her head slowly to confirm it.

"You did what could be done," Zeke told her. "Some problems don't have good solutions."

Jola nodded. "That's not it."

"What's bothering you, then?"

Jola paused, as if considering her words, then burst out with, "It's you. I thought you liked Jerry!"

The expression on Zeke's face changed to one of worry and concern. "Of course, I liked Jerry. Very much, in fact. I'm not sure I see where the problem is."

"Oh, come on." The words just began to tumble out of her. "Jerry just died and you've got everybody carrying on as though it's no big deal. Dammit, I cared about him and I can't just cross him off my scut list and move on to whatever is next. And if you really cared about him, I don't see how you could either."

"Whoa! Jo, have a seat for a minute." Schwartz put up a hand to stop the flow of words.

"No thanks."

"Okay, then. Stand if you like, but listen. Jo, whether I liked Jerry, or even if I didn't, has nothing to do with what we need to do. Just because Jerry is dead does not mean that my responsibilities to him and to his family are over. Far from it. Jerry needs to be cleaned up, so that if his parents want to come in and sit with him for a little while, they won't have to see all the mess a code creates. The paperwork all needs to be done, so that if they want to call a funeral home there won't be a hassle. And, most of all, they need to have someone to sit and talk with when they get here. Ellen Inman is a very angry woman, as I think you know. She needs to talk it out, maybe she needs to yell it out, but there has to be somebody there for her to do it to. Jo, I lose a chunk of my gut every time one of these kids dies, but the hospital is not the place to deal with my feelings. These families don't need a pal to sit and grieve with them. They need a physician who can be with them and see what they need and help take care of those needs. That's our job and you can't do it if you're caught up in your own emotions."

Marienkiewicz looked as though she was ready to cry. "Maybe it would be a good idea if I went downstairs and got some coffee," she said in a low tone.

"Maybe it would," Schwartz replied.

As he watched her retreat down the hallway, Zeke was not pleased with himself. It is all true, he thought, and she has to learn it, unless she wants to come apart at the seams, but it should have been said in private. Not that anyone had been standing right there, he reminded himself, but, somehow, word of conversations like that always spread around hospitals. It will not do Jo's reputation any good. So why, he asked himself, did you, the oh-so-experienced physician, let it happen? Because, he answered himself, I do care about these kids and it got under my skin to have someone say otherwise.

Zeke let his breath out slowly. He still had the note to write and he also had to find and fill out the death certificate. Sitting at the desk worrying about Marienkiewicz was not going to help accomplish either task. As he pulled out a blank death certificate from a drawer his eyes fell on the line labeled "Cause of death." The same question he had faced throughout the case surfaced again in his mind. Why did Jerry have to die? He wished mightily that he could know if it had been the Aspergicin that had caused it. He wished it in no small part because he knew Ellen Inman would be asking the same question.

Jola did go down to the cafeteria where she filled a large mug with coffee, all the while wishing it was beer. Or vodka. Or anything with alcohol in it. The cafeteria was deserted, with the exception of some of the housekeeping crew who were not keeping house. She picked a table in one of the corners and sat there sipping her coffee.

She felt horrible, a little like being sick to her stomach, a little like crying. She could not understand why, which made the feelings even stronger. Jerry was not the first child she had seen die, far from it. True, she had been very fond of Jerry, but he was also not the first child she had been fond of who had died. His death had not even been a surprise. Schwartz had not been sanguine about Jerry's chances for living much longer. He had been quite clear on that point when he spoke with Mrs. Inman the day Jerry had come in for this admission; Jola had been there. So, why did she feel so horrible? Part of it she could blame on Schwartz's attitude, but she had been hurting when the conversation had started, so that could not be the whole explanation. Thinking about it did not help. All she knew was that she did not want to go back up to the floor. She did not even want to be a doctor very much anymore.

Unfortunately, her beeper did not take her feelings into account. When it sounded, she hoped that it would be an outside call, maybe Bobby deciding that he wanted to talk to her again, but even a clinic patient with a silly question would have been fine. Instead it was the floor, with a nurse being insistent about an order that Jola had said she would write before Jerry decided to die and which she had never written.

Schwartz, at least, was not in evidence when she reached the floor. He was, she decided, probably in the parents' lounge with the Inmans. The door was closed with light showing underneath, which supported the hypothesis. There was no chance Jola was going to look in to find out. Let Schwartz have Mrs. Inman to himself for however long it took! She wrote the order, then told the nurses that she was going to the on-call room. Normally, she tried to finish all her notes before going to bed, but just then she did not want to spend a minute longer on the floor than necessary.

The few hours sleep, interrupted three times by calls she increasingly believed could have waited, did not help her mood. Morning rounds were held in the house officer's on-call room and she went through them looking as unmade as the bed she perched on. When it came to Jerry, she said only, "He coded last night and we couldn't get him back. Schwartz was in and saw the family." Just saying those two sentences almost brought her to tears.

The senior resident either did not notice her mood, or he ignored it. He wanted to know if Jerry had been infected and had she gotten a post? Jola did not know the answer to either.

"Oh well," he said. "I don't suppose it really matters, does it?" Then he tore Jerry's index card in two and dropped the pieces in the wastebasket. Jola clamped her jaws shut to avoid vomiting.

After rounds, she walked over to the nursing station and made a show of looking through her patients' order sheets. Jerry's was no longer in the book.

"Rough night, huh?"

She looked up to see Tony C. standing at her shoulder. "I've had better," she managed to say.

"Yeah. Listen, everybody has nights like that, even Superdoc Schwartz I'm sure. Don't worry about it. If you need help with your kids today, just ask."

Sympathy from Tony C. That was a new twist. She had not found sympathy where she expected it, so even coming from Tony, it was welcome. As the day wore on, any sympathy was welcome. She was certain that everyone on the floor, if not in the hospital, had heard about the lecture Schwartz had given her. No one said anything, of course, but she thought they looked at her differently than usual. All her chores seemed more difficult than at any time since the day she graduated medical school. Her brain felt like a blunt instrument. Tony C. actually did help her during the afternoon. She was trying to start an intravenous line in a child, which should have been simple, but each time she hit the vein, it would roll away from her needle. When she finally thought she had the line in, the vein popped and she had to start over. After three tries, the child was screaming out of control and the nurse assigned to hold the child looked about ready to scream herself. That was when Tony stuck his head through the door of the treatment room and offered to start the line. He hit it on the first attempt, which normally would have left Jola chagrined at being shown up, but on this occasion just made her grateful.

After evening rounds were over, she found that she did not have the energy to change back into her street clothes. She replaced the scrub top with her shirt, but left her pants hanging in the locker. It would have been too much effort. She figured she would wear the scrub pants home. When she stepped out of the room, Tony C. was in the hall. He tapped her on the arm as she walked past.

"You look like you could use a drink," he said.

"Probably," she said. "I don't know. Thinking isn't my strong suit right about now."

"Phoney?"

Tom Woodward's eyes goggled open at the word. His mouth was open too, reminding Maureen Delahanty of a goldfish she had once kept in her apartment. The expression was so ludicrous that she delayed saying anything else to see how long it would last.

"Let me put it this way, Bossman," she said once his mouth had closed, "the patients are real, no question about that. It's just that most of them were never treated with Aspergicin, or, at least, not so that you could prove it. Plus, there are plenty of cases that we can prove never got Aspergicin, so there's no chance this is just a horrible case of bad charting."

Woodward was having a hard time thinking. He did not want to believe what Delahanty was saying. It was too impossible, too crazy. Things like this happened at fly-by-night companies run by men with diploma-mill degrees. They did not happen to Dr. Thomas Hart Woodward, a well-trained if undistinguished cardiologist, at one of the world's leading drug firms. He wanted badly to wake up from this nightmare. He pinched himself, but Delahanty was still there.

"In all of his studies?" Woodward's voice was little more than a whisper.

"No," Delahanty said. "I told you about that. It's just the open study."

"Well, that's something."

Not a whole lot, if you ask me, Delahanty thought. Woodward did not ask her.

Instead, he asked, "Have you talked to Kanzel yet?"

"About this? I'm a clinical monitor, not an idiot," she replied. "I figured I'd better see how you want to handle it first." She wanted to ask him how stupid he thought she was. She might have Kanzel nailed better than Al Capone but there was no chance that she would be the first to mention it. It was infinitely safer to let the company bigwigs do that.

Woodward let the barb slide. "Who else knows about this?" he asked.

That was the question Delahanty had been expecting ever since she had started the conversation. "Two of the docs at the medical center know," she said. "One is an intern named Marienkiewicz. The other is Zeke Schwartz."

Delahanty thought she would get the goldfish look again, but she was disappointed.

"Jesus Christ!" Woodward exclaimed. "Of all people to have involved with this study, not to mention with this, this God knows what. How in hell did he get involved?"

"Marienkiewicz was taking care of one of the patients. It turned out she works with Schwartz." The statement was true, if misleading, but it was as close to the real truth as Delahanty felt comfortable giving. "It doesn't really matter now, does it?"

"No, probably not. Do you know what is going to happen?"

"Well, Marienkiewicz won't do anything."

"I know that. I meant Schwartz."

"Nothing right now, I think," she said. "I talked to him about that and he said that he would wait to see what we did. I think you can believe that, although I can't tell you how long he'll wait. I wasn't exactly in a position to get a commitment, if you know what I mean. Schwartz sounded as though he'd like to drop-kick Kanzel all the way to Albania. Speaking of which, what are we going to do, Chief?"

"I don't know. I'm not going to call this one on my own. I need to talk to Jackson. After that, I'll get back to you."

"Sure, no problem. I'll be upstairs writing my trip report."

"No!" Woodward almost shouted it. "You don't write anything until I talk to Jackson." There were visions of subpoenas dancing in his head. "Just do something else until I get back to you. Okay?"

"Sure, Tom. No problem." Her face wore a little grin as she left his office.

The moment Delahanty was out of his office, and the door safely closed, Woodward was on the telephone calling Jackson's office. Woodward was quaking internally and it showed in his hand as he went to pick up the telephone. In all the possible disasters he had imagined himself battling, he had never thought of this scenario. Meldrum's entire position was based on Woodward's interpretation of his data and now he was going to have to say that he could not trust some of the data. If the charts of some of Dr. Kanzel's patients were faked, what about other patients? That would be the obvious question the FDA would raise, and if they started to question the original safety data on Aspergicin in this environment, they might pull the drug off the market simply for political reasons. Woodward wondered if there was an inner city health clinic that needed a cardiologist.

Woodward did not find out in that instant whether he would need such a job because Jackson's secretary told him that Jackson was in a meeting. If Dr. Woodward would call back at about four, she told him, Mr. Jackson might have some free time. Woodward, who was feeling short of breath and just short of panic, could not even envision waiting until four o'clock to discuss the problem. His heart was already pounding in his ears.

"Tell Mr. Jackson that this is urgent," he said to the secretary. He did not care if she heard the anxiety in his voice. It might even make her believe him.

Jackson was on the line a moment later with a cheery, "Hi, Tom. What's the problem?"

Woodward told him in unsparing detail. Afterward, Jackson's reply was neither so quick nor so cheery.

"I'm going to have to make some calls on this," Jackson said. "Can you come down to my office in about an hour and a half? We'll see what needs to be done."

Woodward, in truth, did not want to wait even the ninety minutes. He knew, though, that he would sound like a fool if he said that to Jackson, so he had to agree. He spent the time hidden behind his door doing nothing. Actually, he was not completely idle. He was running through his mind for every contact he could recall having with Kanzel's studies, trying to reassure himself that there had been nothing in the past that should have alerted him to the problem Delahanty found. He was so absorbed in this endless reprise that he almost missed the appointed time for his meeting. As he was walking out the door, it struck him that he should have prepared some notes about the situation, but now it was too late. He would have to do everything from memory.

Woodward received another jolt when he arrived at Jackson's office. Pat Dwyer was there as well. He had thought that one of the lawyers might be there, but not Dwyer. That man, however, had seemed ubiquitous from the day the trouble had started.

"Tom," Jackson said, "please have a seat. I thought Pat should be involved in this also."

The way Jackson said it made Woodward think that someone else had suggested to Jackson that Dwyer should be present. It merely made Woodward more apprehensive. Then Jackson asked Woodward to recapitulate the situation to "bring Pat up to speed on this." When Woodward finished, Jackson took over.

"Other than this incident with Kanzel," he asked Woodward, "how is your study going?"

"Quite well," Woodward answered. "Cooperation has been quite good and we haven't turned up a single instance of liver damage, much less a tumor. Bunch of other things, yes, but none unexpected and, like I said, nothing in the liver."

"Good. You know, I checked with Delahanty and from what she tells me we've actually got data on just about the percentage of patients that we promised the FDA."

Going behind my back! thought Woodward.

The thought must have shown on Woodward's face, because Jackson hastened to reassure him. "I didn't mean to cut you out of the loop there. It's just that I figured you would be busy with this and I wanted an update as of right now. It's an important issue."

Woodward did not see the relationship and said so.

"Look, Tom," Jackson said, "we promised the FDA we would survey X number of patients to make sure that people who got Aspergicin weren't developing liver tumors. That was the deal, right? If there was no problem in this given number of patients, they would accept our position on the tumors."

Woodward nodded.

"Okay. We've essentially done that. Nowhere was it said that so many of the patients had to come from specific investigators. We made some initial estimates of where they would come from, but that was not part of the agreement. You have enough cases to write your report, we'll file it with the FDA and that's that. I think they'll probably want another animal study and some ongoing follow-up of patients who are treated, but we expected that. That's it. We've done 'due diligence' and we don't need Kanzel's patients. At least, not the ones from the open study. I gather from what you said that the other studies he ran checked out okay."

Woodward confirmed the last point, but then he said, "But what are we going to do with this study? The damn patient data is faked! Kanzel's other studies looked good, but after this, I don't know how far I'd trust them unless we go over the data with a fine-toothed comb."

Jackson let out a small sigh. "Tom, there are two separate questions. The immediate issue is this follow-up report to the FDA, for which, I remind you, we have an extremely tight and inelastic deadline. If that report doesn't go in on time, we are in deep shit. Now, to the best of your knowledge, the records in Kanzel's other studies are legit. In any case, there are no liver tumors."

"Yes, but dammit, those studies, including that open one, were part of the package we submitted for the approval of Aspergicin in the first place. And some of that data is phoney. You know what the FDA will probably do. They'll say, okay, you claim part of an investigator's data is fake. We'll believe you had nothing to do with it, but we want to exclude *all* of his data, just to be conservative."

"Which is a problem," Jackson agreed, "but it's a different problem. Tom, what if you throw out all of Kanzel's data, all of it. Would that make you change your mind about whether Aspergicin is safe and effective?"

"No," Woodward said slowly. "Enough people have been treated by now that I think the conclusion is okay. But, the point is, his data is false. That's illegal, if nothing else. After all that bullshit in Generics a few years ago, don't you think they would love to hang a major firm for submitting phoney data?"

"True. But it was Kanzel who made up the data, not us. I grant, it wasn't caught by the monitor, but it sounds like plenty of charts were rigged so that the monitor, who is just checking the data against the source document, didn't catch it. Pat, your guys have worked with Kanzel from the day we got approval. Anything ever seem amiss?"

Dwyer, who had said nothing throughout, merely shook his head.

"So there you are," Jackson finished. "We had no knowledge of it until this morning. I'd say it's Kanzel who has the problem, not us."

"But we know about it *now*," Woodward protested.

"Yeah." Woodward had learned that there were times that Jackson did not want to give a direct answer and that it was best to let the issue, whatever it was, rest. This time, however, he was more afraid of the situation than he was of provoking someone's corporate wrath. "Tom, I'm not suggesting that we forget about it. However, you learned of this today. Does it, in your opinion, pose any safety risk to people using Aspergicin?" Woodward shook his head. "Fine. Then, there is no need to report it immediately. What we need to do is to conduct our own investigation. I imagine we should have Quality Assurance do an audit. Then, once we have all the information, we can file a report."

"Even if that is legal, it's not going to look very good."

"All right." There was an unpleasant edge in Jackson's voice as he said it. "I shouldn't need to point out that our relations with the FDA are rather delicate right now. They look like they were surprised by this, which they were, and they're mad as hell that we let it happen. You have Barcellini in Congress holding his subcommittee hearings right now and he's tearing them apart over the approval process and some of the adverse reactions that have turned up. You can't have it both ways, of course, faster approval and stricter oversight, but it sounds good on the news and then he can rip the shit out of them when it doesn't happen. You let this Kanzel thing become a public issue now, while the hearings are going and before we get this liver business buried, and the FDA is going to be real pissed."

"So much for 'protecting the public.' "

Jackson snorted. "That's baloney and always has been, at least for most of them. It's a matter of covering their own asses. Speaking of which," and here he shot a glance over at Dwyer who stayed silent, "there's another excellent reason for not making a scene just now. Trenton is a big customer. If we go in and embarrass Kanzel, it could cost us. Right now, it's important for Majors to finish the year meeting his sales targets. Blow Kanzel away and we're likely to catch the ricochet."

That did explain it, Woodward thought. They needed to cover up Kanzel's fraud to help the FDA cover up whatever it needed to cover up and so allow the tumor issue to be closed. At the same time, they had to do it to support the chess game Majors was playing with the Meldrum corporate brass. *I wonder what would happen if I thought this stuff was really hurting somebody?* Then, he realized that there was a flaw in Jackson's reasoning.

"It all sounds reasonable," Woodward said, "except for one thing. There are at least two docs down at the medical center who know about this. Do you really think they're going to keep their mouths shut?"

"Actually yes." The answer came from Dwyer and it took Woodward by surprise. "We provide a lot of money to the medical center, everything from grants and fellowships to building programs. I don't think they will be very eager to cause us trouble."

"That may be true of the administration, but one of those docs is Zeke Schwartz. Somehow, I can't see him caring too much about our sensibilities."

"Tom," said Dwyer, "I think Dr. Schwartz will find that he cares very much. If I were you, I wouldn't worry about it at all."

Coming from Pat Dwyer, those words were enough to dissolve whatever remained of Woodward's will. He had, very clearly, been told the limits of his involvement. Woodward rose to leave, with some inane remark about how this clarified everything, but there was as much unease in the pit of his stomach as he had when he first called Jackson.

Chapter 30

ZEKE WAITED for ten days after his conversation with Delahanty. He was not quite sure what he was waiting for. He did not really expect Delahanty to call him to tell him what Meldrum was going to do with the information. It did seem reasonable, however, that whatever Meldrum did should make the news in some fashion, so he watched the papers and scanned the newswires with his computer. After ten days, he decided his patience was exhausted. He had promised Delahanty that he would give her the time Meldrum needed to act on its own, but ten days seemed more than reasonable. It was time, he decided, to act on his own.

That action took the form of a meeting in Worthington's office. He had considered simply confronting Kanzel, but decided against it. He wanted to avoid the appearance of a personal vendetta. Worthington took the news with obvious surprise and then, mostly, silence. He told Zeke, in effect, just what Delahanty had told him a week and a half ago. Worthington wanted to talk to the administration, then he would let Zeke know what was to be done. There followed yet another week of no action, and still nothing from Meldrum.

Consequently, when Worthington stuck his head into Zeke's office on the eighth day to tell him that Schwartz was wanted at a meeting in the Administration wing, Zeke felt certain that some form of action was finally imminent. In his own mind, as he waited for the appointed time, he was uncertain whether the fraudulent Aspergicin data made it any more likely that the drug was responsible for Jerry's death. That, however, was not the foremost concern in his mind. The foremost concern was Kanzel. How could he ever trust what the man said in the future, or even what he had said in the past? How could anyone trust a man like that with patients? Schwartz had spent much time over those two and a half weeks worrying about the answers to those questions. He had come to the conclusion that a doctor like that was a hazard and that the only thing that mattered was removing him from patient care as soon as possible. There would be plenty of time later to sort out what was real and what was bogus.

The clock finally reached the hour he was waiting for. Schwartz pulled a folder that he had prepared just for this meeting. It had a carefully drawn list of the patients whose records had been altered and notes on how it had been done. Then he called the page operator and told her to hold any calls that were not dire emergencies. He left his office with a brisk stride.

The small conference room was full when he arrived, although one chair had been left vacant. The occupants of the room were not quite the ones he had expected. Worthington was there, of course, as was Ogilvie. The Chief of Internal Medicine was there. Also gathered at the table were the hospital's Chief Financial Officer and the General Counsel. Marienkiewicz was not there, which was not too surprising, but neither was Kanzel. Schwartz had assumed that Kanzel would be given an opportunity to rebut the allegations; in fact, he had been rather relishing the idea of the confrontation. Of course, he told himself, it was rather difficult to think of any rebuttal that could be made.

"Okay," he said, settling into the chair, "I'm here. Let's get started."

At the other end of the table, Worthington and Ogilvie exchanged looks. Then Ogilvie opened a folder in front of him, glanced through the pages and cleared his throat.

"Zeke," he said and cleared his throat again. "Sorry. This whole situation is rather awkward."

"I can appreciate that," Schwartz said.

"I'm not sure that you do. Yet." Ogilvie looked directly at Schwartz and said, "Well, I suppose you're right; we should get started. The purpose of this meeting," he went on, "is to review a number of instances of unprofessional conduct on your part, most recently these accusations against Dr. Kanzel, but also going back to your appearance on the Acey Henson show. That episode has resulted in an inquiry from the State Board, which I assure you this hospital takes seriously, even if you do not."

Ogilvie paused to let his words sink in. Schwartz was staring at him, the file folder he had brought completely forgotten. "You look surprised," Ogilvie said.

Zeke had to search for the words before he could reply. "Surprise hardly does it justice," he said. "Certainly I expected to discuss Dr. Kanzel, but if there is unprofessional behavior involved, I would say that it is his fraud and not my reporting of it."

"Please." That was the attorney raising her hand. "As yet there has been no proof of any wrongdoing and I think we should be careful not to speak as if there was."

"If you want proof, that's what I brought," Zeke said, slapping the folder on the table. "Or are you telling me that you aren't interested?"

"It's not that at all." Ogilvie had the sensation that the meeting was going to spin out of control almost before it started. He wanted to prevent that. "Zeke, what you need to consider is priorities. Leon Kanzel is scheduled to retire in two years, actually a bit less. What is to be gained from starting a formal inquiry? It could easily drag on until he's due to retire anyway and what will you have from it? Nothing but embarrassment and ill will all around. I've already spoken to Leon and he's agreed to start wrapping up his clinical activities as soon as possible. I really don't think there is any point in carrying matters further."

Ogilvie looked up from the table and found Schwartz staring at him again. The stare lasted until Ogilvie dropped his eyes.

"You can't really believe that this is all there is to it," Schwartz said. "Maureen Delahanty took the same information I have back to Meldrum. Don't you think they're going to blow a gasket when they realize they've been cheated out of whatever that study cost them?"

It looked as though the lawyer wanted to interrupt again, but neither Ogilvie nor Schwartz paid any attention to her.

"The fact is, Zeke," Ogilvie said, "that Meldrum is not pleased, but Meldrum is also not going to do anything. If they did, it would have to involve the FDA and I'm sure you realize that they don't want that right now. Nobody at Meldrum is going to say anything."

"That was not the understanding I had from Delahanty when she left,"

Schwartz retorted. "From what I know of her, I can't believe she would be satisfied with keeping her mouth shut."

"I'm afraid you're quite wrong there," Ogilvie said. "I imagine Ms. Delahanty is quite satisfied." Schwartz was staring at him again, but this time Ogilvie ignored it. "She received a bonus from Meldrum for her work and, in fact, was promoted two grades. Of course," he said softly, "promotions like that usually come with transfers. In her case, it was to Meldrum's Australasia subsidiary which, I gather, had an urgent need for a manager. I doubt she will be back in this country for several years."

Hearing that, Schwartz began to realize that the meeting had not been organized by a group of incompetents, out of touch with reality. Instead, he began to think that he was the one out of touch with reality.

"What about Marienkiewicz?" he asked.

It was Worthington who answered him. "Dr. Marienkiewicz may, eventually, make a competent physician. However, if she wants to complete this residency program, she is going to need to focus her energies on her work and not on frivolous side projects. We've had a little talk and she understands her priorities completely."

"Is that your way of intimidating her?"

"Zeke, that is a poor choice of words." Worthington looked genuinely hurt. "Her problems in the Emergency Room and on the patient floors are well documented."

It was becoming all too clear to Schwartz. Marienkiewicz was vulnerable to pressure. Delahanty probably was not, but she could be tricked, not even realizing that she had been bought. That left only himself, which explained the crazy charges that Ogilvie seemed to have concocted. Why would they go so far to help Meldrum bury the scandal? That answer was there too.

"You need Meldrum's money to keep your programs going," he accused Ogilvie. "You can't afford to embarrass them."

Ogilvie flushed but refused to answer the charge. "This is not a finance meeting," he said.

"No, of course not," said Schwartz. "It's a kangaroo court and the objective is to keep me quiet."

"No, Zeke," Worthington said, "you can say anything you like. However, you don't have tenure here and I doubt that you will get it. In the meantime, if the outcome of this meeting requires us to start a formal inquiry, well, you understand what the results of that will be."

Zeke looked around the table at the others. Each one found some other occupation for his or her eyes as Schwartz turned. No one met his gaze. They did not speak either. The silence was left waiting for Zeke Schwartz. He could see the ultimate conclusion. Say the wrong word, Zeke, and they'll pillory you. Sure, he could go shout about fraud at the top of his lungs to anyone who would listen. It would all sound like sour grapes from a man thrown out for his own breach of conduct. He could not buy his safety, though, by simply keeping quiet, either. They could not hold trumped-up charges over his head forever, the one from the State Board in particular.

"What all of this boils down to," he said into the silence, "is that you would all like to see Zeke Schwartz resign." Naturally, he thought, with a memo on his unprofessional conduct to be kept confidential unless he talked. That way, it would look as though he had left to avoid public charges, so the charges would be effective in a way they would not be if he stayed at the medical center and everything was dropped.

The silence continued after he spoke. On the other side of the table, Worthington shifted uncomfortably in his chair. Schwartz saw the movement and snapped at him.

"That's what this is all about, isn't it, Barlow?" His voice grew sharper as he spoke. "Zeke Schwartz needs to resign and go away so the medical center can stop irritating Meldrum Products because you need the money they are holding out to fix the finances you've all bungled so badly. Isn't that so?"

"I wouldn't put it like that, Zeke," Worthington said.

"Probably you wouldn't. But, you are here to ask me to resign. Right?"

"It would be best, Zeke."

"Best for whom?" came the terse retort.

"Best for you, Zeke," said Worthington. His eyes seemed preoccupied with the intertwined hands in his lap. "You've worked very hard here and, clinically, you've achieved a lot. I take nothing away from you. But politics is not your forte. Leaving here won't cripple you, far from it, and you know it. You'll have no difficulty obtaining another position. At least, that will be true as long as it is not necessary to pursue Mr. Ogilvie's charges."

"I might add," put in Ogilvie, "that under those circumstances you would leave here with the superb recommendation which, as Barlow has pointed out, your clinical work deserves. I suspect the last laugh will be on us, since you will probably end up with a much better position than the one you have here."

Schwartz watched the man chuckle softly as he spoke, as if inviting Schwartz to see the humor in the situation. If he could not see the humor, he did see the truth. There were never many pediatric oncologists, the nature of the specialty saw to that. Even if the number of specialists needed was low, the number of good ones available was even lower. Schwartz could find another job. Easily. He could find a job where there was adequate support, where he did not need to work killing hours, where he could really teach the younger doctors what he knew, instead of dropping an idea or two on the run. That was the carrot. Leave quietly and we will take care of you. It occurred to him that they were counting on him to do what he always did when it was his money or his time at stake. Cave in. Do whatever he was asked to do. All the things he would never do if it were his patients at stake and not him. Except, in a way, it was the kids who were at stake. Who would be there for Jodie or for the next Jerry, or for any of the others? Who was going to care, beyond the simple mechanics of listening to chests and writing orders in charts? Not the people in that room. He knew that. He recalled something Acey had told him one evening. In a jam, she had said, kick him in the balls, or scratch his eyes, or do whatever else it took, because you could not afford to be a nice guy. Nice guys not only finished last, they got fucked before they were finished. It was strange, he thought, that with all his education and training, the best advice he could remember came from a girl who had grown up as a streetfighter. Zeke was tired of being a nice guy. Ogilvie saw Schwartz's face change and his chuckle died abruptly.

"I have a better idea," Zeke said softly.

It was a minute before Worthington managed to ask what that was.

"Fire me."

Another awkward silence followed that statement until Worthington said, "Zeke, we can do that. I wouldn't like it because, personally, I rather like you, but if you force the issue that is what will happen. Think it through, Zeke. Even if you force an investigation, which you may, Kanzel may be retired before it happens and if not"—Worthington shrugged—"the FDA is likely to just bar him from using investigational drugs again. Whatever damage you do to Meldrum and to this center will hardly match the damage you'll do to yourself."

"Oh, I don't quite agree with that," Schwartz said. "You know, I looked into the money that wasn't there, for my program I mean. Hell, we've actually discussed it before, so we all know what I'm talking about. The hospital got it all right, it was part of a federal grant. But it seems that it got spread around, buying some equipment here, supporting a Fellow in Surgery there, I assume to cover other money that you mismanaged. The reason doesn't matter. Misappropriation of government money is a crime. And I very honestly don't think it will take long to get an investigation started. I don't think it will take any time at all."

Zeke paused there to look around the room again. Every face but his had gone red. The Chief Financial Officer looked as though he wanted to crawl under the table.

"Mr. Ogilvie," Schwartz said, "what do you think will happen when people find out that the head of this medical center tries to order physicians to switch to inferior treatments because the insurance company will pay for it that way and, what the hell, the kid might die anyway, so who's to know?"

"I never said that!" Ogilvie blustered.

"Of course you did," Schwartz answered back, "and we both know which kid we were talking about."

By some effort of will, Ogilvie managed to keep his voice nearly level. "I do recall having a conversation with you about reimbursement, but I would never have said what you claim. You can't believe that anyone would take your unsupported word for something like that."

"I don't have to," Zeke said with a smile. "I taped the conversation."

"What!"

"Word of honor." Zeke felt like laughing in Ogilvie's face.

"Zeke, this is blackmail. You have to know that. I can't believe you're capable of this kind of betrayal."

Schwartz gave him an ironic grin. "I really don't think we should be passing out labels like blackmail, should we? Anyway, what was that old saying? 'If it prosper, none dare call it treason.' This will succeed, I assure you."

"Where is the tape?" Ogilvie ground out.

"Acey Henson has it down at WCZY. Go ahead, fire me. The nationally syndicated shows are picking up on what she broadcasts these days, so it won't just be something that happens around here. People in every god-damn state are going to get an earful of the way you do business. How will it play? 'Hospital tries to cover up mismanagement by stealing government money and gypping sick kids of their medicine.' I think investigations will follow in rather short order. No, there will be resignations today, gentlemen, but mine will not be one of them."

Ogilvie was unable to respond. He sat silent, his fists clenched as tightly as his jaw. The rest of the table was silent too, so Schwartz got up to leave. Worthington stopped him as he was about to go through the door.

"Zeke, don't do this," he said. "The repercussions will be far greater than you think. Not just for the medical center. There will be consequences for you too."

"Frankly, gentlemen, I don't give a damn," said Zeke Schwartz and closed the door in their faces.

Schwartz went striding through the corridors at a clip that forced people in his way to scatter or risk being stepped on. He did not stop until he reached 4 North. From the length of the corridor, he saw the intern called Tony C. standing by the nursing station. Schwartz walked up just as Tony was leaving.

"Tony," he called out, "wait a sec."

Tony turned back to face Schwartz. "What's up, Dr. Schwartz? You got an admission?"

Schwartz shook his head. "No. I'm looking for Jo Marienkiewicz. Is she on the floor?"

Schwartz was not prepared for the expression that formed on Tony's face, eyes wide in surprise. "Dr. Schwartz, haven't you heard what's been going on?"

"No. I've been a little busy today. Why don't you fill me in?"

"Uh, sure." Tony sounded very unsure of himself. "Jo got called into Worthington's office this morning."

"I know that, Tony. What else is going on?"

"Well," Tony was having trouble with the words. "Well, I don't know what went on in there, but we figure it must have been kind of nasty. Anyway, Jo came out of there, told somebody she was leaving and split. Nobody's seen her since, it's like she just took off. It's really been a mess up here with her patients and she was supposed to be admitting today too."

"What! What are you telling me, that she just up and left the hospital?"

"Yeah, well, word is that Worthington told her she wasn't doing too well in the program and she really went ballistic. I think she quit, just like I was telling you."

"How can you be so sure of that, Tony?"

"Oh come on, Dr. Schwartz," Tony said, "you know the problems she had, some of them at least. I mean, we all have problems with internship and I'm sure others think about quitting, but we keep going and we get it done. It's not like we cut out and dump the load on somebody else. Some people can take it and some can't. I guess she can't."

"Jesus," Schwartz said. He was feeling sick to his stomach. "How are the rest of you doing with this?"

"Okay, I guess," said Tony. "For myself, I just worked with her a few times. It's not like I knew her very well."

Schwartz thanked him for the information, then turned for his office, albeit at a much slower pace than before. What do I do now? Up to the last ten minutes he had thought he had won. The confrontation was over. There would be at least three resignations from the people in the room: Worthington, Ogilvie, and the finance officer whose name he had forgotten. He had no doubt of it. Kanzel would be gone too, just as soon as he heard the outcome of the meeting. So what? He still did not know if Aspergicin had killed Jerry and the other two kids. Ellen Inman would get an answer from the court, maybe five years from now, but that would be less of an answer and more simple vengeance. Schwartz wanted to know the answer and he was not sure that starting an investigation was going to provide it. Except, he thought, that it was no longer as simple as what Aspergicin might have done. The people in that room had been ready to ruin him and anyone else who stood in their way. Hell, they had tried to ruin Marienkiewicz, and might well have succeeded from the look of it. They would have ruined him, too, had he not exploded. Schwartz wondered where Marienkiewicz had gone and whether there was any way to salvage the situation. Acey was right. No more Mr. Nice Guy. He knew what he was going to do. He just needed to find Marienkiewicz first.

The House Officers' lounge was really just a conference room that had been redecorated. A few of the chairs at the table had cushions; a coffee maker and microwave oven sat on a shelf along one wall; and there was a television set at the far wall, bolted to the shelf and chained to the wall.

Jola was standing at the table, her back to the door, when Schwartz came in. Her attention was focused on a small backpack, which was crammed full of papers, books and various medical tools. She was trying to stuff her pediatrics textbook into the remaining space in the pack and it would not fit. Occasionally, as she struggled with it, her glasses would slip down her nose. She would pause to resettle them, then resume pushing the book into a space far smaller than it needed. One seam of the backpack looked as though it was ready to split.

"What are you doing?" Schwartz asked.

Jola jumped at the words. She had been so intent on her backpack that she had not noticed him. She turned to face him with her hair in disarray and her glasses out of place again. Her face looked as though she had been crying.

"I'm packing," she said sharply. Then she stopped to adjust her glasses.

"Tony said you were leaving."

"Yeah, well, I guess he's right about that," she said. "Just as soon as I can get my ass out the door."

"You want to tell me why?"

She turned back to the table and said over her shoulder, "Not particularly."

"Oh come on, Kay Vitch. Talk to me, here."

"Goddammit!" she said whirling back to face him, "don't call me that. My name is Jola. Okay?"

Schwartz backed up a step, surprised at the fury in her voice. "Actually, I thought your name was Jo."

"Not really," she said, the anger gone. "Look, Dr. Schwartz, what difference does it make? I'm out of here and that's that."

"You still haven't told me why."

"Why do you think?" she retorted. Her voice was more weary than it was angry. "It seems like I just can't cut it here, so I told the Chief Resident that he could take his goddamn program and his goddamn hospital and shove them in his goddamn ass. Or words to that effect. Goddamn it, Schwartz, all I wanted to do was be a doctor. That's all I wanted, all that really mattered. I guess I'll just have to do it someplace else."

"Marienkiewicz, nobody is going to throw you out."

"Yeah, sure."

"I mean it," Schwartz insisted. "You said that being a doc is real important to you. Well, if that's so, don't walk away from it. You're good at it, Marienkiewicz. Don't throw it away."

"I hate to tell you," she said, "but not everybody shares your opinion. I just had His Highness, Barlow Worthington, tell me just how lousy I am. Too slow in the Emergency Room, don't work well on a team, too much time on side projects. Do you have any idea what it feels like to get torn apart like that? And then, at the end, he was going to be so generous. We're not going to kick you out now, Marienkiewicz. Oh no. You can be on probation until the end of your internship. How stupid do you think I am, Schwartz? I'll work like a slave until June and *then* he'll kick me out, when it won't cause a hole in the schedule. Fuck that! And fuck you, too."

"Marienkiewicz, will you slow down a moment and listen to me? That bullshit isn't about you, it's about Meldrum. It's got nothing to do with you."

"That's very comforting," she said. "Worthington says I'm gone, I'm gone. The reason doesn't matter."

"Except it won't happen like that. Worthington is resigning today. What he said doesn't mean a damn thing, not any more. Not unless you do something stupid, like run away."

Marienkiewicz looked at Schwartz as though she could not comprehend what he said. "What do you mean, 'Worthington is resigning'?" she demanded.

"Just what I said," he replied. "This whole business was about covering up for Meldrum and Kanzel. They tried the same thing with me, tried to force me out. It didn't work."

"You expect me to believe that you just said 'I won't go' and they folded up?"

"I wish it had been that simple," Schwartz said. "Actually, it was more like blackmail. It wasn't a pretty sight. But, it's done. There's no reason for you to quit."

"But."

"But nothing. Do you expect me to have Tony take care of Jodie, Kay Vitch?"

She smiled at that. "No, I suppose not. But what about the Chief Resident? After what I told him . . ."

"You let me worry about the Chief Resident," Schwartz said. "He and I will have a little talk. Now, are you staying?"

"I suppose so," she said. She hefted the textbook and tossed it onto the table. "It wouldn't fit in the pack anyway."

EXCERPT FROM THE *WALL STREET JOURNAL* _____

The pharmaceutical industry was rocked yesterday by reports that as many as two-thirds of the patient reports in a key study of Aspergicin had been faked. This study was conducted by Dr. Leon Kanzel, Chief of Infectious Disease at the Central New Jersey Medical Center. In the wake of these reports, Dr. Kanzel, Mr. Ben Ogilvie, Chief Hospital Administrator, and at least two other members of the staff have resigned. For Meldrum Products, the maker of Aspergicin, the unwelcome news comes on the heels of a difficult summer. It began with the disclosure that Aspergicin had leaked into a creek running behind the manufacturing plant and was being linked to the development of a rare liver cancer in three children living nearby. Meldrum has consistently denied that any association exists.

The new revelations cast further doubt on whether Aspergicin, once hailed as a wonder drug for patients with weakened immune systems, will even remain on the market. In response to inquiries about this, Dr. Thomas Woodward of Meldrum Products stated that the company planned to continue marketing Aspergicin. According to Dr. Woodward, the study was only a "supportive study and the present developments in no way impact on the determination of Aspergicin's safety and efficacy." Dr. Woodward maintained that there was "absolutely no link" between this study and the earlier reports associating Aspergicin with liver cancer.

Not all observers were so sanguine, however. One of them was Senator Alfonso Barcellini (D-New Jersey), who chairs the subcommittee currently investigating the pharmaceutical industry. "It is inconceivable to me," he said at a news conference yesterday, "that a crucial piece of evidence regarding the safety of this drug can turn out to be fabrication without raising serious questions about Meldrum's response to earlier concerns."

Barcellini made it clear that he would find out what Meldrum knew and when they knew it. He also wanted to know what the FDA knew and when they knew it and why they had done nothing about it.

The news sent Meldrum's stock plunging four dollars a share on the New York Stock Exchange and triggered a mini sell-off in other pharmaceutical issues as well.

TRENTON, NEW JERSEY _____

Schwartz walked into his office without really paying attention to his surroundings. He marginally saw Doris on the telephone and breezed past her until he was halted by a quick, "Wait a minute. He just walked in."

"If it's Mrs. Shaw," he said, intending to continue on into his office, "just tell her that I will call her this evening after five." At that moment, he had no stomach for reviewing the long list of vitamins Mrs. Shaw had assembled for the purpose of deciding which ones the Shaw's four-year-old daughter could take.

"It's not Mrs. Shaw," Doris said. "It's Dr. Woodward from Meldrum Products."

That brought Schwartz to a stop. He did not go into his office at all, but walked over and took the receiver from Doris.

"What do you want?" His tone was barely civil.

"Simple," Woodward said. "You once told me that you were only interested in knowing if Aspergicin was involved in those tumors. Is that still what you are interested in, or are you looking for blood?"

Schwartz tightened his grip on the receiver. He saw Doris watching him and wished she were elsewhere. He tried to indicate that she should leave, but she conveniently misinterpreted his hand signals.

"Is this going to be a confession?" he asked Woodward.

"What? Don't be ridiculous. What I'm saying is that I have whatever data is available. Do you want to see it?"

Schwartz said, "Yes," followed almost immediately by, "Why are you doing this now?"

There was a short laugh. "Let's just say I'm sufficiently pissed off. You're most of the reason all this shit is flying, but all anybody here seems to care about are their little power games. That may be all fine for them, but I'm the one who's left holding the bag when the *Wall Street Journal* or anybody else calls and I'm sick of it. I can't say anything, but you can—hell, that's about all you've been doing—so I'm going to let you see the data and then you can say anything about it you damn please. Which is not to say I'm stupid. If you get this, you did not get it from me. That has to be clear."

Schwartz had no hesitation. "Not a problem. Why don't you meet me here?"

"No. I can't do that. Too many people might know me, or one of our reps might be in the hospital."

"Jesus Christ, Woodward. You're paranoid."

"I am not paranoid. I can't come to the medical center. It has to be somewhere I won't be recognized."

"This is getting ridiculous," Schwartz said. "I gave up playing spies twenty years ago."

"Schwartz, I'm offering you this because I don't like the way certain things are being handled. That does not mean that I am eager to be unemployed. You are going to have to humor me."

Eventually, they agreed on the parking lot of one of Somerville's shopping plazas. It was only after he hung up that Schwartz realized he had no one to sign out to. He could hardly ask Worthington to cover the service while he went out. In the end, he had to drive to Somerville with his beeper on and, once there, sit in the parking lot hoping Woodward would arrive before it went off.

Woodward did pull in only a few minutes after Schwartz, although it seemed much longer while he was sitting in the car. They greeted each other coolly from a car's width apart.

"I hope you don't want me to call you Deep Throat," Schwartz said.

"By no means." Woodward's anger had carried him this far, but his antipathy to Schwartz was beginning to cancel it out. It left him acutely aware of the risk he was taking. Woodward walked around to the back of his car and opened the trunk. Inside were stacks of small binders.

"This is what there is," Woodward said. "The reports on Aspergicin from the time we started marketing it to now and the results of the follow-up study I did. There's also the sampling results from the creek. You're welcome to go through it. You won't find a damn thing."

Schwartz looked at the books a bit dubiously. "Aren't things like this registered or something?"

Woodward's laugh was harsh. "Now who's playing spy? Actually, there's an interesting flaw in the security system. The computer will record every time the database is accessed, and who does it, and the final signed copies of reports like these are all numbered with a record of who has which number. However, nobody keeps track of the drafts and I always keep a copy of mine. There are some minor changes in the wording from the finals, but the data is all the same. Now, sales figures, they shred every extra copy, but not reports like these. Well, yes or no?"

"Yes," said Zeke Schwartz.

Chapter 31

NORMALLY, JIM Morrison would have been immensely pleased to look in the *New York Times* and see that Quad Industries stock had closed at over forty-three dollars a share. QI had not traded so high since before the big crash in October 1987. Its current price meant that Morrison's considerable holdings had increased by almost half in just a few months. Unfortunately, these were not normal circumstances. QI stock was not trading so high because the company was suddenly doing very well, or even because people thought that it would in the near future. The run in the stock had been triggered solely by Thigpen's assault on the company. The latest upsurge, a rise of five dollars a share in the last three days, had come along with a rumor that Meldrum Products had decided to tender their block. Morrison knew how to gauge the reaction of the Street to takeover talk. The Street was betting that the rumor was right. They were betting that QI would not survive.

Morrison, much to his disgust, was beginning to agree with the Street's assessment. The Meldrum block, supposedly the linchpin of QI's defenses, probably was a lost cause. In fact, it had probably been so ever since Acey Henson opened her mouth early in the summer. Any doubts Morrison might have had vanished the day before. He had sent Meldrum an offer for QI to buy half their block. It had been rejected the same day. Ames had simply snorted and said that Meldrum was probably suspicious of QI being able to raise the needed money. The point was reasonable, and might even have been true had Morrison tried to implement the plan, but Meldrum had rejected the idea too rapidly. They could not have found out, that fast, that the financing was shaky. Ergo, Meldrum was no longer interested in working with QI. That was why Morrison was so sure the Street rumors were correct. Ames refused to see it, but just because Dick Ames was being stubborn did not mean that he was right. None of this meant that Morrison was ready to quit. It just meant that he was desperate.

Desperate times called for desperate measures. That was why, on that particular afternoon, Morrison left QI's New York offices early in the afternoon. His destination was WCZY in Flemington. The move was made on a flimsy basis. Howard Firman, the station manager, had called QI's office that morning. He had been reading the stories about the takeover attempt and wanted to tell someone at headquarters that he knew John Lawrence Thigpen from high school. Did anyone at corporate think that would be useful, Firman had wanted to know. Information like that was passed to Morrison's office and, with his other options dwindling, Morrison returned the call. It took Morrison only a few minutes to conclude that Firman was useless. That was the same conclusion, he recalled, that he had reached during the unsuccessful attempt to silence Henson over the summer. Two unexpected bits of information, however, had fallen from the conversation. Thigpen had actually been at WCZY not too many days before Acey Henson had launched her attack against Meldrum. In addition, while he was at WCZY, Thigpen had met Acey Henson. A switch in Morrison's brain had gone "click" when he heard that. He wondered if there was some way he could turn it to his advantage. That reasoning took him to Flemington in the afternoon, where he sat in Acey Henson's office waiting for her.

When Acey arrived, she stopped dead in the doorway as Morrison stood up. From a distance of five feet, they eyed each other warily. The contrast could not have been greater: Morrison in his dark blue suit and close-cropped gray hair, Acey in fraying jeans and Hard Rock Café tee shirt with streaks of red and purple running through her hair. One of us must look very out of place, Morrison thought.

"I'm Jim Morrison from QI," he said extending his hand.

Acey took the proffered hand and gave it a firm shake. "I know the name," she said.

Acey had been expecting some form of corporate response to her continued broadcasts. She assumed that this was it. Morrison, on the other hand, from the moment he saw her eyes and heard her voice, felt all his political instincts shouting for caution. Be careful with this one, they said, be very careful. He quickly discarded a half-dozen approaches that he had considered and decided to be blunt.

"I need to talk with you about the Meldrum leak story," he said.

Acey's lips pressed into a thin line before she answered. "I've already had one discussion about that. With Mr. Ames."

"I know all about that," Morrison said, as indeed he did. "I am not here to try to reverse the outcome of that meeting. It's far too late for that anyway. Actually, I was hoping to get some information from you."

"What sort of information?"

"Background, if you will. Close the door please."

Acey did and took the opportunity to pull out a cigarette. Then she turned back to face Morrison.

"Okay," she said, "what can I do for you?"

"First," said Morrison, "let me show you the picture as it exists. Bear in mind that our discussion is confidential. If even a hint gets out, much less on the air, I will have you fired. In fact, it would be a perfect excuse, if you know what I mean." Acey nodded. "Good. You are aware that Quad Industries is the subject of a takeover attempt?"

"I read the papers." She gestured toward her desk where six different titles were in evidence.

"How familiar are you with the guy orchestrating it?"

"I'm not."

"Sure you are. His name is John Lawrence Thigpen and I know that you've met him."

Acey stared at him, trying to place the name. She recognized it from the newspapers, but not as an acquaintance. Then she made the connection. Thigpen had been the name of the man Howard had brought to the station one night earlier in the summer. It seemed like a year ago.

She nodded her head very slightly. "You're right. I did meet him here once, although I'd forgotten it until now. What's the point?"

"Simple, really," Morrison said. "I need to know what he wanted from you and what you actually did."

"That's simple," Acey laughed. "He wanted to get laid and I told him no."

"I'm afraid I find that hard to believe."

"What is it that you find so hard to believe, Mr. Morrison? That he was interested in screwing me, or that I wouldn't put out?"

Morrison allowed himself a small smile. "No, neither one. I just don't believe that the sole subject of the meeting was sex."

"Why not?"

"Henson, I don't have time to play games." Morrison felt his frustration rise and battled to control it. "Your story on the Meldrum leak has gone a long way to undermine QI's ability to fight off Thigpen. You met with him not long before you broke the story and he went after QI as soon as the public interest in it started to build. It's only logical that there is a connection."

"The story was about Meldrum. The takeover is about QI."

"Correct."

Acey shook her head. It didn't make sense, or did it? Her listeners normally had little or no interest in the affairs of corporations, unless they directly affected the counties along the Delaware, but she had kept clippings on the QI story because they owned the station. There was something she had read that she could not quite remember. Ignoring Morrison for the moment, she pulled open a file drawer and yanked out a folder containing a bunch of newspaper articles.

"Ah!" she said, still focused on the contents of the file. "Meldrum owns QI stock. A lot of it, I guess. Is that the connection? And you think I was trying to . . . ?" She broke off and laughed in Morrison's face. "I'll be damned. I was wondering what Ames was so damned bothered about. That explains why you wanted the story killed."

"Precisely. And also why we could not simply fire you. Even if you didn't make the connection, I'm sure dear Mr. Thigpen would have lost no time in pointing it out. Although, I should add, nothing has been forgotten. There will be a payback, unless you help us now." That assumes, Morrison said to himself, that QI survives in the first place.

Acey lit the cigarette she had been holding. "Okay. Let's forget all the history for a moment. What all this boils down to is that if I give you what you want, that will make up for running the story in the first place. Right?"

"Basically."

"And if I tell you he just wanted to get laid?"

Morrison frowned. "As soon as the publicity dies down, or the takeover bid is stopped, you're history."

"Figures. And what in particular, are you looking for?"

"Did Thigpen give you the data on the leak that night or arrange for you to get it? What did he pay you or promise you in return for running the story?"

"What would you do with the info, if I had it?" Acey asked.

"For starters," Morrison said, "I can see tying Thigpen up in court on stock manipulation charges. If we can trace the information on the leak to him, we may be able to hit him with some more mundane stuff, too, like theft."

Acey let out a sigh and a fair amount of smoke with it. "You know, I didn't take to Mr. Thigpen when he was here and I'd hardly call myself his friend, but the fact is that all he wanted was to get laid. As I recall, he didn't offer to pay for that, much less anything else."

Morrison gritted his teeth. "I can top whatever he is paying you."

"He ain't paying me," Acey said. "I guess that's about the only difference between the two of you."

Morrison stared at her as though by the intensity of that stare he could force the truth out of her. He had no way of telling whether she was being loyal to Thigpen or whether she was actually telling the truth. In the end, it did not matter. If she was not going to help him, the reason behind it was irrelevant. Abruptly and silently, he left the office. He would need to talk to Ames, he knew. He could continue to play his games with the stockholders and the lawyers, but there was not much point. If he went that way, he knew what the end result would be. It would be better if he and Ames could arrange to meet with Thigpen. Maybe Thigpen would compromise; maybe he could be tricked. It was worth the attempt.

LOS ANGELES, CALIFORNIA _____

Marilyn Glennoch was waiting for him when Thigpen strolled into the bar at the Los Angeles Airport Hilton. He smiled when he saw her. Marilyn somehow managed to look sensual, in spite of the fact that she was wearing a plaid business suit and had her nose in an open file folder. He wondered how piqued she would be at the way he had rushed her.

"Hi, Glennoch," he said when he reached her table. She looked up at him as though unaware that he had been in the room.

"Afternoon, Johnny." Her voice did not sound angry, but that was not a reliable indicator with her. "Care to tell me what the sudden crisis is?"

"Sure. I'm going to New York to see Ames. Tonight. That's why we had to meet today. I can't wait until I come back."

Glennoch regarded him with an unblinking stare while he said his piece. Then, she closed her file folder and slipped it back into her briefcase. She leaned back into her seat before she said anything.

"Something has happened with the takeover." She said it as a statement, not a question.

"You bet." Thigpen broke into a wide grin. It was fun to let people know you were winning. "A few things happened just right and now Mr. Ames wants to talk."

"I'm just curious," Glennoch said, "what happened all of a sudden like that?"

"I'll tell you. Do you mind if I sit down?"

"Not at all. We are supposed to be meeting aren't we?" She waved him into a seat next to hers.

"We are at that," Thigpen said. "Okay, mostly it's just that Ames is being pushed into a corner and he's just about there. Then, we got a couple of breaks. You remember that kid in New Jersey who got cancer from the Meldrum leak? Well, he died recently. About the same time, some bullshit hit the press about one of the Meldrum Aspergicin studies being forged. Meldrum has all kinds of reasons now to want their money out of QI, and that's especially true since it's worth so much more thanks to Yours Truly and his takeover."

"And this is hot enough for you to take a Friday redeye to New York?"

"It's my game to play, Marilyn." Thigpen's tone suggested that he did not wish to discuss it further. "Were you able to get the information I'll need on the radio stations?"

"Yes." For an instant, it looked as though Glennoch wanted to continue talking about QI and Meldrum but she did not do it. Thigpen had asked her only about the radio stations. She opened her briefcase and withdrew a thick folder.

"This is what I was able to put together for you on the organization and personnel needs of your broadcast group," she said. She opened the folder and selected some sheets to spread on the table. "These provide you with a basic organizational chart for each of the stations and for the headquarters group that will run the company. As you can see, the headquarters group can be quite small. That will keep your expenses down. I have listed on the charts the titles of each of the positions you'll need. Brief job descriptions and the likely salary ranges are in the packet. Where possible, I've listed candidates to fill them. These are either incumbents or potentials. The packet also has some background on the people."

Thigpen studied the charts briefly, then glanced through the supporting material. "What about these positions you have marked with an asterisk?" he asked. His finger lightly touched each of the marked boxes.

Glennoch smiled. "Those are key positions. You have to have them filled, people in place, before you can start operations."

"And the double asterisk here?"

"That's your programming director," Glennoch said. "This is probably your most critical position, given that you don't have any experience yourself. The problem you've got is that since QI never tried to run the stations as a group, each station handled its programming completely independent of the others. No one person had overall responsibility for programming so this job, as I've outlined it, does not currently exist. That's a problem because without someone in this slot, you can't make your group work."

"Okay, Marilyn," Thigpen said, "you've shown me the problem. I hope you can show me the solution."

"It's not simple," she replied. "This kind of position is hard to fill. It's even harder because you need someone familiar with stations this size. Given the time constraints, I'd say your best bet would be a programming director who already works for one of the stations."

"And?"

"Today is your lucky day." She pulled another sheet out of the pack. "One of them, I think, will fit the job. He's got a good track record as a clever and innovative programmer, which you'll need. My sources say that he's the reason his station runs in the black, despite what you might call less than optimal management." She pushed the sheet across to Thigpen.

He picked it up and saw that the name on it was Roger Bannerman. The

man was the programming director for WCZY, Howard's station. Thigpen
tried to hold his laugh in, but was unsuccessful.

"You know him?" Glennoch asked.

"No. I know the station manager. I can believe your assessment."

"You ought to," she said. "One thing to know is that he has been out sick
for a while, some kind of accident from what I understand. From what I'm
told, there's no reason to think it's a long-term problem. I'd go after him.
The others don't measure up."

"Great." Thigpen stacked the papers together again and replaced them in
the folder which he dropped into his case. "That's what I really needed to
know. I want to hit some of these people on this trip. I'll make sure Bannerman is the first one I see after I'm done with Ames."

"Good. I like to hear that confidence, Johnny. It makes me believe that
this is going through."

"Meaning that you'll get the rest of the assignments," he said.

"Of course. Listen, Johnny, if you're taking the redeye, your plane
doesn't leave until much later, right?"

"True."

"That's why I took a room at the airport hotel. Why don't you come
upstairs and relax?"

That was the kind of offer Thigpen was not about to refuse.

Several hours later, he wiggled his back to try and make himself more
comfortable in his airplane seat. The contrast with the king-sized bed he
had recently occupied with Marilyn was only part of the reason for his
squirming. For some reason, all airline seats, even the big cushy first-class
ones he sat in, were uncomfortable from the moment he buckled his seat
belt. Through the window, he watched the plane pull away from the terminal, then turn slowly onto the runway. He could see four other planes in
line ahead of his. Not too bad. Although he never understood why, Thigpen
found himself constrained to watch through the window until the plane
took off. He was fine once the plane was in the air, so he did not think it
was fear of flying. He knew people who were afraid to fly. They would
drink themselves half-insensate in the airport. He never did that. There was
always too much work to do in flight.

At last the plane swung into takeoff position. The engines roared, sending the jet hurtling down the runway. Gradually, the nose of the plane tilted
up, followed by a clunk as the landing gear retracted. Down below, the
nighttime lights of Los Angeles dwindled away. Thigpen let out the breath
he had been holding from the moment the acceleration had pushed him
back into the seat. He could not understand why he always did that either.

The takeoff safely behind him, he pulled down his seat tray and opened his briefcase on it. There was a sheaf of notes and figures on Quad Industries that he needed to review. The flight would deposit him in New York in the morning. There he was to meet with Dick Ames for Saturday breakfast at the New York Athletic Club. Thigpen smiled at the memory of Marilyn's reaction to his schedule. It had made no sense to her that he should agree to such a schedule, not if he truly held the power in the situation. In fact, he had deliberately allowed Ames to insist on a schedule that required Thigpen to fly all night to reach the meeting. He had been smiling all the while Ames had been working over the phone to bully him into it. Ames would come to the meeting believing that Thigpen had given him an advantage by flying overnight. Thigpen slept well on airplanes, however. Ames would also have his flunky, Morrison, there with him while Thigpen would be alone. Thigpen wanted it that way, though, because he wanted to discuss the radio stations. Thigpen did not want any of Kuhnlein's other people involved at this stage. So, Ames would come to the meeting thinking he had rigged it against Thigpen when, in fact, it had been set up just the way John Lawrence Thigpen wanted it. With luck, Ames's guard would be down. Thigpen liked to find every possible advantage in advance.

Thigpen's mind, however, was not on the figures. There might be billions of dollars and thousands of job on two continents at stake, but Thigpen's mind was on his broadcast-group-to-be. There would always be million-dollar paydays, but there might never again be such a chance at his own broadcast group. From underneath the facts and figures, he pulled the folder that Marilyn had given him. He looked through the charts and descriptions again, trying to memorize all the information. They told him his dream could happen. He just needed to make the right preparations. He pulled out the sheet with the information about Roger Bannerman and studied that. The man lived in Philadelphia, an easy trip from New York. Thigpen decided that he would call Bannerman as soon as the meeting with Ames was over. He could not do it beforehand, too much might still go wrong, but he wanted to do it very soon after. He wanted a side agreement with Bannerman well before it became public that QI was to be bought and disassembled. It would never do to have Bannerman run to another job because he was worried about the effect of the QI takeover on his station. He just hoped Marilyn was right about the man.

Marilyn was usually right, of course, that was how she had established her reputation, at least one of her reputations. The other was a different matter. The thought made Thigpen smile broadly. God, it had been a good evening. There had been several of them over the past weeks. Part of him wondered if that was just Marilyn's way of ensuring that she would receive her share of the QI work when the takeover went through—keeping her hand in the action, so to speak. It was possible. Marilyn seemed to regard

sex, in general, as nothing more than the means to guarantee company for
dinner. The idea did not bother Thigpen. If Marilyn thought she was
manipulating him, literally as well as figuratively, he was happy to let her
think so. He enjoyed the manipulating.

Reluctantly, he put Marilyn out of his mind, and the radio stations back
in the briefcase, and picked up the figures on QI. When he walked into that
meeting, he wanted to have all the details about QI fresh in his mind. If
possible, he wanted to avoid referring to notes. It was another psychological ploy he liked for meetings. It would probably work against Ames. Of
course, he had more than just psychological ploys to use on Ames. Meldrum Products would be happy to pull their money out of QI and even
happier to take revenge on Ames for allowing WCZY to turn the leak into a
national scandal. Thigpen could use that as a club when the talks bogged
down. He could walk out of the room with every expectation of taking the
entire company no matter what Ames did. A separate phone call he had
received that afternoon from Morrison reinforced that belief. He was going
to win when he met Ames. He was going to get his radio stations and the
rest of the company, too. He just wished he knew the psychological approach to take with Bannerman.

Chapter 32

"YOU'RE REALLY sure of this?"

"No, dammit, I'm not really sure of it. I don't think I'm really sure of
anything any more."

It was Acey Henson's evening off and, for that reason, the scene was the
living room of her apartment. She sat in a chair taken from her kitchen.
Opposite her, on the couch, sat Zeke Schwartz. Between them, stacked in a
large pile on her already burdened coffee table, were the volumes that had
come from the trunk of Woodward's car. Zeke was glaring at the books,
but Acey was wondering if some of the glare was for her.

"What I am saying," Zeke continued, "is that I have been through these
reports up one way and down another and it's like Woodward said. I don't
find a damn thing."

Acey paused to flick ash into the top of an empty beer can. "Then the Aspergicin didn't cause Jerry's tumor."

"No, I didn't say that either! All I'm saying is that there is nothing in any of these reports that suggests Aspergicin ever caused a tumor like that before. I've also got the sampling reports on Scheuermann's Run and it doesn't look like any of the Aspergicin bugs took up residence there. It makes it unlikely, very, very unlikely, but it's not proof. I'm not sure how you ever prove it unless you find the real culprit, but we've said that before."

"Could Woodward have just given you selected stuff?" Acey wondered. "Kept back all the bad reports, I mean."

"I doubt it," Zeke said. "There are two types of reports in there." He waved at the mass on the table. "There are sporadic cases, people, mostly docs, calling the company to say 'I gave this drug to this patient and such and so happened.' Those are all numbered consecutively and nothing is missing. I can't believe that, a year or two ago, somebody would completely suppress what would have looked like an oddball report, not with some of the wacky stuff that is in here. The other stuff is from their clinical studies, including that follow-up study that caused all the fuss down at the medical center. Those patients all have consecutive numbers, too. It would be too easy for somebody to catch them if they were hiding something. But, the real reason I don't believe anything was hidden is that Woodward doesn't have the balls."

"Okay." Acey let out a big sigh along with a lot of smoke. "What do you want to do? Go back on the show and say 'oops, never mind'?"

"No!"

"Okay. Easy now, easy. This apartment building won't take anything over four on the Richter scale. Zeke, if you're pissed because I got you to go on the show and make a public scene out of this, I'm sorry. Really, I am."

"Huh?" Zeke looked up as though he had been thinking of something else. "Acey, it was my idea to go on the show. If that means I end up looking like a fool, I'll have to live with it. The problem is that I keep flipping back and forth about this damned drug. Did it or didn't it? Right now, I'm thinking that the only way to deal with this mess is to go back and look for something else."

"Well, I'm game for that but"—and she threw her hands up in the air—"that puts us right back at the beginning. Unless you have some new ideas."

"Not really. Just one possibility that I think we should look at. I told you they went looking for bugs in the creek." Acey nodded. "Looking at the dates, I think they did it right after we were on the air asking about it. They took samples below the Meldrum plant, which is where that storm drain cut in, and also near the place Jerry lived. Everything was negative. No bugs, no Aspergicin. The thing is, Jerry once told me that the kids in that neighborhood had a hangout somewhere along the creek. A kid's fort, I guess. It seems to me that the logical place to look would be where the kids were playing and, I'll bet, it's not going to be real near any of the homes."

"Sounds good to me," Acey said. "Do you know where Fort Jerry is?"

"Unfortunately," he answered, "I haven't a clue."

Whatever he might have said about how to find some clues went unsaid because at that moment the telephone rang. The sound was startling because the whereabouts of the telephone was not immediately obvious. Tracking down the noise disclosed the telephone, sitting on the floor, partially hidden under some of Acey's files. Acey grabbed the cord and pulled it over to her chair, scattering the material that had rested on it.

"Yeah?" she said into the receiver.

Her tone changed immediately because the caller was Jimmy and he was upset. It turned out that he had a good reason.

"He wasn't home when I got here," Jimmy said, "which worried me because Rog hasn't been going out at all recently. I started checking the hospitals and, sure enough, he's down at University Hospital. I'm assuming he must have started to feel real bad and called an ambulance."

"Jesus," was all Acey said at first. Then, "He didn't leave you a note, or anything?"

"No, not that I could find. Rog has been pretty forgetful."

"Not important, I suppose, since you found him. How is he?"

"I don't know yet," Jimmy said. "All they told me was that he was going to be admitted. I figured I'd just put together some things he may want and then I'll go see. I thought you would want to know."

"Absolutely, Jimmy. Thank you. I'll be down as soon as I can."

"You don't have to, Acey. It's a long drive."

"I know I don't have to, Jimmy. I said I was coming."

Jimmy did not argue the point further, nor would it have done him any good to try. He did say, "Just one more thing, Acey, before I run. Have you ever heard of a John Thigpen from California?"

At the name Acey's grip on the receiver tightened to the point that her knuckles went white. Just a few days ago, Morrison had come to New Jersey to ask the same question. "I believe I've had the displeasure, once," she said. "Why?"

"He left a message on our answering machine. Said he was coming into Philly and wanted to meet Rog over dinner or a drink to talk about radio stations. I don't recall Rog ever mentioning him, so I was wondering if you knew what this was about."

"Like I said, I met the man once. I have no idea why he would be calling

Rog." It occurred to her that Morrison might have some ideas, but this was not the time to begin discussing them with Jimmy.

"Hmm. I called the hotel he said he would be staying at, but he hasn't checked in yet." Jimmy sounded even more upset. "I left a message that Rog was in University Hospital, which I wish I hadn't done. Rog is going to be pissed."

"I wouldn't worry about it, Jimmy," Acey told him. "Mr. Thigpen will just have to find someone else for dinner or a drink. Now, you get going. I'll meet you there."

She hung up the receiver and turned to face a perplexed Zeke Schwartz. He had, of course, heard only half the conversation. That made it clear that Acey had a problem but gave no clues as to what the problem was.

"What was that all about?" he asked.

"Nothing," she answered. "I'm afraid I have to go out, though. I probably won't be back until late."

"That's a lot of effort for 'nothing.' "

"What can I tell you?" She shrugged her shoulders. She had already started to pull on her jacket when she stopped and turned back to Zeke. "Wait a minute," she said. "You're a doctor."

"No shit, Sherlock. Want to tell me what's going on?"

Acey felt a hesitancy about talking to him, something she had not felt in a long time. Carefully, she said, "I have a friend who is pretty sick and, I guess, had to be hospitalized. I don't know what questions to ask or what the answers would mean. Would you mind coming along to sort through the medical bullshit?"

"That's not a problem," Zeke said. "You should know that. Do you have any idea what's wrong?"

"AIDS, for starters," Acey said very softly.

At the words, the color drained out of Zeke's face leaving behind a look of fright. "How close a friend of yours is he?" he asked.

At first, Acey could not understand his reaction. She had assumed Zeke, or any other doctor, would react to AIDS the same way as any serious illness. Then it dawned on her why Zeke looked scared and she burst out laughing.

"Zeke, Roger would have a laughing fit if he knew what you were thinking, an absolute laughing fit. Don't worry about that. It's not an issue. Will you come?"

"I said I would. There's just one condition."

"What's that?"

"We take my car. I'll be damned if I'm going to ride to Philadelphia on the back of your bike."

They arrived at the waiting room outside the intensive care unit to find Jimmy sitting, legs stretched out in front of him, staring at the ceiling.

"They would only let me visit for fifteen minutes," he said, "which is probably just as well because ten was about as much as I could take. At least, this way, I don't feel like I walked out on him."

"Did they tell you what the problem is?" Acey asked.

"They may have," Jimmy said miserably. "I really wasn't hearing anything. I'd really appreciate it if you would go in. See what's going on, talk to the doctor, then tell me about it. That would help." Jimmy kept his voice fairly level and perhaps looked cool enough to fool most people, but Acey knew all of his little nervous habits. Zeke, too, was accustomed to seeing people under great stress. Both of them knew that Jimmy was not nearly as calm as he was trying to appear.

Once inside the unit, it took only minutes for Zeke to make up his mind. Roger was unaware of his surroundings, hooked to a ventilator that breathed for him. There was a chest X-ray pinned to a light box that Zeke looked at. He checked the medications Roger was receiving, the laboratory values on the flow sheet by the bed, then asked a few questions of the intern. He signaled Acey with his hand to move away from the bedside.

"How bad is he?" she asked.

"Very bad," Zeke said. "I think the odds of him leaving here alive are very small."

"Damn." She bit down hard on her lower lip and tasted blood. "It had to happen sooner or later, didn't it?"

"Yes."

"Ah, shit. Zeke, I'd like to sit with him for a few minutes. Could you go out and tell Jimmy? I, I mean, shit, you're better at doing this than I am and I'm scared."

"No problem."

Zeke went back to the waiting room where Jimmy was in the same position as when they had gone in. "Jim," he said, "my name is Zeke Schwartz. I guess we weren't introduced. I'm a doc from New Jersey."

"Ah, yes," Jimmy said, standing up. "I've heard the name." They shook hands. "Acey would never win any Miss Manners contests, would she?"

"No, I suppose not." Zeke went on to tell Jimmy what he had seen in the unit.

Jimmy took the news quietly, his feelings betrayed only by the way he pulled at the fingers of his left hand. When Zeke finished, Jimmy turned away to face the television in the far corner, although his eyes ignored the characters on its screen.

"I don't really think I can go back in there," he said.

"You don't have to," Zeke told him. "Your friend isn't hurting and he's not aware of who is there or isn't there."

"You say that and I know that but it still feels like a cop-out. The problem is, that's my future I'm seeing in there. I can't face that yet."

They stood silently for a while, Jimmy with his back to Zeke and the door. They might have stood that way for quite some time except for being interrupted by a voice from the doorway.

"Excuse me," it said, "can you tell me how I can get into the ICU?"

They both turned around to find a trim young man clad in a stylish overcoat, a scarf hanging loosely around his neck. Jimmy recognized the voice from his answering machine and welcomed the intrusion as a means of avoiding the vision he had been seeing in his mind.

"Ah, Mr. Thigpen," he said sticking out his hand. "My name is Jim Whittaker. You called Roger Bannerman earlier today."

Thigpen took the proffered hand a bit hesitantly. His own palm was sweaty and he was worried that it would be noticeable. John Lawrence Thigpen hated hospitals. He had been a patient only once, to have his tonsils out at age five, which he hardly remembered, so it was hard to understand the basis of his feeling. It was there nevertheless. Merely stepping inside a hospital gave him the shakes. He would never do so voluntarily. Even when his mother had a heart attack, two years before, his brother had needed to force him into a brief visit. Only Bannerman's importance to his deal had compelled him to enter this hospital. Thigpen's nervousness gave Jimmy a chance to master his own nerves. When he spoke again, he sounded perfectly normal.

"You mentioned that you needed to speak to Roger about the radio station. If you can tell me what it is about, I may be able to help."

"It's really rather confidential," Thigpen said.

"No doubt," said Jimmy. "I'm also his attorney."

"I see." Thigpen licked his lips and decided to take a chance. "I work with Travis Kuhnlein. We're involved in the Quad Industries bid. You may have read about it." Jimmy nodded. "Anyway," Thigpen went on, "I'm exploring the possibility of spinning off the radio stations as a separate company. I wanted to speak with Mr. Bannerman about the possibility of being the programming director. I hope"—he tried to force a little laugh—"that whatever has happened isn't too serious." It was a calculated statement. The QI bid was public knowledge. The radio station spin-off was not exactly public, but both Kuhnlein and Ames knew that it was part of Thigpen's plan. What they did not know was that Thigpen proposed to come out of the deal having the stations to himself and that was the one item he left out of his statement.

"Mr. Thigpen," Jimmy said, "my friend has AIDS and I don't expect him to live much longer. If it's a business deal you had in mind, I'm afraid you're out of luck."

The words hit Thigpen like a sucker punch, the more so for having been said with a total lack of emotion. He looked down at the hand that had just shaken Jimmy's hand, then realized they were watching him do so. His face went scarlet. He recalled Marilyn having mentioned that Bannerman had been ill and wished now that she had investigated more closely. Dammit, he needed Bannerman. He could not lose his stations because some old queer had been doing things he should not have done.

"That can't be," was what Thigpen actually said.

Jimmy laughed in response, although there was no humor in it. "Why can't that be, Mr. Thigpen? Because I don't wear leather or lipstick? Or because someone might think you were a *friend* of ours?"

"N-no," Thigpen stammered. He had, in fact, been thinking along those lines, but he had not meant to say any of it out loud. Desperately, he sought a way out of the bind he had created for himself, all the while becoming aware that he was feeling sick to his stomach. "I didn't mean it that way at all. It's just that this is a key position and from what I had been told about Mr. Bannerman's work, he was the right person to fill it."

Jimmy decided to keep the peace and accepted the explanation at face value. "The fact is," Jimmy went on to say, "Roger has been pretty sick for several months. He really hasn't been doing any work worth mentioning. You might want to talk to the person who's been handling his job."

Thigpen brightened a little at that. If someone had been running things in Bannerman's name, then that was the someone he wanted. Marilyn, obviously, had not noticed the deception. You're slipping, Glennoch, he thought.

"If you can tell me his name," Thigpen said, "I would be glad to talk to him."

"I can do better than that," Jimmy said. "She's standing right behind you."

Thigpen spun around and, when he saw who was standing there, his mouth fell open. Acey Henson had come out of the ICU during the conversation and had walked up behind Thigpen, where she stood quietly listening to the conversation.

Noting Thigpen's reaction, she said, "We were introduced once before, Jimmy. I can see that Mr. Thigpen still remembers me." She did not extend her hand.

Thigpen did remember her. He also remembered using her to bait Howard. At the time, it had seemed harmless. What use could he possibly have foreseen for the goodwill of a small-town radio personality? Yet, if she had been handling Bannerman's work, then she might well be the person he needed. Thigpen had absorbed too many shocks for one evening. His stomach was threatening to rebel. Be careful, Johnny, he told himself. Vomiting on their shoes will not help to close this deal.

"Mr. Thigpen is looking for a programming director for all of QI's radio stations," Jimmy said when it became clear that Thigpen had not recovered sufficient equilibrium to talk. "He was looking for Rog, but I told him he should probably talk to you."

Acey put her hands on her hips. "I was already offered a position under Mr. Thigpen. I didn't take it."

Thigpen's face colored again. "Uh, look," he said, "that was another time and place and it wasn't really directed at you. I hope you realize that."

"Maybe," said Acey Henson. "Are you really offering this job and if you are can you keep your nose out of what you don't know anything about and keep your other body parts where they belong?"

Thigpen could not have turned any redder. "I may be offering the job, if the deal goes through. As for the rest, yes I can."

"Hmph. That's what Benedict Arnold said when they asked if he could hold West Point."

Thigpen ignored the comment. "If this position were to be available," he asked, "would you be interested in it?"

"Maybe," said Acey Henson.

EXCERPT FROM THE *WALL STREET JOURNAL* _____

> In a move that took the financial world by surprise, the Board of Directors of Quad Industries capitulated to Mirage Partners and agreed to the sale of the company. This ends an increasingly bitter struggle for control of the conglomerate that began this summer. It also comes not long after a meeting between Richard Ames, CEO of Quad Industries, and a representative of Mirage Partners was reported to end in acrimonious failure. Mirage Partners is an investment group headed by John Lawrence Thigpen, an associate of Travis Kuhnlein, and is backed largely by money raised through Kuhnlein Investment Services. The group surfaced as a holder of Quad Industries stock shortly after the highly publicized leak at a New Jersey plant belonging to Meldrum Prod-

ucts, the largest shareholder of Quad Industries. Meldrum has blamed a Quad Industries subsidiary for "fueling an atmosphere of hysteria" around the leak. Street sources claim that this incident was the primary reason Meldrum was willing to unite with Mirage Partners against Quad Industries management, although all parties have refused to comment on this.

The agreement came after Mirage Partners threatened to begin a tender offer if the latest bid was rejected. Under the terms of the agreement, holders of Quad Industries common stock will receive $44.00 in cash plus one share of a new convertible preferred for each of their shares. A spokesman for Mirage Partners stated that the group plans to sell off most of the small, non-related businesses that Quad Industries had acquired over many years. The core businesses will be reorganized into a more centralized company and run as a unit. The spokesman refused to comment as to whether this entity might eventually be resold to the public on the grounds that it would be "premature to speculate" in that way.

A second surprise in the announcement was the selection of James Morrison, the current President of Quad Industries, to run the new unit. No mention was made of Richard Ames, and it is rumored that he will retire when the deal closes.

Quad Industries stock closed up $4.75 to $48.50 in heavy trading on the NYSE.

The announcement may have contained two surprises for the business world, but Mr. James Morrison was not surprised. Not by the sale and certainly not by the choice of himself as the man to run the reorganized business.

FLEMINGTON, NEW JERSEY _____

It was twenty past two in the morning and Acey was sitting in the diner up the road from WCZY swirling the last bit of coffee around her cup. Mutely, she pushed the cup across the counter as the waitress passed. That sent the waitress back to the coffee machine to pick up the nearly full carafe that sat there. She refilled Acey's cup and Acey pulled it back across the counter. It was all done without a word.

Acey could not think of a reason for drinking the coffee. In fact, she could not think of the reason she had ordered the first cup. She looked at the surface of the brown liquid from several different angles trying to find her reflection there. She could not do it. The coffee was a poor drink and an even worse mirror. Instead, she pulled out a cigarette.

What the hell was she supposed to do? Seven days had passed since the newspapers had announced that QI was being sold. Six days had passed since the package had arrived from Thigpen. The cover letter within had been very brief. It told her, in case she had somehow missed the news, that the takeover of which Thigpen had spoken was a reality. It also told her that Thigpen was offering her the job. Clipped to the letter was a description of that job. It was, she thought, her best fantasy of a job reduced to paper. Too bad it was being offered by John Lawrence Thigpen. "The favor of an early reply is requested," the letter had concluded. Thank you very much, John Lawrence Mephistopheles, she thought. For six days, she had done nothing. She had not called Thigpen; she had not mentioned the letter to anyone. What do I do? Too bad Roger was dead.

Did she want to go to work for Thigpen, she asked herself. The man was an asshole, of that she was certain. He had treated her like a toy once; he would probably do it again. He was going to cut QI apart and not care about who lost their job. Did she want to work for an asshole? Of course, she argued back at herself, I already work for assholes. Ames and Morrison had been only too ready to fire her. She was certain that, had Thigpen not succeeded in his takeover, they would have fired her. Then, there was Howard. He was not only an asshole, he was incompetent. How was Thigpen any worse than them? Would I rather be out of work? She shuddered at the thought.

The cigarette offered no more inspiration than the coffee. She looked at her watch. It read twenty to three. From the recesses of her mind, she recalled that Zeke had said he would come to her apartment that night. Maybe, she thought, I ought to talk to him.

There was a light on in her apartment when she arrived, but no voice answered her when she opened the door. "Zeke?" she called tentatively. There was no answer.

She found him in the bedroom. He was face down on the bed, sound asleep. He had taken off his shirt, but not his pants. His beeper had been placed on the nightstand next to the bed. Acey put a chair next to the bed and sat there for a while, hoping that Zeke would wake up. He did not. There was only an occasional snore.

"Crap," she said.

Acey got up, walked into the kitchen and pulled a beer from the refrigerator. Then she came back to the bedroom. Zeke had not moved. Deliberately, she pulled the tab on the beer can. It opened with a pop and a fine spray. At the noise, Zeke's eyes opened.

"Acey?" he said, rolling onto his side. "I guess I fell asleep waiting for you."

"I guess," she said. "Zeke, I need to talk to you."

"About what?" He sat up and squinted at the clock. "Christ, Acey, it's after three. Can't it wait?"

"No, it can't," she said. Suddenly, she felt angry at Zeke. "Dammit, if that beeper of yours went off you'd answer it, wouldn't you?"

"Huh?" He looked puzzled. "Of course, I would."

"I know you would. You're so close to that beeper, I'm surprised you left it on the nightstand and didn't keep it in the bed with you."

"What? Acey, what are you talking about?"

Acey could feel her anger rising. It was just like the tide, it kept coming higher and higher. She did not seem to have any control over it. "You know what I mean. Anybody beeps you on that, you answer it, even if it's totally dumb."

"Acey, I'm responsible for a lot of sick kids," he said. "If that goes off, it could be important. I've got no way of knowing until I answer."

"Yeah," she said. "It could be important. I guess I'm not important, though."

"What? Acey, I didn't say that."

"You meant it, though."

"No, I didn't," he protested. "God, three-thirty in the morning is not the time to be having this conversation."

"Oh, is it too late? Well, you can go back to sleep, if you want."

"How am I supposed to do that?" Anger was beginning to show in Zeke's voice as well. "I'm up, I might as well stay up. Before this whole thing started, you wanted to talk about something. What?"

"Never mind," she said. "I don't think you're very interested."

"Acey, right now you have my complete and undivided interest. What is going on?" He pulled his legs under himself to sit Indian-style on the bed.

"Thigpen offered me that job." She clipped the sentence short, then took a swallow of beer.

"You mean the one he was talking about that night at the hospital?" Zeke asked.

"Yes."

"Well, congratulations. Why are you so upset, then?"

"Because I don't know if I should take it."

"Isn't it a good job? From the way he was talking, I thought it sounded pretty good."

"It's a great job," she told him.

"Then what's the problem?"

"Because Thigpen's an asshole," she said. "You don't know what working for an asshole is like because everybody does what you say."

I should only wish, Zeke thought to himself. Aloud, he said, "Is he so much of an asshole that you can't work with him?"

"I don't know," Acey said.

"Christ, Acey." Zeke ran his hands through his hair. "The man is buying control of QI. If you say no, can you stay where you are?"

"I don't know. I doubt it."

"Well, then what are you going to do if you don't take it?"

"I don't know."

"Shit. What am I supposed to tell you, then?"

"Do I take the job?" she demanded.

"How the hell do I know," Zeke shouted. "You haven't given me anything to work with."

Acey's glare turned frosty. "Don't shout at me, Zeke," she said. "I don't like it and I won't take it. You ought to know what I need. But you don't. Zeke, I like you." Her tone, as she said it, was a contrast to the words. "I may even love you, which for me is an astonishing statement, but I just don't think you care that much about me."

Zeke opened his mouth to say something, then closed it again having said nothing. He felt that he was losing the thread of the conversation. "Acey, where did that come from?" he asked. "I don't see how you come to that from anything we've said, so why do you feel that?"

"Oh, come on, Zeke." Acey's face was taut, her voice hard. Inside, her stomach felt cold and twisted. The words seemed to come to her lips of their own accord. "We spend all our free time together, what there is of it. We sleep together, for as much as either one of us sleeps. After all of that, you don't know what I really need and that's because I'm just not that important to you."

"Acey, will you stop giving me riddles for a minute and talk to me? What do you need that you're not getting?"

"Christ!" She spat the word out and stalked over to the door before turning back to face him. "Zeke, sometimes, I just need all of your attention, not just part of it. I never thought I'd hear myself say something like that, but it's my own stupid fault for starting this because you never know where things will go when you get into them. But that's what I need, not all the time, just now and then, and I don't get it. We can be standing in McDonald's and their french fryer timer goes off and there you are reaching for that damn beeper on your belt. Part of your mind is always thinking about Jodie's blood count or Sammy's X-ray or somebody's something else. It's driving me nuts."

"You've never said anything before," he replied, trying to keep his own voice low. "It's not like I've changed. I've always been like this."

"Maybe I've never said it," she said. "That doesn't mean it isn't true." She was not, in fact, sure what was true anymore. Her guts were speaking, not her head, but she couldn't stop it.

"This is a hell of a time to decide to tell me," Zeke said. What had the conversation originally concerned? He could not remember. "Acey, I am what I am. I don't pretend to be anything else and I'm not likely to change."

"Yeah," she said bitterly. "Stupid me for thinking different. That's what I get for not keeping this just professional. The personal stuff never works out."

Zeke was silent for a moment. Then he said, "Is that what you want? Just keep it to business for however long the business goes? Forget the personal stuff?"

"Yes." The word came out clear and definitive. That was not the way she felt inside, though. Part of her wanted to say "No, wait a minute," but she would be damned if she would retreat and look weak. She could not do that.

"I see," was all that Zeke said. He pulled on the clothes that he had left at the side of the bed, then clipped the beeper to his belt. His jacket was hanging from the door knob. He stepped past her without a word to reach it. He put the jacket on and zipped it closed without bothering to button the shirt underneath.

"Look, Zeke," Acey said, "I'm not throwing you out in the middle of the night. You can sack out here."

"That's okay," he said. "I don't think it would be very professional."

She waited in the bedroom until she heard the outside door close. Then she let out the breath she had been holding. Acey looked around the room as if for the first time that evening. The bed was rumpled, but empty. She sat down on it; it was still warm under her hand. There was a half-empty beer can in her hand. She regarded it with suspicion.

"Shit. Piss. Fuck," she said at the beer can. Then she drained it with one swallow. "Shit. Piss. Fuck," she recited again.

She crumpled the empty can in her fist, then flung it against the opposite wall. It bounced back to the middle of the floor. She got off the bed and kicked it. The can struck the wall again, halfway up to the ceiling. "Goddammit!" she yelled. She took two steps to the wall and punched it hard, twice. The blows were hard enough to turn her knuckles red.

"Hey, keep it down over there," yelled a voice from the other side of the wall.

"Oh, stuff it in your ass!" she yelled back. Then she punched the wall again.

Hitting the wall offered no release. She whirled away from it and went back to the bed, where she sat with her head in her hands.

Chapter 33

Zeke felt as though he sleepwalked through the next three days. He went home in the evenings, took a catnap, and awoke at eleven, as had become his custom. However, he no longer had anywhere to go at that hour. He also found it difficult to go back to sleep. During the afternoons, he found himself thinking of calling the station. Stupid thoughts, he told himself. There was no reason to be calling. Before long, he was annoyed with himself for being unable to break those habits. He wished that he had never heard of the Meldrum leak. Jerry Inman was dead, he told himself. Did it really matter, any longer, what had killed him? It was against this back-drop, that he found the clue he had wanted.

It came in a most unexpected manner. As it happened, he was seeing Jodie Schmidt in his clinic, the morning of the fourth day after he walked out of Acey Henson's apartment. He was expecting it to be a difficult visit. Jodie was due for a bone marrow exam, a sensitive test of whether her leukemia was starting to regrow. While it did not take very long for him to read the microscope slides, for the family it was a little like a gladiator on the sand, waiting for the emperor to turn the thumb up or down. That produced plenty of tension, all by itself. Added to that was the fact of Jerry's death. Bad news traveled through the clinic patients with a speed bordering on magical. Zeke did not need to speak to the Schmidts to be certain that they knew Jerry had died. Any child's death was a trauma for all the families who came to the clinic. It forced them to acknowledge how close to the edge they lived. The Schmidts had known the Inmans fairly well, which made it worse.

Nothing was said at first, which did not surprise Zeke. Until the marrow slides had been read, the Schmidts would be thinking only of Jodie. He set up the procedure room quickly, then brought Jodie in with just the nurse for company. Mrs. Schmidt waited in the hall. There was no alternative to the arrangement. The one time Mrs. Schmidt had been in the room, she had fainted, fallen off the stool and driven her teeth into her lower lip to the extent that she needed six stitches. Inside the room, he had Jodie lie prone on the examining table, a blanket roll placed under her hips to give him a better angle. With one gloved hand, he felt along the crest of the large bone that made up the back of her hip, checking for the spot he wanted. He could probably have done without feeling for the position because Jodie had been through the procedure several times before. As a result, the spot on each hip was marked with a small white scar. Zeke liked to check anyway. The needle he used was stouter than a regular needle. It was actually a solid needle nested inside of a hollow one. He spent a minute shooting lidocaine into the area, then pushed the combined needle through the skin and into the bone. A gritty crunch told him that it was in the right place. He pulled the solid needle out, leaving the hollow one sticking out of her hip. Then he screwed a syringe onto the hub of the needle. If a doctor was good with the local anesthetic, and Zeke was, the procedure was uncomfortable but not painful, up to that point. Nothing could prevent the sharp stab of pain when he pulled the marrow out. Zeke had once had a colleague who studied bone marrow and paid volunteers seventy-five dollars a pull for a bit of marrow. He liked to describe it as seventy-five dollars worth of pain. Jodie was quite good about it, which was to say she yelled and called Zeke a string of names that probably originated in a Marine barracks, but she did not move. A minute later, Zeke gave the slides to a technician and put a Band-Aid over the small hole.

"Okay, sport," he said, "you're done. It'll take me about an hour to have everything ready. I'll come see you and your mom then."

Jodie sat up on the table to pull up her pants. Then she wiped away a few tears. "Dr. Zeke, can I ask you something before my mom comes in?" When he nodded, she continued with, "Do you know why Jerry died?"

All at once, Zeke was on guard. A thoughtless answer to a question like that could spawn as much grief as a medical emergency. It was twice as difficult when the question came from a child.

"I think you know that Jerry's tumor came back," he said carefully. "We weren't able to stop it."

Usually, the next question would be, "Will mine come back?" or "Will I die if mine comes back?" It took Zeke totally by surprise when Jodie whispered, "It's my fault."

Zeke looked at her intently. Her face was serious and she was eying the examining room door as though she was concerned that her mother might come through.

"Can you tell me why you think it's your fault?" he asked.

Jodie nodded, then waved to him to come close. She said in a conspiratorial whisper, "Jerry told me about his place. It's a secret, just for the kids who live around there. Jerry said that if you told someone from somewhere else about it, something horrible would happen to you. I got him to tell me about it. See what happened?"

Zeke sat down on the table next to her. When you came down to it, he thought, her logic was not much sillier than the fuss over Aspergicin. "Look, Jodie," he said, "I know you feel bad about Jerry, and I'm sure you feel like you are responsible, but that's not the way things happen. I'm afraid Jerry would still have died even if he had never said a word about it. That is the truth."

Jodie nodded, but her eyes said that she was not ready to accept his explanation. Zeke tried to think of a way to take her mind off Jerry's secret. That was when he remembered the conversation he had with Acey several days before. That secret could be the key to Jerry's death. His grumbling of the past three days, that he wished he could forget the whole affair, was quickly forgotten.

"Jodie, that place could actually be important in what happened to Jerry, not because he told you about it but because of where it is. I need to be able to go look at it to be sure. Can you tell me where it is?"

Jodie shook her head violently. "I can't tell you."

Zeke sighed. "Jodie, I promise you, talking about that place does not make bad things happen to people. Anyway, even if it were true, it's only a secret for the kids who live there, right? You don't live there, so it's not your secret. And it is important."

He could see her relax then and he was certain that it was the slightly skewed logic about not living there that made the difference. Jodie had never been there, but Jerry had told her how to find it. With Scheuermann's Run as a guide, Zeke thought the directions would be good enough. When they finished talking, Jodie gave Zeke a quick hug, then went to join her mother. Zeke went off to see his next patient. Old son, he thought as he walked down the hall, after the promise you just made, you damn well better pray that her marrow looks okay. Fortunately, it did.

In his office, after he had finished seeing his patients, he debated his next move. Obviously, he had to see Jerry's hideaway. Something there could have killed three kids. The problem was whether to call Acey Henson. The story, after all, was as much hers as it was his. The information about Jerry's place was important to that story. He picked up the telephone receiver and put it down twice without making the call.

"The real question is," he asked his telephone, "am I not calling because I don't want to call her or because I'm afraid that I want to call her and it has nothing to do with business?"

"Did you say something in there?" Doris called from the outer office.

"Nothing worth repeating," he replied. "Damn," he said, and punched in Acey's number. Maybe she would not be there.

Acey answered on the second ring with her usual laconic, "Yeah?"

"Acey, this is Zeke Schwartz at the medical center."

"I didn't think there was another one," was the response. "I'm kinda busy."

"I can believe it. Listen, this is business, just business."

"I see."

Zeke wondered if there was disappointment in her voice, disappointment that he only wanted to talk business. It was hard enough to read her expressions in person, but over the phone it was impossible.

"Do you remember that we talked about Jerry's fort?" he asked.

"Yes."

"Okay. I know where it is. I think we should check it out."

"We?"

"This has to do with what killed Jerry," he said. "It's business. Are you still interested in the story?"

"Strictly business," she said.

SCHEUERMANN'S RUN, NEW JERSEY _____

It was a bright and cool Saturday morning when Acey Henson and Zeke Schwartz staged their assault on Jerry's fort. Had it been a real fort and a real assault, it is likely that all their plans would have foundered because there was little cooperation between the two of them. Zeke met Acey at a coffee shop in the town of Scheuermann's Run; neither of them considered the idea of meeting at her apartment reasonable. He could see her sitting at the counter, nursing her coffee, while he parked his car. From her position, it was a certainty that she could see him as well, but she made no move to get up. Instead, Zeke walked in and sat down on an unoccupied stool next to her.

"Good morning," he said after Acey made no move to acknowledge him.

"Good morning," was the response.

"Can I join you for some coffee before we go?" he asked.

"Suit yourself," she said. "Just let me know when you're ready to get started."

"Screw the coffee, then," he said. "Let's just get going."

"Well, can I finish mine first?"

Zeke checked himself before he said anything. They were supposed to do a job this morning, he reminded himself. Starting a shouting match in a coffee shop would accomplish nothing. Not for the first time since telling

Acey about the location of Jerry's fort, Zeke wished he had said nothing. He could have come alone. It would probably have been easier.

"I'll wait in the car," he said. "Come out when you're ready."

Acey nodded her head by way of reply. In fact, she spent no more than two extra minutes in the coffee shop, just long enough to take two more swallows from her cup. It was not empty when she walked out. At the car, she halted by the door, her eyes fixed on the back seat, which was piled high with cardboard boxes.

"What is all that junk?" she asked.

"I'm not sure what we're looking for, or what we may find," he told her. "I brought whatever I could get my hands on."

The boxes were crammed with all manner of things. There were bottles, both glass and plastic, in many different sizes. Stuffed in among the bottles were Ziplock bags. There was a box of latex gloves Zeke had taken from the hospital. There were also two pair of workman's gloves he had purchased in a hardware store, their price tags still attached. One box held several bottles of chemical reagents along with instructions in how to use them to test water. The contents of one box were partially covered by several sheets of stick-on labels. Acey shook her head and got into the front passenger seat.

They drove in silence, broken only once by conversation. "Did you decide to take that job?" Zeke asked as he pulled onto the road.

"What does that have to do with this?"

"Nothing much, I suppose."

"Then it's personal," Acey said. "Let's keep this to business, shall we?"

Those were the last words spoken during the drive. Zeke kept his eyes fixed on the road ahead; Acey with hers off to the side, out the window. Both of them wished they were elsewhere.

Zeke found the road Jodie had described easily enough. It was a spur that joined the main road about a mile and a half past the Inmans' house. It was a narrow road, the yellow line down the middle faded almost to invisibility. The car bounced along over potholes and crumbling patches. The road clearly saw neither much traffic nor many repairs. It headed in the general direction of the waterway, Scheuermann's Run. Less than a mile down the road they saw, through the trees, the hulking outline of a building. Beyond it, the water of Scheuermann's Run was visible.

"This has to be the place Jodie was talking about," Zeke said. "I wonder what it was."

He parked the car on the side of the road. There was a drive leading from the road to the building but it was barred by a rusted gate, chained shut. On either side of the gate, worn grass and bicycle marks showed that the only traffic blocked by the gate was automobiles.

Both of them wondered, as they stepped around the futile gate, what the building represented. It would prove to be an abandoned chemical plant, or maybe a pesticide manufacturer, with metal drums strewn about the premises leaking God knew what. The reality punctured those thoughts. The building was a two-story rectangle of brick and stone set on a concrete foundation near the water's edge. Its windows were boarded up, the front door closed with a heavy padlock. The grounds were wildly overgrown and littered with trash, but it was garden variety trash: bits of rusting metal, broken glass on the walk, pieces of insulation caught in the bushes. None of it looked very ominous. The sign over the door read "Roondick Textiles."

"Mean anything to you?" Zeke asked.

"Nope." At first, it seemed that Acey would limit herself to the one word, but then she said, "I don't claim to know everyone in this part of the state, but I'll wager these guys were out of business before I ever moved here. Hell, even the 'No Trespassing' signs have faded to the point you can barely read 'em."

Zeke gave the door an experimental yank. "Need a damn crowbar to do anything with that," he said. "Which we didn't bring."

"I wouldn't worry about it," Acey said. "The kids certainly didn't go in there. Where to now?"

Zeke shrugged. Your guess is as good as mine." Then, he said, "We know they went swimming around here. Let's try out back."

Behind the building they could see that the small river was converted into a broad lake by a dam placed just past the far end of the building.

"Looks like a perfect spot for kids," Zeke said.

Acey nodded her head in agreement. The shoreline near the building was relatively clear and sloped gently toward the water except for a jumble of rocks to the left that were perfectly suited to jumping in. The far shore was hidden by bushes whose branches trailed in the water.

They circumnavigated the lake, splashing across the river where it narrowed above the lake. Along the way they found more residue of America. There were empty Coke cans and empty Budweiser cans along with several of the plastic rings that held six-packs together. Wedged among the rocks was half of August's Playboy magazine. There were three discarded tires and a mangled bicycle pump. In the end, their shoes were muddy and the bottoms of their trousers were soaked but they had seen nothing worthy of a second look.

They were standing back where they had started when Zeke asked, "I wonder if there is anything *in* that lake?"

"I don't know," said Acey, "but I've got an idea how to find out. I know someone back in town with a small boat."

Acey's contact proved to be an old codger who, despite the early hour, was not entirely sober. After much debate, he agreed to come out to the old Roondick plant with his boat and some nets. It was midday by the time they returned to the lake. They pushed the boat out into the lake, where it looked out of place. The old man sat in the bow with an oar and a can of beer, laughing as Acey and Zeke swept the nets around the sides of the boat. Periodically, the nets would snag on something out of sight and the man would snarl, "Hey there, don't you go tearing my nets!"

"This is pointless," Acey said after a few hours of futile effort. "We certainly haven't found anything, but I don't know if that's because there's nothing down there or because these stupid nets are useless."

"Too true," Zeke agreed. He pushed his hair back with his hand. The movement streaked mud across his forehead. "I just hate to give up now."

That sentiment was not shared by the boatman. He was out of beer and the amusement of watching the two of them flail around in the water had grown thin. They paid him off, helped him put his boat back on its trailer and bade him farewell. That left them standing by the building, much as they had started.

"You look like something in an Army training film," Acey said. There was mud on Zeke's face, his shirt and his pants. The mud was caked in grayish chunks on his shoes.

"You look pretty scuzzy yourself," he replied. There was a smile, visible for just an instant on Acey's face, before she turned away to look back at the lake.

"What now?" she asked.

"The only place I can think to look is inside the building," Zeke said.

"Yeah, but how do we get in?"

"Other doors?"

"Maybe."

There proved to be two of them but they were as sturdily padlocked as the main one.

"Damn!" Zeke pounded the door panels in frustration. They gave off a hollow boom, but the door did not move in its frame. He slapped his hands against his thighs and walked to the front of the building. From there, he looked past the high bushes that crowded the side of the building, down to the low dam and back again. He was almost ready to turn back to the car when something caught his eye. It was a little thing and doubtless he had seen it when they walked around the building before, but its import had not registered then.

"Hey, Acey!" he yelled. "Come here and look at this!"

"This" was a thin track worn clear of grass that ran out of the bushes at the side of the building. From there, it ran toward the lake where it vanished into the high grass. With a whoop, he ran down to his find with Acey close behind. While everything else around the building was overgrown, that track was beaten clear. It must have seen recent use. Zeke pushed into the bushes and found a series of cement steps that led down to a basement door that stood ajar. Above the door was a metal sign bearing a yellow-and-black trefoil.

"I'll be damned," Zeke said. "What a perfect fort. Somebody's old fall-out shelter!"

After a brief pause to retrieve flashlights from the car, they pushed the door wide open and went inside. They found themselves in a moderate-sized room furnished only with a few chairs and a rickety table. The floor was littered with empty soda cans, a few beer cans, comic books and empty peanut shells.

"This is a kid's fort all right," Zeke said. He kicked one of the cans across the floor, scattering peanut shells as it went.

"I'm no expert on the subject," Acey said, "but this looks like a good-sized shelter. I wouldn't think this place would have employed so many people."

"Maybe he was planning to take in people from the area," Zeke suggested. Or, maybe he was paranoid and figured he'd have to stay underground for twenty years."

"Maybe he had a nasty mother-in-law," Acey added. "Whatever, there seems to be another room back there." Her flashlight picked out an open doorway at the back of the shelter.

"Storeroom?"

"Don't know."

They walked over and shone their flashlights into it. At one time it had, indeed, been a storeroom. Its shelves were now empty of everything except dust. Along the back wall, however, the beams picked out a row of stacked barrels. Two of them, on the floor in front of the others, had their tops open. The flashlight beam picked out the black stencil lettering "U.S. Army" on the side of one of the barrels.

"Oh my God." Zeke's words were echoed softly by Acey.

A few strides brought them to the side of the nearest barrel. The light showed more lettering on the barrel. It had come from the PX at a nearby base. Zeke aimed the light into it, his head cautiously following the beam. The barrel was filled with peanuts. A quick look showed that the one next to it was the same. He looked at them silently for a long while before smiling ruefully.

"I think this is it," he said. "I will bet this is it."

Acey's look of confusion was hidden by the darkness. She turned her flashlight on Zeke's face, as if to assure herself that his expression matched his words.

"Doc, did you have your squash microwaved on 'high' back there?" she asked. "I could swear you just identified this barrel of peanuts as toxic waste."

"Could be, Acey. It just could be. However, I've made a fool out of myself once already, so you'll have to understand that I don't want to do it again. What I'd like to do is get a few bagfuls of this stuff and then get out of here."

"And then what?"

"And then," he said, "I'm going to find out what killed Jerry."

"You'll call me when you know something?" Acey asked.

"You mean about this?"

"Yeah, yeah," Acey said. "Just about this business. That's all."

"Of course I will," Zeke said. "Strictly business."

TRENTON, NEW JERSEY _____

Zeke didn't take the bags full of peanuts to the medical center, but instead went to a chemist in one of the University laboratories. There the peanuts were ground into dust, which was then slurried with a variety of solvents. The residue of peanuts was filtered off, leaving a clear solution.

"I'm going to need a few days to play with the chromatography," the chemist told Zeke.

"Which means what?" Zeke asked. "I tinker with people, not chemicals. I haven't done any chromatography since organic chemistry in college and what you've got here doesn't look like what I remember."

The chemist smiled. "That thing," he said pointing to his lab bench, "is a liquid chromatograph." The thing was a metal box, about one and a half feet by two and a half feet in size. An array of dials, switches and plumbing adorned its front. "I'll inject some of the solution into this port," the chemist said, "much the same as the way you give an injection. Anyway, this machine pumps the liquid down this column here under high pressure. Different chemicals stick to the material in the column differently. I've also got several different columns I can use. By varying the liquid I run through here, and the columns, I can separate and identify a lot of things. I've got to do some reading first, though, and then I'll have to play with the system. It's as much an art as it is a science."

Zeke left the peanuts there and returned to the medical center. He went first to the Pathology department where he pulled Carlos out of the laboratory.

"You have some samples of Jerry's liver stored away, don't you?" Zeke asked.

"Of course. Did you find something?"

"Maybe. Just maybe." He told Carlos about his find at the old Roondick plant and his conversation with the chemist. "Can you do anything with the tissue?"

"I think so, Zeke. I'll have to do some research first. When do you need to know?"

"Yesterday."

Carlos gave a little laugh. "So, what else is new? Will the day after tomorrow do?"

"It'll have to," Zeke answered.

Two days later, the chemist had not called but Carlos did. He met Zeke in the pathology laboratory, adjacent to the room where they had first examined Jerry's tumor.

"Have a seat," Carlos said. "I want you to look at something under the fluorescence microscope. I had to call a few people to find out how to rig this thing to show what we want." Carlos's tone indicated that it had not been a simple undertaking.

Zeke fiddled with the focus adjustment on the microscope. "What am I looking at?" he asked.

"This is a slide of Jerry's liver," Carlos said. "It has both tumor and normal liver on it. See the nuclei of these cells, here, here and here?" Carlos moved a stalk on the outside of the microscope. Seen through the lens, a little green arrow appeared and moved in synchrony with the stalk.

"They're blue," Zeke said.

"Correct. With the system set up properly, they fluoresce blue."

"And that means?"

Carlos did not answer the question immediately. Instead, he asked, "Has your chemist friend called?"

"Not yet," Zeke said.

"Well, I think I know what he's going to say, but I'd like to wait until he actually says it. We should also see if we can get an analysis of some of these liver pieces. That would pretty much clinch it."

Ten days went by following their trip to Scheuermann's Run, during which Zeke did not call the station. He did not call Acey's apartment either. She had assumed that two or three days would go by but not ten. As the days passed, she became increasingly concerned about the reason for the silence. The most likely reason, she believed, was that whatever Zeke had thought of when he saw the peanuts had turned out to be wrong. He might feel that, if there was no answer, the project was over and there was nothing to say. That bothered her. It was also possible that Zeke had his answer but was no longer interested in sharing it with her. That bothered her even more. She could have called the center. The issue of what Zeke had found certainly fit even within the silly limits they had put on contacting each other. She could not make the call. She wanted Zeke to call her, regardless of how much it hurt to wait in limbo. Eventually, she convinced herself that he would never call. When the telephone rang on the eleventh day, it caught her off guard.

"Acey?" Zeke's voice said. "Can you come down to the hospital? I need to talk to you."

"Zeke, it's getting a little late in the day," she said. "Have you forgotten? I have to do the news." What she wanted to say was, "Of course!" and run for her motorcycle, but she would not allow herself to do that. She looked at her watch. It was getting late.

"Screw the news," Zeke said.

"Anatomically impossible. You should know that. You're a doctor."

"Jesus, Acey," he said in exasperation, "do you always have to be more difficult than usual? You wanted to know what I found, didn't you? Well, I've got it but now you'd rather do the news."

Acey's grip on the receiver tightened as he spoke. "You know what killed Jerry?"

"I think so."

"Well, what is it? Tell the nosy reporter like a good man."

"Not on the telephone."

"Shit! Doc, my news!"

"Acey, did California fall into the Pacific this afternoon?"

"No."

"Okay. Is the President's wife pregnant?"

"Not that I know of."

"Right. So, why can't you come down here?"

Acey managed not to say the words that were forming in her mind. Instead, she studied her watch. If she hustled, she could reach the hospital, hear what Zeke had to say and still return in time to do a passable job.

"Zeke," she said, "for the sake of whatever children you may hope to have someday, I hope this is good."

Zeke Schwartz was in his office when she arrived. It was in its usual state of disarray, but most of the charts and papers had been moved off the desk to the floor. In their place was the map on which they had originally plotted the locations of the childrens' houses. When she walked in, he leaned back in his chair with his arms behind his head. She noticed that the location of the Roondick textile plant was now marked with a big red circle. Acey moved some papers off a chair and sat down.

"Doc, you look like the jock that ate the cheerleader, so to speak. Are you going to tell me that the peanuts killed Jerry?"

"Yup."

"Jesus. You're serious. And the other two kids?"

"Almost certainly. In fact, the only piece to the puzzle I don't have is how those barrels of peanuts wound up there in the first place."

"Christ, Doc," Acey said, "I've worked that out. I checked into it right after we went out there. You should have called me sooner."

Zeke did not take the bait. "How did it happen?" was all he said.

Acey wished he had said something else, but she answered the question anyway. "There was a staff sergeant at that base a couple of years ago who was running a scam. He was responsible for placing the orders for the PX. What he'd do was order more than the PX needed and divert the excess. He'd cache the stuff in out-of-the-way places all over the area. I guess he made a lot of bucks selling the Army's toilet paper and stuff before he got caught. The peanuts must have been one of his items. Now that I've told you how they got there, would you mind telling me how you can be so certain that a barrel of peanuts is a deadly poison?"

"My pleasure." He sat forward and put his hands on the map. "This whole mess is what comes of being too sure of oneself. You remember, back when we started, I told you how unusual it was to find this cancer in a child?" Acey nodded. "Okay. I probably also mentioned that most of the time people who get this cancer turn out to have had viral hepatitis, either hepatitis B or the one they now call C. In the process, we all seem to have forgotten about what we used to think caused this cancer."

"Peanuts?"

Zeke chuckled. "No, not peanuts, *per se*. Aflatoxin."

"What?"

"Aflatoxin. It's a poison made by certain types of fungus. It causes liver cancer in all types of animals, fish too. The fungus can contaminate stored grain or nuts. Years ago, everyone thought that aflatoxin contamination was responsible for the fact that so many people in Asia got liver cancer. Then people started to study hepatitis and found that the risk really correlated with the virus, not the toxin. Net result, we've all forgotten about aflatoxin causing these tumors, at least in this country. This is what we get for being so smart."

"I take it," Acey said, "that you've proved that the aflatoxin caused this tumor?"

"Yeah. That's what took me so long. I had the peanuts analyzed. They're loaded with aflatoxin. Then, you may not know, we stored blood, urine and tissue samples from Jerry. We usually do that in weird cases, just in case someone gets a bright idea down the road. Anyway, Jerry had aflatoxin in his liver. That's why I'm sure."

"And the other two?"

"There's tissue in Philadelphia from the Delgado boy, so I'll know as soon as it's checked. I can't check the one from Scranton the same way, but take a look at the map. Tell me what you think."

Acey just glanced at the marked locations. "I think the same way you do."

"Thought you would."

"And the Aspergicin leak?"

"Nothing to do with it. I'm sure of that now, too."

"This aflatoxin stuff, then, you eat it and you get cancer?"

"Maybe."

"Dammit, Zeke! You just said these kids ate it and they got cancer."

"That I did." Schwartz looked grim. "Carcinogens cause cancer, but not everyone who is exposed will get it. In fact, most of the time, only a minority ever develops cancer. The problem is, you don't know, in advance, who is going to get it and you don't know when they are going to get it. I wish I knew how many kids used that place."

"Oh, boy."

"Oh, boy indeed. Do I recall you saying something about having a news show to do?"

"Oh my God! The news!" Acey looked frantically at her watch, then relaxed. There was still enough time. "You want me to put this on the air?"

"Why not? It is news, you know. Incidentally, I've already talked with Mrs. Inman, which these days means Mrs. Inman and her lawyer. They're not happy, but they agreed with giving out the information."

"They wanted to stop it?" Acey asked.

"Given a choice, probably. After all, their main interest, these days, has been building a case against Meldrum. This sort of takes it apart. I had to point out that this would come out eventually and they would have no advantage from waiting. Also, there is the very real question of how many other kids ate those peanuts. That got the lawyer thinking about his own liability if they tried to suppress it."

Acey shook her head. "I don't get it. I mean, I can understand the lawyer, but not Mrs. Inman. I would have thought she would be happy to finally have an answer."

"Yeah, except it's not the answer she wanted." Zeke stood up and walked over to look out the window. "Look at what happened to her. Charley got drunk all the time, he lost his job, now he's God knows where. Jerry had a hellish couple of months and now he's dead. Ellen Inman was the one holding everything together for all that time and now she has nothing left. She wants somebody to pay for that, even more than she wants the right answer. Meldrum was a great target and this takes it away. That's why she's not happy. You can't sue Mother Nature."

"Yes, but somebody had to put those peanuts there," Acey said.

"Sure. So what? Peanuts are food, remember. It's not against the law to toss food. There's no way you could prove the peanuts were contaminated when they were put there."

"Okay, Doc, you made your point. Christ, I can't believe those Meldrum scuzzballs really get off the hook."

"I know what you mean," he said. "I can almost agree with Mrs. Inman. It's actually rather bizarre. Two days ago I got a letter from someone in Senator Barcellini's office that they want me to testify at the hearing. I'm going, but what I'm going to say is a bit different from what it would have been last month."

"All right, Doc," she said. "I'll do the piece. Now, I've really got to roll. I've just got one more question. Why couldn't you tell me over the phone?"

Zeke stayed at the window, looking out. "It seemed," he said carefully, "the best excuse I was going to have for seeing you again."

Acey did not turn for the door when he finished. "You really didn't need an excuse," she said softly.

"I wasn't really sure." When he turned back from the window, there were tears in his eyes.

"Do you miss being together?" Acey found her voice was shaky.

"Yes. How about you?"

"Terribly," she said. "What do you think we should do about it?"

"I don't know. You know how I am about the kids here. I doubt that's going to change."

"I didn't think it would," Acey said. "I've got a nasty temper. That's not going to change either."

"So. Do you think we can make allowances for our nuttiness, given that we're going to continue to be what we are?"

"I think so." Acey felt herself starting to shake and suppressed it. "Damn you, Zeke Schwartz, for starting this now. I do have to go back to the station because I do have to do the news. Can you come over to my place tonight after the show? I'd like to talk after I get done talking."

Chapter 34

THE CONGRESSIONAL hearings on the pharmaceutical industry, chaired by Senator Alfonso Barcellini, were in their third week when Zeke Schwartz went to Washington. It was a rather one-sided show. Barcellini had assembled a long list of people with grievances against many companies, not a difficult thing to do. In a country of two hundred and fifty million people, it was not hard to find ones who had been badly injured, or might have been injured, by a drug. Simple mathematics would show that, if there were even the slightest risk to most drugs, there must be more such people than could be heard in even months of hearings. There were also former salesmen from several companies. They told of how vacations were awarded to doctors on the basis of how many prescriptions they wrote for a given drug, and of the little gifts from paperweights to fountain pens that were a routine part of a sales visit. Then there was the official of the American Medical Association, who became ensnared by Barcellini in a debate over how big a gift had to be in order to bribe a doctor into writing a prescription.

"Isn't it like the old story of the prostitute, Doctor," Barcellini said, "who would eagerly go to bed for a thousand dollars but became indignant when offered ten. We're not talking about what you are, we are only trying to establish a price."

Predictably, women's groups were outraged, but the press loved it. There was no one to tell another side of the story. Every pharmaceutical company that had been invited to send a representative had declined. Barcellini played up their absence, although it was clear that he would have preferred to have them in front of him. The FDA fared little better. For every incident with a drug, there was an FDA division to hold responsible. For a time, the parade of Division Directors seemed as forlorn as the long ago townspeople of Salem, in their particular witch hunt.

The Aspergicin case had been scheduled toward the end of the planned hearings. The room in the Capitol building was packed. At one end of the room sat the committee, behind desks and nameplates, microphones mounted in front of them. Barcellini sat in the middle, a portly, balding man who wore old-fashioned, black rimmed glasses. He seemed at ease in the crowd of witnesses, reporters, and cameras, although only his staff knew the effort expended each day to keep the television lights from reflecting brightly off the top of his head. Facing the committee was a table for the current witness, with space for an attorney or two. That was placed directly across from Barcellini. In favored positions on either side were the reporters. Crammed into the space behind them were the spectators.

The Aspergicin hearing opened with Barcellini announcing that Meldrum Products had also declined to provide a representative to testify. Just after he said that, a scuffle broke out in the spectator area when a small group of people unfurled a banner that said, "Just say 'No' to drugs." They were led away by the marshals, but not before the cameras had captured the banner on videotape. The first witness turned out to be Ellen Inman. Even before she was sworn in, the bright television lights were on, raising the temperature in the room. Barcellini led her gently through the story of Jerry's last summer. It was a story that needed no embellishment to be moving. After Ellen Inman came Dr. Elizabeth Jessup, introduced by Barcellini as the person who "should have been protecting little Jerry Inman." Their exchanges bordered on the unfriendly. Dr. Jones from the CDC was called as well. The committee had not planned to call him when the hearing was planned, but they had not anticipated the reports from New Jersey claiming that aflatoxin, rather than Aspergicin, had poisoned Jerry Inman. Dr. Jones put on an elaborate show, with charts and graphs, of the information assembled by the CDC on the subject. He put most of the audience to sleep and the television lights were turned off.

Then it was Zeke Schwartz's turn. There was a stir in the room when his name was called. The newspapers had, for two days, been rehashing what he had said over the summer and speculating about what he might say in front of the committee. The television lights went on again.

At first they reviewed what Schwartz had said during the course of the summer. There was nothing new said, it was simply for the record and for the cameras. Then Barcellini said, "Dr. Schwartz, is it true that Meldrum Products recently established a fellowship in your department at the medical center?"

"Yes it is," Schwartz said, "but the plans were made many months ago."

"But the funding was not provided until recently," Barcellini insisted.

"That is correct."

"I see. Dr. Schwartz, if you were in my position, don't you think it would seem odd that you have changed your mind about this case just in time to get this funding from Meldrum?"

Schwartz stared across the table. "Are you implying," he shot back, "that I was bribed by Meldrum to change my story?"

"I didn't put it that way," Barcellini said, "but since you do, were you?"

"That is ridiculous!"

"Is it, Dr. Schwartz?" Barcellini asked. "We have heard about doctors receiving golf clubs, plane trips, dinners, you name it. Now, by all accounts, you are a dedicated clinician and I, personally, doubt that you would be swayed by such things, but a fellowship program to help the kids in your clinic is a different matter, isn't it. Everyone has their price, even your American Medical Association agrees with that."

"I suppose, Senator, that kind of behavior seems natural to someone who has spent as many years in politics as you, but no, I was not bribed."

The room fell silent, even the chatter in the spectator area stopped. The reporters edged forward on their seats, hoping a shouting match was imminent. Barcellini disappointed them.

"Then why," he asked quietly, "did you publicly state one thing earlier in the summer and something else now?"

"Simple," Schwartz said. "I jumped to the wrong conclusion when I didn't have enough information. I'm well aware of that. I'm not going to let that stop me from putting it straight now."

"So, the conclusion you wish to give this committee is that aflatoxin caused those cancers. You're sure of that now?"

"Yes."

"No chance you're wrong again?"

"This isn't a campaign promise, Senator. The boys were exposed to the aflatoxin. The two cases where we have tissue samples show the toxin in their livers."

"However," Barcellini countered, "they were also exposed to Aspergicin."

"No question about that," Schwartz said, "but Aspergicin has never been shown to cause tumors. Aflatoxin is a known carcinogen."

Barcellini lifted his glasses in order to wipe his eyes with thumb and forefinger. "Perhaps you have missed some of the testimony, Dr. Schwartz, although I could have sworn you were here. We have just heard Dr. Jones from the CDC review the data on aflatoxin. Certainly, in the past, we have considered aflatoxin a carcinogen in humans, but I think Dr. Jones has made it clear that this has been disproven. Aflatoxin does not cause cancer in humans. Perhaps, Dr. Schwartz, you are not as current as you should be." There was, perhaps, a trace of condescension in Barcellini's voice.

Schwartz bristled. "Senator, you cannot prove or disprove a cause-and-effect relationship with epidemiology. What Dr. Jones has shown in such great and soporific detail is that there is a lot of hepatocellular carcinoma in areas that have lots of hepatitis, that people with this liver cancer tend to have had hepatitis, and that people who have had hepatitis have a higher risk of getting this cancer than people who haven't had hepatitis. Fine. I'm not trying to dispute the point that hepatitis can lead to liver cancer. But." Schwartz paused and, in the moment of that pause, the room became absolutely silent. "This is not the same thing as showing that aflatoxin does *not* cause liver cancer. Aflatoxin causes cancer in animals. We know this. There was aflatoxin in Jerry Inman's liver and I now have reports of other liver tumors where aflatoxin was found. There are recent reports of a specific gene mutation caused by aflatoxin and you can find that mutation in some liver cancers. How much do you want? I find it astonishing that you can just wave this evidence away, especially in a country where people go ballistic when they hear that a huge dose of anything might cause a tumor in a rat or two. These are facts, not estimates of incidence rates and fancy epidemiological theories and if Dr. Jones doesn't know enough to fit his theory to the facts, instead of the other way around, then I don't understand what his purpose is or he is just an idiot."

A titter ran through the audience while Barcellini called for quiet. The reporters made sure they had the second half of Schwartz's last sentence marked as a sound bite for the evening news.

"We can do without name-calling here," Barcellini said. "You mentioned other reports. Where are they from?"

"A number of African patients," Schwartz said. "Mostly from Kenya, I believe, although the analysis was done in England."

"Kenya?" Barcellini did not completely suppress his laugh. "How did you find out about them?"

"They are in the published literature, as Dr. Jones should have known had he bothered to look."

"Can we leave your opinion of Dr. Jones out of it for a moment? The *fact* is"—and Barcellini stressed the word—"that you have no way of judging the quality of this work."

"And how should I judge it," Schwartz retorted, "by comparison maybe to the high quality of our federally funded research as exemplified by people like John Darsee and Leon Kanzel?"

Barcellini's face darkened at that. "You should remember, Dr. Schwartz, that Dr. Kanzel was a paid investigator for Meldrum Products."

"Yeah, but he also did a lot of work with NIH money, a helluva lot of work. How much of that is real? Christ, some of Kanzel's work has been used to set practice guidelines! Are they correct, and how much work and how long will it take to find out? Please don't tell me about quality of work."

Once again, the reporters leaned forward to capture the argument. Once again, Barcellini disappointed them.

"Dr. Schwartz," he said, "I think we have moved somewhat afield of our original purpose for this hearing. I would like to thank you for your opinions regarding this case and for taking the time from your heavy schedule."

With that, the committee dismissed Zeke Schwartz. The reporters decided that he could not match Oliver North, but he would be good enough for ninety seconds at six o'clock.

It took Zeke several minutes to get clear, first of the committee room itself, then of the gaggle of reporters who shoved microphones in his face in the corridor. They trailed him part of the way down the corridor, giving up only when it became clear that he would say nothing worth recording. He leaned against the wall while they dispersed, trying to catch his breath. He waited a little longer, until he saw Acey coming down the corridor to meet him.

"Boy, am I glad you could take the time to come down with me," he told her.

"My pleasure," she said. "How did you like your fifteen minutes of fame?"

"Hated it. As far as I'm concerned, people who like the spotlight are welcome to it. You know, we really moved heaven and earth to solve this case and I'll bet the only thing anybody heard is that we were wrong. It's a bit like making the prom queen and then finding out she has the clap."

"Hey, Doc," she said, "nobody starts out with all the right answers. You got it right in the end."

"I suppose."

"Tell me something, though," she asked, "where did that bit about funding from Meldrum come from?"

Zeke looked rueful. "There was a note in the paper recently about Meldrum. You probably saw it. The company decided to pin the responsibility for the Aspergicin mess on some guy named Buford. I never heard of him, but obviously they needed a fall guy and he was it. In addition to telling about how he got canned, it mentioned that they made Pat Dwyer a Vice President. I still needed that fellowship and I figured, under the circumstances, he would be real happy to help out. At least, the clinic would get something good from that jerk. I guess my timing sucked."

"A mild understatement Doc, a very mild understatement."

Zeke grinned. "Wouldn't Barcellini love to know the real reason behind that deal. Oh well, what did you think of that dog-and-pony show?"

"Me? I think the Senator has a low wattage bulb. Either that, or he just wants to screw Meldrum and doesn't care about what really happened."

"Maybe a little of both." Zeke took a deep breath and tried to relax his muscles. Acey could feel them rigid beneath the hand she put on his arm. "It's so damn exasperating," he said. "Five, six years ago, there would have been no questions. It would have fit with our preconceived notions. Today, though, the CDC has decided that aflatoxin does not cause cancer and you can't tell 'em otherwise. Of course," he added wryly, "maybe it's just as well. If they really believed me, we'd probably have a panic like the time there was that grain contamination. They'd probably try to impound every damn peanut in the country."

Acey wondered out loud if there were enough peanuts to completely fill the Capitol building. They both had a good laugh at the mental image that created. Preoccupied by visions of peanuts flowing out of the dome, they did not hear the footsteps in the corridor. Zeke jumped in surprise when a hand touched him on the shoulder. He spun around to face a robust man who appeared to be in his mid-twenties.

"I'm sorry, Dr. Schwartz, I didn't mean to startle you," the man said. "Let me introduce myself. I'm Brad Sampson. I'm one of Senator Barcellini's staffers."

"Okay," Acey said, "you work for Barcellini. What do you do?"

Sampson had been looking at Zeke when he spoke and, except for a brief flick of his eyes to Acey, he kept his gaze there. "I do most of the analysis and writing on health care issues for the Senator," he said. The importance he attached to the position was evident from his voice.

"Does that mean," Zeke asked, "that you are the one responsible for briefing the Senator so well on Dr. Jones's position?"

Sampson flushed. "It seemed to us that the question had been definitively answered."

Zeke laughed out loud. He no longer felt tense. "I don't think many things are ever 'definitively answered' in medicine," he said. "Hell, we're still arguing about when a person is really dead and you would think that one is obvious. You didn't come over to continue the argument in the hall, I hope."

"No sir." Sampson shook his head. "I wanted to make certain that you realize the Senator does not wish to have an antagonistic relationship with you. He considers you key to this proceeding."

"I assume that means he doesn't want me to take it personally," Zeke said. Sampson nodded. "Well," Zeke continued, "I may be key but I think I'm key to the other side."

"Not necessarily," Sampson said. There was an eagerness in his voice that told both Schwartz and Henson that the man had reached his main issue. "The real issue here is that the pharmaceutical companies in this country have been getting away with murder. Sometimes literally. The Senator sees this as the perfect opportunity to rein them in. That's the purpose behind these hearings."

"Except," Acey said, "in this case they didn't."

"Please don't interrupt me, honey." Sampson did not bother to look at her when he spoke. "Even if there is some question of interpretation here, that is not really important. What is important is controlling these companies. Politically, the timing is perfect; the country is ready for it. We can do it. All I'm asking, Dr. Schwartz, is that you back off a little. Don't take such a hard line. If there is room for argument, fine. That's perfectly okay."

Zeke rubbed at his chin. Then he looked over at Acey before he spoke. She was impassive. "It seems to me that not too long ago I was being pressured to lay off the argument that Aspergicin caused these cancers. Now, you want me to back off from the argument that Aspergicin did not cause the cancers."

"Surely you see the point," Sampson insisted. "You must see the point. Your own career was nearly destroyed by this affair. These companies cannot be trusted. We must establish control."

" 'We must establish control,' " Zeke repeated. "Is this your position or the Senator's?"

"The Senator's, of course," Sampson replied.

"But you write all the analysis on health care issues, isn't that right?"

"Yes, I said that." Sampson said it again. There was pride in his voice.

"So, basically, you're the key to what the Senator knows or doesn't know about health care." Sampson did not reply but the expression on his face made it clear what the answer was. No false modesty here, Zeke thought.

"Sampson," Zeke said, "what kind of degree do you have?"

"I have a Bachelor's in Political Science from the University of Pennsylvania," he said. "Is that a problem?"

"Okay," Zeke said, "why don't we cut through all the chaff here. Can you tell me in a simple sentence what you want me to do?"

"I need to know if you will work with us," Sampson said. "At the least, I want to know that you won't work against us. There are all sorts of reasons to put a leash on these damn companies, but most of them are technical or involve digging through lots of numbers. Things like that have no hold on people's imaginations. People don't get excited about columns of numbers. The Inman case, though, that hits every American where it hurts. We can use that to push through the changes we need."

"Jerry Inman was a nice little kid," Schwartz said softly. "He's not a tool for you to use."

Sampson's face flushed, more from anger than embarrassment, Schwartz thought. "Do I take that to mean that you plan to oppose us? That's not wise, Dr. Schwartz. You're not dealing with some superannuated hospital administrators here. You play hardball with us, you could wind up running a one-man clinic in Buffalo Breath, Montana, and be lucky to have that."

Schwartz stared into Sampson's eyes. For a minute neither man spoke nor moved.

"Mr. Sampson," Schwartz said quietly, "aside from the fact that I don't like what you're doing, if you go ahead and pin this all on Aspergicin, everybody is going to forget all about those peanuts. Weren't you listening in the hearing room? We don't know how many kids ate those nuts. I can't guess how many of them will get sick or how long it will take."

"But if it was the Aspergicin," Sampson replied, "it would be the same ones getting sick. For our purposes, there's no difference."

"But there *is* a difference. Maybe it will be easier to find kids who ate peanuts than it will be to find kids who swam in a lake that they've been told had chemicals dumped in it. Kids are funny sometimes, when you try to find out what they've done. If it's only one kid we don't find until he's too far gone, it's one too many. But forget that. Maybe we would find all of them. It's still no good. If people think Aspergicin is responsible, we'll lose the drug for sure. How many people will die because we can't treat their infections anymore? How long before we get another drug that's as good? I take care of a little girl who would be dead if it weren't for Aspergicin. I think that is important to remember."

"I didn't say it wasn't important, Dr. Schwartz. Only that, in the scheme of things, other things are more important right now. You know, you can't make an omelet without breaking a few eggs."

"Spare me the clichés, Sampson." Schwartz had to struggle to avoid shouting. "First of all, people aren't eggs and, second, it's not for you to be deciding who is expendable. You do as you please. Just don't expect me to do your dirty work." He turned away from the younger man and walked down the hall.

Sampson moved to follow him, but Acey put a hand on his arm. He tried to shake her off and discovered that her grip was too strong. "What do you want, girlie?" he snapped. There was no cordiality left in his voice.

"I don't want anything," Acey said. "I just want to point out something to you. I handle programming for a broadcast group with radio stations across the country. How would you like your sexual habits to be a talk-show topic everywhere in the US?"

"What the fuck are you talking about!" Sampson exploded. "I don't know you. You don't know anything about me."

"But I could find out," Acey said. "I probably do my background work more carefully than you. That's assuming, of course, that I bother to do any background before I shoot my mouth off."

Sampson goggled at her. "That would be slander. I'll . . ."

"You'll what?" Acey cut him off. "Oh, sure, you might eventually *prove* that you don't do anything too kinky or deviant, although I wonder how you do something like that. I doubt you'll still be working in Washington by that time, though. You play hardball with me, I'll cut your nuts off, little boy." Acey gave him a sweet-looking smile. "You have a nice day now," she said and patted his arm. Then she left him there.

Neither of them spoke until they were no longer in earshot of Senator Barcellini's staffer. Acey judged the length of corridor carefully, then whacked Schwartz in his ribs with her elbow. When he looked at her, she gave him the thumbs up sign.

"Acey, what did you tell that kid back there?" he asked.

"Oh, Sampson?" Acey had mischief in her eyes as she related the conversation. "Of course," she concluded, "I might need a microscope to find his balls in order to cut them off. One look at his face and you know he won't take any risks himself."

"I can take care of myself, you know."

"I know that." Acey paused while she searched Zeke's face to see if he was really angry. He looked a little tense. "I had reasons too."

"Yeah, I heard the 'honey' crack."

Acey nodded. "Not a smart move. The one you didn't hear was even dumber."

"He doesn't strike me as being smart in general. It's such a joke. He's just an Ivy League wanna-be dictator who probably learned everything he knows about health care in some sensitivity seminar and he sees himself as the architect of health care policy. He's found all the levers he needs to use: Barcellini, who uses his analyses, the flap over Aspergicin, and never mind what the truth is. It doesn't matter that he doesn't know anything about medicine, or even much about people. He's going to decide what's best for everybody else. On second thought, it's not a joke. It's kind of sad actually."

Acey was not laughing any more. She was leaning against the wall, looking at the cold stone, thinking of the history in the building. Her mood changed with the suddenness of a toggle switch being thrown.

"You know, Zeke, it all sucks," she said. "Nobody cares what killed Jerry. They just saw something they could use. Sampson and his Senator playing politics. Thigpen out to grab QI. The Meldrum jerks playing their company games. I feel like we did everything but storm the gates of heaven to solve this, except nobody noticed and nobody cared. What good did it do? Jerry is still dead. The other kids are still dead. Roger is dead."

"We used it, too, if you remember, Acey. You wanted a hot story and I wanted to give Meldrum a swift kick. We both got what we wanted."

"Is that supposed to make me feel better?" Acey asked. "I guess getting what you want isn't always so great. They fired Howard at the station, you know. The man was such an incompetent ass, I always thought I'd jump for joy if they canned him, really rub his nose in it, but watching him pack up and leave was so pathetic. That on top of taking the job with Thigpen just made me feel dirty."

"Come on, Acey," Zeke said, "it's not as though nothing good came out of this."

"Name one thing."

They walked out onto the portico of the Capitol. The day had almost disappeared while they were in the hearing room. Ahead of them, now, the evening sun turned the sky orange behind the Washington Monument.

"Nice view," Zeke said. "Backlit spire against that sky."

"You're changing the subject," Acey said. "Name me one good thing out of this."

Zeke stood with his eyes on the monument. "I rather thought we were pretty good for each other," he said.

"Yeah, but that's yesterday's news, isn't it, Zeke?" Acey's voice was almost harsh. Her hand went into her pocket and came out with a cigarette, which she lit. "Yeah, we were friends and lovers, and then we weren't. Sure, we made a great team, did a fine job, if you ignore some of the incidental catastrophe we created. But the job's done; the story's over. You go back to your clinic and I'll go back to my office. I suppose we can wave to each other and make conversation at public functions."

Zeke was still gazing into the sky, which was now perceptibly darkening. "I was thinking that it had nothing to do with jobs or stories. We're just good together. We miss each other when we're not."

"Things like that don't last, Doc."

"Why not? We do okay. Why can't things like that last?"

Acey shrugged. "Not in my life, they don't."

"That's not a very positive attitude." Zeke leaned forward onto the marble railing. "Some things can last. You ever think about getting married?"

At the question, Acey's eyes narrowed. "Is this a hypothetical question, or is there some specific reason behind it?"

"Assume it's hypothetical."

"Oh. The thought has occurred to me. Naturally. I could do that and keep doing what I'm doing."

"Anybody in particular?"

"Is this a hypothetical anybody or a somebody?"

"Anybody. Or somebody. Or me, for example."

"Hypothetically you?"

"Jesus, Acey, why are you always so damn difficult?"

"I was born difficult. Now, is there a hypothesis you want me to consider or is there another question here?"

"Dammit, Alice Catherine, I'm asking if you want to get married!"

"Call me Alice Catherine again and there won't be any point in you getting married."

"Now you're changing the subject. Come on. Do you or won't you?"

"Shit." Acey inhaled on her cigarette. Then she held it out in front of her while the smoke blew out. "Yeah. I do, believe it or not." She threw the cigarette on the marble and ground it under her heel.

Together, they sat hand in hand on the steps of the Capitol watching the sun set on Washington.